THE

GATEKEEPER'S

SONS

Eva Pohler

Published by Green Press

THE GATEKEEPER'S SONS, Copyright 2012 Eva Pohler

FIRST EDITION

Book Cover Design by Keri Knutson of Alchemy Book Covers and Design

Library of Congress Cataloging-in-Publication has been applied for

ISBN-13: 978-0615685960
ISBN-10: 061568596X

Other Books by Eva Pohler

The Gatekeeper's Challenge: The Gatekeeper's Saga, Book Two

The Gatekeeper's Daughter: The Gatekeeper's Saga, Book Three

The Gatekeeper's House: The Gatekeeper's Saga, Book Four

The Gatekeeper's Secret: The Gatekeeper's Saga, Book Five

The Gatekeeper's Promise: The Gatekeeper's Saga, Book Six

The Gatekeeper's Bride: A Prequel to The Gatekeeper's Saga

Hypnos: A Gatekeeper's Spin-Off, Book One

Hunting Prometheus: A Gatekeeper's Spin-Off, Book Two

Storming Olympus: A Gatekeeper's Spin-Off, Book Three

Charon's Quest: A Gatekeeper's Saga Novel

Vampire Addiction: The Vampires of Athens, Book One

Vampire Ascension: The Vampires of Athens, Book Two

Vampire Affliction: The Vampires of Athens, Book Three

The Purgatorium: The Purgatorium, Book One

Gray's Domain: The Purgatorium, Book Two

The Calibans: The Purgatorium, Book Three

The Mystery Box: A Soccer Mom's Nightmare

The Mystery Tomb: An Archaeologist's Nightmare

The Mystery Man: A College Student's Nightmare

Secrets of the Greek Revival: Mystery House #1

The Case of the Abandoned Warehouse: Mystery House #2

French Quarter Clues: Mystery House #3

Chapter One: The Drowning

Therese Mills peeled the white gloves off her sweaty hands as soon as she and her parents were in the car. Now that her mother's thing was over, she could finally get home and out of this blue dress. It was like being in a straightjacket.

Anything for Mom, of course.

What the…

A man glared at her through her backseat window. She jumped up, sat back, blinked. The man vanished, but when she blinked again, she could still see the eerie face behind her lids: the scruffy black beard and dark, haunting eyes.

"Thanks again for making tonight so special," her mother, apparently not seeing the man, said from the passenger seat as her father started the engine. "You two being there meant a lot to me."

"Did you see that man?" Therese peered through her window for the face.

"What?" Her mother also looked. "What man?"

"What man, Therese?" her father asked.

"Never mind."

Therese did not find it unusual that her mother hadn't noticed the man. Although her mother was a brilliant scientist, she wasn't the most observant person.

Just last spring after all the snow had finally melted around their house in the Colorado mountains, and Therese and her mother had been able to enjoy their wooden deck with the melted lake spread out in front of them and the forest rising up the mountains behind them, Therese had spotted the wild horse and foal she had seen just before winter. They both had reddish brown coats with a white stripe between their eyes, the foal nestled beside its mother's legs, staring intently at Therese without moving. The animals stood beneath one of two magnificent elm trees ten feet from their back door—the tree her mother said had gotten the Dutch elm disease. Therese relaxed with her mother at the wooden table on the deck, each of them with a mug of coffee in the bright Sunday morning. Her mother had the paper but wasn't reading it. She had that look on her face when she was thinking of a scientific formula or method that she planned to try in her lab. Therese stared again at the horse and didn't move. She whispered, "Mom."

Her mother hadn't heard.

"Mom, the wild horses," she whispered again.

Therese looked from the beautiful creatures to her mother, who sat staring in space, transfixed, like a person hypnotized.

"Mom, are you deaf?" she blurted out, and then she heard the horses flee back up the mountain into the tall pines. She caught a glimpse of the foal's reddish-brown rump, and that was that.

As Therese strapped on her seatbelt, she also considered the possibility that she had only *imagined* the man in the window. She was, after all, prone to use her imagination and fully capable of making daydreams as real as reality, as she had, just now, with her memory of the horses.

Her phone vibrated. A text from Jen read, "Heat sheets r n call me when u get home." Awesome, she thought. Therese was anxious to see who would share her heat in tomorrow's championship meet. She hoped she would be swimming breaststroke in the top heat against Lacey Holzmann from Pagosa Springs. She wanted to beat her this time.

She searched outside her window for the scruffy face but saw only a line of headlights as others, like they, exited the parking lot of the concert hall. Maybe she *had* only imagined the man. It was getting dark. The mountains across campus were barely visible as dusk turned into night.

"We're both so proud of you, Honey," Therese's dad said from behind the wheel.

Therese probably got her imaginative talent from her father, who was a successful crime fiction writer. As soon as his first book made the *New York Times* bestsellers list, he moved his family out into their big log cabin in the San Juan Mountains.

Therese saw her father eyeing her in the rearview mirror. "Aren't we, sweetie pie?"

She wondered at her father's need to praise her mother all the time. Didn't her mother already know she was brilliant and that her husband and daughter looked up to her? "Absolutely. You're awesome, Mom."

Therese's phone vibrated again. A text from Paul read, "Wat r u waring?"

She cringed and murmured, "Oooh. How gross." She couldn't believe he had got her number. He had been stalking her around campus just before school let out for the summer.

Before she had a chance to delete the text, Therese heard the rear window behind her head explode. "What the…" Glass shards pricked at her neck and bare shoulders. The car swerved left and right. She looked back to see the window behind her busted. The line of headlights had dispersed into chaos, horns blasting, people shouting.

"What the hell was that?" her father yelled. "Oh my God! Linda! Linda!"

"Dad, what's wrong? Is Mom…"

Another explosion rang out, and something zipped just past Therese's head.

"Therese? Are you okay? Get down!"

"What's happening? What's going on?" Therese cowered in the back seat as a third explosion sounded, this time near the windshield. Therese could barely breathe. She gasped for air, her heart about to explode.

"Stay down! Someone's shooting at us!" her father shouted.

The car swerved, slowed, and turned. The smell of burned rubber permeated the air. Therese's head whipped back as her father gunned the accelerator. Her fingers trembled so wildly, she was barely able to punch the correct numbers on her phone. She messed up twice and had to start over. Finally she pressed them in slow motion: 911. It seemed an eternity before a woman answered on the other end.

"Nine-one-one, is this an emergency?"

"Someone's shooting at us! You've got to help us. We're leaving Fort Lewis College. Dad, where are we?"

"Heading toward Huck Finn Pond."

"Huck Finn Pond!" Therese screamed into the phone as the car swerved, her seatbelt digging into her hip. Then she noticed the blood dripping down the back of her mother's neck and onto her mother's silk scarf. "Oh, my God! Mom? Mom, are you okay?"

"She'll be okay, Therese!" her father shouted.

"Oh my God! I think my mom's been shot! You've got to do something! You've got to help us!"

A crushing sound shot through the car, and Therese felt herself jolted hard to the right. She hit her head on the window and dropped the cell phone. When she bent over and tried to pick it up, the back end of the car lurched upward like a seesaw, and her head hit the back of her mother's seat in front of her. She sat up and saw they were sailing through the air over the lake. The front end of the car hit the water, causing her head to flop forward and back. She heard the air hissing through the airbags as they inflated in the front end. She was so stunned, she couldn't speak. She watched in silent shock as water crept into the front end of the car, up to her father's neck, the untied bowtie of his tuxedo floating around him. The front airbags pressed against her father's cheek, her mother's face. Water spilled over the front seat and onto the floorboard in back where she sat elevated higher than her parents.

4

She unfastened her seatbelt and leaned over and looked down at her mother in horror. A bullet had put a hole in the back of her neck, and blood rushed from it. Her head lay against the airbag turned to one side, toward Therese's father. Her eyes were open and she was gasping for air, but blood was pouring from her mouth and choking her.

"Mom! Oh my God! Mom!" Therese's teeth chattered uncontrollably as her mother strained to look at her. She reached down and caressed her mother's hair. "Mom! Oh my God!"

She realized her father had been shouting her name for several seconds. "Listen to me, Therese! Therese! Try to open your window. Therese! Try to get out of the car!"

His voice sounded like it did when he was cheering her on from the deck of the pool at her swim meets. "Keep going, Therese! You're looking good! Kick! Pull!"

Except now it was tinged with desperation.

"I'm not leaving without you and Mom! I'm scared! Dad, please! Can't you get out?" Her teeth continued to chatter.

The water level rose to his mouth. He shook his head. "I'm stuck!" He shouted through the water. His eyes widened as the water crept to his nose. He was drowning right in front of her.

"Dad! Dad!"

In a state of frenzy, he turned from side to side, only the top of his head visible.

Therese watched in silent shock.

She looked at her mother. Her mother's eyes met hers briefly, then closed as the water washed over all but her red hair. Unlike her father, her mother didn't move, but simply relinquished herself to the water. Her hair danced like seaweed, like long veins of blood. Therese became aware of the coldness of the water that had been sucking her down. Its cold fingers crept up to her shoulders. Her white gloves floated beside her, pointing at her. *You! Do something!*

She took a deep breath and went underwater toward her father. She couldn't see in the dark, so she pushed against the airbag and felt around for the harness. The belt was undone, but the steering shaft was crushed across her father's lap. She pulled with all her might on the steering wheel. It didn't move. She tried to puncture the airbag but without luck. Then she yanked on her father's lifeless arm. She couldn't lift him from the seat.

Another memory shot through her mind: She was pulling her father's arm, coaxing him from his recliner. "Come see the deer," she was saying. She was small—maybe six. "Come on, Dad. Come see." He had laughed and made a comment about her chipmunk cheeks and dimples, that he'd do anything to see those dimples. She pulled at his arm and he laughed and climbed out of his chair to follow her outside.

But now she could not get her father to follow her.

She felt her mother's hand and flinched. She found it again. It was as cold as the water and as limp as a dead fish. She hugged her mother, held on to her for dear life till her brain hurt and she needed air.

Therese popped back up near the top of the car for air, but there was none. She hitched her body up and hit her head on the roof of the car. She then noticed a bright light shine on her through her backseat window. She thought she saw someone swimming toward her. She heard another crash and a surge of water, but she needed air! Panic overtook her like a wild beast, and she opened her eyes as far as they would open, writhed her body against every molecule in reach, and strained her mouth wide open. Her lungs filled with burning water, the cold water burning her like fire. She gagged on the water, gagged, kicked, went wild with fear, and then stopped and gave in to the darkness.

Chapter Two: Thanatos

Humans didn't realize how lucky they were, Than thought as he took the woman's hand. At least, if they were mostly good, they could live a brief life with some kinds of freedoms and then spend eternity in a dreamlike trance, unaware of the monotony around them.

"Just this way," he said to the woman and the man as they floundered above the abyss, disoriented, like all of them were at this stage of the journey.

"What about Therese?" the woman asked. "Where's Therese?"

Than sighed. He couldn't imagine the pain they almost always showed on their faces. He couldn't imagine it because he had never felt it. At least it was temporary. The Lethe, the river of forgetfulness that flowed from the Acheron, would soon ease that pain, so long as these two souls were destined to the Fields of Elysium. The judges would soon decide.

"It's not too much further," Than murmured. "Come along."

"But what about our daughter?" the man asked.

The three of them now hovered up to the muddy bank where Charon waited on his raft. Than brought them down and allowed some of the water to wash up against their feet. It would help fog their memory until they reached the Lethe.

"Oh, that's cold," the woman said softly. "But it feels nice."

"Very nice," the man agreed.

Than gave a curt nod. "Time to board."

Charon nodded back as he dug his slender pole into the mud to hold the raft steady. He rarely spoke, with his nearly bald head, long, white mustache, and pale, cracked skin, and seemed more a cog in the wheel than any of them, churning on and on, back and forth, up the river and down, in

7

an endless cycle. Than supposed Charon's existence was still worse than his own. At least Than got to travel the world. Charon saw the same sights day in and day out. His life never varied.

Than put a hand on the shoulder of each of the passengers, knowing it would comfort them. Yes, he thought again, humans were lucky. A brief, exciting life trumped a dull eternity. As his father always said, nothing ever changed. A few details might, but the big picture always remained the same. Than realized that none of the gods was really all that different from Sisyphus who, each day, must face his rock.

But what if things could change? Than wondered, not for the first time. He sighed and once again shook his head and waited as the raft approached the gate.

Chapter Three: Sleep

Therese opened her eyes and found herself standing on a cool, muddy bank. Fog curled around her, and through it she could see water in front of her, and it flowed in a narrow gorge between two ominous granite mountains. "Mom! Dad!" Her screams were stifled by the thick fog. "Mom! Dad!" She looked around the empty bank. Her bare feet sunk into the itchy mud. Where were her shoes? Her white gloves were back on her hands, her gown perfectly dry, and her hair back up in its fat clip. Tall blades of grass as high as her knees grew in tufts along the shore. Mosquitoes swarmed over one area of the water. Three large boulders leaned in a cluster on the left side of the shore against the base of a steep, massive wall of rock. How did she get here?

She waded into the icy lake. The cold water crept up her thighs. She couldn't see Huck Finn Bridge. Nothing looked familiar, but she had to find her parents. Isn't this where they went under in the car? She dove into the freezing water.

Long, snakelike tendrils of hydrilla weeds grabbed and scratched at her ankles. She flinched, kicking her legs all about.

"She's moving," a familiar voice above her said.

"Therese?"

She resurfaced. "Who said that?" Her voice was only a whisper, though she tried to speak loudly. It was hard for her to move her mouth. "Who, who said that?"

When no answer came, she dove back into the icy lake. "Mom! Dad!" Why was she looking for them? Her memory went fuzzy. "Mom? Dad?" She could talk underwater as though she were talking through air. She could breathe without water entering her mouth. How strange, she thought to herself. She felt as though she had turned into some kind of mer-creature.

The lake transformed into a beautiful world of colorful coral, tropical fish, and sunken treasure chests.

She swam back to the muddy shore. "I must be dreaming." She walked over to the three boulders and sat on one of them. "Or I'm dead." She pulled off the wet gloves and tossed them on the ground.

Therese jumped into the air and swam a breaststroke through the fog, like she always did to test if she was dreaming. She went up above the curling, iridescent moisture where she could see the twinkling stars. Therese turned somersaults, forward and backward, dolphin-kicked a loop-de-loop, and then floated on her back. "Yep. I'm either dreaming or I'm dead."

She made the fog disappear, so she could see all around her. She reached up and touched a sparkling star, turned it into a diamond ring, and put it on her finger. Then she plucked her flute out of the air and played a Handel sonata. The flute felt comfortable in her hands, the cool, shiny metal beneath her fingers. The tones flowed smoothly as she blew, moving from one fingering to the next with perfect fluidity.

"I've never seen anyone like you," a voice came beside her.

Therese stopped playing. She hadn't willed him, as she had willed other guys to appear in dreams past, but she was glad he was there floating in the night sky alongside her. His thick golden hair covered his ears and fell on his forehead almost into his eyes. His eyes were blue, his skin fair, and his lips moist and peach. They parted into a smile.

"Are you checking me out?" he asked.

Therese blushed. "This is my dream, isn't it? Or am I dead?"

"You're not dead."

"So I'm dreaming, then. I can do whatever I want." She tossed the flute and willed her parents to appear, and they did.

"Mom! Dad!" She flew across the sky and into their arms. They were still in their formal wear. Her mother's neck, face, and scarf were perfectly clean, and she smelled like Haiku, her favorite fragrance. Her father smelled like musk, like the deodorant he always wore. Unlike Therese, her parents wore their shoes. Therese decided she should have her new shoes back, so she willed them to appear on her feet.

"Fascinating," the boy said. He wore a white, opened shirt, and his tight abs gleamed in the moonlight. White loose pants covered his legs, and he wore brown sandals on his feet.

Therese willed his shirt off, and the shirt disappeared.

The boy laughed. "You have so much control. Very few people are lucid dreamers, and I've never known anyone like you."

Therese turned to her parents. "I thought you were dead."

"Silly girl. Of course not," her mother scolded. "Give me a kiss."

She kissed her mother's cheek. It felt warm and soft and fully alive.

"Who's your friend?" her father asked.

Now that Therese had been comforted by her parents, she could let them go for a while. "I'll be home later. 'Kay?"

"Not too late," her father said.

Therese willed him to take it back.

"Whenever you get home is fine," he said.

Her parents vanished, causing a vague sense of panic to quell her excitement over the boy, but she pushed the panic down, reminding herself this was just a dream. She turned to the sexy guy, still shirtless, beside her. "So what's your name?"

"I have many. Most people call me Hip, short for Hypnos."

Okay, that's strange. Whatever. "Hip. I'm Therese."

"Are we going to make out now, or what?" He took her in his arms. "Your beauty, as well as your power, draws me. Is this a projection, or your real image?"

Therese had willed many sexy guys to appear in her dreams and have romances with her, but even there, she had kissed and made out with them on her own terms, and in the awake, real world, kissing was still a faraway anticipation. The eager look in the boy's face made her wary.

She pushed him back. "Why are you in such a hurry?" She looked over her body. She decided to make her boobs bigger. She smiled down at the soft, round flesh protruding from the top of her blue formal gown. Nice cleavage, she thought. "How's that?"

He threw his head back and guffawed. Then he shook his head, regaining his composure, and said, "I liked them better before."

"You've got to be kidding." She blushed and deflated herself. "It's my dream, not yours, but okay."

"No kidding. And I like your dimples. You've got a cute round face and full lips. I wouldn't mind kissing them."

Another voice sounded above her. "Therese?"

"Who *is* that? Who keeps calling me?"

A vague inkling of a car in a lake threatened to impose itself into memory, but Therese turned back to the boy and took in his beauty, forgetting all else.

Hip said, "They're trying to wake you up. But I'm not ready for you to go yet. You're such a nice diversion from what can sometimes be my dreary existence."

"How old are you?" She turned and floated on her back and looked down her body at him where he hovered near her shoes.

"Ancient."

"You look eighteen. I'm fifteen. I'll be a sophomore this year."

Down below, she noticed a raft floating across what she now saw was a river. There were four people on it, but she couldn't make out who they were. She swam the breaststroke through the air toward the water to get a better view. Her teeth felt loose. They started to crumble. She willed her teeth back into her mouth and licked them to be sure they were set correctly. Satisfied, she smiled.

12

Hip was fast behind her. "You're so incredible. People usually wake up when their teeth fall out."

She saw an old man standing on the raft dragging a long paddle through the water. Alongside him stood two familiar people and one other she didn't know. "It's my mom and dad. Hey, wait up." She flew above them, but they didn't seem to notice her.

The old man and the other passenger, whom she could now see was another guy, as cute as Hip, looked up at her. He looked sad and serious, like the silent moody type. His eyes were blue, and his hair was nearly black. He's so awesomely beautiful, she thought. He wore loose white pants and an opened white shirt like Hip had worn earlier, and, as with Hip, she willed the shirt to disappear. The boy looked startled, but her parents didn't react. They stood expressionless on the raft.

Hip laughed at the other boy's bewilderment. "That's my brother, Thanatos. Everyone calls him Than. I'm pretty sure that's a first for him."

"He looks a lot like you."

"We're twins, but not identical. I got the sense of humor, the easygoing disposition, and the charm with all the ladies. He got, well, not a whole lot, actually. I suppose he's trustworthy. My father says dependable and responsible, but those are pretty boring qualities, if you ask me. I sometimes feel sorry for him."

"What's he doing with my parents?"

"He's taking them to the Underworld, where all the dead go."

"My parents aren't dead." Again, the vague inkling threatened to return to memory, but Therese shook her head. She willed herself back home in her own cozy bed with her dog, Clifford, curled beside her. Hip was not with her.

"Time to wake up," she said to Clifford.

The brown and white fox terrier licked her cheek.

13

Therese tossed back her comforter and climbed out of the bed, the warm, wooden floor familiar beneath her feet. She dropped some hamster food into Puffy's hamster cage and turned on the lamp over her Russian tortoise's tank.

"Good morning, Jewels," Therese said.

The tortoise winked at her.

Therese headed downstairs. Clifford bounded behind her, as usual. Her parents were in the kitchen sitting at the granite bar drinking coffee and reading the paper, as on any Saturday morning.

They were still in their pajamas, but she was in her blue formal gown.

She replaced the gown with a nightshirt. *Poof.* There, better.

"Good morning," she said to her parents.

She went through the screened front porch and out into what she was expecting to be the sunny morning on their wooden deck in the mountains but was instead the night sky over the foggy river. Hip greeted her.

"Nice outfit."

"So this really is just a dream," she said. "None of it's real."

"What makes a dream any less real?" he challenged.

"Hip, let her go!" the boy from below on the raft warned. "They need to revive her or she's going to die!"

"Therese?" a voice came from somewhere above.

Than flew up and pulled Therese away from Hip. "Let her go, brother. You're endangering her life."

Therese felt weak and she tried to wriggle free but nearly fell from the air.

Than held her up. "You shouldn't be here," he whispered, close to her ear. He sent a shiver down her spine, but his breath was sweet.

She didn't like the direction this dream was going. In the dreams in which she was about to die, she usually bolted into the air and changed the

14

events into something happy. Although she couldn't find the strength to jump up and twirl around, she did manage to throw her arms around the good-looking boy holding onto her. She could make the dream into a new romance. "My dream," she managed to say as she clung to him. She put her lips against his lips. "You're…so…lovely."

"Whoa, brother," Hip said. "Today's full of all kinds of firsts for you, man."

Than seemed shocked. He looked at her like she was an alien. "You can't do this," he said, but he didn't push her away. His eyes closed, he sighed, and, almost reluctantly, it seemed, he put his strong arms around Therese, who felt weaker. She could feel his mouth near her forehead. A sound came from his throat, something like a groan.

She liked being in his arms. "You're…so…lovely," she murmured, growing weaker and weaker.

"Take her back." Than seemed to be fighting an inner battle. "I'm to take her parents, but not her. It's not her time."

Therese willed herself up. "My parents? Where are you taking them?"

Than looked into her questioning eyes. He looked as though he wanted to kiss her. She wanted to kiss him, too. His face moved closer. She nearly lost her breath. But her parents! She flew from his arms and down to the raft.

"Charon, don't board her!" Than growled, fast on her heels. "She's not to go across."

"Mom! Dad!"

Her parents didn't seem to hear her.

"This is my dream, dammit. Look at me!"

Her parents turned toward her. "Therese?"

Than gave Therese a look of astonishment. "How did you do that?"

Therese flew down to her parents.

15

Strong arms went around her and pulled her away from the raft. The brothers were on either side of her. She was fighting a futile battle. The brothers were much too strong for her to break free from them.

Than smiled. "You're right. She's a powerful soul. I've never known someone to follow loved ones down this far."

"You're forgetting Orpheus and Hercules," Hip pointed out.

"But they were demigods." Than's hands tightened their grip on Therese. Hip started to say something, but Than interrupted, "And Odysseus was sent down, so he doesn't count, either." Hip opened his mouth, but as before, Than was too quick with his retort, "And Aeneas had a guide and a golden bough, unlike this girl who came all on her own with no bribes."

Hip finally got his say, "I *told* you this girl was powerful. You're *making* my case, brother." He pulled Therese closer to him. "I want to keep her."

Therese wondered if they could possibly be talking about her. *Powerful?* She was anything but, as her inability to break free from them proved.

Than frowned. "If you try, she'll die, and then what fascinates you about her will be lost."

"Therese?" the voice from above called.

"Let her go!" Than implored.

Hip moved his lips to Therese's ear. "Seek me out in your dreams. I want to find you again. Look for me. Call for me."

Chapter Four: A Warning

Still jarred by his brother's foolish risk, Than waited in the poppies, until he fell asleep, and then he sought out Hip in the dream world.

Than knew exactly what Hip would be doing when he found him.

"I'll get you, my pretty! And you're little dog, too!" Hip's voice rang out over the abyss.

"Maybe not exactly," Than thought, rolling his eyes at his brother's projection of a little green woman in a pointed black cap. "Hey, witch!"

Hip turned in surprise and spoke in the voice of an old hag. "What are you doing here? I'm kind of in the middle of something."

Than looked at the pretty girl cowering in fear before his brother. Then he asked his brother, still in his witch form, "Since when has this been your style? What happened to lover boy?"

"Now come on, brother," Hip said. "I've been doing this for over a millennium. Shows how often you come to see me."

"What exactly is this?" Than asked. "I don't think that particular character has been around for over a millennium."

"Details, details," Hip said. "I'm talking strategy here, not the details."

"Scare them to death?"

"Never to death, brother. Then you'd get them. I just scare them enough to want a protector." Hip changed his witchy projection back to himself and spoke in his own voice. "There, there, Melody. I'll save you from that nasty witch."

The girl ran into Hip's arms.

Hip gave Than a smirk and a wink. "Works every time," he said over the girl's head.

Hip's mouth fell on the girl's. "Nice," Hip said in between kisses.

Than remembered the feeling of Therese's arms around him, her lips pressed against his.

Hip read his thoughts before Than could block him. As twins, they had a special insight into one another's minds.

"Aha!" Hip laughed, tossing the girl to the side. "That's why you're here. All these centuries you have chastised me, looked down on me for making the most of my lot by having a little fun with the girls, a little harmless fun…"

"Not always harmless," Than murmured.

Melody faded into the background.

"And here you are now, wanting some tail now that you've had a small taste. What a hypocrite!"

"Tail? Is that what you so irreverently call human beings? They're not playthings."

"Oh? Says who?" Hip folded his arms at his chest. "Get off your high horse."

"They're our responsibility, not our amusement."

"They are both, Than. That's your problem. You take everything too seriously. You need to learn to have a little fun."

"Switch jobs with me for a day and then tell me how that's possible!"

"Broken record, bro'! That's what you are! A scratched disc. I didn't choose our lots. All I can say is, you need to make the most of yours, and you don't."

Than moved closer to Hip, putting his face inches from his brother's. "And you need to be more careful. You almost killed that girl before her time."

"You're just mad that I get to go to her now, and you don't."

"Leave her alone, Hip. I mean it. She's been through a hard time, losing her parents."

Hip moved his face so close to Than's, that they almost touched. "That's exactly why she needs me, to help divert the pain. And believe me, bro', I'll show her a good time."

Than shoved his brother out of his face.

Hip flew back to retaliate, but then didn't. He smiled, took a relaxed stance. "Lighten up. I'll leave her alone."

"Good." Than backed off, about to leave, about to wake in the field of poppies.

"I've never seen you like this before," Hip teased. "If I didn't know better, I'd think you like this girl, Therese."

Than ignored him and opened his eyes. Another death beckoned him to China. But as he met the old man to lead him to Charon's raft, his mind went back to the red-haired girl who had kissed him.

Chapter Five: Figments and the Underworld

"She's waking up! Sheila! She's waking up!"

"Tell Dr. Burton her patient is waking up."

Therese grabbed the plastic tubing in her mouth and yanked. It scratched her throat, and tears welled in her eyes. Hands in latex gloves guided the tubing out and away. Therese gagged, heaved a dry heave. The latex-gloved hands held out a cup.

"Take a sip of water."

Therese put her parched lips to the cup and sipped. Her neck hurt when she lifted her head, so she lay back again. She blinked and looked up, squinting against the bright lights. She cleared her throat. The crud was still there. She cleared again. Took another sip. Ow, my neck.

"Therese, can you hear me?" It was her Aunt Carol, her mother's sister from San Antonio. What had happened to the brothers? They were right here, so close to her. How could they vanish like that? Carol kissed Therese on the forehead. "Oh, sweetheart!" Therese felt a flutter of kisses sweep over her cheeks. "Oh, Therese! I'm so glad you're finally awake!"

Why would Carol be here without her parents? "Where's Mom and Dad?"

Carol took her hand and squeezed it. "First tell me how you feel. The nurse needs to know."

She looked around the room. Machines beeped beside her. An I.V. ran through a needle in her hand. A nurse stood beside her aunt.

"My neck hurts." Then she added. "I'm so cold."

Carol pulled the covers up around Therese. "Can we get her another blanket, Sheila?" Carol said to the nurse.

Sheila left the bed and opened a nearby cabinet.

"Anything else hurt?" Sheila asked.

"I don't think so." Therese cleared her throat again. "Where's Mom and Dad?"

Another woman entered the room in a white coat.

Carol said, "Oh, Doctor, I'm so glad you're here."

She nodded hello and took a small flashlight from her front pocket. "Hi there, Therese. I'm Dr. Burton."

"Where are my parents?"

Sheila unfolded a thin white cotton blanket and added it to the heap of covers already atop Therese. Although the three persons in the room, including her aunt, looked at her with the kindest eyes, she had a sudden feeling of dread dragging her down like a heavy weight into a sea of gloom.

"Your parents didn't make it, Therese," Carol said, squeezing her hand. "They died in the crash. I'm so sorry."

Therese's mouth dropped open. Despite the dread and the inkling memory she had suppressed, she was utterly surprised. "But I just saw them. They were right there with me, hugging me, kissing me. I saw them plain as day!" Then, against her will, she remembered the shooting, the car plunging into the lake, and her parents drowning in front of her. She saw her father writhing in the water and her mother's yielding face. She felt panic gripping at her chest. She was all alone. Her mother and her father were gone. A silent scream of terror rose in her throat, but she pushed it down.

She wanted to be a little girl again sitting in her father's lap, curled in her mother's arms. She wanted to be a tiny thing making sand castles with her parents at the Great Sand Dunes, canoeing and kayaking on the lake and down the river, making snow people and snow animals in front of their house. She wanted to feel the warmth of her father on a summer evening standing on their deck around their house with binoculars turned toward the mountains beyond the reservoir in front of their house. She wanted to bake brownies with her mother one more time. She didn't need to lick the bowl;

21

she didn't need to eat a bite; she just wanted her mother there telling her what to do with the big wooden spoon and array of ingredients. She just wanted to hear her mother's voice one more time. She wanted to be a baby again, safe and swaddled, and listening to her mother's sweet lullabies:

Sweet Therese, my precious girl; you're my love, my life, my world.

Then she remembered the boys, the brothers, and her parents on the raft with the old man. It had been a dream, hadn't it? But at least she could be with them there. She wanted to be with them any way she could. She closed her eyes and tried to go back to the dream.

"Therese, try to stay awake," the doctor said, shining the flashlight in her eyes as she held open each lid, one at a time. "I need to check your reflexes." The doctor tapped an instrument against Therese's elbow, then her knee, her foot.

No, she thought. I want to die. I want to go be with my parents. She closed her eyes again.

Sheila strapped a band around Therese's upper arm. The band expanded and squeezed Therese's arm, hurting her, forcing her awake again.

"Where are my mom and dad?"

Carol gave the doctor a look of concern and then stroked the bangs from Therese's eyes. "Oh, sweetheart. They didn't make it. They're in a better place."

Her aunt's hair was red and straight like her mother's, but shorter, in a stylish bob, the front ends slightly longer than the back. Her eyes were the same blue as her mother's and her eyebrows had the same arch. Even their slender noses looked alike. Therese was grateful Carol was with her. She loved her aunt like a big sister and had relished every Christmas and spring break and summer vacation they had ever spent together either in San Antonio or here in Durango. She held her aunt's hand and allowed the flood of tears to pour from her eyes. "But Carol, where are they? I mean their bodies. Are they in the lake?" The sobs shook her. She thought she might be sick.

The band released its pressure on her arm.

"Her vitals are normal," Sheila informed the doctor.

"Oh, thank God!" Carol cried. She squeezed Therese's hand.

"Tell Lieutenant Hobson he can come tomorrow," the doctor told Sheila. "Let's give her today to rest."

"Yes, Doctor," the nurse left the room.

Carol caressed Therese's forehead. "You've been in a coma for a week. We've already buried your parents."

Therese tried to understand what her aunt had just said.

"I'll check on her again later." The doctor excused herself.

Therese turned to Carol. "A week?"

Carol nodded. "I've been staying at your house. Puffy, Jewels, and Clifford are fine."

"It's really been a whole week? I missed the championship meet?" As if that really mattered now.

She briefly wondered if her swim team had won, but then indifference set in. It no longer mattered anyway. Her parents were dead. Nothing mattered anymore. She closed her eyes and tried again to find her parents in her dream.

Therese quickly realized she was wearing nothing but a t-shirt. No shorts, no undies, no socks and shoes—as if socks and shoes mattered when she was wearing no shorts and undies. She pulled the t-shirt over her hips and sat, crisscross, in the middle of the gymnasium floor. The entire freshman class soon noticed her. They stopped playing basketball on the half court. They piled into the stands, all pointing, staring, and laughing at Therese sitting there in the center of the gym floor with her shirt pulled over her naked bottom. Soon the entire student body, all 1, 352 students, sat in the stands laughing.

Even Vicki Stern, the new girl Therese had befriended because she felt sorry for her, pointed and laughed.

To complicate matters, Puffy, Therese's hamster, was loose and running across the floor.

"Get Puffy!" Therese cried out. "Save him! He could get hurt!"

No one, not even Jen, came to her aid.

"Wait a minute," Therese whispered. "I'm not a freshman anymore. It's summer. And I would never forget to put on shorts and undies. This must be a dream." She willed herself into a pair of jeans. To be sure it was a dream, she jumped into the air and swam the breaststroke toward the ceiling. She swooped down, picked up Puffy, and soared back into the air. She kissed her hamster on the head. "Where do you think you're going, mister?"

She dove down to the gym floor, made an announcement over the microphone that everyone was to return to class, and looked across the room for Jen. "There you are. Ready to drive me home?"

Jen drove her truck toward Therese's house, toward the outskirts of Durango. They rode over the Animus River and into the San Juan Mountains.

Therese tried to remember the important thing she was supposed to do. Didn't it have something to do with finding her parents, or someone who could help her find her parents?

Without transition, she found herself in the back seat of Jen's pickup with the steering wheel in her hand. She was trying to see from the back, but was having trouble. She strained her neck as she approached an intersection flanked by tall pines. She turned to the left. The road looked as though it was winding in impossible dimensions. The steering wheel came loose and the pickup swerved out of control.

"What are you doing?" Jen asked.

24

Therese let go of the broken steering wheel, jumped out of the window with Puffy in her hands, and dolphin-kicked up to the clouds over Durango. "I'm taking control again. I call the shots in my dream. Which reminds me: I need to find Hip." Therese kissed Puffy and told him to go home like a good little hamster. "Feed Jewels and Clifford," she told him.

Puffy gave her a thumb's up and said, *"No problemo."* Then *poof*: Puffy disappeared.

Therese waved goodbye to Jen.

Jen's Toyota pickup sailed away, just like Chitty-chitty-bang-bang, the flying car from her favorite childhood movie.

Now off to find Hip, Therese thought. She flew the breaststroke over the tall pines and cypresses of the mountains near her home. "Hip! Hip! Where are you?"

"Over here!"

She couldn't see him, so she ran toward the sound of his voice. She was running down a long corridor with white floors and white walls and lots of closed doors. This must be a hospital, she thought. She ran faster, sure Hip was ahead, his golden hair just visible as he turned a corner. She turned the corner expecting to see him, but he wasn't there.

"Hip!"

No answer.

She kept running down the winding hallway. Now down a flight of steps. She could just see the golden hair as the figure rounded the landing to the next flight of stairs. Then she cried, "Hip! Enough of this!" and she stopped dead in her tracks.

The hospital setting faded away, and she was floating over the foggy river between the massive granite rocks of the gorge.

Hip floated in front of her. "You're amazing." He took her in his arms and kissed her lips. "I'm so impressed." He kissed her again. "Most people just keep on running. They don't even know why, and they never think to stop."

"You've got lipstick on your cheek," Therese said, pushing him away. "Have you been kissing another girl?"

Hip sighed. "Look, this may be your dream, but I'm the sleep guide." The lipstick disappeared. "I usually get my way when I appear in people's dreams, and I say we make out, no questions asked. Got it?"

He went for her, but she slipped past him and dolphin-kicked several feet away. "Then you're with the wrong girl."

Hip looked amused. "No. You're different. I like that."

Therese wondered in what way she was different. She was probably the most flat-chested girl going into tenth grade, her thighs were losing the gap between them and curving out past her hips, her nose could use the hands of a good plastic surgeon, and she was prone to daydream, which drove her teachers crazy. Despite her popularity as a fun person, the only boys who ever liked her—aside from Paul who was downright strange— were the ones she conjured up in her dreams, but she hadn't conjured up Hip, had she?

"Tell you what," Therese said. "I'll let you kiss me again if you answer a few of my questions first."

"Deal. Shoot."

"Where did your brother take my parents?"

"To the Underworld, where all the dead go. Your parents made it to the Elysian Fields—kind of a paradise. I've seen them. They're happy. But they can never leave that place now."

"Then how come I've been able to will them here?" Therese made her parents appear.

"Hey, sweetie pie," her father kissed her head. He was wearing a t-shirt and his favorite jeans with holes in the knees.

26

"How was band practice?" her mother asked, wearing a pair of sweats that did nothing to diminish her beauty.

Why can't I look like that? Therese thought. "I didn't go," Therese replied.

"What? Why not?" her mom asked.

"They're just figments," Hip interrupted.

Therese and her parents looked at Hip.

"What do you mean?" Therese asked.

Hip crossed his arms and leaned back. "Your parents' souls have passed on to the Underworld, and once Cerberus, my dad's three-headed dog, lets them in, he won't let them out. The images of your parents here are figments. Figments are nymph-like creatures that reflect the dreamer's unconscious images. They have no reflection of their own in a mirror, so you can always test it out if you're not sure. Watch this." Hip pulled a hand-held mirror from out of the sky and held it up to Therese's parents. The mirror was blank where the reflection of her parents should have been. "See? No reflection." Then he shouted, "Figments, I command you to show yourselves!"

Therese's parents turned into eel-like creatures with scales and long, winding bodies. They curled around the air and then zipped away, giggling.

Therese hung her head.

Hip moved his arms around her waist. "Don't I get my kiss now, or do you have other questions?"

"How can I get my parents back?"

"You can't. Only two other people in history have ever tried to retrieve a loved one from the Underworld, and both attempts turned out badly. Besides, that's my brother's area of expertise, not mine."

"Can you take me to your brother?"

He snickered and shook his head. "No one ever wants to find Death."

27

"Your brother is Death?"

"Most call him Than."

"*He* was Death?"

"Look, I can give you a bird's eye tour of the Underworld. I can even show you your parents from above. But I can't actually take you into the Underworld proper while you're alive. The other day when you met my brother, you were very near to dying. That's the only way a person can come into contact with him."

"That's so sad," Therese said.

"What do you mean?"

"Doesn't he have any friends?"

Hip shrugged. "Our sisters, I guess."

Therese bit her lip. "Well, I guess we can start with the tour."

Hip moved in close to her again. "First I get my kiss." He pressed his lips against hers. His breath was like mint. She closed her eyes and brushed her lips across his.

"Nice," he said. "Let's do that again."

Therese pulled back. "First the tour."

Hip took her hand and led her down to the river. A few feet away she could see the old man on the raft, his long white mustache, slight and slumped shoulders, and red peasant robe visible through the fog. He used his stick to pull away from the bank with two other passengers, one whom she recognized.

"That old man is Charon," Hip said. "He ferries the souls across the Acheron River where it meets the Styx River at the gates to the Underworld. My brother retrieves the souls from the world of the living and accompanies them until they're settled in."

"Than!" Therese called.

He looked up at her, astonished.

"She wants a tour," Hip explained.

28

Hip didn't wait for his brother's reply. He took Therese's hand and pulled her past the raft, down the river to where it entered a dark cave. Sitting near the mouth of the cave was a creature about six feet tall, black as night, with a sweeping dragon tail, and three ferocious heads resembling those of a French bulldog: tall batlike ears, pug upturned noses, large frowning mouths with slight under-bites exposing white sharp teeth, and plenty of loose skin and wrinkles around the three necks. The eyes on the heads looked red and unfriendly, but Therese had never met an animal she hadn't tried to befriend.

"That's Cerberus," Hip said. "He guards the gate." A massive iron gate, maybe a hundred feet above the water, and who knew how many feet below, stood just past Cerberus tightly fastened. "Only the gods can go in *and* out, so I can't take you through, but I can show you what's down there by making the upper part of the caverns transparent."

"Gods? You and your brother are gods?"

Hip gave her a smug grin. "That's correct. Hades, the god of the Underworld, the gatekeeper, is our father, despite some misguided myths you people have about our origins."

"I've heard of Hades, but I've never heard of you and your brother," Therese stated matter-of-factly, which seemed to offend Hip.

He grabbed her arm in a tight grip. "Come on."

"Wait," Therese insisted when Hip pulled her onward. "Can I say hello to Cerberus?"

Hip's mouth dropped open. "You actually want to?"

"Yeah. Why not?" She let go of Hip's hand and floated closer to the creature. "Hello there, Cerberus. Are you a friendly thing? May I pet you?"

The three-headed dog leaned toward her and wagged its dragon tail.

"I wouldn't do that if I were you," Hip warned as he caught up to her. "He can be pretty vicious. And he's always suspicious about being tricked, especially after what happened with Orpheus and Hercules."

29

Therese wanted to ask about Orpheus and Hercules, but Cerberus now bared his teeth and uttered a low growl from all three heads.

"Why did you have to mention them? Look what you've done!"

"Come on." Hip pulled Therese past the creature, above the enormous gate, and over the mouth of the cave. "There's a lot more to see."

They flew over rocky terrain with the night sky above them and the stars and crescent moon piercing through the fog now and then. Beneath them, the layers of rock vanished, and Therese could see several large chambers attached by tunnels through which five different rivers flowed. One of the rivers was alight with flames, illuminating the many chambers.

Hip explained that the first chamber, just passed Cerberus, was the room of judgment, where three judges worked together to determine whether a soul was worthy of the Elysian Fields. If a soul was found to be unworthy, the judges would then determine which punishment in Tartarus would be most fitting. Some of these punishments were terrible, like that for Tantalus, who stood in water up to his neck but could never drink and saw fruit above his head but could never grasp it. Others were laborious, but not too unlike the world of the living, like Sisyphus, who was doomed to roll a huge rock uphill all day only to watch it roll to the bottom of the hill where he must start again. Some souls were doomed to remain in Tartarus for all eternity, Hip explained; but others, after their debts were paid, could travel over to the Elysian Fields. Tartarus was narrow and long like a great hall, just past the room of judgment. It seemed to stretch endlessly in two directions further than Therese could see.

Hip then pointed out Erebus, a chamber just after Tartarus and much deeper, though also smaller in circumference, perhaps fifty feet wide at most. He explained that victims of terrible crimes were often sent there through the Lethe, the river of forgetfulness, to forget the heinous crimes that tortured them in life. Mostly abused children and women, suicides, and prisoners of war went there before they were eventually led up and out into the Elysian

Fields. Therese could see people below in the dim light lying in their clothes in a shallow pool of water as though sunbathing.

The fields were vast and amazing, covered in beautiful flowers of white, pink, and purple. There were trees and something like sunshine, but more of a purplish-pink veil of light that added beauty to all it touched. The Lethe River met its banks, and spread in small streams marbling through the fields, which meant that the souls who frolicked there had only the vaguest recollection of a previous life. Therese could see hundreds of souls all doing different things. Some read or slumbered under trees, others danced or swam or ate at huge tables covered with massive amounts of food. Others played sports like golf and tennis. A few children flew kites. Hip explained that the kites, the trees, the food, and the books and things were merely shared illusions, part of an ongoing dream for the dead. The Elysian Fields, like Tartarus, seemed to stretch infinitely in two directions, the boundaries invisible to her eyes.

She squinted at a couple sitting on the bank with their feet dangling in the river. They were her parents.

"Can I speak to them?" she asked Hip.

"They won't hear you from up here," he answered. "And we can't go down to them below. Besides, chances are they won't remember you."

Therese couldn't bear the thought of her own parents forgetting her. She burst into tears. "Take me to your brother, so he can tell me what I need to do to get my parents out of here."

"I haven't even showed you my parents' palace. It's the most fascinating place of all."

She saw the old boatman docked at the gate just past Cerberus. She flew down to find Than.

"Therese, wait!" Hip warned. "If you follow the raft in, you can't come out. You'll die, and then there's certainly no way to save your parents."

31

She stopped and looked back at Hip.

This is only a dream, isn't it, she thought. There's nothing real about any of this.

"Therese! Wake up!"

"Wait!" Hip called. "What about my kiss?"

"Therese! Sweetheart, wake up!"

Chapter Six: Distractions

Than left Charon and headed to Mexico to escort the souls of three teenagers who had died in an earthquake. He would be making several more trips there over the next few days as the frail human bodies gradually expired. He had disintegrated and dispatched himself to four other locations--Turkey, Japan, Iraq, and Egypt. It was a busy day, busier than usual, and because of the disintegration, he found it a little more difficult to keep his mind on his duties.

Therese had come back, had called out his name. He knew she wanted her parents, like so many of the survivors whose family members he carried away. Than had learned to block those futile prayers, "Spare my sister," "Bring my child back to me," "Let my husband be alive when we find him," and so forth. He had blocked them because there was nothing he could do about them. Therese's prayers were no different. He could not help her.

Yet, he couldn't forget the feel of her soulful arms around him, the sensations of her warm lips against his, and the scent of her sweet breath. No one—human or god—had ever touched him like that. His mother must have when he was a baby, but he had no memory of it. If Therese's spirit were capable of making him feel so much sensual pleasure, how much more pleasurable could she make him feel in the flesh?

Only now did he become aware of what he had been missing.

He disintegrated and dispatched another part of himself to the poppy field beside Hip's rooms. Than wanted to re-enter the dream world and talk some more to his brother, even on this busiest of days.

Chapter Seven: Visitors

Therese blinked her eyes as Carol leaned over her saying, "Wake up, sweetheart. The lieutenant is here."

Carol smelled like her mother. She smelled like Haiku perfume and Jergen's lotion.

A memory of her aunt teaching her to blow into the flute distracted her for a moment. They had given one another manicures and pedicures, and when the polish had dried, Therese had asked to try the flute, which Carol had played in high school years before. She had the scent of Haiku and Jergen's even then.

"Therese?"

"I'm still in the hospital? What day is it?" Therese tried to sit up. Her neck was stiff, but slightly better. She rubbed it and noticed the IV was still attached to her hand.

"It's Tuesday morning. You woke up from your coma yesterday," Carol said. "There's a tray of breakfast for you here. Are you hungry? You slept through yesterday's dinner."

Therese looked across the room at a short, round man with gray hair and razor stubble. He wore a policeman's uniform and looked to be in his late fifties.

"Maybe I'll eat something later."

"Hi there, Therese." The lieutenant approached her bed. The smell of body odor wafted above her head. "How are you feeling?"

"My neck is stiff, but I'm okay." She pulled the covers up around her.

"Good. I'm glad to hear that." He scratched the stubble on his chin. "Look, I know what happened to you was pretty scary. I'm really sorry it happened. But I want you to know that I'm going to do everything I can to find out who did this, okay?"

Therese nodded as the tears welled in her eyes.

"I'm Lieutenant Hobson with the Durango Police Department." Beads of sweat forming on his forehead dripped around his temples as if he had run all the way to the hospital.

"Hi."

"What can you tell me about what happened? What do you remember?"

She told them what she could, and then cleared her throat, her mouth suddenly dry, her chest tight. "I couldn't save them."

Carol stroked Therese's arm. "It's not your fault, sweetheart."

Therese grabbed Carol's arm. Panic overtook her as it had beneath the water trapped in her mother's car. Her throat burned, like it had when the water rushed through her lungs and she had hit at every space around her. "Tell me I'm dreaming!" Therese wailed. "Tell me I'm going to wake up and it will all be over!"

Carol kissed her cheek and started crying. "I wish I could."

The lieutenant took a small notepad and pen from his front shirt pocket and gave Therese a moment to recover. Then he cleared his throat and said, "Can you remember anything else?"

The face. It popped into her head and startled her as much as it had the night her parents were killed. "I might have been imagining this, but right before the shooting, I thought I saw a gruff-looking face outside my car window. It was a man."

"A man's face? Can you tell me what he looked like?"

"His skin was dark."

"Black?"

"No."

"Native American?"

"No, oh, I don't know. He had dark brown eyes, black hair, kind of short, like yours, and a scruffy beard."

"How old would you say he was?"

"I don't know. Not too old. Younger than my dad."

"Would you describe him as heavy-set, thin, tall, short?"

"I just saw his face. I don't know."

"Do you think you can remember enough details about his face to work with an artist from my department?"

"I can try."

"Anything else you can remember? Anything at all?"

"Right before I went out, I saw a bright light and someone swimming toward me."

The lieutenant nodded. "Yeah, that would have been the rescue crew. They went in and pulled you out of the car."

"Oh." She wondered if they got her parents out then, too.

"Therese, do you know if either of your parents had any enemies?"

"What? You mean you don't think this was just some random school shooting? An angry student gone postal? Like Columbine?"

"That's a possibility, Therese," the lieutenant said. "But your car seems to have been the primary target. Other people suffered some minor injuries when the perpetrator drove recklessly through the parking lot, but your car was the only one shot at."

The hair on her neck stood up and she felt her heart go wild. She could hardly breathe. She never imagined someone would want to murder her parents.

"Do you know if your parents had ever received any threatening phone calls, emails, or letters?"

36

"No, sir. I don't know of anything like that. My dad got letters and emails from his readers, but they were fans, not enemies. My mom's students all loved her. Both of my parents were well liked by everybody, I think. I can't imagine why anyone would want them, want them..." She lost her voice and broke into sobs again. "I'm sorry."

The lieutenant closed his notepad and stuffed it back into his front shirt pocket. Then he added his ballpoint pen. "Thanks, Therese. I'll follow up with you again soon. I'll have an artist meet with you for that description later today, while your memory is fresh."

A panicky feeling threatened to surge through Therese again. "Lieutenant Hobson?"

"Yes?"

"What do you know so far? Who do you think did this?"

"I shouldn't discuss the case with you, Therese. You just focus on getting better."

"That's not fair." Therese's voice was desperate. "I have a right to know. They were my parents."

"Get some rest, and I'll come back and tell you something when I know more. Maybe your description of the face will give us the lead we need." The lieutenant reached out and took her hand, shook it, patted it, and said, "You take care, now. Call me if you think of anything else."

"Okay." She wiped the tears streaming down the sides of her face.

The lieutenant handed his card to Carol.

"Thank you, Lieutenant," Carol said.

Just as the lieutenant walked out of the hospital room, Therese's three best friends—Jen, Ray, and Todd—walked inside carrying balloons and a toy stuffed animal lemur.

"She's really awake!" Jen cried, rushing in and grabbing Therese's hand.

"Hi guys," Carol said. "Therese? Are you sure you're ready for company?"

"Yes, I'm sure. I need some cheering up."

"Well, if you're really sure…"

"I'm sure."

"Then I'm going downstairs for a bit. Enjoy your visit."

Once Carol left the room, Ray said, "Todd wanted to get you the lemur. You should have seen him moaning and groaning in the shop if either one of us picked up anything else. So if you don't like it, blame him." Ray was tall, chubby, and Native American.

"I love it. He's cute."

"His hands have velcro," Todd said. "You can wear him around your neck, like this." Todd put the lemur's long, skinny black arms around his neck and attached them. "You can wear him here in front," he moved the monkey to his back, "or back here. It's quite a fashion statement." Todd was tall and thin with sandy-blonde hair and a face full of acne.

"Just what everyone wants, Todd," Ray said. "A monkey on their back."

Therese and Jen laughed.

"I like him guys," Therese said. "Let me have him." She was glad they hadn't said anything about her parents. For a little while, she wanted to pretend everything was normal again.

Todd handed the lemur over. "He's going to miss me. He wants me to come visit."

Therese smiled. "I guess I can allow visitations."

"When I called yesterday, your aunt said your neck has been hurting. Are you any better today?" Jen asked as she tied the balloons to the railing at the foot of the hospital bed.

"Some. Still stiff." Then she thought, *please don't say anything about my parents*. "How did we do at the championship meet?"

"Pagosa Springs won by thirteen points," Jen said. "We came in second. Bayfield got third."

"Did Lacey swim breaststroke in the first heat?"

"Yeah. She got first. You would have beaten her though, I just know it," Jen reassured her.

"Maybe. I guess we'll never know."

"There's always next summer," Todd said. "Hey, listen. I finished rebuilding the engine for my truck."

"The fifty-seven Chevy?" Therese asked. "Are you serious?"

"You should see it," Ray cut in. "He painted it yellow, of all the colors in the universe."

"I like yellow," Therese said.

"It looks awesome," Jen added. "Todd's going to take us for a ride as soon as you get out."

"Hey," Todd said, coming close to her, his face taking on a more serious expression. "I haven't told you yet how sorry I am about your parents. I know you already know it, but I wanted to say it, you know?"

"I know." Therese clenched her jaw as she fought off tears. She supposed she couldn't go on pretending, and it was nice to know he cared.

"Me, too," Ray murmured. "What he said."

"Me, too," Jen said, taking Therese's hand.

"Thanks guys."

Her three friends stood there now in awkward silence, brushing away tears they didn't want one another to see. Luckily, Carol eventually returned and asked the visitors how they were doing, shifting the focus from Therese. She lay there in the bed wiping more tears from her face.

Her friends chatted with her and her aunt for a few more minutes, and then they said their goodbyes. Therese put the lemur's long, furry arms around her stiff neck and closed her eyes.

Carol said, "Your lunch is here. You never ate your breakfast. Do you think you can eat something now?"

"I think so."

A different nurse was standing over Therese with a tray. She moved a few things on the rolling bedside table and set it down. "Today we have a turkey sandwich, vegetable soup, fruit cup, and chocolate pudding."

"Thanks," Therese said.

The nurse studied the machines near Therese's bed. "Everything looks in order. My name's Letty. Just call if you need anything. How's your neck?"

"Better. Still a bit stiff."

"I can give you something for the pain."

"Okay."

"I'll bring it in a while, give you time to eat." Letty left the room.

Carol gave Therese an update about her pets while Therese ate. They chatted about school and Therese's friends. Therese really didn't feel like talking, but she could see it made Carol feel better. The food tasted good. She hadn't realized how hungry she was. Not long after she finished her pudding cup, Letty returned with the medication.

"Thank you," Therese said.

"You're welcome, mija." The nurse removed the empty tray and left the room.

Carol must have noticed the tears welling in Therese's eyes, for she leaned over the bed and took Therese's hand. "You know, when your grandpa died, even though we knew it was coming, it was so hard. It felt like a part of me died with him. And then when your grandma died two years ago...gosh, I can't even believe it's already been two years. Then all I had left were you and your mother. Now that my big sister's gone, well, Therese, you're all the family I have left."

Therese sucked in her lips as she watched the tears slide down her aunt's cheeks. "And you're all I have left."

"I'm coming to live with you, Therese. I've already moved out of my San Antonio apartment. I hope that's what you want."

Therese hadn't thought that far ahead. She was still trying to get used to the idea that her parents were, that her parents had....she couldn't even think the idea through in her mind.

"I mean, I could take you with me to San Antonio, but you have your life here, and I can live anywhere. Since I work from home, my boss has no problem with me coming to Durango. Now that grandma's gone, there's really nothing keeping me there."

"What about Richard? And I'm sure you have friends."

"Richard and I will work something out. We've dated long distance before. Absence makes the heart grow fonder, you know." Carol gave Therese a smile.

"I do love my house," Therese murmured.

"I do, too," Carol said.

"I guess we can see how things go, right?"

"Oh, sure. We don't have to decide anything today." Carol kissed Therese's cheek. "You know, I've always been so grateful for you in my life. I don't know when or if I'll ever have children, and having you for my niece has kind of fulfilled that maternal part of me. I know I can't replace your mother—and I don't want to—but I want you to know I will be there for you. I'm not just a babysitter. I'm not just a temporary fix. I'm here for you for the long haul, through thick and thin, and the works. Okay?"

Therese nodded, more tears piling up in the corners of her eyes again.

"Now, sweetheart, I can ask them to bring me one of those hideaway beds and sleep here with you tonight if you want me to. I've been staying at the house because of Clifford, but he can go a night without me if you want me to stay here now that you're staying awake for longer periods of time."

"No," Therese said. "I'd be worried about Clifford. Go ahead and go home. I'm just gonna go right back to sleep."

"Good. You need the rest," Carol said.

Therese sighed, nodded.

Carol nodded too. "I'll come back this evening to check on you again. Go to sleep."

"Okay. Thanks."

Carol kissed her forehead and stroked her hair. Then she crossed the room and waved one more time before disappearing through the door.

Therese sat in her ninth grade AP English classroom with the rest of her classmates taking a multiple choice exam, but none of the questions made sense. They seemed written in a different language. Therese pressed her pencil into the bubble next to "E. None of the above," but the lead on her pencil broke. She raised her hand. Mrs. Spencer stood with her back to the class writing something on the dry erase board and didn't notice.

"Excuse me," Therese said.

When Mrs. Spencer turned around, Therese saw she wasn't Mrs. Spencer at all. Her eyes were red, her ears pointed, and when she opened her mouth to ask, "Yes?" blood dripped from her lips.

She's a zombie, Therese thought, frozen in her chair.

She looked around the room. They were all zombies.

That's when she knew she was dreaming.

"I need to find Hip," Therese reminded herself, so she took off flying from the school, looking for the Underworld.

Then her parents appeared in front of her, and she couldn't resist stopping midair and looking at them. Could they possibly be her real parents?

"Mom? Dad?"

They smiled and held out their arms. She ran to them and felt their warm embrace. Then another zombie appeared and ruined the delusion. Therese willed it to disappear.

"You're just figments, aren't you?" she asked her parents softly, stepping away from them just a bit, but not too far.

Her mom and dad shrugged.

"Tell me you're real!" Therese commanded.

"We're real?" her father laughed. "What are you talking about? Of course we're real."

The zombie English teacher approached, scolding Therese, "You didn't finish the test, young lady!"

Reluctantly and full of sadness, Therese said, "Figments, I command you to show yourselves."

Her parents and the evil teacher transformed into eels, giggled, and flew away, leaving Therese hovering in the air alone in the middle of nothingness.

"Hip!" she shouted at the top of her lungs, full of anger. "Hip! I need you!"

The handsome twin appeared. "You called?" he had a smirk on his face.

"I want to rescue my parents from the Underworld, and I want you to help me."

"Impossible," he said. "And you owe me a kiss."

He moved against her and touched his lips to hers. She froze, waiting.

"Aw, what kind of kiss was that?"

"If you're not going to help me, go away."

"You've got a lot of nerve, giving commands to a god. I could kill you, you know."

She looked him dead in the eye. "Do it."

He rolled his eyes. "My brother would cause trouble for me." He backed off and shook his head. "He's obsessed with you, Therese. He can't stop thinking about you. He thinks he's in love with you. He's trying to work out some kind of deal with our father."

"What are you talking about?"

"Than? My twin brother? The one you threw yourself at saying, 'You're so lovely. You're so lovely!' Ring a bell?" He crossed his arms and sulked.

"You mean the god of death?" she asked with some hesitation. This was sounding a little crazy. Maybe this wasn't Hip. Maybe he was a figment. "Figment! I command you to show yourself!"

Hip rolled his eyes again and said, "Give it a rest. I never should have taught you that."

"Hip, please tell me what you're trying to say."

"My brother's coming for you."

"What? The god of death is coming for me?"

Pound, pound, pound!

"What was that?" Therese asked.

"No! Don't wake up! I want a real kiss this time!"

Pound, pound, pound!

"Hello?" a woman's voice called out.

Therese opened her eyes and saw an ultra-thin woman with chocolate skin and blonde hair and outlandishly colorful clothing enter the hospital room. She carried a sketch pad.

"Therese?"

Therese gave her a nod and then winced from the pain. Her neck was better but still tender.

"I'm Margo Brewster. Lieutenant Hobson sent me over to sketch a suspect."

44

"Oh, yeah."

"How you feelin'?" The artist sat down in the chair next to the bed and opened her pad to a blank page. She pulled a pencil from behind her ear, which was studded with rings.

"Okay."

"Well, I'm so sorry you're here and can't imagine what things are like for you, but I'm here to help, okay?" A little diamond shone on the side of one nostril.

"Okay." Therese described the face she had seen in her car window as best as she could, fighting the tears without success.

The artist would show her the drawing in progress, and ask, "Eyes like this? No, how 'bout more like this? Okay." And then, "So, okay, more of a pointed jaw, like this?"

Eventually they came up with something that Therese thought looked eerily like the man she saw before the shooting began. Chills ran down her spine. "That's him. Wow, you're really good."

Letty came in and checked on Therese, took her temperature, checked the machines, and asked how she was feeling. "Do you need more medicine for your pain, mija?"

"Yes, please."

Letty left the room.

Margo Brewster was nice, but Therese was glad when she left and Letty gave her the pills, and she could close her eyes again and go to sleep.

When she found herself running through the hospital, Therese was immediately suspicious. She stopped at the end of a hallway and walked into a room. Todd, Ray, and Jen lounged around on living room furniture laughing at something on the television.

"Hey," Todd said. "Look who finally made it."

45

Therese sensed something behind her, outside of the door in the hallway. It felt bad, dangerous, frightening. She sprung to the door and pushed it closed, but it didn't have a lock. In fact, the door didn't even fit properly in the door frame, as it was bordered by a one-inch gap all the way around. Even the hinges seemed loose. Whatever was out there would have no problem getting inside.

Therese quickly recognized that she wasn't in a hospital room, but in her grandmother's house back in San Antonio. Strangely, she recalled that her grandparents had both passed away—her grandfather several years ago and her grandmother in more recent years. So she wondered now how she could be standing in their living room trying to keep their front door from being busted open.

A bright light spilled through the one-inch gap around the door.

"What is that?" Jen asked.

"I have a bad feeling about this," Todd added.

"Very good, Obi Wan Kenobi," Ray sneered.

"Wait a minute!" Therese burst out. "This can't really be happening." She jumped into the air and turned a somersault. Then she turned to her friends. "Figments, I command you to show yourselves!"

Three scaly, eel-like creatures flew about in a tizzy, giggling wildly.

Then the door crashed in and the bright light illuminated the room. The three figments rushed out through the opening and into the light. Out of the light a figure emerged.

"Figment, I command you to show yourself!" Therese said.

"None but my father commands me." The figure stepped within inches of her. He was tall and muscular and wore a fierce look on his beautiful face.

It was Than.

Therese dropped with weakness to her grandmother's old green carpeting, which still smelled like wet dog. Than rushed to her side and

46

helped her to sit up. She leaned against him. Her grandmother's blue merle Australian Shepherd, who had died the same year as her grandmother, strolled over to Therese and licked her cheek.

"Hello, Blue," Therese said to the dog in a faint, weak voice.

"I don't have much time, so listen," Than said. "I came to tell you three things."

Therese felt inexplicably drawn to him. "Am I dying?"

"Not if I can help it," he replied. "Now shut up and listen to me."

His cold, hard glare suddenly frightened her, so she kept her mouth shut, her eyes wide.

"First, I've asked the Furies to seek you out. Look for them in the waking world of the living. They can help you solve your parents' murder."

"Who or what is a Fury?" She felt faint.

"I'll let them explain. You could die if I don't hurry. Let me speak."

She gave him a weak nod.

"Second, don't let my brother keep teasing you. He respects your powers but not you, and I don't like it."

Therese managed a smile. "Jealous?" She would never be so bold outside of her dreams.

"Absolutely." He looked deeply into her eyes, his face close to hers.

"Do you want to kiss me?" The air left her body and her mouth flooded with moisture.

"Absolutely."

She closed her eyes and leaned in.

"Listen," he said, swallowing hard. "I haven't stopped thinking about you since that day you kissed me, and that brings me to the third thing I want to say. Thank you for your affection. Know that I stay away, not because I want to, but because if I don't, you'll die."

Therese found it hard to breathe. "Don't go," she barely managed to say. "I want to die. I want to be with my parents. And then you and I could,

47

we could spend some time getting to know each other." She was really faint now, on the verge of collapse.

He leaned close and took a breath of her scent. Then he clenched his jaw. "You're not the same when you die. You lose your free will, and that's what is so attractive about you. It's what sets you apart from the others. You have a strong will."

Therese gasped for air and none came.

Than vanished.

Therese heard a loud beeping sound next to her ear. She gasped and gasped, and finally her lungs opened up and the air rushed in, burning her chest. Someone rushed up beside her.

"Mija!" the nurse shrieked. "You okay?"

Therese lay on the hospital bed. Was she awake? "Figment, I command you to show yourself!" she said to the Letty.

The nurse bent her brows. "Mija, what are you talking about?"

"Oh. I thought I was dreaming." Okay, Therese thought. I'm not saying that ever again.

Letty looked at the oxygen monitor. "Well, what is wrong with this thing? It was beeping like crazy just a second ago, but now it looks fine." She checked the probe taped to Therese's big toe. "Maybe it's come loose. Well, it looks alright. You feel alright?"

Therese nodded. "I'm fine."

"Well, alright then. Call me if you need me. I'll be back in a little while with your dinner tray." The nurse left the room.

Chapter Eight: A Deal with the Gatekeeper

"**W**hy should I do this?" Hades asked from his jewel encrusted throne. The one beside him was empty because Persephone was gone in the summertime. Her absence made Than's father irritable. This wasn't the best time to ask for favors.

In fact, the cavernous room of golden walls inlaid with precious stones was usually brimming with bustle as Persephone and Hecate discussed the affairs of the Upperworld and of Mount Olympus. With his mother and her assistant gone, the chamber echoed with the silence of slinking shadows caused by sleeping bats that barely moved and would not fly till nightfall. The nearly vacant castle had not even ghosts to move the air, for all the souls were in their proper places, and even the formidable form of Hades could not fill the room. Hades, who now slouched and picked at his beard, would, in a few months' time, with the first chill of autumn, sit erect and commanding and proud like a peacock before his mate. Despondence, however, was his only companion until then.

Than spoke with confidence. "Because I can help the Furies find the killer and bring him to justice."

"They can do it without you. So I say again, why should I do this?" Hades's voice was not ignited. He sounded bored and unmoved. "You know it's impossible for Hypnos to disintegrate between two duties. He'd have to take your place."

Than grasped for ideas. "Hermes at one time conducted the dead."

"He's busy with other duties now. He can't possibly take on your job."

"Humans can go without dreams for a few weeks while Hip escorts the souls."

49

"Why, Thanatos? Dreams are more important than you seem to realize. Humans need dreams to work through the range of experiences and emotions they deal with during their waking hours. Without dreams, they'd shut down, die early deaths, and that's not how I want to build my kingdom. I want honorable souls. Just souls. The unjust ones can usually learn to be honorable with a series of behavior modification courses, courtesy of your sisters."

"And Sisyphus? Tantalus?"

"Serve to amuse."

"Amuse, Father? Are you amused by their suffering?"

"When it's deserved. I find it both amusing and satisfying."

Than caught on to a glimmer of hope. Hades was known for saying that life wasn't fair, but death was. Over the centuries, Hades had made it his utmost goal to level justice at every soul that crossed his path, complaining that Zeus showed favoritism and that most of humankind suffered for it. "You are just, Father, and it is for this reason you should let me go to earth as a mortal and force my brother to take my place escorting the dead. You know that, of the two of us, my brother got the better lot."

"So it is with me and my brothers. Do you think I chose the Underworld?" He moved his hand above him through the air as if to dismiss the splendid emeralds and diamonds and rubies around him. The golden palace would be a pleasure from which any lesser god would willingly rule, but the open skies and the expansive seas were superior in the eyes of Than's father. "Don't you think I'd prefer the sky or the waters? You must learn to accept your calling. Believe me, you'll be much better off."

"But you have mom, at least for half of the year. Hip has the company of hundreds, thousands of girls. I can think of no other god, save Charon, who is expected to live a lonely existence without end, and even he finds companionship from time to time in Cerberus, who's like a puppy to him. Why shouldn't I have a chance to find a queen? You have the power to

50

grant me this request. You have the authority to make my lot more equal to that of the other gods of my rank. You should do this because you are just and because you can."

At that moment, Hermes entered the room. "Excuse me, Lord Hades. Should I come back later?"

"No. We're finished for now. What do you have?"

"Hello, Than."

Than gave a nod to his cousin but was in no mood for light conversation.

Hermes turned back to Hades. "A message from Poseidon regarding the small colony of white abalone beneath the coast of California. As you may know, the white abalone are headed for extinction, and because this particular colony is underground, Poseidon wants to be sure you stand beside him on his conservation efforts."

"Of course. He knows I support diversity. How dull of him to send you all this way."

"Something's brewing, my lord," Hermes said. "I think he fears your alliance won't last."

"Do you have wind of it?"

"I know nothing yet. I'll report back when I know something."

"Yes. Do that." Hades rubbed at his temple.

Than moved closer to his father as Hermes left the room. "I'm sorry to have burdened you further with my request. I know you have a lot of business to manage."

"You may think I don't care about your happiness, son, but I do, and in this matter, you are right. You deserve a chance to find a queen, and I do have the power to grant you this chance. So be it. You have forty days and no more."

Than's mouth fell open. "Thank you, Father."

"Wait. There is something she must do. Remember, nothing in this world is free."

Chapter Nine: Back Home

Even though Therese felt pretty sure the saga in her dreams was imaginary, she couldn't stop herself from getting on the Internet as soon as Carol brought her home from the hospital two days later. She had to use her laptop, though, which was slower than her parents' computer, because that computer had been taken by the police for their investigation.

Her neck had finally loosened up, and she could walk around without much pain. She could even run up the stairs to her room. She should have played around with Clifford, her little brown and white fox terrier, who was obviously starved for her affection. She should have let Jewels climb up her chest to nestle against her neck as she did most evenings while Therese read a good book. She should have taken Puffy from his cage and allowed him to scamper around in her hair, which she fanned out for him over the bed like a curtain, her arms carefully hovering over him lest he scurry out of reach. The chipmunks were in need of sunflower seeds, the deer their corn, and the wild horses the apples she tossed out behind her house. But Therese put off all these things, usually so important to her, to log on and surf the net for information about the Underworld.

A part of her knew her obsession with her dreams was a distraction. Her brain didn't want to think about what her house would feel like without her parents in it. Her brain didn't want her to go downstairs and into the kitchen on Saturday morning and find only Carol sitting with the paper at the granite countertop. As much as she loved Carol, Therese's brain wanted more.

She googled "Underworld mythology" and was surprised by all the links that appeared on her search results page. She clicked on the first link: "Hades, brother of Zeus and Poseidon, was the king of the Underworld, which he ruled with his bride Persephone, whom he kidnapped and made his queen. Guarded by Cerberus, a three-headed dog, the Underworld was underground and separated from the land of the living by five rivers, one of which was the Acheron, across which the dead were ferried."

Therese sat bewildered as she read articles describing many of the features about which she had dreamed. Not all the sources agreed on the details, but there were enough commonalities about them and her "tour" that made her hair stand on end: Charon, the old boatman; Tartarus and the Elysian Fields; Lethe, the river of forgetfulness; Sisyphus and his huge rock. Maybe she had read this stuff somewhere before?

A particular passage soon caught her eye: "Thanatos, also known as Orcus and Mors, was the god of Death. The son of Night and twin brother of Hypnos (Sleep), he was believed to be a beautiful young man but, because of his ghastly task, was very unpopular with both man and gods."

Therese's heart pounded in her chest. She felt she might be sick. Surely she had read this stuff before? Of course she had, she thought, taking a deep breath and slowly releasing it.

One article depicted Hades and his sons as evil demons. Therese shuddered. Then she clicked on another link. An image of the Grim Reaper, also named Death, tall and hooded with a gruesome face, long, thin hands, one of which held a scythe, made Therese flinch.

Clifford must have sensed her anxiety, because he jumped on the bed beside her, shook his stubby tail, and looked pleadingly into her eyes.

"You want to go outside?" she asked.

He immediately pranced around her room, full of eager excitement, running through the cluster of balloons that were beginning to sag. Puffy hopped onto his wheel and ran with enthusiasm, even though he usually waited to exercise at night. Even Jewels poked her head over the side of her plastic tank to peek at the activity around her.

Therese carefully took her tortoise into her hands and placed her against her chest. "You can come another time, Jewels." She stroked the shell and then put the tortoise back on its log in the tank with the hot lamp shining.

As she and Clifford went down the stairs—he like a speeding bullet and she a little more slowly than usual—panic gripped Therese's heart. She had almost forgotten. She had almost expected her parents to be downstairs reading or watching TV. She stopped on the bottom step and looked past the kitchen to the empty living room. Where was Carol?

Therese went to the deck outside, followed by Clifford. Carol sat at the wooden table talking on the phone, her body turned toward the reservoir side, away from the giant elms in back. The sun was just over the lake, heading toward its rest behind the mountains on the other side. The sky was a clear blue, and though it was still a long time till dusk, some of the animals were making themselves visible. There were always the birds hopping from tree to tree, twittering anxiously about this and that. But now there were also the chipmunks scampering around, and across from them, two deer plucked grass beneath the trees.

"Of course, Lieutenant," Carol said. "We'll be there." Carol pushed the end button on the portable phone. "No cell reception out here, I guess." She waved the receiver. "It's been a long time since I've been land-locked."

"We're lucky we get good Internet service out here. We had to use dial up until just a few months ago."

"Ugh."

"Did the lieutenant have any news?"

"They want us to come for a line up tomorrow, to see if you can identify the man whose face you saw, you know."

"They think they got the killer? Already?"

Carol tilted her head to the side. "The man you saw may not be the killer. They think they got him, though. His picture was in their system. They

55

went to his apartment and brought him in for questioning and have enough to detain him overnight. He *could* be the killer. They don't know yet."

"Oh." Clifford lifted his paws to Therese's jean-clad shins. "Okay, boy. Let's go."

"Where are you going?"

"Just for a walk through the woods where Clifford likes to do his business. We'll be right back."

Therese realized as she led Clifford off the back steps of the wrap-around deck that Carol probably would have liked an invitation to join them, but Therese didn't want human company just yet. She wanted to retreat like she always did to the mountain forest with her dog and the wild animals for company.

Clifford frolicked around in front of her, sniffing this tree and that, as she headed up the mountain through the pines, aspens, and cypresses. A cardinal swept down and landed five feet away on a cypress branch. Therese inspected the feeder on the elm by the back deck. Empty. If she wanted to watch the birds through the kitchen window while washing dishes, she'd need to refill it. She looked more closely at the elm. One of its branches had turned completely yellow. Her mother had told her it had Dutch elm disease and the tree would slowly die if they didn't cut off the dead branch and treat the roots, but her parents hadn't had a chance to do anything about it. They kept saying later this summer...

She headed back up the trail after Clifford. She stepped over little round pellets, evidence that more deer had been visiting.

The national forest climbed behind her property for miles, and she rarely ran into another person on her walks. Only five homes stretched the expanse between Lemon Reservoir and the national forest, and the homes were more than half a mile apart. On the end lot on their northern side with twenty-five acres of private ranch land was Jen's house. It was three quarters of a mile down the dirt road that separated the houses from the reservoir, and

Jen's mother ran the trail rides up through the forest in spring and summer, so, occasionally, Therese could hear them calling out commands to their animals. Usually the woods were quiet, like they were now.

Up ahead, Clifford started growling and barking. Therese caught up with him where he stood crouching in the woods.

"What is it, Clifford? Do you see a deer? You think you're so vicious, don't you, boy? But you and I know the truth."

Therese glimpsed a sudden movement ten feet away that was nothing like a deer. It seemed larger, like a bear, but human. "Who's there?"

Clifford's growl grew more intense, and he bared his teeth, backing away toward Therese.

Could a stranger be roaming around the forest?

Or worse, could her parents' killer be after *her*?

"Come on, Clifford! Let's get out of here!" Therese ran, but the dog stayed planted, baring his teeth and growling viciously.

"Clifford, come!" Therese's heart beat wildly, her throat felt dry, and her body numbed.

Still Clifford growled.

Therese ran over to Clifford and swept him up in her arms. Then, in her peripheral vision, she saw the figure move, closer this time.

"Therese!" It was a woman's voice, but it did not belong to her aunt.

Therese held on to Clifford and scrambled down the trail to her house, her head and neck throbbing with pain. Her foot caught on an aspen root, and she fell to the ground, hurting her knee and the palms of both hands. Clifford leapt from her arms as she fell, and he bounded back up the trail.

"No, Clifford!" She sprung to her feet and followed her dog. "Come back here, boy! Please! Come!"

From the corner of her eyes, she saw the figure move between two trees. Clifford yelped and ran down the trail, back to the house. Before

Therese turned to follow him, she saw a woman wearing a short brown leather skirt and brown knee-high boots. She had pale skin and blonde rogue curls falling from a high bun. Therese thought she saw a bird perched on the woman's shoulder, but she couldn't be sure, because Therese had turned around so quickly and ran so fast that she couldn't be sure of what she had seen. She knew it was a woman, and that was all. A woman who had said her name.

"Call the lieutenant! Call 911!" Therese cried to her aunt, who still sat on the wooden table looking out toward the reservoir. "But come inside! Lock the doors!"

"Therese?" Carol jumped up. "What's wrong?"

"Come inside! *Now!*"

It seemed to take Carol forever and a day to follow Therese in through the kitchen door, but when she did, Therese slammed it shut, locked it, and turned the dead bolt, which was not easy because they hardly ever used it. Therese then ran to the front door and did the same. "Check the downstairs windows!" Therese yelled. "All of them!"

"What is going on, Therese! Tell me what happened!"

Why couldn't grownups ever just do what kids asked of them without asking a million questions? "Please, Carol! I saw someone out there. She looked really weird. And she called my name."

Carol went to the bedrooms to check the locks on the windows, but not without saying, "Calm down, honey. It's probably nothing. Maybe a neighbor you didn't recognize?"

Therese finished checking the last window and then found her aunt in the guest bedroom. She pointed a finger at her aunt and shouted, "You either think I'm paranoid or you're acting brave because you think you need to for my benefit! Well, I think I have a right to be paranoid. And if you're just acting brave, don't."

She left the room and sat on the sofa, which faced the kitchen, and stared at the back door. Clifford jumped into her lap.

"Therese, I'm sorry." Carol crossed the room and sat on the other end of the sofa.

"I know my own neighborhood," Therese said, still worked up.

"You're right. I'll call the lieutenant. I'm a little scared now, too."

It was dusk when the lieutenant arrived with another officer in tow. They came inside, accepted glasses of iced tea, and listened to Therese's account of what happened earlier in the woods.

The lieutenant said, "To be on the safe side, I'll post an officer on guard for a week or so to keep an eye on the place. Officer Morgan here will stay tonight. I'll see you both in the morning for the line up. Let Officer Morgan know if you hear or see anything the least bit suspicious to you, okay?"

"We will," Carol said, following the lieutenant to the door. "Thank you so much."

Officer Morgan slept on a cot on the back deck, so Therese felt a little more at ease, even though she couldn't take Clifford out to pee without him barking up a storm.

At night, when it was time to go to sleep, she was glad the officer was there below her on the deck outside. She lay there with Clifford and first thought of the fear. The woman had looked so strange. Even her voice was strange. Then Therese thought of the despair, and she fought off the panicky feeling until it won, and she sobbed and sobbed until she finally fell asleep.

Therese was riding on a carousel at a carnival on a painted horse moving up and down to accordion music when Hip appeared and said, "My brother is coming for you."

"But he said he'd kill me if he came to me," Therese said.

59

"Only when he's acting as the guide for the dead. He's getting our father to make me take over that loathsome job. I'm not looking forward to it, and I guess I have you to thank for it."

"I don't get it. You're going to be the new guide for the dead?"

"Just temporarily, so Than can come for you."

"And then what?"

Hip shrugged. "I think he wants you to become his queen of the dead." Then he said, "Why don't you become my queen instead?"

Therese laughed. "You're not the marrying kind, Hip. I can see that."

The next morning after breakfast, Carol drove Therese to the Durango Police Department. Lieutenant Hobson met them at the front desk and escorted them into a dimly lit room that smelled like her father's cigars. Through a window on one wall, they could see six men being led into an adjacent room. Each wore a number around his neck. Two of the men were tall and the others closer to average size. One had a big belly. All six men had dark skin and beards, though the beards were of varying lengths and tidiness. Therese recognized the face she had seen the day of the shooting. Seeing him sent shivers all down her spine and made the hair on the back of her neck stand on end. She could barely breathe. There was no question in her mind. He was there the night of the shooting.

Had he killed her parents? She looked at him with hatred and fear as tears slid down her cheeks. Had he been responsible for ruining her life forever? She wanted to break through the glass and strangle him. "Number four," she finally said with confidence. "Definitely number four."

"You're sure?" the lieutenant asked.

"Positive."

The lieutenant spoke into a machine and said, "Thanks. You can lead them out now."

As the men turned to follow the officer out of the small chamber, Therese saw a reflection in the window of a woman standing behind her. The reflection appeared out of nowhere and looked exactly like the woman in the woods from the day before—the woman who called her name and may or may not have been carrying a snake. There was definitely a large bird perched on the shoulder of the woman in the reflection, and the woman was smiling and nodding, apparently at Therese. Therese quickly turned, gasping, but there was no one behind her.

"What's wrong?" Carol asked, standing beside her.

"What? Oh, nothing. Can we go home now?"

Chapter Ten: Setting Up

Late at night, Than listened for her voice among the multitude praying to him. So many voices all at once, "Please don't take my son! He's all I have!" and "Don't let the cancer take her. Help her to recover." As if he had a choice. People are born, they live, and they die, and there was little the gods could do to alter their experiences. In many ways, Than thought, the gods were the slaves of humans, each with a duty to help maintain the world and to keep all of its creation in balance. The gods served the world and its inhabitants, not the other way around.

At last he heard her voice echoing above the mountains of Colorado. He flew to her and listened.

"I hope my parents feel no pain," Therese whispered, and her voice lifted up to him and into the clouds like sweet, soft music, like something his mother might have once sung to him. "I hope my dream was true, and they really are in the beautiful Elysian Fields, perfectly happy."

Than looked down upon Therese where she sat on her bed with her little dog. "I miss them, Clifford," she said out loud. "I miss them so much!" She hugged her dog and sobbed.

A knock at her bedroom door brought her beautiful face up again. "Yes?"

"Can I come in?" A woman, a redhead, too, stood behind the door.

As Therese and the other woman spoke, Than wondered if he were acting too hastily in his decision to pursue Therese. She was, after all, the one and only girl he had ever met alive. Once he changed into mortal form, he could meet other girls and make a more informed decision. What was so special about Therese? As soon as he had asked himself the question, he answered it: she was the only soul in the centuries of his existence to have willed herself to the outskirts of the Underworld and to get close enough to him to touch him. This alone set her apart. Also. she hadn't come to him in a proud, arrogant, threatening way. She hadn't realized she had left the dream world and was close to dying herself. She had believed herself to be the author of her own dream, and in that dream, she wanted her parents alive. Who wouldn't? If she had exerted her will and demonstrated strength, she had done so in ignorance. She had not set out to challenge him.

She hadn't come like Sisyphus to bind him so humans could not die. She hadn't come like Hercules to steal Cerberus. She had not come like Orpheus first to persuade with song and then to defy a broken agreement.

She had come, put her arms around him, and told him he was lovely—so lovely—and she had kissed him. Who in the history of time had ever done that to Death?

And the deal with Hades required Therese to do something that not just any mortal could do. He wasn't sure that even Therese could do it.

Plus, he had only forty days. Why had his father chosen forty days? To Than, this seemed an arbitrary number. Why not one hundred? Why not twenty? At any rate, forty days seemed hardly enough time to make a selection among the billions of girls on earth. No, unless Therese was less than she seemed, he would spend his time courting her. He would not do like his father had his mother and take her unwillingly. Than had seen how her resentment had poisoned her relationship with his father. He wanted to win Therese's heart.

From the conversation below him, he came to understand that the woman was Therese's aunt, Carol, and this woman was now encouraging Therese to visit her friend, Jen. Than soon learned where Jen lived, and so he turned his attention to her, to see if he could use her in his efforts to meet Therese in the flesh.

When he found her, he was surprised to hear her praying to him. Most mortals prayed to a different god, unless they or someone they loved were dying or already dead. But this young woman was asking for death?

"Everything would be easier for everyone else if you just took me. Then he could come back, and they'd all be a happy."

Than saw a way to befriend Therese. He would first study Jen and her family.

Chapter Eleven: Invitations

A few weeks passed since Therese had identified the man she saw the day of the shooting, and, after mostly lying around in bed and spending time with her pets, she finally returned to the woods with Clifford. She didn't go as far as usual, but she went a little ways, and Carol stood on the back deck watching her in full view. The police were no longer standing guard at the house, and Therese could finally take Clifford out to do his business without a leash and without him barking and growling and driving her mad. The wild animals, which had not come around while the officers were here, returned to eat the sunflower seeds Therese sprinkled across the deck and railing.

Jen had called several days ago and had begged Therese to come and groom the horses with her, and Therese decided today she felt like going.

Carol turned on to the gravelly drive leading up to Jen's house. Clifford leaned his head out of Therese's open window, his tongue hanging happily from his mouth, his stubby tail wagging. Clifford loved to come to Jen's and run around the ranch, though he wasn't allowed in the pen. He knew Jen's family and their horses, and they knew him, and so everyone got along just fine. Therese loved to come too. She looked at the big log cabin, similar to her own, on the right of the property, and the barn and pen to the left. On the opposite side of the pen from the house, two pastures spread out to the north at the base of the mountains. A stream cut across the entire property behind the house and pen, and through the center of the pastures. Tied to the base of the front wooden steps of the house was a lone goat, which bleated as Jen opened the front door and skipped down the five steps to the ground.

Jen's blonde hair was pulled up in a high ponytail, and she wore a white tank top and old blue jeans and boots. Therese felt a wave of jealousy at Jen's beauty but shrugged it off as soon as Jen called to her in her friendly voice, "Hey there! You're finally here!"

When Therese opened her car door, Clifford sprang out to meet Jen. The goat bleated its objections, and Clifford cowered away from it.

"Hey there, boy!" Jen pet Clifford when he greeted her with his front paws on her legs. Then Clifford ambled down to his favorite hangout: the stream at the back of the property, which was full of trout.

Therese turned to Carol. "Thanks for the ride."

"Sure. Call me if you want a ride home. First I'm running into Durango to get a few more groceries, but I'll be back in a couple of hours."

Therese stepped out of the car, but before she closed the door, Carol asked, "You sure you don't want me to run you by the cemetery later? You still haven't visited your parents' graves. It's been over a month since we buried them."

"I'm sure. I'm not ready to do that yet." She wished her aunt wouldn't have brought this up now. She'd been close to happy and excited, but now she was filled with dread.

"Okay. Bye, sweetheart."

Therese closed the car door and turned to her friend. "It's nice to be out of the house. Thanks for inviting me."

"Hey, listen. My mom was wondering if you want a job. The two brothers she hired this spring had a death in the family. She hired a new temp a week ago, but she still needs one more hand, just until she can find someone more permanent. Up to it?"

Therese shrugged. It would be a lot of hard work, which could be both good and bad. "Would she need me every day?"

"Pretty much. She pays ten an hour." Jen led her across the gravel drive past the barn toward the partially sheltered pen where the dozen horses hung out.

"I don't know. If she can't find anyone else, maybe." Then to Clifford, who had come back to check on her, she said, "No boy, not in the pen. You know better."

"Please say yes. We could hang out."

"How early in the morning?"

"Okay, you wouldn't have to do the early morning stuff."

They reached the pen and the General greeted her with a sniff. He stretched his long gray neck over the fence for what he knew would be a soft stroke. He was the biggest of the horses, a huge gray gelding. Jen and her brothers sometimes called him the elephant. "Hey, General," Therese said, rubbing the side of his face.

"We bring the horses in at nine for grooming before they start their first trail ride of the day. My brothers and the new handler are in there finishing up now. We'll need help with the grooming and tack so they're ready to go by eleven. You could leave after that."

"So nine to eleven? That's not bad. Let me think about it." She could use some of her own mad money, and twenty dollars a day for just a couple of hours of her time seemed like a good deal, and a good distraction. She loved grooming the horses.

Jen added, "After my mom's trail rides, we exercise them hard before dinner, when we turn them out to pasture again till dark. We could use another rider then, too, from like four to five. Not necessarily every day. Just when you can."

One of Jen's two brothers appeared in the middle of the pen from behind the shelter. He was the tallest and oldest of the Holt kids and had blond hair like his sister, which he kept short around his face like a bowl. He graduated last May and would be attending college in the fall. "Hey, Therese."

"Hi Pete."

"Oh, hey, Therese!" the other brother, who would be a freshman this year, called as he popped up from behind a horse. He wore the same blond bowl on his head as his brother, but the freckles that peppered his cheeks were more prominent.

"Hi Bobby."

"Sorry about your parents," Pete, the older one, said.

"Yeah. Thanks." She bit the inside of her bottom lip.

Then Bobby asked, "Hey, have you met Than?"

Another boy, slightly taller than Pete with dark wavy hair and a bigger build, stepped out of the shelter and into the middle of the pen and the horses.

It was the Than from her dreams.

Jen must have noticed the look on her friend's face, because she asked, "Do you guys know each other?"

"You look familiar." Than strolled up to the fence in his blue jeans and tight white t-shirt.

"No, I don't think we've met," Therese said. It couldn't be. It just couldn't be him. But how many people had she known named Than? Her knees felt like they might buckle.

Than extended his hand. "Well, then, it's a pleasure to finally meet you, Therese. I've heard a lot about you, thanks to Bobby here."

Bobby's face turned crimson as she gave the new guy her hand, and she couldn't pull it away fast enough. Than seemed to be laughing at her behind his smile, enjoying her pain and confusion and Bobby's embarrassment. She decided she did not like him.

"It's nice to meet you, too," she lied.

Jen opened the gate of the pen. "We're half way done with the grooming."

"Can I groom Sugar?" Therese asked.

"Than's finishing her up now," Pete said. "Can you take Hershey?"

68

Without warning, Clifford ran through the gate and leapt into Than's arms. He licked Than all over his face. The General spooked back, causing a domino effect as two other horses, Ace and Chestnut, reared and snorted. Fear gripped Therese as she recognized the danger. But Than tossed Clifford to Therese, grabbed the General's mane, and whispered something in his ear. The General settled, which calmed the other horses, and Therese finally released her breath.

"Bad boy! Go back to the stream! Go catch a fish!" she scolded Clifford, turning him out of the pen. She said to Jen, "I'm so sorry. I don't know what came over him. He should know better than that." Then she looked up at Than with suspicion and awe. Why had Clifford run to him? And how had he settled the horses so quickly?

"Wow, Than," Jen said. "How did you do that?"

Than shrugged and said he had a way with horses, but Therese still felt as though he were laughing at her, as though the threat of danger had been her fault because she couldn't control her dog, and she had needed Than to save the day. She took up a brush and went over to Hershey, a mare whose coat, as the name implied, was like chocolaty brown silk.

"Hey girl," Therese said in a soothing voice. "Did you miss me?" Therese could feel Than's eyes on her, but she tried her best to ignore him. He was too sexy for her, anyway, and much too arrogant and self-assured. Jen had probably already staked her claim on him, and she was probably more his type, so naturally beautiful. As Therese brushed through Hershey's coat, she wondered if it had been a mere coincidence that Than looked like the Than in her dreams. Or, maybe he didn't, and somehow she was now imposing the image of him on her memory.

Therese bent over to brush Hershey's belly, and her rear-end bumped against Than, who was passing behind her. She popped upright, the blood rushing to her face, and muttered, "Excuse me." He said nothing, but when she snatched a glance his way, she could see he looked pleased with himself.

Had her subconscious somehow *sensed* she would be meeting him? Had it been a prophetic vision? And if so, what had it meant?

After they finished grooming and saddling the horses, Jen's mom came out of the barn where she had been working to formally offer Therese the job and to thank her for accepting it. She was surprised to hear Therese wouldn't be coming at dawn to help with the barn and pen cleaning, but Jen quickly explained that she planned to work every morning instead of splitting the chores with her brothers. Jen's surreptitious glance toward Than confirmed Therese's suspicion that Jen was interested in him, and this explained Jen's sudden eagerness to work more. Mrs. Holt seemed pleased with the arrangement, since she paid Jen less than ten an hour.

Jen invited Therese to stay for lunch when her mom and Pete took the first riders on the trail. "We're just having frozen pizzas," Jen explained, "but it would be fun to chat."

Clifford was splashing around in the stream behind Jen's house chasing trout he would never catch, but perfectly entertained, nevertheless. Luckily, he was too preoccupied to bother the riders walking up the drive toward the pen. "Sure," Therese said.

Jen surprised Therese by asking Than if he wanted to stay, too.

"Maybe next time," he said. "I promised my sisters I'd eat with them today."

He waved goodbye as he left, on foot, down the gravel drive, where cars were now parked in a line, and south up the dirt road toward Therese's house. Therese and Jen both watched him until he was out of sight. Even a few of the trail riders waiting to mount stole glances at him.

Then Jen said, "Is he drop-dead gorgeous, or what?"

Therese shrugged.

"How can you take such a casual attitude toward his splendid good looks? Does this mean I don't have to fight you for him?"

"What about Matthew?" Therese referred to the boy Jen had been with most of their freshman year.

"He hasn't called much this summer. I think he's lost interest."

"Maybe he's just busy or on vacation."

Jen asked again, "So you're not interested?"

They walked up the steps toward the front door, Bobby close behind. "He's all yours," Therese said, though, as soon as the words came out, she felt nauseous.

"Well, I won't hold my breath," Jen said. "He was checking you out the whole time we were grooming in the pen. I think he prefers you."

Bobby squeezed by Jen and went down the hall. "I'm outta here."

Jen laughed at her brother.

"That's impossible," Therese said when they were alone. "I mean, God, look at you."

"Oh, shut up. You always talk yourself down. I would kill for your curly hair and pouty lips."

"You can get a perm and botox—not that you need it. I wish I had your boobs."

"You've got boobs!"

"Nubs." She cupped her hands around her half-lemons and looked enviously at Jen's full oranges.

"Cute nubs. And some people develop later than others. Plus, there's always implants," Jen laughed.

"Yeah, right." Therese rolled her eyes and took a seat at the kitchen table. "So, where's Than going? Did he really walk here?" Just saying the name sent a shiver down her spine.

Jen grabbed some paper plates from the pantry and put three around the table, though just now Bobby was watching television in the other room. "He and his sisters are renting the Melner cabin for the summer."

"The *Melner* cabin?" It was about a half-mile south up the road from Therese's house, the third of the five houses across from the reservoir. The Melner's had turned their home into a vacation getaway, and although Therese was used to different people staying there throughout the year, she found it upsetting that Than was one of them. She recalled the image of the Grim Reaper on her computer screen and shuddered. It was just a coincidence, she reminded herself.

"Yeah, you guys are neighbors," Jen giggled.

"If his family can afford the cabin, why's he working for your mom this week?"

"For the same reasons you are, I guess." The oven started beeping—it was hot now—so Jen put the frozen pizza directly on the center rack. "He said that he enjoyed working with horses and that he wanted to get in touch with nature." She laughed. "I'm part of nature. He can get in touch with *me*."

Therese laughed with her. It felt good being with her friend like this. Jen could be bossy and stubborn, but she was so worth it.

Jen closed the oven door and asked, "Diet Coke?"

"Sounds great." She took the ice-cold can from her friend and popped open the tab. The cold pop felt good going down her throat. The grooming had worked up a thirst. "So where's he from?"

"He said he's from down south. At first he said 'down under,' and we thought he meant Australia, even though he doesn't have the accent. But he said he meant down south, from Texas. From what we gathered, he used to work on a ferry."

Therese choked on the Diet Coke and broke into a fit of coughing.

"You okay?" Jen asked, patting Therese on the back.

Therese eventually nodded. "Wrong pipe," she explained when she could.

Carol dropped Therese and Clifford at the Holt ranch again the next morning. Carol had been thrilled about Therese's new job, saying it was just what she needed to get her mind off...things. Therese was partly glad that she would be out of Carol's hair this week and keeping herself entertained with her best friend and the horses, but she was also partly annoyed by Than's appearance, especially since the more she thought about it, the more she was sure he looked *exactly* like the Than in her dreams.

"Come on, boy!" she called to Clifford, as she climbed from the car. Then she said to Carol, "I'll call if I need a ride."

As Therese walked up the gravelly drive with Clifford stopping to pee on every tree, she thought more about her discoveries last night. When she couldn't sleep, she had gone on the Internet and googled "the Furies." One article had this to say: "The Furies are three sisters: Alecto (The Unceasing), Megaera (The Avenger of Jealousy and Hatred), and Tisiphone (The Avenger of Murder). They are the goddesses of revenge, sometimes called the daughters of the Night. They haunt criminals until they go insane and die. The Furies are untiring and persistent in their pursuit. They are impartial and indifferent, merely carrying out their duty. They continue to torment wrongdoers even after death. In some traditions, they are the daughters of Hades and Persephone, rulers of the Underworld, and their brothers are Hypnos (Sleep) and Thanatos (Death). The Furies are known for tormenting sinners under the command of Hades and for pursuing criminals on Earth until their victims have been rightfully avenged."

In her dream weeks ago, Than had said he was sending the Furies to the waking world of the living to help her solve her parents' murder. Therese now shuddered at the prospect.

Of course, it had only been a silly dream, something her subconscious must have conjured up based on this mythology she must have read a long time ago and had forgotten all about.

As she approached Jen's house, Clifford turned around back down the gravelly drive and took off across the dirt road toward the reservoir. Boulders and short aspens made a kind of barrier between the road and the water until the road reached Jen's house. Across from the Holts' was a big field of tall grass, and out in the middle of the grass this morning was a lone figure. Clifford was running toward it.

"Come back, Clifford!" Therese followed her dog into the grass. She was stunned when she saw Than, soaked from head to toe, walking toward her with his clothes bundled in his hands. All he was wearing were his wet white boxers and boots.

"Good Morning, Therese," he said when he got closer.

She couldn't avoid looking at his golden body—his golden *naked* body, for the wet boxers didn't leave much to the imagination. His skin wasn't what you would call *tan*, but it seemed to almost *glow*.

"How are you today?" Than asked.

She could tell he was amused by her reaction, which she hadn't been able to disguise. Her eyes were about to pop out of her head.

"Fine," she said, turning away. "Come on, Clifford."

"That water felt so good," Than said. "Do you go swimming in the lake often?"

Not often enough, she thought. She'd only been a few times this summer, and that was before…her life had changed. "Not often."

"That's too bad. I'd go every day if I could. I had no idea how beautiful everything is up here, how nice the sunshine feels, the water, the cool mountain air when the wind blows. I love listening to the birds, too. I think I've found seven different species in this forest alone." He caught up to her now and walked beside her.

"They don't have those things down in Texas?"

"What? Oh, well not like this."

74

Therese noticed that Clifford walked beside Than, putting Than between them. Clifford never took to strangers this quickly. "Come on, Clifford," she said again, a little jealous that he wasn't trotting alongside her instead of *him*. "Don't you have barn and pen duty this morning?" Therese asked Than with a touch of hostility as they reached the dirt road and headed toward the gravel drive.

"We finished. I worked up a sweat and thought I'd come cool off a bit before grooming the horses. You should join me tomorrow. Come a little earlier."

He stopped on the gravel drive to put on his shirt. Therese took the opportunity to study his tight ruffle of abs but looked away as soon as his head was visible again. Then he knocked off his boots and climbed into his jeans. Therese didn't know whether she should stand there and wait for him or keep walking toward the pen, so she walked on, but at a slow pace.

"Come on, boy!" she said to Clifford.

Clifford decided to wait for Than, but, in no time, both boy and dog had caught up to her as she reached for the gate to the pen. "No, Clifford," she warned.

"Mornin' Therese," Bobby called brightly from behind the yellowish-brown horse named Ace.

"Hey, Bobby." Therese quickly closed the gate behind Than. "Go play, boy," she said to Clifford. "Where's Jen?"

"She'll be out in a minute," Mrs. Holt called from the shelter. "She's on the phone. Mornin' Therese."

Therese stepped under the aluminum structure. "Mornin', Mrs. Holt. Who do you need me to start on?"

Jen's mother had her gray-blonde hair cut short, like her sons, in a bowl around her leathery freckled face. She was beautiful once, but she stopped caring about her skin in the elements, and the sun had taken its toll.

Plus, she smoked and looked slightly underweight, and the lines in her face were deep. "Bobby said you prefer Sugar."

Therese liked all the horses, but Sugar, the white mare, never resisted Therese's requests. The General, Chestnut, Rambo, and Rusty were the most stubborn of the herd, all constantly vying for the upper ranks in the pecking order, and Therese didn't like having to hit or kick or growl at the animals to get their cooperation. Sugar, Ace, and Dumbo had mild dispositions and seemed indifferent to rank and status. Therese took up a brush and said in a gentle, even tone, "Hi, Sugar, girl. You already look so pretty today." She took the brush to Sugar's withers. "You're not nearly as dirty as Hershey was yesterday."

Bobby laughed, "That's because she's a lazy girl. She just stands around and sleeps all mornin', don't you, girl."

Therese noticed Than was just a few feet away from her, eyeing her with a smug look on his face. What had she done to give him the impression she was interested in him? She was confused by how confident he seemed to be that he had some kind of an effect on her. Well, she'd have to show him. He didn't need to know that he *did* have an effect on her, that his very presence had suddenly made her more self-conscious than she could ever remember being, but she could very well control herself and make Than think otherwise. She wanted to wipe that all-too-confident grin right off his face, even though his dark wavy hair, now wet and clinging to his beautiful face, set off the crystal blue of his eyes. She took a deep breath and focused on the animal. Sugar soothed her; the contact with the warm mare and the look of her friendly eyes made a feeling of peace wash over Therese. "You're such a good girl, even if you are lazy."

"Ace, on the other hand, is a roller, aren't you boy?" Bobby said to the yellowish-brown horse. "If you could get one more weed stuck in your coat, I'd be surprised."

"Oh, come on now," Mrs. Holt said. "You're being too hard on Sugar. She's not lazy. She and Satellite groom each other, don't you, Satellite. That's why you're so clean."

Satellite was pure white and seemed to have a bond with Sugar. Therese often noticed them standing head to tail flicking away the flies and licking off the grass and dirt from one another's coats.

"Where's Pete?" Therese asked.

"He's practicing today," Mrs. Holt said. "His band is performing at the Wildhorse Saloon in Durango tomorrow evening."

"That's awesome!" Therese knew Pete dreamed of making it big with his music and that, as much as he loved horses, he probably wouldn't come back to work on the ranch after college. "I bet he's about to pop."

"He's pretty excited," Bobby said.

"We're all going after supper," Mrs. Holt said. "You're welcome to come with us." Then she added, "You, too, Than."

"Thanks, Mrs. Holt," Than said. "That sounds very entertaining."

Before Therese could reply, she heard Jen greeting Clifford on her way to the pen. "Good boy!" she was saying. "You go catch a fish! Catch a fish!" Then she came in through the gate and came up beside Therese. "Hey. How's it going?"

"Okay," Therese lied. She couldn't very well say she'd cried herself to sleep because she missed her parents so terribly and that she'd felt restless the whole night long. She couldn't say what she had discovered about the Furies and how suspicious she felt about Than showing up here not long after her strange dreams. "What's up?"

Jen grabbed a brush and started working on Annie, a red mare who happened to be on the other side of Than from Therese. "We're all going to the Wildhorse Saloon tomorrow night. You *have* to come with us. Ray and Todd might go, too."

77

"Ray and Todd are going?" Therese perked up. She loved hanging out with them. They always managed to make her laugh.

"Yeah, I was just on the phone with Todd. Pete's band is performing."

"That's what your mom said." Although Therese didn't like the idea of being there with Than and his arrogance, she could use a good dose of company from her friends, a distraction from all the anguish and longing and dread, especially at night, when she had more time to think. She patted Sugar's front leg for the hoof. Therese picked out a small pebble wedged against the shoe.

"So are you going?" Than asked.

He looked Therese directly in the eyes, all signs of smugness gone. Therese's mouth opened with surprise. He really seemed to like her. Therese shot a glance at Jen and from the look on her face realized she had drawn the same conclusion. "Um, I'll ask my aunt."

Mrs. Holt said, "Pete would be glad if you could make it. Tell your aunt to call me if she has any questions."

"Yes, m'am, I will." Therese squatted down to work on Sugar's legs.

"Oh, and I have a favor to ask, Therese," Mrs. Holt said. "Could you help us ride later today before supper? With Pete gone, we could use the extra hand."

Therese frowned. Riding made her nervous. She hated kicking and shouting the commands. But she didn't want to let down Mrs. Holt. "I'm sure my aunt won't mind. She's working anyway."

"Great," Mrs. Holt said. "Sure do appreciate it. We already exercised Sugar yesterday, but Dumbo's a gentle ride. You can ride him."

Therese finished grooming Sugar, a little knot forming in her stomach now over having to ride later today. She rode last summer a few times because Jen had pleaded with her and then stooped to bribing, but a year is a long time. "Who should I work on now?" Therese asked.

Mrs. Holt told her to groom Dumbo, so they could get better acquainted.

"Stay clean, Sugar." Therese petted the horse's cheek and neck. "You look so pretty. Yes, you do."

Therese spotted Dumbo on the other side of Jen, behind Annie. Dumbo was the youngest of the males and the new stallion, added to the group after Benji was put down last summer. His ears were slightly bigger than those of the other horses, hence his name. Just now they were pointed forward and his muzzle was extended toward Therese and sniffing at her with curiosity like Clifford sometimes did with visitors. "Hi there, Dumbo. Remember me? I'm Therese." She took the brush to Dumbo's withers and pet his neck with her other hand. "You're a handsome boy, and from the look of you, you're a roller like Ace, aren't you?" She started pulling weeds and stickers from his thick mane.

Bobby snickered. "You should see 'em at night before we bring 'em in. He and Ace are like puppies the way they roll around in the grass and chase each other across the pasture."

"I bet that's fun to watch," Than put in. "I'd like to see that some time."

"You're welcome to come and watch the horses any evening," Mrs. Holt said. "Just stay outside the fence. If they see you in with them, they'll get upset. They like their routine."

"Maybe I'll come by this evening," Than said.

"Come just before dusk," Bobby said. "That's when all the fun starts." Then Bobby added. "Therese, you should come too."

"I'll have to see how I feel after riding. I haven't done it in so long, I may be sore."

Mrs. Holt let out a loud guffaw that made Therese jump. "No sugar. You won't be sore tonight. You'll feel it in the mornin'."

Therese looked at Dumbo's eyes, and he looked back at her with a knowing smile, as if to say, "You'll be alright." Therese rubbed his face and put her cheek against his. Dumbo nuzzled up to her and softly whinnied.

"He likes you," Bobby said.

After Therese helped saddle the horses for the first trail ride of the day, Jen asked if she wanted to stay again for lunch. They were standing near the gravel drive beneath the shade of a cluster of cypresses as the cars were pulling up—the first riders of the day.

Therese's eyes were on her dog, who noticed the cars and was coming up from the stream to investigate. "Come here, Clifford! Come, now!" He bounded over to her like a good boy. She picked him up to avoid conflict. Then she turned to Jen. "Thanks for the invitation, but I better get some rest at home if I'm coming back this afternoon. What time does your mom need me? Four?"

"Yeah. You're really only riding for about half an hour, but by the time you remove the tack and turn 'em out, an hour's gone by before you know it." Then Jen added, "Don't feel like you have to do it if you're not up to it. I don't mind riding an extra hour tonight. I don't think my mom knows how nervous you get."

"Thanks, Jen, but I'll give it a try. I'll call you if I chicken out. Can I use your phone to call my aunt? She won't let me walk."

Than came up from behind her. "Would she mind if I walked you home?"

She shrugged. "I guess that would be okay." She tried to seem indifferent, but her heart was pounding so loudly that she worried he might be able to hear it. She knew she should call and ask permission, but she knew the answer would likely be no, and she wanted to walk with him. They said goodbye to the Holts and headed down the drive toward the dirt road. Clifford wriggled in her arms and then settled.

"You have a gift with animals," Than said, stroking Clifford. "I like to watch you interact with them."

"Thanks," she said, unable to prevent herself from giving him a genuine smile. Being an animal lover was probably the thing she liked most about herself. "You're pretty good with animals, too. Clifford has never taken to a stranger the way he has with you, like yesterday when he jumped in your arms."

"I don't get to spend much time around animals." They stepped out onto the dirt road between the houses and the lake, so Therese let Clifford down as Than continued. "I wish it were otherwise. The horses and the birds and even your little dog have brought me a lot of pleasure these past two days."

Therese didn't know what to say. All of this was so unexpected. She had taken Than to be arrogant and maybe even selfish, but he sounded sincere. "I couldn't live without animals," she said.

Than frowned. Then he turned to her and said, "Being around people has been a pleasant change, too. I tend to be a loner, except for my sisters' company."

"That's too bad. But you can always change."

He sighed, gave her a sad smile, and shook his head. "Some things never change."

She wondered what he meant, but she was afraid to pry, so she looked across the reservoir to the mountains on the other side. The sun was almost at high noon, and everything sparkled under its brilliant light.

"I never get tired of this view," Therese said. "I feel so lucky to live here." Then she thought of who else used to live here, and the tears welled. Panic gripped her heart, but she took a deep breath and let it out slowly. She wasn't going to cry.

"I know you must miss them," Than said softly. "Bobby told me. I wish I could say I know how you feel."

"Are your parents staying in the Melner cabin with you?" Therese wanted to change the subject.

"No. My dad had to work and my mom is visiting my grandmother."

They were silent for a while, both looking out over the lake and at Clifford stopping again to pee on every other tree. When they reached Therese's gravel driveway, they slowed down and came to a stop. "What does your dad do?"

He stuck his hands in his pockets and let out a deep breath. "Hmm. Well, my dad, he manages a large operation, and my mom helps him during parts of the year. It's difficult to explain."

"So he never gets to get away?"

"Never. In fact, this is my very first trip away from home, and I had to beg and make promises." He laughed. "My dad's a good guy. Please don't misunderstand. But he's got a huge responsibility, and, well, it's difficult for him to be flexible."

Therese noticed Clifford had gone on ahead of her toward the house. "Well, I'm glad you got to come out here. It's beautiful country and the Holts are an awesome family. And the horses are so incredible."

"I'm glad, too." He took a step closer to her. "I'm glad I got to meet you."

Therese felt the blood rush to her face, and she looked down, shuffling around the gravel of her driveway with her sneaker. "Thanks. I'm glad I got to meet you, too." She looked up to see him grinning down at her.

"So I guess I'll see you later this afternoon, when it's time to exercise the horses."

"Yeah." She wanted to add, "Unless I chicken out," but she didn't.

"See you later." He turned and headed toward the Melner cabin.

She watched him walk away, enjoying the view.

Chapter Twelve: Mortal Sensations

Being human certainly had its advantages, Than thought as he walked away from Therese toward his cabin. For one thing, he never realized how much more humans than gods experience the world. As often as he had been all over the planet, he had never felt the sun on his back. He had never experienced the cold water of a lake or river running through his fingers. He had never heard the beautiful music of the birds. Than realized his primal senses were more finely-tuned when in mortal form, while his mind was more finely tuned when in godly form. In other words, he had never felt so much in all his life.

He wondered if the lower one went in the animal kingdom, the more this was true. Did horses feel more than humans? Beetles more than horses?

He stopped before a pine tree and pressed his nose close to its tickling branches. He breathed in the fresh, astringent scent with immeasurable pleasure. The path was alight with voices of insects, birds, and rodents, like an orchestra unaware of its audience and so unlike the quiet desolation of the Underworld. Even as Than travelled across the globe for souls day in and day out, he had not heard these insect sounds or felt the freshness of this air or basked in the heat of this sun. Before turning up the gravelly drive to his log cabin, he went to the reservoir once again to kick off his boots and dip his feet into the cool water. In the Underworld, he was surrounded by rivers but in none of them could he indulge his senses like he could now as a man.

Therese had baffled him. Earlier in the pen, she shouted prayers at him that had made it hard for him to keep a straight face. She had said, "What are you looking at? You think you're so sexy? So what if you are? Quit looking at me like that! You're a jerk, aren't you?"

It had amazed him how quickly these prayers that she unwittingly hurled at him changed as the afternoon went on. By the next day, by time he was walking her home, she directed other thoughts his way, "Who are you? Why do you like me? How can someone like you be interested in someone like me?"

He couldn't read her thoughts, but prayers that she sent his way were crystal clear, even if she did not know he heard them.

When he reached his cabin, he found it empty. Meg and Tizzie were rarely there, always busy hunting. Apparently they had a new lead in the case and would be gone for a while. Than felt a little guilty, now, as he thought of their constant work. His sisters enjoyed their job, but did they ever get a break? Who was he to have this extended vacation where he could revel in the sensual pleasures the earth had to offer?

Than sat on the sofa and immediately felt his brother's appearance.

Hip appeared on the opposite end of the sofa. "I was just wondering the same thing myself, brother," Hip said.

"I have no sympathy for you, lover boy."

"I don't blame you. Your job sucks. The past three weeks have been absolutely odious. I wonder how you've suffered through the past centuries without complaining before now."

Than shrugged. "It's not so bad as you make it out, Hip. There's satisfaction in bringing an end to earthly pain and suffering, which is almost always present at death. Don't you think?"

"Absolutely not. It's perfectly depressing. Not a bright spot anywhere to be found. I came to beg you to give me a day's reprieve, just a day, so I can have a little fun in the dream world, just to tide me over these next horrible days to come."

Than frowned. "I suppose I can find a day to do it. Let me think on it and get back with you." Than didn't want to risk the possibility of his father shortening his visit because of a complaining brother.

84

"Have I told you lately that I love you, bro'?" Hip jumped up and disappeared, smiling.

Chapter Thirteen: News

Carol looked up from the couch where she had been working on her laptop as soon as Therese and Clifford entered the house. "Oh, good. You're home. Hungry?"

Carol must have assumed one of the Holts had given her a ride, and Therese didn't say otherwise. "Not yet."

"Well, the lieutenant is coming by for a bit, so I guess we can wait till after his visit to have lunch."

Therese plopped onto the couch beside Carol and then winced. She kept forgetting about her neck. It felt good most of the time, but plopping on couches reminded her that her neck was still a little sore, and today's exercise probably made it a little more so. "Why is he coming?"

"He said he had some news and wanted to discuss it with us. He'll be here in about twenty minutes or so."

"I'll go shower and change."

Later, Therese opened the door and let the lieutenant inside. He was sweating again, and she wondered if he had a health problem.

"Did that man kill my parents?" she asked.

"Sweetheart, let the lieutenant come in and sit down."

"I don't blame her," Lieutenant Hobson said as he crossed the room. "I'd want answers, too, if I were her. He took the seat Carol offered him beside the fireplace.

"Can I get you something to drink? Iced tea? Lemonade?" Carol asked.

"Iced tea sounds nice. No sugar, please. I'm diabetic."

Therese sat on the sofa across from the lieutenant and waited until Carol returned with his drink. Once Carol was beside her on the couch, Therese asked, "What news do you have for us?"

"Well, I've established a couple of possible motives. Your father's most recent novel was based on a crime committed by a felon released a month ago from the federal prison in Three Rivers, Texas. My team has been tracking this man's whereabouts, and, as soon as we've located him, we'll bring him in for questioning."

"What about the man in the line up?" Therese asked.

"Another motive involves your mother's work. She was being honored at the university for her role in leading a team of students close to finding an antidote for the mutated anthrax toxin C. Maybe there are folks out there who wanted to slow down its discovery."

Therese's mouth dropped open. Her head started spinning and she closed her eyes.

"We've questioned a lot of people from the university and have pretty much ruled out disgruntled students and colleagues."

Therese opened her eyes. "What about the man in the lineup?" she said again.

"Sweetheart, be patient," Carol said. "He's getting to that."

"Yes. He's confessed to the shooting."

"Oh my gosh!" Therese cried. "He really did it!" She couldn't believe she had seen the killer before he committed his gruesome deed. Maybe if she had gotten her parents to see him, maybe she could have somehow prevented, maybe..." She broke into tears. She felt panicky and so alone. She wanted her mother and father!

"The shooter claims he was working for someone else," the lieutenant said, "and that's as far as we've gotten. We don't know who this other person is or why he was after your parents. But we know we've got the shooter, and we're in the process of offering him a deal to talk." The lieutenant finished his tea and set the glass down on the end table beside the chair. "That's all I have for now, but I wanted to tell you in person. I'll call as soon as we break this guy."

Therese shuddered. That man *had* killed her parents. She couldn't get his deranged face out of her mind. She shuddered again as the tears streamed down her cheeks. "I'm going upstairs," she said, before the lieutenant had left.

Sometime later, Carol came upstairs into Therese's room. "I'm so sorry you have to go through all this," Carol said gently, sitting beside her on the bed.

Therese didn't reply.

Carol stroked Therese's hair. "Can I fix you something to eat?"

"Maybe in a little bit."

"Richard's coming tomorrow night to stay with us through the weekend," Carol said, obviously trying to lighten the mood. "It'll be nice to have a man around."

"He's coming tomorrow night?"

Carol frowned. "I hope that's okay. What's wrong?"

"Nothing." Therese patted Clifford, who lay on the bed beside her. "I'm glad he's coming and everything. It's just that the Holts invited me to the Wildhorse Saloon tomorrow night. Pete's band is playing. Pete is Jen's older brother."

"That sounds like fun. Rich and I could join you after I pick him up from the airport."

"Oh, that would be so great. I need to get out of here, you know? You really want to go?"

"Sure!"

"Awesome," she said this softly, unable to show enthusiasm, but she really was glad they would all be going out. "I'll can Jen."

"I'll go fix a salad. Come down when you're ready." Carol left the room.

Therese sat up and reached for the phone on her nightstand. Jewels poked her head up from her log with a piece of spinach hanging from her mouth.

"You're still eating?" Therese teased, wiping a tear from her cheek. "Is it good?"

Jewels answered with a loud crunch.

Therese looked over at Puffy, who was asleep in the little tower on the top of his plastic house. She could just make him out through the bedding he had carried up there. She would need to clean out his cage soon. She dialed Jen's number. Jen was pleased with the news. Therese didn't mention anything about the lieutenant's visit nor did she mention the panicky feeling that had gripped her heart.

Carol called up the stairs to let Therese know the salad was ready, but Therese wasn't hungry. She had just finished cleaning out Puffy and Jewels's houses, which always messed with her appetite.

"Do you mind if I play my flute?" Therese called down. She hadn't played since before…everything changed.

"Of course not, sweetheart. You go right ahead."

Before she could get out her instrument, the phone rang, so she picked it up, and found it was Vicki Stern calling.

"Hi Vicki."

"What's going on?"

"I'm getting ready to practice my flute. What's going on with you?"

"Nothing."

Therese waited for Vicki to say why she was calling, hoping it wasn't to share her regrets, and when she didn't, Therese asked, "Have you seen any movies lately?"

"Nope. Want to go with me tomorrow night?"

Therese cringed. "I'm sorry. I'm going to…I have other plans. We're going to the Wildhorse Saloon, if you want to meet us. A whole bunch of us will be there."

"Hmm. I don't really like crowds. What about Thursday?"

"I'll check with my aunt and call you back. Okay?"

"Okay."

"By then.

"Bye."

Therese slid the black instrument case and fold-up music stand from beneath her bed, set up the stand, and got her sheet music out from a desk drawer. What did she feel like playing? She had received a one in a UIL solo and ensemble contest last spring playing a Handel sonata. She took it out now and put it on the music stand. Then she assembled the three pieces of her silver flute. She hadn't played in so long, and she realized now as she blew the air across the mouth piece how much she had been missing it. Playing relaxed her, fulfilled her, and brought her pleasure. She launched into the sonata full of emotions.

She hadn't played very far into the song when she started crying. She wasn't sobbing and shaking as she had done each night since she woke from the coma. Instead, the tears simply fell down her face, like water dripping from a broken faucet. She could no longer see the sheet music, but she didn't need to. She played the song by memory, moving her fingers quickly and effectively, a trill here, an eight-note rise there, and a whole note pause. She bent her brows and threw her heart into the song. She sang in her mind to the rising melodic scale: *They are still with me, in my heart and in my soul. They are a part of me forever.*

She kept repeating the words in time with the melody: *They are a part of me forever.*

90

A movement in the woods outside her second-story window caught her attention. She stopped playing and went to the window. At first she didn't see anything, so she almost went back to sit on her bed and continue playing, but as she was about to turn away, she caught a flash of white and blue.

"Oh my God, it's Than," she said to herself. "What's he doing out there?"

As if he had heard her, he looked up and waved. He looked huge, even beside the giant diseased elm.

She opened the window. "Hey, Than. What are you doing?"

He walked down the side of the mountain toward the back of her house and looked up. "I was taking a walk when I heard music. I came this way to find out where it was coming from. It's beautiful. Is it coming from you?"

She blushed and nodded. "Hold on a minute, and I'll come down." Then she turned to Clifford, who sat curled on her pillow on the bed. "That's not your pillow, boy. Why do you always have to lie down on *my* pillow? Yours is right there beside you! And you have another over there on the floor! You greedy boy." Then she laughed, suddenly joyful, and petted him. "You want to go outside?"

Clifford leapt from the bed, scattering the limp, pathetic balloons, and headed downstairs. Therese followed with her flute, anxious to show off her talent to Than.

Carol looked up from the granite counter as Therese came down the stairs. She was eating her salad. "Who is that guy?" she asked. She must have seen him through the kitchen window.

"He's staying in the Melner cabin. I met him at the Holts'. He's working for them this week, too."

"He looks like a god," Carol said. "How old is he?"

91

Therese shivered at her aunt's choice of words, pushing down the memories of her dreams. "Eighteen, I think. I'm not sure."

Carol looked as though she was about to say more, but she took another bite of her salad instead.

Therese went out the back kitchen door and onto the deck to meet him. "So you can hear me all the way at the Melner cabin? That's embarrassing. I thought having the window closed would keep the sound from carrying."

Clifford put his paws up on Than's shins.

"Hi, Clifford," Than said, patting the dog. Then he answered Therese. "I was actually closer to your place than mine. I don't really know if you can hear it all the way at the cabin. But I hope so. I haven't heard music like that in a long, long time, which is crazy because both of my parents are big fans of music." Then he asked, "Will you play some more for me?"

Now she was shaking. She had planned to show off, but now that it came down to it, she didn't know if she could control the movements of her fingers. They shook much more than they had at the UIL contest last spring. "Um, I don't know."

"Please?"

His crystal blue eyes were just too persuasive for her to say no, so she led him to the side of the house to the wooden table and offered him a chair. She sat across from him, with her back to the side of the house, took a deep breath, and played. Everything came out all wrong. Then she took a deep breath, tried to forget his presence, turned to face the reservoir, and played again. Automatically, her mind picked up the words where she had left off: *They are with me, in my heart and soul. They are part of me forever.*

When she had finished the complete sonata without having made a single error, she looked up at him and smiled.

He clapped his hands. "I loved it. You put so much of yourself into the music. It's almost like you're voice is singing in place of the flute, or as if the flute were an extension of yourself."

"Thanks." She didn't know what else to say. She was much too nervous to think beyond playing for him. A chipmunk ran up onto the deck and saved her from an awkward silence. "SShh," she whispered, and pointed to the little furry animal just behind one of the other four chairs at the table.

Than's smile at the sight of the animal took her breath away. What a gorgeous smile.

Therese scooped a few sunflower seeds from the clay pot on the table and dropped them on the deck. The chipmunk froze for a few seconds, and then he went for the seeds. Therese looked up at Than and watched him while he watched the chipmunk. His smile could kill.

She shuddered at her own choice of words.

Clifford came bounding onto the deck from the forest and scared the chipmunk away.

"Bad boy!" Therese scolded. "Time for you to go inside."

"No, let him stay. It's not his fault. He's just following his natural instincts, doing his job."

"Yeah, I guess you're right." To Clifford she said, "I'm sorry boy. You can stay outside." Then she said, "Actually, we could all go inside. I could introduce you to my aunt. Do you want anything to eat or drink?"

"No, that's okay. I don't want to bother you. I just wanted to hear you play."

"It's no bother. Really." She mentally crossed her fingers for luck. She wanted him to stay. Stay, she willed. Stay.

"Well, if you're sure."

She smiled. "Come in. My aunt's just inside having lunch." Therese led Than to the front of the house, through the screened front porch, and inside the living room.

Carol seemed pleased Therese brought Than in to meet her, and she immediately offered to make him a salad just like hers. Therese insisted her aunt sit down. "I know how to make salad," she said. So Therese chopped up some spinach, green leaf lettuce, bok choy, white cabbage, green onion, and a few radishes. Then she sprinkled on some toasted sesame seeds, Chinese noodles, and Ginger dressing. She divided it up into two bowls and gave one to Than where he sat beside her aunt at the countertop. Therese stood up and ate at the bar across from them.

She enjoyed watching his face after he took his first bite. She could tell he liked it.

"I've never tasted anything like this salad before," he said. "It's delicious."

Therese watched him take great pleasure in every bite. "It's so easy," she said. "It's not like I made you a five course meal."

"Oh, offer him a drink, sweetheart," Carol said.

"Sorry." Therese opened a cabinet behind her and took out two glasses. "What do we have?"

"There's iced tea in the fridge. Than, do you like iced tea?"

"I've never tried it, but I'd love to have some."

Therese knew they had iced tea in Texas. What was with this guy? Did his parents keep him in a cave or something? The memory of her dream popped into her head, so she pushed it back out with a shudder. Silly, silly dream.

Carol and Therese both chuckled as they watched Than try the tea.

He frowned and licked his lips.

"You don't like it?" Therese asked.

"It's bitter."

Carol crossed the room. "Try some sugar." She brought the sugar canister over and put a couple of teaspoons in his glass, mixed it, brought the spoon out. "Try it now."

94

Therese put her hand over her mouth to hide the huge grin she couldn't stop from forming on her face. He obviously liked tea with sugar. He drank down half the glass in one gulp.

"I think I like sugar," he said. Then he gulped down the rest of the glass.

Chapter Fourteen: Therese's Prayers

Than realized as he put down the glass of tea on the kitchen bar that Therese was praying to him again. Sometimes it was difficult for him to discern whether she was praying or speaking out loud, for when he was this close to her, as he was now, with her face less than two feet away, he could hear the voice and the prayers with the same pitch, clarity, and volume; whereas, from a far distance the prayers were clearer to him than speech. He also knew that she wasn't aware that her prayers to him were heard, for she hadn't yet accepted the fact of who he was. The human mind interested him in this way, in its ability to play tricks on its owner. As far as Than knew, gods were unable to achieve such feats of self deceit as humans.

Her prayers to him this afternoon, so different from earlier, went something like this, "You are such a breath of fresh air to me after all that's happened. I hope you stay around a while. I hope I get to know you. You are so cute, Than. So cute and so sweet. What crystal blue eyes you have. What muscles. And the way you fill out your jeans, oh! Never mind! Stop it, Therese! Oh, don't look at me like that."

Than had to work hard not to react to the words she did not say out loud, but just now he found himself blushing and wanting badly to press his lips to hers like she had done to him that night they met.

He didn't want to leave, especially with her silent pleading, but he had to give a few hours to helping his sisters track down the killer—after all, that was his selling point to his father in getting permission to come up here. He couldn't neglect that duty.

"Thanks for the lunch," he said. "It was delicious."

"You're welcome any time," Carol said.

Than stood up from the bar stool as Therese took his empty bowl and glass and put them in the sink behind her.

Therese said, "I'm going for a walk with Clifford. If you're not doing anything, you could come along." Then she prayed, "Please say yes."

Than stepped around the bar and looked through the window to follow Therese's gaze. Her back was to him as she stood at the sink. He wondered what she was looking at. Then he heard her pray, "Save that tree. Don't let it die." He saw she was looking at an Elm, one of two that towered behind the house.

"Is that tree special to you?" he asked, again forgetting that she had made her request silently.

She turned to look at him in surprise. "What? Oh, yes. It's got the Dutch Elm disease. My parents were going to try to save it. I guess I'd hate to see it die… too."

Than awkwardly patted her shoulder where he had touched countless souls before on their journey down the river, but her warm skin and the tension between them made him uneasy. He looked out the window at the tree. He said, "I wish I could join you for your walk, but I have to go help my sisters with something. I'll see you this evening, though, okay?"

"Darn," she prayed in her head. "But I like that you help your family."

He almost made the mistake of responding to this silent statement. "Thanks…again for the lunch, and for playing your flute for me," he corrected himself. "I'll see you later."

Her hair smelled so fresh and her body felt so warm beside him, that he had a hard time pulling himself away from her company to the dreaded deed of hunting with the Furies.

Chapter Fifteen: Another Tragedy

She pulled on her oldest pair of Justin Ropers, glossed her lips, and headed down the stairs, her hair loose and flying behind her. The smell of her peach shampoo made her feel fresh. She ran her fingers through her curls. Her dad used to say how he loved her hair and that it was the perfect combination of Therese's mother's red hair and his own mother's curly hair.

"Sorry, Clifford," she said to him at the front door. "You have to stay this time. You're not allowed on the pasture."

Carol was typing furiously on her laptop while she sat on the living room sofa. "I'll drive you," Carol said, jumping up. "I'm not ready for you to walk alone yet, especially if Clifford's not going."

Than appeared at the door to the screened porch. "Hi there. I was wondering if you want to walk up to the Holts' together."

Therese turned back to her aunt. "That okay?"

Carol hesitated, then smiled. "I guess so. Just call me when you get there."

The sun had fallen behind a thin layer of clouds. It usually rained for a few minutes every afternoon, often with thunder and lightning, and Therese wondered now as she and Than turned onto the dirt road from her gravel driveway if it would today. She hoped not. She was nervous enough about riding without adding rain into the mix.

Than hadn't changed from his tight white t-shirt and jeans, but he looked refreshed and clean and, even under the cloud cover, brilliant.

"Thanks again for the salad and the recipe," he said. "I told my sister Tizzie about it. She might go into Durango tomorrow for the ingredients and try to make it herself."

"Be sure to tell her to buy you some tea bags and sugar," Therese said. "You seemed to like that a lot, too."

"Yes. Especially the sugar."

He asked why Clifford wasn't with her, and she explained that he'd want to follow them into the pasture and how that was dangerous for the horses. "Small dogs tend to spook horses. They can handle the big dogs, but because horses have a lot of blind spots, the littler animals tend to freak them out."

"I *see*," he said, apparently attempting a pun.

Therese shook her head and chuckled. "That was really bad."

"You're right. It was." He chuckled too.

Although she had initially thought him to be arrogant and selfish, she found him easy to talk to as they made their way down the road. He asked her about her hobbies and she talked a bit about swim team and band and the times she liked to spend in the forest with the animals. When she asked about him, he shrugged.

"I've realized these past few days how little I know myself," he said cryptically.

When they reached the ranch, Mrs. Holt, Bobby, and Jen were already in the pen saddling up five of the horses.

"Hey, guys," Bobby greeted them. "Think it's gonna pour?"

"I hope not." Therese put on her long-sleeved shirt.

"Don't worry," Jen said. "The horses love the rain. It won't bother them or anything."

"It'll just make them stinky," Mrs. Holt said. "Somethin' we have to look forward to come mornin'."

"Oh, I'm supposed to call my aunt." Therese turned toward the house.

"Use the phone in the barn," Mrs. Holt said.

Therese found the dusty, old-fashioned dial phone mounted to the wall and called her aunt to let her know she had made it safely. Then she returned to the pen with the others.

They led their horses from the gate on the pasture side of the pen, on the opposite side from the barn and the house, and Bobby closed and secured the gate. Hershey and Ace put their heads over the fence and brayed their objections. They wanted to come, too.

Than turned and said something to the two horses that Therese could not hear. She inwardly laughed. He liked talking to them as much as she did. Despite his inability to describe himself, she was learning a lot about him. He loved the outdoors, especially the water, and he loved animals. She looked forward to learning a few more things.

Therese approached Dumbo, and he nuzzled against her. She put her hand out for him to sniff. He caressed her hand with his mouth and then nuzzled her palm. She stroked his face, whispering, "Thanks. I needed that."

As soon as Therese mounted Dumbo, the nervous anxiety made her chest feel tight. Jen must have noticed, because she came up beside her and said, "Just follow me. You've got nothing to worry about."

Jen started at a walk, and without Therese having to say "Go," or squeeze Dumbo's sides, the horse followed. Therese relaxed. Maybe this would be easier than she had thought.

"You're doing good, boy," Therese said as she stroked Dumbo's neck. She watched Jen moving gracefully ahead of her on Sassy, as though she and her horse were one fluid organism. Jen made it look so easy.

Than came up beside her on Midnight. "You okay?"

"So far so good." She gave him a brave smile. She could do this.

Bobby and Mrs. Holt had already gone on ahead across the stream where it narrowed and up where the pasture began on an incline up the mountain. Jen now took Sassy up to a trot, and, without warning, Dumbo followed suit. Therese held on to the saddle horn and hugged Dumbo with

100

her thighs. She managed not to shriek, but her heart was beating a million miles an hour as the adrenaline pumped through her. Than and Midnight were soon beside her again.

"This is fun, don't you think?" he asked.

Therese was bouncing hard on Dumbo, so she stiffened her legs against the stirrups and pulled her bottom up, practically in a standing position. "As long as Dumbo follows Sassy, I'm alright." She didn't admit it was like riding a scary rollercoaster.

Drops of rain began to fall and a sudden streak of light illuminated the clouds above them.

Great, Therese thought. Just what I need.

A moment later, the roar of thunder followed.

Jen and Sassy approached the stream, so Jen slowed down to a walk. Dumbo slowed, and Midnight beside him. They took turns jumping across the narrowest part and then joined Bobby and Mrs. Holt in the trees on the other side. They kept the horses at a walk as they followed the trail through the trees near the fence line. The trees offered some protection from the rain, but not much. Another streak of light shot across the sky, and the thunder followed. Therese wondered how the horses would react if the thunder got loud and if they were safer in the trees or if they should head back across the stream to the open part of the pasture, but she didn't say anything, sure Mrs. Holt would know best. She couldn't help but feel even more nervous, though.

They walked the horses through the trees, weaving up and down, occasionally having to jump across a low dip or fallen log. Therese focused on talking with Dumbo, to ease her nerves and to let Dumbo get to know her.

"You're doing great, Dumbo. You're such a good boy." Therese stroked his mane, which was now clean of all sticker burs and weeds thanks to her hard work this morning. "Wait." She said to him when Jen paused up ahead. "Wait." She gently pulled the reins and released, and Dumbo obeyed.

They jumped over a steep incline, one at a time, and then weaved back down through the trees back in the direction of the stream. Here again Therese asked Dumbo to wait his turn to cross the stream, and he did. Then Mrs. Holt took Rambo back up to a trot. Bobby and the General were fast behind. Jen followed with Sassy, then Therese on Dumbo, and Than and Midnight brought up the rear. From the trot, the horses in front moved to a canter. When Dumbo took off to catch up with the others, Therese felt the adrenaline surge through her. This was the scariest part. They galloped at high speed across the open pasture with the rain hitting her in the face. Lightening continued to streak the sky and the thunder to crash. Therese wanted to squeeze her eyes shut, but she was too afraid that Dumbo would scrape her leg along the fence or take her beneath tree branches that would whack her in the face. She heard Than say something to her, but she couldn't speak; she had to concentrate on holding onto the saddle horn, her legs rigid against the stirrups.

Mrs. Holt reached the fence line and turned Rambo south and followed the fence toward the dirt road in front of the house. They all followed Rambo and turned with the fence line, now parallel to the dirt road, still at a full canter. As they reached the pen where they had started, Mrs. Holt took Rambo down to a trot, but kept going, back up toward the stream. The rest of them followed. When she reached the stream, Mrs. Holt slowed Rambo down to a walk and led him along the stream to where it grew about six feet wide. She stopped him and told him to drink. Bobby brought the General beside her and did the same. Dumbo followed Sassy to the other side of Rambo from the General. Midnight came up beside Therese, and all the horses had their fill of water.

The stream in front of them danced with each raindrop. Therese saw several trout diving under rocks in the shallow water away from the muzzles of the horses. Clifford would have a field day here. She was glad for this chance to catch her breath. She looked up at Than and was surprised to see his face turned up to the rain, his eyes closed, and a smile lingering on his lips. His dark, wavy hair blew in the wind and caressed his strong jaw line. She longed to reach out and touch him.

Mrs. Holt led Rambo away from the stream back toward the open pasture. Jen and Bobby followed. Dumbo and Midnight continued to drink, and Than seemed oblivious to the departure of the others, his face still turned up to meet the rain. Therese just sat and watched him.

Than opened his eyes when thunder crashed again. He looked over at Therese, and they shared a smile of embarrassment. He noticed the others had gone several yards away to the open pasture, so he said, "Come on Midnight," and he gently pulled her reins to one side to lead her away.

Therese mimicked Than. "Come on, Dumbo." But Dumbo stubbornly refused to come. He pulled up a tuft of grass that had been growing near the stream to feed. "Come on, Boy!" Therese said a little more forcefully. Instead, Dumbo walked further up along the stream and fed on more stalks of grass. "Great." Therese glanced back at the others. Than was waiting for her about twenty yards away, but the others were already cantering along the fence line again.

Meanwhile, Dumbo refused to listen. "Come on, Dumbo!" Therese gently touched the stirrups against his sides. He went further up the stream, pulling long tufts of yellow grass. Before Therese knew what was happening, Dumbo reared up and down, over and over, braying loudly. She screamed in horror, "Whoa, Dumbo! Whoa, boy!" His back right hoof slid on the bank and into the stream; she could hear the rocks slipping, the hoof sliding, and then the leg belted beneath him, and he fell sideways toward the stream. Therese screamed in terror and pushed both feet against the stirrups, and she managed to stay on top of Dumbo as he rolled into the water on his side. She pulled her right foot loose and pushed with her left to avoid falling under the horse. She fell on the opposite side of him, on the bank among rocks and grass, on her left side. She rolled when she fell and came to a stop at Than's

103

feet. Her elbow and hip hurt, not to mention her neck, and she was terrified for Dumbo.

"Are you okay?" Than knelt beside her with wide eyes.

She sat up, dazed. Then she looked into the stream. Dumbo hadn't moved from his side in the water. His head was lifted toward the sky, and he was whining with pain. "Dumbo!" Therese jumped to her feet and went to the horse. "Oh, no! Oh my God! Than, I think he's really hurt!"

Than held Therese back, and as she tried to pull away she saw a snake hissing in the grass at his feet. He grabbed the snake behind its head with one hand, and then he flung it nearly a hundred yards down the stream away from them.

Therese was in too much shock to wonder how he could throw it so far. "That snake must have been what spooked him," Therese said. "It's okay boy!" She couldn't take his loud cries. She felt so helpless.

Soon Mrs. Holt and the others returned.

"Oh no!" Jen cried from on top of Sassy.

"What happened?" Mrs. Holt dismounted Rambo. She quickly went into the stream and squatted in the water next to Dumbo to assess his injuries while Therese and Than told the story. Therese was in tears before they had finished. Than put his hand on her shoulder.

"Are you hurt, Therese?" Mrs. Holt asked.

Therese shook her head. "I'm fine." Then she said, "I'm so sorry, Mrs. Holt. I'm so, sorry! Do you think he's going to be okay?"

"Bobby, go to the barn and call Dr. Gilbert. Ask him if he can come right away. Tell him it's an emergency. The rest of you take the other horses back to the pen and remove their tack. Then turn all the horses out to the second pasture. Jen, lead Therese on Rambo. I'll stay here with Dumbo."

Bobby took off on the General across the field.

"Is it bad?" Therese asked.

"We'll know more once the vet takes a look at him," Mrs. Holt replied.

Another crash of thunder cracked overhead as the sad party obeyed Mrs. Holt's orders. Therese couldn't stop crying. On top of her worry over Dumbo, she was scared to death to ride Rambo, even though Jen held a lead and would be in complete control.

"Try not to worry," Than said as he helped her mount the huge horse.

After they had returned to the pen and removed the tack from the horses, Jen went to turn them all out to the second pasture while Than led Therese, still in tears and beside herself, toward the house. Bobby got them clean towels. The thunder shower had passed, but they were soaked. They went inside to wait for the vet. Therese called Carol to tell her what happened and why she'd be late, and Carol made her promise over and over that she was telling the truth about not being hurt.

"I really am okay," she said into the phone. "At least, physically." Then the sobs came over her again in another wave. Than put his arm around her where they sat on a wooden bench in the entryway with towels draped over their shoulders. "I'll call you when I'm ready to come home."

After a while, Jen ran inside to say the vet was here, and so Bobby, Therese, and Than jogged behind her out across the first pasture where Dumbo lay in the water, no longer whining, totally exhausted, but still on his side. Mrs. Holt was soaked with her hand on Dumbo's cheek as the vet, shin-deep in water and using a flashlight, did his best to examine his patient.

As the group of teens got closer, Dr. Gilbert was telling Mrs. Holt that he was giving Dumbo a sedative and pain killer solution so that he could more safely maneuver around the animal. The water was shallow enough so he wouldn't drown. Therese watched in horror as the vet stuck the giant needle into Dumbo's neck. Dumbo flinched, but within seconds closed his eyes and lay still. The vet propped Dumbo's head up on a rock to keep it out of the water.

Bobby wrapped a dry towel around his mother's shoulders and convinced her to come out of the stream. Therese looked into Mrs. Holt's anguished face and said again how sorry she was.

Mrs. Holt gave Therese a big hug and said, "Please don't feel for a minute that this is any fault of yours. This could have happened to any rider."

But it happened to me, Therese thought.

The group stood on the banks of the stream watching as the vet conducted his exam. Therese became aware—vaguely at first and then more acutely—that Than had his arm protectively around her shoulders again. Jen came up and put her arm around Therese's waist from the other side. Bobby stood close to his mother with a hand on her back.

Eventually, the vet stood up and walked over to them. "It's not good," he said. "Maybe the kids should go inside."

Mrs. Holt looked at Therese. "Than, would you please take Therese back to the house? The others can stay."

"Please, Mrs. Holt. I want to stay, too."

Mrs. Holt hesitated. Then she looked at the vet and nodded. "It's okay, Dr. Gilbert. Go ahead."

"Well, Dumbo has two broken legs, his right front and his left hind. His left hind leg is broken in two places, and I think a couple of ribs may be cracked as well."

"Oh no," Bobby groaned.

"What do you recommend we do about it?" Mrs. Holt asked.

"I hate to say it, Steph, but I think we're gonna have to put him down."

"No!" Therese yelled.

Everyone looked at her, Than tightening his hold around her shoulders.

"Stay calm for the others," he said softly in her ear.

"What's the alternative?" Mrs. Holt asked.

"A slow and painful death," the vet replied. "He'll never recover."

A blanket of dread and grief wrapped itself around Therese. This couldn't be happening, she thought. She covered her mouth with her hand.

Mrs. Holt walked back out into the stream beside Dumbo. She kissed his still and quiet cheek. "Alright, kids. Time to go back to the house. I'll stay here with Dr. Gilbert. Than and Therese, it's business as usual in the mornin', okay?"

Therese slowly nodded. That would be hard to do.

When the four teenagers got back to the house, Than asked Therese if he could walk her home, and she said yes, glad for the company. She could have called her aunt, which would have been a good choice since she was wet and cold and really upset, but she wanted to be with Than. He had become quite good at comforting her.

She hugged Jen and Bobby before she and Than headed home, apologizing over and over for something she knew wasn't her fault but had nevertheless left her with a horrible feeling of dread. She and Than were quiet most of the way. Dusk was falling, and the deer had come out in the tall grass across the road. Therese watched them with blank eyes.

Than broke their silence. "That's the first time I've seen firsthand what happens when a person or animal dies. I've never seen how hard it is for those they leave behind."

Therese's thoughts went from Dumbo to her parents. She clenched her jaw to stay back the tears. "Very hard," she muttered.

"I really am sorry, Therese," his voice was low and husky. He stopped and took her hand. "I'm so sorry people and animals have to die. I wish there were another way."

He seemed more upset than she had realized, as on the verge of punching something, and she wanted badly to fling herself into his arms and let them each wash away the other's pain, but she checked herself. "Thanks."

He released her hand and walked her up to her front screened porch. "Will you come early tomorrow for a swim?" he asked.

"I don't think so."

"You need to do something to heal the pain," he said.

"You see your first death, and now you're an expert," she snapped, and then immediately regretted it. "I'm sorry."

"It's okay. See you in the morning."

Therese went inside to find Carol wrapped in a blanket on the living room couch watching a movie. "You alright?" Carol asked.

"I'm tired. I'm going to bed."

"Are you sure? You don't want to talk about it?"

"I'm sure."

Clifford jumped from the couch beside Carol and followed Therese up the stairs. She turned off Jewel's lamp and told her good night. Puffy was in his wheel already at work. Therese climbed out of her soggy clothes and went to her bathroom to take a long hot shower. Clifford stood outside the shower curtain waiting, as though he sensed she was upset and needed a friend.

Once she was dry and in her nightshirt, Therese cuddled with Clifford on her bed. She felt bad for snapping at Than when he was only trying to help. She was also worried he might not like her anymore. Why did she have to be so rude? She took the stringy stuffed animal toy lemur from where it hung on the headboard post and wrapped it around her neck. She couldn't stop her mind from replaying the tragedy with Dumbo over and over. Her mind went from the tragic events on the pasture to those at Huck Finn Pond. Therese closed her eyes, wishing she could die, too.

Before she had fallen completely asleep, she felt a presence other than her pets in her room, and her eyes snapped open. The moonlight washing into her room wasn't bright, and she could see no one. She could have sworn she felt someone standing over her bed looking down at her, about to touch her face. She stopped breathing to listen, but after seeing and hearing nothing more but Puffy running in his wheel, she closed her eyes and told herself it must have been a dream.

Chapter Sixteen: Doubts and Confliction

After leaving Therese safely at her door, Than went to her room and, in invisible mode, conversed with the hamster and the tortoise.

"I love her," he said in each of their tongues. "And she's hurt. Please comfort her. Can you please?"

"If she picks me up!" The hamster said, as he ran round and round. "Good human! Good human! I've known others, and she's good! If she picks me up, I'll lick her with my tongue!"

Than turned to the tortoise, which now said, "She's loving and tender. So gentle and loyal. I try as best as I can to let her know I love her, too."

A noise came, and then Therese entered. Than softly thanked the animals, and listened as the tortoise said a bit more. Then Than took his leave.

He soared down past the abyss, past Cerberus and the gate and down to his father's chamber in such a state of fury that the bats swirled down from their perch and made their escape into the cold night earlier than was usual. Although Hades must have foreseen his son's arrival, he still showed surprise at his son's rage, the son whom he was used to seeing as the more temperate of his two boys. A tinge of guilt ran through Than as he told himself to show more control.

His sister Alecto stood in the shadows beside their father. Her fire-red hair stood up in a Mohawk and contrasted with her deep black, beautiful eyes. A choker of black stones adorned her neck and similar stones served as buttons in her leather jacket and tight leather pants and high-heeled boots.

"Thanatos?" Hades asked. "Alecto was just apprising me of her progress in a number of the Furies' pursuits, including the killer of your girlfriend's parents. But something tells me you are not here for a report."

"Have you found him?" he asked his sister.

She shook her head.

"Why are you here?" Hades asked Than.

Than tried to think how to put his sorrow and his shame and his desperation into words, but no words seemed to fit the caged and raw emotion he had never before felt. Finally, seeing his father was in a patient mood, Than swallowed and said, with more control and less rage than he felt, "I used to envy the humans their short lives. Their deaths make their lives more meaningful."

"You no longer think it now?"

"I still think it, Father. Death is better than immortality, a yoke only we gods must bear."

"I can't see your thoughts, son. You must speak them."

"Death is good for those who die, but not for those left behind. Why haven't I understood before tonight the depth of that pain? If a horse could raise so much anguish in my mortal heart, I can only imagine what the loss of a parent or child would do. Father, I've ignored countless prayers from billions of souls because I felt there was nothing I could do; but I'm a god. Surely there is something?"

Hades looked down his thin nose at Than. He scratched at his beard and, Than could see, stifled a smile.

"Are you laughing at me?" Than said, moving dangerously close to his father.

Alecto stepped back, further into the shadows.

"Not at you. At the whole cosmos."

"What is that supposed to mean?" Than asked.

"Son, nothing is free. Everything comes with a cost. As you have said, the mortal creatures of the world, at least the good ones, are fortunate that their lives end and their souls spend the rest of eternity in near oblivion; unlike we who must endure our mundane tasks forever. You said yourself that the brevity of their conscious lives makes their journey more meaningful than ours. We are like caged hamsters in a wheel, spinning, spinning, spinning. Humans have but one spin, one go, one bright moment and then the flame goes out.

"The advantage of mortality is clear to us, but not to them, and that is why those left behind suffer. They miss the company of their loved ones, but it is the feeling that the deceased no longer exist that hurts the most. This is the cost mortals must pay. Let me put it to you this way: Mortality is better than immortality, but only the immortal have the ability to see this, and there lies both the irony and the cost of human happiness."

Than shook his head. "So there really is nothing then? Nothing we can do to ease that cost?"

"If there is a way we gods can ease that burden, it is by inspiring this understanding into the human heart. I don't know if it is possible, though. They have such limited minds."

Than sat at the foot of his father's throne on the hard, cold rock awash with defeat.

Hades asked, "A horse's death has brought you to me in fits?"

Than looked up, ashamed. "Hip winked at me as he took the soul of the creature, completely ignorant of the pain we were feeling. How many times have I been so calloused as that?"

"Never. You and your brother are very unlike each other, as I am to mine."

"It wasn't the horse's death that hurt so much as the pain I could feel in the humans left behind. That and the overwhelming feeling of helplessness. And also the rage that I, a god, could do nothing."

Hades smiled. "I am familiar with the feeling. I suppose it is good that gods are humbled now and then."

Than said nothing.

"How goes it with the girl?" Hades asked.

Than, used to being honest for so many centuries, could not find it in his heart to lie. He glanced at Alecto, unsure if he wanted her to hear, but went on and said, "I love her, but I'm having second thoughts about teaching her to love me."

Hades lifted a brow. "You find her unworthy?"

"No. Just the opposite."

"I find that insulting and despicable. Don't weary me this way."

Than stood up. "You don't understand me because I can hardly explain myself. What I'm trying to say is that she loves the Upperworld and its inhabitants more than most humans, and I worry I would make her into a despondent wife down here."

"There is no other kind of wife down here," Hades said. "Remember that."

Chapter Seventeen: The Wildhorse Saloon

Therese woke up sore Wednesday morning. She climbed out of bed, stiff and in pain. She replayed the events of the previous evening over in her head and shuddered. Maybe she should stay home. She picked up the phone and called Jen.

"My mom warned me you would call," Jen said on the phone. "But she says it's really important that you come this morning. You'll heal a lot faster if you do. Moping around all day will make it worse. My mom had to threaten Bobby for the same reason."

"But I'm in pain," Therese objected. "I hadn't gone riding in a year. And I fell down and hurt myself, remember?"

"We can't make you come," Jen said, "but my mom will be very disappointed and really upset. It's your choice. Don't forget we still have the Wildhorse Saloon tonight. I've gotta go."

Therese groaned. She couldn't have the entire Holt family angry with her, especially when she still felt guilty over what had happened. She kept thinking if only she had been in better control of Dumbo, things might have happened differently. Reluctantly, she threw on some clothes and sneakers and headed downstairs. She shared some breakfast with her aunt before they and Clifford climbed into Carol's car. She kept her eyes out for Than as she absently made two braids in her hair, but didn't see him along the dirt road. When they reached the tall grass across from the Holts' house, she craned her neck to see if he might be swimming. His golden figure glided through the water. After she climbed from the car and thanked her aunt, she followed Clifford across the field to the lake where Than was swimming.

"Come in," he said when he saw her watching him from the bank where his clothes sat piled in a heap. "It feels great." His eyes sparkled in the sunlight, and his wet hair and body glistened.

Sometimes a weird feeling that he was merely a product of her imagination made her long to touch him to make sure he was real. "I didn't wear a suit." She was relieved he wasn't mad about the way she had snapped at him yesterday. "But maybe another time."

He swam toward the shore and stood up where the water grew shallow. His skin glowed as the sun behind her sprayed its rays across his wet body. Therese turned away from his beauty. Sadness still hung over her.

"You okay?" he asked.

"I'm sorry I snapped at you yesterday." Her voice cracked.

"No apology necessary."

She waited for him while he climbed into his clothes. She tried not to steal glances at him, but she failed miserably. Clifford came up to Than for some affection.

"Hi, Clifford." Than patted the dog's head. Then he turned to Therese. "Ready?"

They walked across the tall grass and dirt road to the gravel drive leading to the Holt house. Than asked her a few more questions, like what was Clifford like as a puppy and she as a little girl. He laughed when she told him about the time she lost Jewels in the woods and had actually called 911 and the person on the phone thought Therese was talking about a younger sister.

"I got in a lot of trouble for that," she said. She looked over at him and took in his grin. It unnerved her, but she managed to ask, "Have you ever gotten into trouble?"

"Never," he said.

"Never ever?"

"Nope. I've always been good. My brother, on the other hand, well, that's another story."

"You have a brother?"

"A twin. But we're not identical. I got the good looks, the sense of humor, and the charm. He got the more devilish qualities."

Although Than was laughing, like he was only joking, Therese froze in her tracks.

"What's wrong?" he asked.

She'd heard something like that before. A chill moved down her back. "Um, nothing." She shook her head, reminding herself that what she was about to suspect was entirely impossible, but as she looked at Than through the corner of her eye, she could have sworn he was laughing at her.

Jen and Bobby were coming from the house at the same time Than and Therese approached the pen. Mrs. Holt was already in the pen working on the General.

"Mornin', Than. Mornin', Therese," Mrs. Holt said.

"Mornin', Mrs. Holt," they replied.

"Than, you go ahead and get started on Rambo. Therese, Sugar's waiting for you."

Jen and Than entered the pen and shared their good mornings all around. Jen said she had just gotten off the phone with Ray who said he and Todd would definitely be joining them at the Wildhorse Saloon tonight to hear Pete's performance. No one mentioned anything about what had happened the night before.

Mrs. Holt drove up in her Suburban at seven o'clock Wednesday evening. Therese climbed down the front wooden steps and entered on the passenger side. Bobby sat in the passenger seat wearing his cowboy hat and a short-sleeved Western shirt. He smelled like soap and had a huge grin on his freckled face as Therese climbed into the seat behind him. Jen laughed as

116

soon as she saw what Therese was wearing because they wore almost the same thing: same dark blue shade of boot-cut jeans, same red Justin Roper boots, and nearly identical white blouses, except that Therese's had a round neckline whereas Jen's had a v. Both wore their long hair down, and although Jen's was straight blonde and Therese's was curly red, they fell to the same length, to the center of their backs.

"We do this all the time," Jen said.

"It's almost eerie." Therese grinned.

"Are you wearing Oscar De La Renta, too?" Jen asked.

Therese shook her head. "No, it's, um, it's called Haiku. It's what my mom wore. I've been wearing it a lot lately."

The two girls looked away from one another.

"It smells nice," Mrs. Holt offered.

Therese's heart skipped a beat when she referred to her mother, but now that they were pulling up the gravel drive to the Melner cabin, it sped up considerably, more than making up for the skipped beat.

Jen explained, "Than and one of his sisters are riding with us. His other sister had plans."

Mrs. Holt's reaction expressed Therese's same sentiments when she said, "Lordy, Lordy, look at those two."

Than's sister wore a tight black leather mini-skirt, black go-go boots, and a red silk blouse with spaghetti straps. Her blonde curls were wound together in a thick bun on her head, a few strands spilling out of the bun down to the nape of her neck in a wild cascade. Her lips matched the red in the blouse. The rest of her rather fierce face seemed void of makeup. Her skin glowed like her brother's, but hers was fairer, almost white.

Like the white witch from Narnia, Therese thought.

Even in that conspicuous outfit, Than's sister could not outshine her brother. His clean dark wavy hair gleamed with golden highlights in the evening sun and danced against his strong jaw line. His pale blue cotton polo

117

seemed to match the crystal in his eyes, and together with his white trousers, emphasized the golden hues of his magnificent skin. His brown boots and matching belt were the same shade as his hair. Therese climbed out of her seat and into the back to make room for them.

Before Jen could do the same, Than said, "Jen, why don't you stay there with my sister. I'll climb in back. I don't mind at all."

Jen's face looked like a mixture of giddiness and jealousy.

Then Than said, "Everybody, this is my sister, Meg."

They took turns introducing themselves to Than's sister, who was courteous if not friendly. "A pleasure," she said.

Therese could barely breathe in the third seat next to the golden boy. She almost thought, "Golden god," but then her memory of the dreams and the fear of insanity made her shrug that word out of her mind. It made more sense to her that she had felt him coming, that she had had some kind of prophetic dream about a new crush, than that she could have been communicating with gods.

He gave her a friendly smile, and this made Therese shiver with excitement.

"You look and smell so nice," he whispered.

"So do you," Therese replied, unable to think of anything original with her heart going a million miles an hour against her rib cage.

Meg turned around in her seat and gave him a disapproving glare. Than looked away from Meg and from Therese to stare out of the window.

Meg's face looked vaguely familiar to Therese: Her pale skin and unruly blonde hair and dark red lips. "Oh my God!"

Everyone turned to look at Therese.

"Is something wrong?" Mrs. Holt glanced at her from the rearview mirror.

"No. No, nothing's wrong." She bit the inside of her bottom lip, not wanting to utter her thoughts. Than's sister looked uncannily similar to the

118

strange looking woman in the forest who had called her name and frightened poor Clifford a few weeks ago. How embarrassing if she had simply been frightened by a guest at the Melner cabin. On the other hand, how would Meg have known Therese's name?

But hadn't she also seen her reflection in the glass at the police department? No. Of course not.

Than said, "The sun looks so beautiful when it drops behind those mountains across the lake. The pines seem to twinkle."

Bobby chuckled and shook his head. "I've never heard that one. Twinkling pines, huh?"

Jen snickered.

Than glanced at Therese, and she gave him another smile. She didn't like the way Bobby and Jen had laughed at him. "I know exactly what you mean," she whispered. "I never get tired of sunsets here."

Meg, who spoke without turning, startled Therese with her loud condemning voice, "If you've seen one, you've seen them all. They never vary."

Jen glanced back at Therese to give her the "What's with her?" look. Than caught it too and chuckled.

The drive to the dance hall from Lemon Reservoir Dam took a little less than twenty minutes down winding country roads flanked by tall trees. Therese felt Than looking at her when he wasn't watching the scenery through his window. She liked the attention and was beginning to allow herself to believe he really could like her. Normally, this would be enough to make her nervous, but compounded with that were her insane and persistent suspicions about his connection to her bizarre dreams.

As they pulled into the parking lot, pretty bare since it was still early and a Wednesday night, Therese asked Jen, "Todd and Ray are still coming, aren't they?"

"Yeah, they said they were. Oh, look! They're in Todd's truck!"

The bright yellow fifty-seven Chevy pickup towered over the other vehicles from its heightened position on a lift kit including giant mag tires with thirty-inch rims. Jen and Therese piled out of the suburban and rushed over to meet their friends.

"Come on," Therese called to the others. "You guys have got to see this!"

"Hello, down there!" Todd shouted through his window as the truck bounded into a parking space. He rolled up his window when he came to a stop.

"Oh my God!" Therese and Jen giggled, shaking their heads in disbelief.

Bobby and Than came up behind with Mrs. Holt and Meg bringing up the rear.

Therese laughed as she watched the long and lanky Todd jump more than a meter to the ground from the monster truck.

"Of all the colors in the universe," Ray said laughing. He came around the cab to join the group gathered on the driver's side. "I kept expecting the truck to transform into a giant robot."

"It's awesome!" Therese exclaimed. "I mean, wow, Todd!"

"You don't think it's a little extravagant?" Jen asked. "It's a bit big."

Therese gave Jen a warning look. *Don't hurt his feelings*, her look said.

"That's kind of the idea," Ray said. Then he added, "Think he's compensating?"

Todd slapped Ray on the back. "Thanks a lot, Ray. Don't forget I'm your ride home."

Therese noticed the second and third looks Ray and Todd gave to the newest members of their group. Jen introduced them, and then they all went inside the saloon. Everyone but Mrs. Holt had to wear a special red bracelet made for minors. Therese was relieved to learn that Than wasn't twenty-one.

She wondered how old he was. She thought maybe eighteen. She thought she might get up the nerve to ask him tonight.

Pete's band was still setting up equipment on the stage, so the music that carried throughout the dance hall was a prerecorded mix of songs usually played over the radio. Just now, Lady GaGa's voice had Jen jumping up and down.

"I love this song! Let's go dance!" Jen pinched Therese's hand and pulled her toward the dance floor.

Therese grabbed Ray's hand and shouted, "Help! You guys have to come, too!"

Ray and Todd made it to the edge of the dance floor but refused to go any further. Only a few others were dancing, as the place was pretty empty. Jen pulled Therese onto the floor, and Therese, not wanting to disappoint her friend, cheerfully made a fool out of herself as she bounced her hips and swayed her shoulders to the music. She stole a quick glance at Than to confirm he was watching. She could feel him laughing at her, but his eyes seemed pleased, like he was admiring her.

Jen sang with the song, waving her arms in the air.

Pete flashed them a smile when he noticed them on the floor. He gave Therese a thumb's up, so she mimicked it back to him. As embarrassed as she was to be one of the few people dancing, she also, and unexpectedly, felt free. Just a few weeks ago, she wouldn't have thought it possible to smile and have fun. She knew it was temporary—that tonight in the quiet of her bedroom—well, not complete quiet, for Puffy would be exercising in his wheel—she would not be able to avoid the flood of memories that would fill her with dread and bring that panicky feeling gripping at her chest. She wouldn't think of that now!

"P-p-p-poker face!" she cried. She could do this. She could go on pretending that everything was fine and she was free.

Therese stayed out on the dance floor with Jen for one more song, and then the two of them joined the others at the bar where they all got pops. Therese was relieved for the sake of Pete and his band by the arrival of more and more patrons as the hour grew later. By eight o'clock, there was a decent crowd, and swirls of cigarette smoke began to fill the air, Mrs. Holt contributing her fair share of it. The sheer number of bodies on the dance floor brought the place alive.

Therese was glad when Pete's smooth voice penetrated the dance hall from the sound system in perfect harmony with his background singers. She watched with delight as he plucked the strings of his guitar without missing a note, looking handsome in his white cowboy hat and starched denim shirt and jeans. The microphone was perched on a stand, and Pete swayed behind it, strumming the guitar. He winked at her, which made her smile. He had always been the big brother she never had, and she wanted everything to be just right for him tonight. His voice rang out to an old Mac Davis song her father used to sing, "Oh Lord It's Hard To Be Humble."

Therese pushed down the memories of her father to think instead of Than. The song described him to a tee. He was perfect in every way.

Her thoughts were interrupted when Todd was at her side asking to dance.

"Sure," she said and took his hand as she followed him to the dance floor.

Waltzes were the easiest dance to follow, in Therese's opinion, and Todd was a strong lead. He twirled her around the dance floor, giving her that fake feeling of freedom again. She smiled when she saw Bobby and Jen join them and the other couples moving across the floor with the smoke and the laughter and Pete's smooth voice. She glanced back at Than, and a thrill moved through her entire body when she saw he was looking back at her.

When the song ended, Todd asked for another dance—a polka to "The Yellow Rose of Texas"—and Therese loved to polka, so she gratefully accepted. Round and round they went, flying across the floor. Todd was good at this too. As he turned her once again, she noticed Carol and Richard standing next to Mrs. Holt. Carol had tears in her eyes and a huge smile, obviously relieved to see Therese could still have fun in a world where her parents no longer existed. Carol's tears sobered Therese, though she knew her aunt would be utterly grieved by that knowledge, so she bravely smiled and gave a quick wave before Todd pulled her around again. When the song ended, Todd ushered her off the dance floor to join their friends.

"Thanks, Todd. Come here so I can introduce you to my aunt and her boyfriend."

Therese introduced Carol and Richard to the group, though they had met the Holts briefly last Christmas, and Carol had met them one other time years ago, before Jen's father had left. Richard stood a foot taller than her aunt, about six-four, the same height as Than, and his chocolate complexion and dark brown eyes shimmered in the sparkling light thrown off by the disco globe above them.

"An investigative journalist?" Mrs. Holt asked as she shook Richard's hand. "How interesting. Political or criminal?"

"Mostly political, but a bit of both."

After the introductions and Richard's attempt to field Mrs. Holt's barrage of questions about the war and the president and Homeland Security, Richard pulled Carol out onto the wooden floor to dance the Texas Two-Step to a George Strait song, Pete's voice easily matching the inflections of the original.

"Jen, ready?" Todd asked.

"Let's go," Jen beamed.

Therese was aware of Than when he stepped beside her to watch the band and the dancers.

"Can you teach me to do that?" he asked.

123

"What? Dance?" her mouth dropped open. Was this god—no, not god—was this really hot guy asking her to teach him to dance?

"Yes."

She could feel the blood rush to her face as a nervous giggle popped from her throat. "Um, I don't know. I guess so. Have you ever Country-Western danced before?"

"Never. I've never danced, period." He bent his brows and looked troubled. "These past few days I've come to realize how much I've missed out on while living down, down in the south."

She scrutinized his lovely face. She knew people danced in Texas, but she didn't mention it. He looked like an angel flung down from Heaven. His soft frown moved her. "Sure. I can teach you, but maybe we should go outside and practice before we try it on the dance floor. We wouldn't want to get run over out in the crowd."

She told Mrs. Holt what they were doing before leading Than outside, but not before noticing the glare Meg cast them as they left.

"I don't think your sister likes me," Therese said once they stepped from the smoke-filled dance hall and out into the cool night air. Stars twinkled down on them from the clear sky, and the full moon illuminated the otherwise dark parking lot. The gravel crunched beneath their boots. Somewhere, far off in the distance, a dog was barking.

"It's not you," he said.

She studied his face. "Then what?"

"She's worried about me forming attachments. We can't stay long."

Therese cleared her throat as she looked for a spot on the edge of the parking lot. "When do you leave?"

"My father gave us forty days. He was quite firm about that."

It was approaching the end of July. "So how long do you have left?"

"We've got about two weeks."

She had only two more weeks to spend with him? "Are you going to school in the fall?" she asked.

"Back to work."

"Down south?"

"Yes."

"What do you do for your father's business?"

He sighed. "It's complicated."

Therese stopped in the open space at the end of the lot and squared herself in front of Than. He was so tall. He towered over her. She felt a little shaky. She decided not to pry.

The dog's barking seemed to grow louder, and the two of them looked in the direction of its barking and giggled.

"He sounds scarier than Cerberus," Than said.

The hair stood up on the back of Therese's neck and she froze. "What did you just say?"

"I said teach me to dance already. We've been out here for ages."

She knew that wasn't what he had said, but she decided to dismiss it. Maybe he was a fan of Greek mythology.

"I'm going to teach you the waltz first because it's the easiest. You can basically march in place, one foot and then the other, and not miss a step. You don't have to spin around until you get the hang of it. Here, put your hand on my waist." His warm hand on her body made her tingle with pleasure. She put one hand on his shoulder and took his free hand with the other. "If a girl is a good follower, she will put her fingers against the backside of your shoulder like this and her thumb against the front side of your shoulder like this." His shoulder was thick with muscle. She couldn't prevent her fingers from trembling slightly. "That way she can feel if you're going to lead her backward or forward. She can also tell what you're going to do by the pressure you put on her other hand with your hand, and here, too, at her waist. You have to use your hands, along with your body, to talk to her, to tell her what to do."

"So I'm supposed to tell you what to do with my body, and you're supposed to follow?" he asked with a wry smile.

She broke into a grin. "Are we still talking about dancing?"

He lifted his chin and laughed. Then he looked at her. "I like you so much."

She bit her lip and looked down. He'd just told her he was leaving. Why let her heart get broken in two? "Okay, so the steps are in counts of threes, but like I said, it's like marching: one two three, one two three."

He tried it out and she followed, but he paused when he should have kept going, causing her to crash into his chest.

She righted herself. "Sorry."

"My fault." He swallowed hard. "Let's try that again."

"Ow!" She pulled her foot out from underneath his boot. "It's okay."

"Are you hurt?" His face was full of concern.

She couldn't feel anything with his face so close to hers. He could have chopped off her leg, and she wouldn't have known it standing here looking into his crystal blue eyes, his mouth so close to hers. "I'm okay. But I forgot to explain that the guy should always start with his left foot."

After a smoother start, he seemed a natural leader: firm, but sensitive to her movements. He moved her across the parking lot effortlessly now, the gravel crunching beneath them and that dog in the distance incessantly barking.

"You're very good," she said. "The best leaders don't try to master their partners. It's like a cooperation of wills."

"I like that," he said. "A cooperation of wills. I like that a lot."

He picked up on the movement quickly and after a few minutes tried to mimic what he had seen Todd doing with her on the dance floor earlier.

"Wow, you're a fast learner."

126

"You're a good teacher." He twirled her around.

"What are you doing in Colorado, besides working with horses? I mean, why'd you come?"

"I'm waiting for you to recognize me."

Her mouth dropped open and a shudder worked its way down her spine. She stopped dancing, pulling herself away from him. She took several steps back. "But we just met two days ago."

He frowned and looked at the ground. "Have you really already forgotten? Don't you remember putting your arms around me and," his voice faltered, but he swallowed and found it again, "giving me my first kiss?"

She stopped breathing.

"I haven't forgotten," he added, looking into her eyes. "I will remember it for all eternity."

She shook her head and took several steps backward. "Do you have me confused with someone else? Or are you making stuff up? I'm sure I would have remembered that. I haven't even *had* my first kiss."

"If we had more time, I'd take things slowly. I don't have you confused with anyone, and I'm not making stuff up. You kissed me in your dream that night I took your parents' souls."

She staggered back against a parked car, nearly falling. Her entire body trembled with fear. The hair on her neck stood on end. She found it difficult to speak. "And now you've come to take me, too?" She swallowed hard. "Good. I want to go."

He took a step closer. "I've come to help you avenge their murder."

"But, but the lieutenant has already…"

He stood only inches away from her. "He wasn't the master mind. The real villain is still out there."

She pushed herself up with the help of the parked car. She knew that. But how did he? Her knees were weak, and she could barely stand. "I don't care about the real villain. I want to be with my parents. Take me, too." She stumbled forward and into Than's arms. "Take me to them," she said again.

He kissed the top of her hair. "I told you, you wouldn't be the same if I did."

"I don't care," she whispered breathlessly.

"That's not why I'm here."

"Therese?" It was Jen calling for her through the dark parking lot. "Therese? Than? Are you guys out here?"

Than steadied Therese onto her feet. "Are you okay?"

She gave a near-hysterical laugh. "No! I'm not okay. I'm losing my mind."

"Therese?" Jen's voice was closer now. "Oh, there you are. Sorry. I didn't mean to interrupt. Pete's about to play his last song of the night."

Therese turned to her friend and tried to hide her misery. "Already?"

"Yeah. It's almost ten. The place shuts down early on weeknights."

Therese nodded. "Of course I want to hear it. That's why we came." She took a step forward, but her knees buckled, and she fell on the ground.

"Geez, are you alright?" Jen asked.

"Um, yeah. Just tired,'" she replied as Than helped her to her feet. "Still a little sore from yesterday."

He kept his hand around her waist as he led her back to the Wildhorse Saloon. Once inside, their group gave them suspicious looks as she and Than joined them on the side of the dance floor, but no look was more scrutinizing than Meg's.

Pete's smooth voice soothed Therese as it carried through the building.

"It's a waltz," Than whispered in her ear. "Can we try it? Please?"

At first she shook her head. She could barely walk. How could he expect her to dance? But when she looked up into his pleading eyes, she couldn't resist him. "Okay."

128

Therese could feel the stares of everyone in their group as Than took her in his steady arms and practically carried her across the dance floor to Anne Murray's beautiful song, a wedding song, she thought. It was called, "Can I Have this Dance for the rest of My Life?"

He was leaving in two weeks, but just as she had in the ride over here, she felt herself falling for this sensitive, beautiful guy who claimed to be a god. She was crazy, or maybe he was, or maybe both of them shared an insane delusion between them.

By the end of the song, though, she felt better and could actually return Than's smile. She clapped along with the others to congratulate Pete, but then, before leaving the floor and rejoining the others, she whispered to Than, "This can't be real, can it?"

He whispered back, his breath hot but somehow managing to send chills down her scalp and neck, "Give yourself time to process it. I'll see you in the morning."

He walked her over to her aunt and the rest of the group to say their goodbyes. Therese rode in the backseat of her aunt's red Toyota Corolla and stared out the window at the darkness around her. She tried to push off into the sky to turn somersaults, but she remained planted beneath the seatbelt. It hadn't been a dream. It hadn't been a dream at all.

Chapter Eighteen: Hunting with Alecto

After the dance, Than hovered with Alecto, both of them invisible in the air conditioned air above a man at a desk in a small room at the back of a shoe store in Indianapolis. The shoe store was closed for the night, so there were only two others in the shop, taking inventory of their stock. The man Than and Alecto knew as Steve McAdams had short brown hair and a suit that was old and too small with a slight brown stain on its lapel. He was about forty and the ring on his pudgy finger signaled that he was married. He was filling out forms with a ball point pen that bled black ink on the side of his hand.

The two gods materialized outside his door and knocked.

"Yeah?" the man called. "I'm busy. What is it?"

The two gods entered. "Federal agents." They flashed badges. "We have a few questions."

"And what is this about?" He sat up, flustered, tossing the pen on the desk.

"Do you recognize this man?" Alecto showed him a picture of Kaveh Grahib, the man that had shot Therese's mother and caused the death of both of her parents.

Steve McAdams shook his head. "No. Who is he?"

"Think carefully," Alecto said in a threatening voice. "Be sure before you reply."

"His name is Kaveh Grahib," Than said. "Ever heard of him?"

The man looked at Than and then back at Alecto, whose eyes were narrowed and appeared to be shooting invisible darts into the man's skull.

"No," Steve McAdams said. "Why? Should I?"

Alecto walked across the room and put both hands on the desk, leaning her face toward the man's within a foot of his. He leaned back as far as he could in his chair.

"I swear I don't know him."

The room began to shake, and hot steam jets shot up from the Lethe River through the floor on each side of the man's chair.

"What the...?" the man flinched and cowered further back in his chair.

Pouring up from the two jets were swarms of black snakes, hissing and darting their tongues as they quickly curled their way up from the floor, onto the legs of the man, and up to his wrists and neck.

"Ah! Ah! What's happening? What the hell is happening?"

"Think carefully," Alecto said again. "Are you sure you do not know of this man?"

"Help!" the man screamed, but Than knew his cries were futile, for Alecto had already immobilized the two others in the store with her acrid steam from the Lethe, putting them in a funk they would not recall.

The steam enveloped the man.

"I swear I don't know him!"

Alecto stood up and turned to Than. "He's not the one."

Immediately the snakes rushed back down from the man back into the holes in the floor from whence they came. The man fell in a stupor on his desk covered with the foul steam. The jets stopped and the steam began to dissipate. Than and Alecto left the man, but not through the door.

Chapter Nineteen: Questions and Answers

After a warm shower, Therese lay in her nightshirt in bed with Clifford curled up beside her near her waist. Than said to give herself time to process what he had told her outside the Wildhorse Saloon, but how does one process such information? He's the god of death? His sisters are the Furies? They've come to Earth to avenge her parents' murder?

She couldn't sleep, so she took the remote from her nightstand and turned on the television tucked in a small armoire beside her desk. Puffy stopped in his wheel to see what the bright lights were all about. "Sorry," she said to him. "I know it's late." Puffy liked to work in silence and darkness.

Puffy continued on his wheel as she flipped through the channels and finally settled on an old *George Lopez* episode she had already seen. She tried to distract herself with the humor before her, but her eyes left the television to stare at the light reflecting on the ceiling. This whole business with Than as the god of death couldn't be real, could it? Had she lost her mind? The death of her parents had taken a toll on her sanity, right? She'd become a deranged lunatic.

The hair on the back of her neck stood on end. Clifford's ears pricked up. Therese was vaguely aware that Puffy had frozen, like a chipmunk in the middle of the road. She and Clifford jumped to their feet at the same instant. Standing across the room in the same pale blue polo and jeans he had worn earlier was Than, the supposed god of death.

Clifford sat back down on his haunches and wagged his stub of a tail.

She didn't move. "How did you get in?"

Than gave her a wry smile. "I'm a god."

"Why are you here? Did you decide to take me after all?" She was suddenly not so certain she was ready to go.

"I came to check on you. I was worried." He moved toward the bed. The smell of cigarette smoke and alcohol lingered in his clothes from the dance hall. "Mind if I sit down for a while?"

Laughter roared on the television, but Therese wasn't laughing. "I guess not. Go ahead."

He sat at the foot of her bed, and she returned to the headboard against her pillows by Clifford. She tucked her feet closer to her body to avoid touching him.

"I knew you wouldn't be able to sleep and that you'd have questions, so I decided to come to see if I could help put your mind at ease. I know this is hard for you."

"You have no idea. How could you?"

His mouth tightened into a frown. "I suppose you're right. I can't know how you feel."

"How can you be here, anyway? Don't you have a job to do? Is nobody dying while you're here handling horses?" Her voice had a touch of hostility in it. Then she remembered Dumbo. "Why couldn't you do anything to save Dumbo?"

He gave her a weak smile. "So I was right. You do have questions."

"And you haven't answered any of them," she said sharply.

"There was nothing I could do about the horse. I'm sorry. I don't kill living things; I merely guide their souls after they die. I have nothing to do with the timing."

"Couldn't you pull some strings?"

"No." He cleared his throat. "As to your other question, I made a deal with my dad. I told him if he'd make my brother, Hip, take my place as the guide for the dead, I would come to Earth and help my sisters find your parents' murderer and avenge their deaths. He gave me a time limit because

133

while Hip is doing my job, humans have restless nights without dreams, and Zeus won't tolerate that for long."

That explained why she hadn't been able to reenter the dream lately. "But why would your father care about avenging my parents' death?"

Than shifted by lifting one bent leg partly on the bed and turning to face her, his back to the television. "My father is a just god and his priority is justice for the souls in his care. When humans fail to find justice for the dead, he and my sisters step in. The lieutenant needs help finding the person who orchestrated your parents' death. My sisters, Tizzie and Meg, are working on the case. I plan to help as well, but first I wanted to get to know you."

"Why?"

He moved closer to her on the bed, sending her heart into arrhythmia. "Don't laugh, okay?"

Laugh at a god? she thought. Yeah, right. "I won't."

"My mother may have given me some affection when I was young, but I don't remember it. The other gods on Mount Olympus rarely visit the Underworld. They only come if they want a favor. They know my job is necessary, and I suppose they're glad it's me doing it and not them, especially Hermes who did it before me, but that doesn't stop them from looking down at me with contempt. And the humans I encounter have already died. They have no love for me.

"But that night I took your parents and you came close to dying yourself, that night you swept down from the sky from out of nowhere and took me into your arms, that night you kissed me, well, that night changed me."

Therese pulled her knees into her chest with her covers around her. Than moved closer, his face inches from hers. She couldn't tell if she was frightened or aroused. Maybe she was both.

His mouth seemed to twitch with anxiety. "Before that night, I didn't know what I was missing, but once you showed me what affection was like, I

134

needed more. So, to be honest, my true motive in coming to Earth was to seek you out."

Therese couldn't speak. She didn't know what to say. She sat there, stunned.

"I knew I wouldn't kill you—at least, I didn't think I would. As I've said before, you wouldn't be the same. I don't think I'd like having a wife with little personality and no freedom."

"Wife?" Therese whispered.

"Just listen," he said. "After that day your parents died, I went to my father to see what it would take to make you a god. As a god, you would retain your personality and free will and could live with me in the Underworld unchanged. I reminded my father how he got my mother, Persephone. Are you familiar with that story?"

Therese shook her head. "Vaguely. I don't recall." She still hadn't gotten past the word "wife."

Than pulled off one of his boots. "Do you mind?"

Like she would deny a god. "Make yourself comfortable," she murmured.

He pulled off his other boot and then brought both legs straight in front of him on the bed, crossed, stretched over the tan and white comforter nearly to her headboard. Therese shifted over to give him more room, still unable to believe. He didn't sound like a god. Shouldn't a god speak differently? In her mind she said, "You sound so human."

"We've been around humans for centuries. Why wouldn't gods sound like humans?"

Her eyes shot up to his. He could hear her?

He crossed his arms at his chest. "My mom, Persephone, is the daughter of the goddess of the harvest known as Demeter. Technically, she's Zeus's sister. The genealogy of the gods is…complicated. Anyway, one day Persephone was walking along with some friends when she was drawn by a

135

cluster of white daffodils. Persephone was picking the daffodils near a cliff edge separated from her friends when my father came riding by in his chariot and swept her up without stopping. He plunged the chariot over the cliff edge into this giant chasm in the earth and took her down with him to the Underworld where he made her marry him and become his wife."

"That's so cruel." She pulled her legs closer to her chest, hugging them with her arms. "Your dad sounds like a jerk." Did she just say that out loud? To a god? She sucked on her lips. Keep your mouth shut, she said to herself.

"Hades thought if she could just get to know him, she would fall in love with him. See, like me, he had little contact with the other gods, and all the humans he knew were already dead. He was lonely."

"I don't think that justifies…"

"I know," he snapped.

Therese's eyes widened. Shut up, she said to herself again.

"My grandmother, Demeter, looked all over for Persephone, but no one would tell her the truth because they feared my father. She even disguised herself and came to Earth and lived for a while with a human family, but her misery made the Earth barren, and people and animals were beginning to die along with the vegetation. So my father's brother, Zeus, decided to take the matter into his own hands and force my father to let Persephone go. By that time, Persephone had grown fond of Hades, but she missed her mother and was anxious to see her. Before Persephone left, my father offered her a pomegranate seed, which is one of the most powerful foods you can eat, as a farewell blessing. She graciously took his offering without knowing it was another trap. By taking his food, Persephone was obligated to return."

Therese shuddered, still convinced Hades was a jerk.

"Zeus, trying to please everyone, commanded Persephone to live with Hades in the Underworld as his queen for six months out of every year,

136

and the rest of time she could spend on Mount Olympus with her mother, Demeter. That's why humans have to deal with fall and winter every year: For six months, Demeter sinks into depression and mourns the loss of her daughter. Most of the vegetation dies. Demeter never gets over losing my mom."

Therese thought of her own parents down in the Underworld, permanently. At least Demeter had the six months each year. Therese would take that deal. She had nothing. She released her knees and sat up crisscrossing her legs. Clifford crawled over into her lap. "What does your mother's story have to do with me? My parents are already down there. My aunt wasn't expecting to have to finish raising me. It would be better for everyone if I died, too."

Than moved along the foot of the bed so that he was lying on his side propped on an elbow, his head resting in his hand. "You know that's not true." He gave her a gentle smile. "Your aunt, your friends, and your pets would all miss you."

"They'd get over it." She pet Clifford as tears came into her eyes and spilled down her cheeks.

Than reached across the bed and wiped the tears from her face and then lay back on his side. "My brother told me I should come to Earth and have my way with as many girls as I wanted, to sow my wild oats, he said; but that's not my style. There's only one girl I'm interested in."

Therese's heart sped up. "You can't really mean me?"

He smiled, apparently amused. "Why not?"

"I'm the first girl you've met. How can you be so sure there isn't someone better? And you hardly know me. And I'm, I'm nothing compared to many girls I know." She couldn't believe she had blurted all that out. She felt her face flush red.

"Earlier I said the humans I come into contact with are dead, but I have still seen the living from afar. I have travelled all over the earth and

137

have seen all kinds of people. You are the sweetest, most natural, most vibrant person I have ever observed." He reached across the bed and touched her hand.

"That's impossible," she whispered.

He laughed out loud. "Jen's right. You're way too hard on yourself."

Her eyebrows flew up. Had he listened in on their conversations?

"And you seem to have no clue about your natural abilities."

"Abilities?"

He laughed again. "The way you communicate with animals, the way you read people's thoughts, the way you naturally know what to say to make others at ease. You are so full of life and aware of the nature around you. Ironically, you are the exact opposite of the dead I ferry. And that makes you utterly attractive to me in every way." He leaned in and touched his lips to her cheek. She felt her heart beat erratically and her lungs fill with air which she couldn't release.

He sat back and smiled shyly at her, and then he frowned with doubt, but she didn't know what to say. "So, anyway, I reminded my father of his own loneliness before finding my mother and asked him to consider making you a god. He said there is a way."

"What is it?" Therese asked with enthusiasm. "Please tell me. I want to know."

His face turned bitter. "It's not worth doing just to see your parents. I'm telling you, they aren't the same. They probably won't remember you."

She slid on her knees and then lay down on the bed across from him, mimicking his position propped on her elbow. Clifford moved between them. Therese and Than both pet Clifford as she struggled to put into words what she was feeling. "That's not my only reason," she finally said in a soft voice. "I want to be with you, too."

He looked up at her with surprise, but he didn't seem convinced. "I know you liked me before, but now that you know who I am, you still want to be around me?"

Therese gave him a shy nod.

"I was under the impression you despised me, like everyone else." His face was full of anguish.

"No. I don't. I was just frightened."

"I don't believe you," he said.

She stopped petting Clifford to take his hand. It felt big and moist and warm in hers.

He gently squeezed her hand and closed his eyes. "That feels so nice." Then he jumped from the bed. "Your aunt is coming. I better go. Come early tomorrow."

He vanished into thin air just as Carol knocked on the bedroom door.

"Can I come in?" Carol asked.

Therese was momentarily jarred. "Um, yes. Come in," she finally said.

Carol poked her head in the room. "Richard and I are going to bed. I just wanted to say goodnight. I had a good time tonight, and I hope you did, too."

Therese managed a smile for her aunt's sake. "I did. I really did."

"Good. I'll see you in the morning." Carol closed the door behind her.

Therese sat up on her bed hoping Than would reappear. When a half hour passed and he still hadn't come, she turned off the television and tried her best to go to sleep.

Early Thursday morning after toast and eggs, Carol and Richard dropped Therese off in front of the Holts' place.

139

"Have fun in Durango," Therese said as she climbed from the car. A feeling of guilt for leaving Clifford alone in the house made Therese frown, but she knew he'd find ways to entertain himself.

The sun peeked over the forest behind Jen's. The road was mostly in shade and the morning air was cool, maybe too cool for swimming, she thought. Instead of heading up the drive to the Holts', she walked across the dirt road and through the grassy field in search of Than. She wore her bathing suit beneath her shorts and tank top in case she felt brave enough to swim with him.

When she reached the lake, she looked for him. She even called his name. A mother duck and her ducklings scurried away from the bank, but there was no sign of Than. Disappointed, she turned away from the water and headed across the tall grass to Jen's.

She wondered what Than had meant when he had said there was a way to make her a god. She still couldn't believe he had come to Earth to seek her out. Maybe he had been changed by her affection, but affection could be found from many sources. She still felt like he was settling when he could have someone better.

When Therese approached the pen, she found it empty of people. Ace came to the fence and stretched his yellow-brown neck out to her. "Where is everybody, Ace?"

"You're early," Pete called from the barn. "Than and I are just finishing up in here." He appeared at the barn door, shirtless. Therese stole a cursory glance over his well-formed chest. "Jen, Bobby, and my mom went inside for a short break." He gave her a big smile as she moved closer.

"You were awesome last night," she said. "I'm so excited for you."

He gave her a sweaty hug that smelled of earth and hay. "You're a sweetheart for saying that."

Than appeared at the door, tense, as though Pete's embrace upset him. He also wore no shirt, and she could immediately see there was no

140

comparison. How could you compare a mere man to a god? "Hey, Therese," he said with reserve in his voice.

"Hi, Than." She felt shy. "I looked for you at the lake."

"I was just about to head over there," he said, brightening. "I need to cool off after all that barn work."

"That's a great idea," Pete said to Than. "Mind if I join you?"

"Not at all, Pete."

Therese could see the disappointment in Than's face, and she herself felt let down. She was anxious to find out how she could become a god. "I'll just come along and watch you guys from the bank. I'm not hot enough to get in that cold water yet."

"Believe me, you're hot enough," Pete teased.

Therese felt her face flush red and could make no reply.

Pete mussed her hair.

She walked between the two tall boys across the dirt road and the field of grass. As they walked, Pete talked about his hopes for his band. It was difficult for her to hear what he said. She wasn't used to being pinned between two gorgeous guys—one a god, no less. She tried to keep her breath steady as they approached the water and the two boys stripped off their boots and jeans. Pete's boxers were gray, and Than wore white again.

She laughed when the two boys decided to make a race of it as they jumped out into the deeper part and swam freestyle till they were out in the middle. She smiled with delight as they dunked each other, playing like bear cubs vying for fish.

"Come in!" Than shouted during a reprieve from their game. "It feels great."

"Maybe later!" she shouted back. "After I work up a sweat!"

They swam back to the shallows and stood up, water dripping down their glistening bodies—the one thick and glowing, the other almost as tall,

141

tan, and well-formed by human standards. Therese looked away. It was just too much to take in.

The boys climbed into their jeans and boots and the three of them headed back to the pen to begin their work on the horses. Thoughts of Dumbo sobered Therese as she took a brush to Sugar.

"Hey pretty girl," she said to Sugar.

Jen, Bobby, and Mrs. Holt soon joined them from the house.

"Hi Therese!" Jen noticed Than and Pete were both soaked and shirtless. "Go for a swim, guys?" She took a brush to Sassy.

Pete laughed from behind the General. "Yeah. Than here nearly drowned me." He must have recalled the fact that Therese's parents' drowned, because she caught a glimpse of his face behind the horse as he turned red and said no more.

Therese shuddered, but Than was soon there to distract her. "I sure had fun at the Wildhorse Saloon last night. I wouldn't mind going again sometime."

Bobby piped up. "Me, too. That was a blast. Hey, Mom. Can we go again tomorrow night?" Bobby held the brush midair, above Chestnut's back, waiting for his mother's answer.

"I don't know, Bobby," Mrs. Holt replied as she dug something from Rusty's hoof. "It gets pretty crowded on Friday nights."

"Oh, come on, Mom," Jen joined in. "Pete could take us if you don't want to go. Couldn't you Pete?"

"Sure. I don't mind."

"Maybe so," Mrs. Holt said without committing to anything. But both Jen and Bobby exchanged smiles. They knew "maybe so" meant "yes."

When Jen finished with Sassy, she came over to Therese and said in a confidential voice, "Matthew called late last night and invited me to lunch today. I'm a little nervous."

Therese stood up. "Are you excited? I mean, are you glad he called?"

"Yeah. It was like we hadn't stopped talking all this time. He said he had pictures to show me. He just got back from Alaska. I'm pissed that he didn't call before he left, though." She picked Sassy's hair from the brush.

"Language," Mrs. Holt warned.

"Sorry, Mom," Jen said.

Therese continued their conversation in a whisper. "Maybe he'll explain why. He wouldn't have called last night if he weren't still interested." Therese patted on Sugar's leg for the hoof. Therese inspected the shoe while she waited for Jen's reply.

Jen shrugged. "You really think so?"

"Yes, I do."

"I'm meeting him at Hondo's for chicken fried steak. I'm dropping Bobby at Gamestop to get him off my back. He's been bugging me to take him all week. Matthew offered to come pick me up, but since Bobby wanted to go to town...anyway, that's why I'm meeting him." Jen went over to Annie, the red mare, and started brushing her back. "What did you get into, girl?"

Jen and Bobby went inside to wash up after the last horse was saddled and ready for the first trail ride. Pete and Mrs. Holt started helping the riders mount their horses, one at a time. Than and Therese waved their goodbyes and headed home. Than stopped her on the dirt road in front of Jen's house.

"Are we going swimming?" he asked with a smile.

Therese grinned back. "I'm up for it if you are. But only if you promise to answer a few more questions."

"I was planning on it anyway. Let's go." He took her hand in his and walked with her across the field.

Therese felt giddy with excitement. His big warm hand surrounding hers made her shiver with delight. Their arms brushed every so often, sending tingles of pleasure down her skin. She became even more excited when they reached the bank of the reservoir and Than kicked off his boots and jeans. She pulled off her tank top with shaky arms and stepped out of her shorts. She left her sneakers on so her feet wouldn't get hurt on the rocks on the bottom of the lake.

She stood there, embarrassed, in her two-piece bathing suit while he looked over her body. She felt good about her flat stomach and curvy hips, but, even though Jen said she was crazy, she didn't like her blossoming thighs and the lemon halves she had for boobs.

Than walked up to her in his white boxers and, with one finger, pulled up the strap that had fallen from her shoulder. "You're so beautiful," he said in a soft voice. Then, without any warning, he took her waist in his hands and carried her into the water.

She screamed with pleasure. "It's like ice!"

"Nice, isn't it?" He took her out where she couldn't stand and then released her waist to tread water.

She treaded beside him. "You said you'd answer my questions first, you cheater!" She splashed water against his face.

"Cheater? You didn't specify the order!"

He splashed her back, and it felt like a tidal wave had washed over her. She sputtered and gagged on the water that had unexpectedly entered her mouth. Her hair flattened in her face.

"Sorry about that," he laughed.

She had the feeling he wasn't sorry at all. She shivered with the cold of the water but managed to stick out her tongue at him in mock anger.

He put his hands on her waist again and towed her to shallower water, where she could stand, the gentle waves clearing her chin. The water came up to his nipples, and she could see from the look of them that he was cold, too.

"I don't need your help," she teased. "I'm an awesome swimmer."

"Is that right?"

"Wanna race?"

He laughed. "Let me get this straight. You are challenging a god to a race?"

"You raced with Pete."

"That wasn't a real race. I wouldn't dare show my true speed and give myself away."

She narrowed her eyes. "Show me. I want to see."

"Others might be watching."

"Please?"

He laughed. "Who could resist you anything?" He dove under and swam freestyle in a flash of white to the other side of the reservoir and back before she had counted to ten.

She opened her mouth with surprise. "Oh my God!"

"You can call me Than," he said slyly.

She splashed him again. "Time to pay up. What did your father tell you when you asked him how to make me a god?"

His face grew somber. "Do you have to ruin the fun?"

"You promised."

"Fine. He said if you personally avenge your parents' death, if *you* take the life of the one responsible so that he or she can be properly punished in the Underworld, he will make you a god."

She narrowed her eyes again. "So if I avenge the death of my parents, I can become like you?"

He frowned. "But it's a bad idea. I thought about it all night. I don't want you to do it."

"You're kidding, right? Who wouldn't want to be a god?"

145

"Not just any god, Therese. A god of the Underworld. Even my mother can only handle it six months out of the year. Hades isn't offering you the same bargain."

"I don't care. I told you. I want to be with you." Then she shivered. "Unless you've changed your mind." Maybe he didn't want to be with her, now that he had a chance to know her and to see that there are other, more beautiful, fish in the sea.

He put his arms around her waist and put his face inches from hers. She felt light headed and weak kneed. "You've got it all wrong," he said. "Once I thought more about the way you were with nature and the animals, I realized you belonged among the living. Therese, the Underworld would be a dull place for someone like you. There aren't any animals except the delusions created by the psyches of the dead. You said yourself you couldn't live without animals. The souls of dead animals are like those of dead humans—without freedom and full of delusions."

Even though she could barely control her arms because of the trembling, she put them around his neck and pressed her body against his, so warm compared to the ice cold water. "It should be my decision."

He licked his lips and looked at her mouth. "Then you've got a lot to think about." He gave her a playful smile and then picked her up in his hands and tossed her high across the water.

She had a feeling as she flew above the water, squealing like a pig, that he hadn't used his full strength. She plunged into the water as though she had been on a high slide in a water park. She swam underwater back to him, and when she returned to the surface, she dipped her head back to pull her hair from her face, looked right into his eyes, and said, with her own playful smile, "You're gonna pay for that."

She dove under water and pulled his legs out from under him, but when his head went under, he merely looked at her and laughed. He could

146

breathe underwater and talk underwater. She shook her head at him, folded her arms to show she was pouting, and resurfaced.

"What's wrong?" he laughed as he came up to meet her face.

"You've got to have a weakness. It's not fair otherwise. Achilles had his heels."

He pulled her into his arms and she gladly yielded into his warm embrace. "I do have a weakness now."

She didn't need to ask what he meant, even though she couldn't believe it was true. How could such a remarkable being feel so strongly about her?

He walked with her to the bank and said, "Wait here. I'll be right back." She blinked and he was gone.

"Than?" She felt totally unnerved. It was creepy, surreal. He had been standing right in front of her and now he was gone. She suddenly felt the need to sit down, but before she could move, Than reappeared, and he was holding a quilt in his hands.

Her mouth dropped open as she watched him spread the blanket out a few feet from the bank in the tall grass.

"What did you just do?" she asked.

He grinned and shook his head. "Give me a break, Therese. You don't expect much from the gods, do you." It wasn't a question.

"Um, I've just never personally known one. I'm trying to adjust. Excuse my human ignorance." She hadn't meant that to come out as mean as it sounded.

"I'm sorry," he said. He had fixed the blanket neatly across the grass, and now he reached over to her and took her hand. "I need to be patient. I'm so unused to the company of living mortals." He pulled her close and kissed her cheek. "Why don't we dry off in the sun before heading home?"

She lay down on her back beside him. Both of them turned their faces up to the sun, eyes closed. He held her hand, and she couldn't decide which was warmer: he or the golden orb above them.

"Tell me about your parents," he asked suddenly.

His question took her by surprise. She was almost always thinking about her parents, longing for them, but over the past several minutes they hadn't crossed her mind. "What do you want to know?"

"What was your mom like? Tell me about her first. Was she like you?"

Therese gave a short laugh. "She was nothing like me. She loved solving problems, you know, problems in science and discovering answers to things. Ironically, she was afraid of unreasonable things, like heights, planes, and elevators. She hated escalators, too. She was even a little afraid of the water, I think, and I love the water. I feel the most at home there. I sometimes think if I had a previous life, I must have been a dolphin. My mom and nature didn't get along. I sometimes got the feeling that as a scientist she was trying to conquer nature by understanding it. She was scared of spiders and snakes, I'm talking about ones that aren't even poisonous. A lizard would have her in hysterics." Therese laughed. "Dad and I used to have a lot of fun with that."

"What was your dad like?"

"He was more like me. We used to go on hikes. Nearly every evening we'd sit on our deck with our binoculars and study the wildlife across the reservoir. My dad was a writer, so sometimes months would go by and I'd hardly see him, but then he'd finish a book and we'd have months together before he'd start on another. The thing I liked most about my dad was that he was the best practical joker I've ever known, and luckily my mom, and not me, was his most common victim. But I think she liked being victimized in a strange kind of way. He always made us laugh. My dad and I were often in collusion together against my mom, but she never minded. She even seemed to like it."

The memories swept over Therese and she nearly forgot where she was and what she was doing as she relived brief moments with her parents. She giggled when she remembered the time she and her dad got her mom with the plastic rat they had planted beneath the kitchen sink.

Than squeezed her hand and brought her back, and she looked at him with gratitude. "This is the first time I've gone down memory lane with any kind of joy since the shooting. You have a way of keeping me happy and on the bright side of things."

He returned her warm smile. "I'm glad. You already know what you do to me."

"No I don't. What is that exactly?"

He closed his eyes and turned his face back to the sun. She watched him, studied every line and feature of his golden face and chest as he spoke. "You make me feel human, in a very good way."

"What do you mean?"

"Humans often envy the gods because of our power, but the truth is we have far more responsibilities than freedoms. We have duties, obligations we can't neglect without significantly affecting the world—the whole world and the life on it. My entire life has been about serving. I have been a dutiful son to my father. This is the first time in my ancient history that I have ever done something solely for me, and it feels great. It makes me realize that I need to strike a balance, more like my brother, who has always managed to find time for both work and play."

Therese laughed. "That's an understatement. I'm not sure he works nearly as much as he plays."

"You're wrong. Dreams are more important than most humans realize. Hip plays around a lot, but he also works hard to make sure people are inspired, fulfilled, provoked, challenged, comforted. It's a big responsibility."

Therese was quiet while she let that information sink in. She hadn't thought of Hip as rendering an important service. She had only seen him as a playboy. "It sounds like you love your brother."

"I do. I love all the members in my family."

She turned on her side and put her free hand—the hand he wasn't holding—on his heart. She wondered if it beat like a human heart. She could feel it thumping in a regular, humanlike rhythm beneath his chest, and it picked up speed as she moved her hand across his skin.

"I don't want this afternoon to end. I hope my aunt's not worried."

"She and her boyfriend have lost track of time sightseeing in Durango."

"That's so weird that you know that."

He laughed softly.

"Do you really have to leave so soon?" she asked.

"Yes, I do."

"But what if we don't find the person behind the shooting? What if I can't avenge my parent's murderer in time?"

He opened his eyes and looked at her. "Would that make you sad?"

She nodded. She never liked someone so much and couldn't imagine it ending so soon. "I want more time with you. I'm just getting to know you. Can't you use your powers to freeze time for everyone else or something?"

He chuckled and his body moved beneath her hand.

"What's so funny?"

"You freak out when I disappear and reappear, but you expect me to stop time."

She laughed, too. "But why can't you? You're a god."

"Like I said, we have more responsibilities than freedoms. I doubt even Zeus could pull that one off."

150

From high above, a streak of light flew from the sky and struck a boulder not twenty feet from where they lay, sending sparks and smoke and a loud crack in all directions in the echoing valley. The boulder was split in half and was as black as coal.

"Holy crap!" Therese cried, falling against Than. "What was that?"

"Oops. My apologies," he muttered, but it didn't sound like he was talking to her. "I made someone angry."

"That scared me to death. Does that happen often?"

"No. Never to me. But this is an exceptional time in my life."

Therese now realized she had flattened her body against Than, on top of him from the waist up. He wrapped his arms around her and held her against him. Heat surged through her. She reached her lips to his.

His mouth was warm and wet. A tingling sensation surged through her and she could hear nothing but her heart thudding in her ears.

He said softly, "If I could stop time for you, I would."

In her mind, she said, "I'd rather die than be parted from you," and then he looked at her with shock, as though he had heard her thoughts.

"What?" she asked, mortified by the possibility that he could read her mind.

He leaned his head back and closed his eyes. "I can't stand the thought of causing you pain."

"Then don't." Her words sounded hostile.

He opened his eyes again and looked at her. "Should I go away before your feelings…"

"No!"

He cracked a smile. "Does this mean you've decided?"

She couldn't help but return his smile despite the conflicting emotions coursing through her. "First, I want to meet your sisters."

Chapter Twenty: Hunting with Tizzie

Than and Tizze flew above hundreds of humans in an airport terminal in San Diego. Some sat at tables inside small cafes and sandwich shops. Others sat crammed together near gates. Still others walked quickly through the corridors dragging their bags on wheels behind them. The man they knew as Steve McAdams had short, blond hair and blue eyes and sat sharply dressed in a crisp white shirt, unbuttoned at the neck, black trousers, and shiny black shoes. He sat looking at a cell phone with another man, about the same age, mid-thirties, also sharply dressed but with dark, curly hair and glasses. Both men held their heads together looking at the phone and laughing.

"This should be fun," Tizzie said to Than as they landed before the men and made themselves visible.

Tizzie stood in her tight black leather pants and silver halter top and tall black boots. She spread out her arms and legs and closed her eyes and smiled. The men looked up at her and then looked at Than and then looked at each other, perplexed. Tizze opened her eyes and smiled at the men as dozens of wolves appeared in the terminal around them.

The humans were shocked and stopped what they were doing and backed into areas away from the hounds, and as the hounds lifted their heads into the air and howled their loud, screeching, blood-curdling cries, the humans dropped whatever they were holding and cupped both hands to their ears.

The two men before Tizzie also dropped the phone and cupped their ears, tears streaming from their eyes.

"Hear me, Steve McAdams?" Tizzie said coolly, barely perceptible to Than over the howls of the hounds.

The flustered, frightened man nodded.

"Do you know this man, Kaveh Grahib?" She made an image appear in the air over her head, an image of him in his jail cell slumped on a cot, staring into space.

Steven McAdams shook his head.

Tizzie beckoned one of her hounds to her side and then he bared his fangs at the man as he uttered a threatening growl.

"Be truthful Steven," Tizzie warned. "I do not like men who lie."

Steven McAdams looked at the growling hound and then back up at Tizzie, still cupping his ears and streaming tears. "I don't know him!" he shouted but could be heard by none save the two gods.

Tizzie lifted her arms higher in the air, and at once the howling stopped. The humans stared blankly as the wolves descended upon the humans in a rush and a flash, licking each one with a forgetting serum before vanishing into thin air. Than and Tizzie also vanished as Than heard her voice mutter with profound disappointment, "He's not the one."

Chapter Twenty-One: The Furies

Therese was glad when she came home Thursday afternoon to find herself alone—except for the company of her pets—because she could hardly contain her excitement. She couldn't wait to have more of her questions answered, to find out what the Furies were like, and to spend more time with Than.

The phone rang just after she had stripped down for a shower, but she picked it up in case it was Carol, or better, Than. It was Vicki Stern.

"So can you go to the movies tonight?"

Therese had completely forgotten her promise to call Vicki back. "I'm sorry. I've actually got plans again. I was invited to have supper with another friend."

"But I asked you first, Therese."

"This is a family thing that came up. I'm sorry. My aunt's in town and…"

"You just said it was a friend."

"A friend of the family. Hey, let's shoot for next week, okay?"

"Okay."

"Bye now."

"Bye."

"Ugh," Therese said to herself. What was she going to do with that girl?

After her shower, she threw on a comfy t-shirt and shorts and went downstairs to make a batch of brownies to take to tonight's dinner. She hummed as she poured the chocolate batter into a pan and popped the pan in the preheated oven. Although she was humming "Poker Face," it dawned on her that she wasn't faking this new feeling of liberty as she had on the dance

154

floor. Something about Than's presence and his apparent love for her had freed her from the dark depression that had threatened to overtake her. She still wanted to go to the Underworld, but now she could do it without dying. She could be with her parents *and* the sweetest, sexiest guy she had ever met.

Things hadn't turned out so badly for her after all.

As she made herself a peanut butter and jelly sandwich, she wondered if she truly loved Than. There was no doubt that she was enamored with him, no doubt that she crushed on him harder than anyone she had ever met, no doubt that she longed to be with him every second he was away from her. But could she really say she *loved* him when she barely knew him? And if her answer was yes, as crazy as that would sound, did she love him enough to spend all of eternity with him?

She took her plate and glass of milk with her upstairs so she could log on to her laptop to learn more about Thanatos and the Furies. She found a passage from an ancient poet named Hesiod who described Than and his brother this way:

And there the children of dark Night have their dwellings, Sleep and Death, awful gods. The glowing Sun never looks upon them with his beams, neither as he goes up into heaven, nor as he comes down from heaven. And the former of them roams peacefully over the earth and the sea's broad back and is kindly to men; but the other has a heart of iron, and his spirit within him is pitiless as bronze: whomsoever of men he has once seized he holds fast: and he is hateful even to the deathless gods.

A new doubt worked its way into Therese's head as she processed the description. Could Than be deceiving her only to show his true self once she's his wife and it's too late for her to change her mind? Was he like his father, Hades, willing to trick her into becoming his queen of death?

Impossible, she thought.

She came across three different images depicting him. One showed him wielding a sword, wearing a shaggy beard and head of curly black hair.

155

His ugly face looked fierce, unrelenting, and cruel. The second image was one she had seen that day she had come home from the hospital: the Grim Reaper, thin like a skeleton, cloaked in black, bearing a deadly scythe. The third image still wasn't her Than, but was closer to how she viewed him: a winged boy, like Cupid, maybe sixteen or seventeen years old, with a sweet air about him.

Therese knew these were all human interpretations of him and not factual renditions, but, nevertheless, uncertainty about his identity gripped her heart and made her anxious. Her anxiety increased when she read that the Furies had wreaths of snakes in their hair and blood dripping from their eyes and were horrible to behold. Meg had been beautiful. Had she somehow disguised herself?

After more reading, the oven timer beeped, so she went downstairs to take the brownies out and let them cool on the stove top. What a strange circumstance she found herself in: baking brownies for a handful of gods from the Underworld.

The ringing of the telephone startled her from where she had been standing in the kitchen deep in thought. She hoped it wasn't Vicki. She picked up the phone. "Hello?"

It was Carol calling to check on her, which gave Therese the opportunity to tell her about her supper plans. Carol seemed relieved, for she and Richard had lost track of time and now wouldn't need to rush back home. Therese hung up and went upstairs to her closet to figure out what to wear. Nothing in her wardrobe seemed good enough for a dinner with gods.

Standing there in the small walk-in closet, she thought of her mother. Normally, she would ask her what she should wear, for her mother seemed to know the latest style, maybe because she worked around college kids every day. Mom could be oblivious to so many things around her, but she had seemed to always notice fashion.

156

Therese went back downstairs to the master bedroom. Across the hall from it was a guest bedroom, where Carol was staying. Neither Carol nor Therese was ready to disturb the master bedroom. Therese had taken the bottle of Haiku perfume, but had touched nothing else.

Now as she stood there, perfectly alone, she went to her parents' bed and lay down on her belly with her face in her mother's pillow, taking in her scent. She took her dad's pillow and practically inhaled it. His scent washed over her along with a current of tears. She pulled back the covers and crawled beneath them and wrapped herself in their smells. She closed her eyes, willing herself to dream, but there was nothing. After about twenty minutes, she climbed from the bed, not troubling to make it up again, and went into her parents' closet where their scents were even stronger. She gingerly touched their garments. Would she ever wear something of her mother's without falling apart? Could she dare part with her father's clothes by giving them to charity?

She left the closet and went to her mother's dresser. She opened the tiny drawers of her wooden jewelry box, a gift from Therese's father before Therese was born. She took a diamond necklace from one of the drawers and held it up to her throat, gazing at her reflection in the dresser mirror. Twelve round stones linked together on a delicate golden chain made a beautiful choker around her neck. Maybe one of these days she would find an occasion to wear it. Maybe she would take it with her when she became the goddess of death.

She laughed nervously. "I have lost my mind," she whispered.

Therese tucked the necklace back into its drawer, closed the drawer, and went back upstairs. She was surprised to find Clifford had not come down with her, but had chosen to stay on her bed. She hadn't given much thought to how much he probably missed her parents, too. She now shuddered at the thought of leaving him and Jewels and Puffy forever.

157

Therese returned to her own closet again. She finally chose a short red skirt and tight white, short-sleeved sweater that she thought made her boobs look bigger. She slipped on her white wedge sandals and looked over herself in the mirror. She picked up her hair to see which looked better—down or up—and decided to stick with it down, the way her father liked it.

Her heart felt tight as she wondered if she should have told someone the truth about her hosts tonight. What if they killed her and took her down to the Underworld before she could say goodbye? What would her aunt and the Holts think if Therese never returned? Should she leave a note just in case?

I'm being paranoid, she thought. Than would never hurt me.

Therese went to the kitchen to cut up the brownies and put them on a platter. She folded plastic wrap across them to keep away bugs during her walk through the forest to the Melner cabin. She looked like a normal girl headed toward a normal neighborhood potluck, or something; not a possibly deranged girl with illusions of eating with gods.

She put the platter down on the counter and swept her dog up in her arms. "I love you, Clifford. Be a good boy. I'll be home soon."

Than gave Therese a bashful smile when he answered the door in his khaki shorts and a short-sleeved denim shirt. She was glad she had come. She didn't care what happened to her. She wanted to be with him.

"What is this?" he asked of the platter she handed him.

"Brownies. Have you ever tasted some?"

"You obviously aren't talking about nymphs." He looked confused.

Therese threw back her head and laughed. "Chocolate and sugar. They're for dessert."

He gave her a sheepish grin as he led her through the living area and into the kitchen. He sat the brownies down on the kitchen bar. "Thanks. I can't wait to taste them."

158

The Melner cabin was similar to her house in that the living room and kitchen were open to one another. But in the Melner cabin, the stairs started near the front entrance instead of the back. At the back of the house, off of the kitchen, where Therese's stairs would be, a door led to a dining room. A huge bay window opened to the forest climbing the mountain behind the house. Therese could see a flagstone patio and grill outside.

Than's two sisters were already gathered waiting for her with the table set. They stood up when she entered, their round eyes shining with the light of the crystal chandelier hanging over the center of the beautiful table scape.

Therese recognized Meg even though her thick blonde curls were loosed from their usual bun and spilling out down the length of her back. Her beautiful face was without makeup, and Therese now realized that her lips were naturally deep red. Meg wore the black go-go boots from the night before with a short black fitted dress. Unlike last night, she wore red ruby studs in her ears, matching stones in rings on her fingers, and one enormous blood-red ruby pendant around her neck. She looked fiercely beautiful.

A little much for a dinner at home, though, Therese thought.

The other sister—Tizzie, Therese presumed—had equally long, thick hair, but hers was jet black, and her curls were individual serpentine ringlets, as though she had curled her hair and then not brushed it out. Her face was darker complexioned, and her eyes were black like her hair. She had dark eyebrows with a delicate arch and deep red lips. She also wore no makeup and yet possessed an eerie kind of beauty. Tizzie wore tight black leather pants, black stiletto heels, and a silver halter top that tied around her neck, leaving her dark back bare. Shimmery emeralds hung from her ears, and smaller ones linked in several loose, jangling bracelets around both wrists.

Therese felt she had underdressed.

Than pulled out a chair from the table. "Please, sit down."

When Therese sat, the Furies sat, too.

"Therese, these are my sisters. You've met Megaera, or Meg for short."

Meg gave a courteous, but distant, nod.

"This is Tisiphone. Everyone calls her Tizzie," Than said.

"Welcome to our table," Tizzie spoke without smiling. "Our brother told us you wanted to meet us. I must say you are the very first human to ever make such a request."

Meg's sneer sent a shiver down Therese's back.

"Thanks for having me," Therese managed to say. "Everything looks delicious, and the table spread is absolutely beautiful."

"What nice manners," Tizzie commented.

Meg added. "We've been known to punish those without them."

Than cleared his throat. "Why don't we eat?"

Therese saw that the salad was like the one she had made for Than. Along with the salad was a bowl of vegetable soup and a plate with fried potato patties.

"We're vegetarians," Than explained. "I hope you like the food."

Therese took a sip of the soup with her spoon. "Mmm. Delicious. I tend to be vegetarian myself—not strictly, but usually." She cut a piece of the potato patty with her fork and gave it a taste. It melted in her mouth. "Oh my goodness. So this is what gods eat?"

Than said, "We usually eat ambrosia and nectar, but when in Rome…"

Therese smiled. "Oh yes. Right." She was terrified now of appearing impolite. She continued to eat in silence.

After several minutes of cutting and scraping and drinking and chewing, Meg prompted her, "Than says you have questions."

Therese stammered, "I, I hope you won't think it rude of me."

Tizzie said, almost demanded, her arched brows raised with curiosity, "What do you want to know?"

160

Therese wasn't sure where to begin. "Maybe you could tell me what you've learned so far about my parents' killer."

This question apparently pleased both sisters, for they gave her lascivious smiles.

Tizzie spoke, "Every night I go and torment the man who pulled the trigger that shot the bullet into your mother's neck"

Therese shuddered.

"That is why I could not go dancing last night," Tizzie added.

Well, of course, Therese thought. That sounded perfectly normal. She couldn't go dancing because she was too busy tormenting a man in jail.

Tizzie continued, "This man's name is Kaveh Grahib. He lies in his cell while I fill him with anguish and dread and terror. I whisper in his ear to tell me the details of the plotter. I climb on top of him and let my snakes slither on his clammy skin. Blood drips from my eyes when he resists, and my legs squeeze him until he cannot breathe. So far, I have only a name, but it won't be long before I track the plotter down."

Therese's appetite left her, and she sat chilled and afraid. "What is the name he gave you?"

Tizzie looked at Than, and Than nodded, so she said, "Steven McAdams. I know he is American, but that is all. Tonight I will find out more." She gave her lusty smile.

Meg scowled at Therese. "It's rude not to finish your plate."

Therese took a sip of the soup and tried her best to finish the rest.

"Maybe we should change the subject," Than suggested. "Why don't you two tell her what it's like living in the dark abyss that is the Underworld. She'd like to be better informed before making the decision I discussed with you."

"It's actually quite fun on days when I go to Tartarus and torment the evildoers for their sins on Earth," Meg said.

Therese shivered and let out a just-audible moan.

161

Than's smile faded. "Listen, Therese, my sisters may take satisfaction in their work, but they, unlike the souls they torment, are not evil." Then he bent his brow at Meg, "Could you tone it down a little?"

Tizzie smirked. "Well, I have to admit, I enjoy my job. Than's right: It is *very* satisfying. But I also like the precious stones our father has mined from deep underground. He gives them to us as gifts when we are especially swift with his just payment." She lifted one of her arms to jangle the emerald bracelets.

Than frowned. "Now let's not go in the opposite direction with extremes, Tizzie. I don't want her to be terrified, but I also don't want her under any delusions of grandeur. The Underworld is a loathsome place, even if there are a few perks. There aren't any animal companions or beautiful plants. No sunrises and sunsets. Everything is cold and lifeless."

"That's not so," Tizzie objected. "Cerberus is there, who can be quite entertaining when provoked, and so are Swift and Sure, Father's two black stallions that pull his chariot. They look fierce with their red eyes and huge bodies, but they are sweet when they are eating pomegranate seeds from my hand. And as far as real plants, you're forgetting the poppies around Hypnos's abode—albeit, they make you want to go straight to sleep."

"And don't forget the asphodel along the Elysian Fields," Meg added. "Those fragrant white flowers are real even if everything else there isn't. And the rivers are real, and they're really quite beautiful and serene when neither I nor my sisters are using them as weapons of torture." The edges of her lips twisted up into a half smile.

Therese narrowed her eyes at Than. "Your sisters don't make the Underworld sound nearly as bad as you do." Then she frowned. Maybe he doesn't want me after all.

As if he had read her mind, he took her hand in his and gave it a warm squeeze. "I would love for you to come with me, but I want you to be sure. I want you to know what you're getting into."

162

So he's not like his father, she thought. He's not going to trick me like Hades did Persephone.

"And Cerberus can be kind if you bring him cakes," Tizzie offered. "Though Alecto never should have given that information to Orpheus."

"You have to admit, dear sister, how fun it was to see him torn to pieces," Meg snickered.

"Not for me. I saw no justice in it."

Meg spoke though grit teeth. "It was his due dessert for how he tricked us all."

Therese asked them to tell her the story of Orpheus, so Tizzie began.

"First you must know that the very first musicians were gods. Though Athena didn't play, she invented the flute. Hermes made the lyre and gave it to Apollo, and when he plays, we all lose our thoughts to his beautiful music. Hermes also invented a shepherd's pipe, which he plays himself, quite well, actually, when he's not running errands or going on adventures with Zeus; and Pan, Hermes's little goat-footed son, made a pipe of reeds that sings the songs of nightingales when he blows through it.

"The Muses play no instrument, but their voices are the loveliest of any I have heard in my long existence. I tell you all of this because despite the superiority of the gods to humans in all ways, there was one demigod—part human and part god—who nearly equaled the gods in musical talent, and that, of course, was Orpheus.

"Wherever Orpheus played his lyre and sang his sweet voice, the animals—even the rocks—followed. Every nymph of the woods where he travelled was in love with him, but he had interest for none until his eyes fell on Eurydice. She, like the others, could not resist his song, and she loved him immediately. They were married in the woods among all those who loved them, but right after the wedding, when Eurydice went walking through a meadow with her bridesmaids, she was bitten by a viper and instantly killed.

163

"They say even the rocks wept. Orpheus's grief was impossible to endure. He hastened to the Underworld, set on charming everyone there with his song. Our sister Alecto was the first one to be moved by his beautiful voice and the melody emanating from his lyre. She gave him cakes to feed to Cerberus. Once through the gates, his music charmed the judges next, and then Meg and me, the tormenters in Tartarus. For the first time, I think, we wept with tears. Sisyphus got to sit down on his rock, and Tantalus forgot his hunger and thirst. Our father Hades and our mother Persephone came from their chambers to hear the melodious sounds.

"Orpheus sang a song about the bud being plucked before its bloom and his wish to borrow, not take, his love for a little while. Iron tears fell down my father's face, and my mother kissed his softened cheek. They beckoned Than to bring forth Eurydice, but gave Orpheus this condition: He could not look back at his love until they were through the gates of the Underworld and across the Acheron."

Meg took up the story here, "Orpheus had little faith, it seemed. Eurydice was behind him, followed by our brother, as they climbed through the caverns above the river. As Orpheus passed Cerberus and jumped onto Charon's waiting ferry, he looked back, extending his hand, and in that moment, my brother, under my father's strict command, pulled Eurydice back down into the darkness."

Therese shuddered and glanced at Than, whose mouth was turned down in a frown.

Meg jeered, "Orpheus did not keep his end of the bargain, and he should have gone on back with the fact of his failure; however, in a desperate rage equal to Zeus, he tried to force his way back into the Underworld. When his entrance was refused, he finally gave up and wandered off until a band of Maenads—women frenzied with the wine of Dionysus—found him and tore him limb from limb, flinging his severed head into the river."

Therese looked away from Meg's awful smile. She felt sorry for Orpheus, suspecting he hadn't meant to betray his deal with Hades.

Than spoke up here, "I found his soul and took him directly to Eurydice, and they are there now together, though as I've told you, they aren't quite the same as when they were alive."

The change of subject had done nothing to bring back Therese's appetite, but she chewed on the potato patties lest she appear rude. She forced the food down with the glass of tea, which she tasted now for the first time. She nearly choked. It was sugary sweet, just the way Than apparently liked it. The corners of her mouth curved up into a smile when she recalled the way he had relished his sweet tea at her house two days ago.

The sugar reminded her of the brownies. "Oh, Than, the brownies. Should I get them and serve them to you and your sisters?"

The girls exchanged confused looks.

"She's not referring to nymphs," Than explained. "Her brownies are something called chocolate." He stood up from his chair. "I'll get them."

Both girls produced their lustful smiles. Apparently they were familiar with chocolate.

Than brought the platter to the table and passed it around. Therese watched him take his first bite of the chewy, fudgy square. He closed his eyes and uttered something like a moan. "Oh, my," he said once he'd swallowed. He took another bite. "I can't believe I've lived so many centuries without chocolate."

"And we're always so busy," Tizzie said, still smiling. "We rarely take the time on Earth to enjoy its pleasures."

"Well, well, well," Meg said after finishing her square. "I think Therese has discovered a bribing tool. If you ever have a request for me, bring me chocolate." She took another square and shoved it whole into her dark red mouth.

After Than ate a third brownie, he pushed his plate away from him and took Therese's hand in his. "So, Therese, will you go with me tomorrow night to the Wildhorse Saloon and teach me more about dancing?"

"On one condition," she said, with a bargainer's smile that would have made Hades proud. "I want to meet your parents."

The three siblings looked at one another with astonishment.

Then Than said, "Maybe if you offer to play your flute for them, they'll come."

"Music and chocolate," Meg said. "A killer combination."

"No pun intended." Tizzie laughed.

Chapter Twenty-Two: The Wildhorse Saloon Revisited

Therese felt strange Friday evening squished in the backseat of her aunt's old red Toyota Corolla between two gods, Than and Meg, on their way to the Wildhorse Saloon to meet the Holt kids, Ray, and Todd. Richard kept stealing glances behind him at the eccentric beauty beside her, dressed as she was in a red leather short suit, black go-go boots, and her blood-red rubies on her earlobes and around her neck. Although Therese had been proud of how she looked in her olive cotton camisole and her Levi boot-cut jeans, she now felt totally eclipsed.

Tizzie had promised to meet them later after her tormenting obligation. Therese imagined her hovered over her victim with a swarm of snakes dropping from her head. Would the blood still be dripping from her eyes when she arrived at the saloon? Therese shuddered.

"Are you okay?" Than whispered close to her ear. His warm breath sent chills across her scalp and down the nape of her neck. Because her red curls were up tonight in a high pony tail, she could feel Than's warm breath caressing her neck as he spoke. "Are you cold?"

"I'm fine," she said. "Just a little nervous."

"Do I make you nervous?" he whispered.

She made a little nod, but then breathed, "In a good way."

He gave her a broad smile, showing his perfect white teeth, and took her hand in his. Therese quivered with desire.

"Can you drive a little faster?" Meg asked coldly.

Carol looked at her in the rearview mirror. "I'm going the speed limit."

Meg rolled her eyes. "Great."

Therese wondered how Meg could get away with punishing people for forgetting their manners and be so rude herself. "I'm sorry we don't have more room," Therese offered.

"It's quite alright." Meg's voice was not kind.

"That's not what's getting on her nerves," Than whispered. "She's jealous of how smitten I am with you."

"Than," Meg threatened. "There's no need to speak rudely of others."

Richard gave another uncomfortable glance back at Therese's companions.

When they arrived at the Wildhorse Saloon close to eight o'clock, Todd's giant yellow truck stood out as a beacon in the parking lot, but neither Pete's truck nor Mrs. Holt's Suburban was among the three dozen other vehicles. Therese texted Todd while she led the group inside the dance hall, a wave of cigarette smoke accosting her like a stifling blanket. She tried to hold back the cough gagging her throat. Ten or so couples danced a fast polka around the wooden dance floor in front of the empty stage where Pete's band had performed two nights ago. More people gathered around the two bars—one on either side of the hall—and two or three older men, sitting on stools alone, looked drunk. Todd and Ray turned from where they stood in line at one of the bars and waved, their red minor bracelets dancing around their wrists. Therese waved back and led her group across the dance hall toward them.

After their initial hellos and some talk about Todd's truck and when Therese would get her ride—since she had missed the maiden voyage—they stood around awkwardly sipping their straws and watching the dancers on the floor across the room. One of the older men who had been sitting alone and apparently drunk approached Meg and asked for a dance. Therese was surprised when Meg consented, but Meg's mocking expression made her wonder about the Fury's motive.

The new song was a waltz, and Therese could feel Than turning toward her to ask, but before he had his words out, Todd grabbed her hand and said, "Let's go!"

Therese gave Than a look of apology as she allowed Todd to pull her out onto the floor. He glided her easily around and around with his thin but strong frame, and soon Therese was having fun and laughing out loud, especially at Todd who was now telling her all about his family's trip to California and the strange people they met there. He gave a glance at Meg as they passed her and her drunken partner and said, "Though we have a few strange folks right here in Durango."

He wanted to know more about Meg and Than. Although Therese was just a bit tempted to tell the truth—Than was the god of death and his sister was one of three tormenting avengers known as the Furies—she decided to hold her tongue, shrug, and say, "They're guests at the Melner cabin. I don't know much about them." She knew she wasn't telling him anything he didn't already know.

"Be careful with this guy," Todd said. "I have a bad feeling about him."

"Okay, Obi Wan Kenobi." She laughed.

She wondered exactly what it could be that gave Todd this negative impression of Than. Had Todd sensed something different about him?

When the song ended, he asked for another dance, but she thanked him and said she was thirsty, maybe later, so they joined the others and finished their pops.

About that time, Pete, Bobby, Jen, and Matthew appeared. Therese thought Jen and Matthew looked like they were back on, the hot item they had been for most of their freshman year. She couldn't help but suspect that Matthew had wanted his summer free, in case someone new came along, perhaps while he vacationed in Alaska, but now that school was only a few

169

weeks away, he'd reclaimed her. She didn't particularly care for his behavior, but she was glad Jen looked happy.

As Jen introduced Matthew to those in the group he had not yet met, Pete turned with a look of excitement to Therese. "This is an old Bob Wills song! Let's go swing. How 'bout it?"

Therese couldn't say no. She loved the Western Swing, and Pete was a great dancer. She also loved the idea of showing off for Than.

Pete pulled her around the floor with authority, easily leading her away from him, to him, away from him, and back to him. He swung her under his arm and around his back and picked her up in the air like she was a rag doll.

As soon as the song was over, she excused herself and ran straight to the restroom. Jen followed closely behind. Luckily there wasn't a line.

Once they were out of the stalls and washing their hands at the sink, Therese asked, "You've forgiven Matthew?"

"Yeah," Jen smiled guiltily. Her hair was in a ponytail tonight, too. It was like they could read each other's minds. "He said he didn't mean to get back with me, but he just couldn't force himself to stay away."

Therese's forehead wrinkled with doubt, not because her friend wasn't beautiful and sweet and capable of making it hard for boys to stay away from her, but because she tended to be too gullible when it came to Matthew.

Jen asked, "So what's with you and Than? Do you guys like each other?"

Therese couldn't stop the smile from crossing her face. "I don't know. I think so."

"Has he kissed you?"

Therese watched herself blush in the mirror. "Yes. And he had me over for supper last night."

"And you didn't tell me? How did it go?" Jen dried her hands on a paper towel and then dropped the towel in the trash can.

Therese told her friend a few of the details.

Jen sighed. "Sounds like he really likes you." Then she added, "Don't tell Pete I told you this, but I think he's jealous."

"You mean Bobby."

"No. Pete."

Therese's mouth dropped open as she stared at her friend's reflection beside her in the mirror. "No way. Did Pete say something?"

"No, but I know my brother."

"You're imagining things. Pete's like a big brother to me."

"Whatever you say."

When they rejoined the group, Carol and Richard were out on the dance floor and, much to Therese's astonishment, so were Bobby and Meg. Ray was telling Than a story, but Than seemed to be only half listening as he kept his eyes on Therese. Before she could make it to Than's side to hear what Ray was saying, Todd grabbed her arm and said, "Let's go. I love this song."

Therese glanced at Than over her shoulder, but he had politely turned to listen to Ray.

Matthew and Jen joined them on the floor. It was a Texas Two Step to a George Strait song.

As soon as it was over, Pete took Therese from Todd for a polka. She felt the sweat dripping down her face, the small ringlets of her hair that hadn't made it into her ponytail sticking to the nape of her neck. Her hands were slippery in Pete's dry hands, but he held fast to her as he swung her around, closer, she now realized, than he had before.

As she danced round and round with Pete, Therese wondered if there could be even a smidgen of truth in Jen's assessment of her brother. Pete smiled at her, laughing when they barely missed running into another couple,

171

or when Therese nearly lost her balance and he had to catch her. Yet his smiles and laughter seemed no different to her tonight than they had any other day. Had there always been something there, just beneath the surface? If Than hadn't stepped into her life, Jen's revelation would have excited Therese. She had hero-worshiped Pete all her life—she'd liked the kind of music he liked, played the sports he played, watched the shows he watched. He was gorgeous, just like his sister, his blond bowl-cut hair framing a strong face and blue eyes. But it had all been a sister-brotherly love, hadn't it?

She tried to see Than, but the Friday night crowd had thickened, and he was lost in the swarm of bodies and smoke. When the song ended, Therese thanked Pete and went looking for Than, but before she could reach him, Bobby snagged her hand and asked for a dance. This was a Texas Two-Step, Bobby's specialty, for he hadn't yet developed the same level of skills in the polka, swing, or waltz as his older brother and Todd possessed.

The song ended, and a new one played throughout the hall. Therese felt a tap on her shoulder, and she turned midstride to find Than there smiling at her. "A waltz. Shall we?"

"Yes." She smiled back, a thrill coming over her. Then she thanked Bobby, who went straight to Meg.

Alan Jackson's voice brought a lump to Therese's throat as Than took her in his arms and with near-expert control led her in the slow waltz.

As if Than knew what she was thinking, he said, close to her ear, his warm breath sending chills across her cheek and bare neck, "This song describes my feelings exactly. I was worried I wouldn't get my turn with you. I'm glad it came on this song."

She leaned her head against his chest and closed her eyes, unable to look at his sweet longing. It seemed too surreal. All of it. Was she still in a coma, and all this was a dream? Could she jump into the air and turn somersaults?

Before she had time to answer her own questions, Meg and Tizzie rushed to their side and began talking fervently in Than's ears. Therese was unable to hear what they were saying.

"How long?" he asked, his brow bent with worry.

"There's no time to lose," Tizzie answered.

The group moved from the dance floor, Therese all the while wondering what was going on. "What's the matter?" she asked when they stopped between the bar and the exit.

Tizzie answered, "I made your parents' killer talk, but we don't have time to explain. You stay here."

"Where are you going?" Therese was horrified.

"Back to your house," Than explained. "McAdams has men there waiting for you."

"They're waiting for your aunt, too," Meg added coolly.

"Clifford! My pets!" Therese felt sick. "Oh, please let them be okay!"

"We're on our way now," Than assured her. "We'll come back and let you know when you can return home."

"Take me!"

"It's too dangerous," he said. "Stay here with your friends, where it's safe."

She followed them through the exit and out to the parking lot. She forgot about god travel and expected them to take a car, but when they went to the dark part of the lot and simply vanished, she sighed, and a feeling of helplessness washed over her.

Therese knew she should listen to Than and his sisters and stay put, but she was in agony over what might be happening to her pets, especially Clifford, who would have been barking like crazy at the intruders' approach. Would they have killed her very best friend? She couldn't wait here for who knew how long. She had to go see for herself. But she didn't want to

173

endanger Carol and Richard by asking them to drive her home. They would go into her house and directly into danger. The Holts wouldn't have room for her if they came in Pete's truck, plus Matthew and Jen were having too much fun. Unless she revealed the true reason she wanted to go, she wouldn't have their cooperation.

Maybe Todd would take her! He would be bored by now, with Jen dancing exclusively with Matthew and with Therese unavailable. Todd was too shy to approach girls he didn't know. She could ask him to drop her off and to not even bother to drive up the long gravelly driveway to her house. He would be safe, she hoped.

She ran back inside the dance hall, stopped in the entrance, and turned her head from side to side. The crowd was too thick to spot him, even though he was tall. She texted him as she picked her way through the crowd and the noise, feeling more and more desperate. In her haste, she accidentally knocked into someone's drink, and some of it spilled on her shirt. She weaved through the bodies and smoke, a wave of panic threatening to overtake her. Then she saw Ray.

She practically ran to him. "Where's Todd?"

"Bathroom. Why? What's wrong?" Her face must have looked bad, because Ray, usually quick to joke around, showed sudden concern.

"I don't feel well. I was going to see if he'd take me home. He promised me a ride in his truck sometime. I thought maybe tonight. I don't want to ruin my aunt's good time. Maybe you'd like to come, too? Y'all can come right back."

"Sounds good to me. I'm bored anyway. But I don't know about Todd. He loves this place. Where are your new friends?"

"They had to leave."

A flicker of understanding and suspicion crossed Ray's face. "And they wouldn't give you a ride? Some friends."

"It was a family emergency. That's why I don't feel well. I'm worried about them."

"What happened?"

"I don't really know. They were in too much of a hurry to explain."

"Maybe there was no emergency."

She shook her head. "It was too obvious. They were so upset."

Todd joined them then, and Therese turned and explained everything she had told Ray to him. Would he take her?

"I don't know. You want me to take you for a ride in my pride and joy? That's tough. Hmm." A smile illuminated his face. "Do I want to show off my new stereo? Hmm. This is a hard one."

She gave him a pleading smile.

Todd shrugged. "Alright. Let's go."

"Great!" Relief came but still could not outdo the approaching panic. "Thank you so much! I'll be right back. I have to tell Carol."

Therese found Carol and Richard on the dance floor and was about to tell them the same story she had told Ray and Todd when she realized Carol would insist on taking her home if Therese were upset, so she stopped, mid-sentence and said, "I've been dying to take a ride in Todd's new truck. He's ready to leave, though. Can he take me now to get a shake from McDonald's and then on home? Than and Meg already got a ride. Their sister came and got them."

Carol's face lit up even brighter than Todd's had, probably because she was relieved to see Therese having fun with friends. "Of course. We'll be home right behind you."

"Don't rush," Therese said. "We'll hang out at McDonald's for a while before heading home."

"Sounds great!" Carol said.

Therese felt awful about the lie as she ran through the crowd back to Todd and Ray without even bothering to explain to any of the Holts. She was

175

in too much of a hurry to leave so she could check on her pets and her house and see what was going on. She would text Jen on the way. She was tempted to call 911 as she picked through the crowd but decided the Furies and the god of death could handle the situation better than humans. Once she found Todd and Ray, they left the dance hall, climbed into Todd's ostentatiously high truck with her in the middle in the bench seat, and took off.

Todd turned on the stereo, and Therese oooed and awed over the sound, the feel of the ride, the restoration to the dash, the paint job, and anything else she could think of to show her gratitude and hide her anxiety as they drove through the winding country roads to her house. The height from their perspective did lend a strange sense of power despite the panic threatening to burst inside her. More than anything now, she wanted to be a god, so she could better protect those she loved.

Chapter Twenty-Three: Meg's Falcon

Than waited above the abyss as, first, Alecto sprang up from the granite below with a wild look of hatred, made more horrific by the blood dripping from her beautiful, dark eyes. Next came Tizzie with a shrill cry of outrage, echoed by the howl of the great hound on whose back the Fury was straddled. Finally, up came Meg with a large falcon on her shoulder, its toothed beak dripping with blood from a recent kill.

They left the abyss and quickly emerged inside Therese's house, where the dog Clifford lay dying on the floor.

Than hastened to the dog's side and grunted, knowing what the dog's death would mean for Therese. He disintegrated and dispatched himself straightaway to Aphrodite at Mount Olympus to beg for her help.

The other Than remained with his sisters to catch and torment the men who were waiting in the shadows to ambush Therese and her aunt.

There were four of them, for Than could easily sense their presence-- one for each of them, he thought, smiling. He finally understood the pleasure his sisters took in their duties. He couldn't wait to strangle the man he had heard talking about Therese.

The man had said, "So young and pretty," as he had looked at a photo of her on her dresser. "I wonder if she's a virgin. I can't wait to pinch her pretty flesh." Than had shuddered with rage and clenched his teeth at hearing those words from the man's filthy mouth.

Alecto brought the first scrawny, little human up by the neck from the master bedroom where he had been filling his pockets with jewelry, including a diamond necklace now falling from his flailing hand. Meg came up from the basement with a hairy blonde whose blue eyes now opened wide with fright, the whites of his eyes like perfect circles. He was the only fair-skinned man among them. The others were brown skinned, like Grahib.

Tizzie held her man from the back, putting her beautiful face against the side of his face and allowing the snakes that were once her hair to curl around him from behind. Than found his man in Therese's room holding the tortoise, so he had to be careful. In invisible mode, he extracted the animal from the human and then bound his hands behind his back with a leather belt. He brought his man to the main living room, where his sisters and their prey had gathered.

He watched with profound satisfaction as Meg took her falcon from her shoulder onto her finger and ordered him, "Do it!"

The falcon went up to the man that Tizzie held entwined by her snake hair, which hissed at the man and flicked its many tongues. The falcon took his toothed beak and viciously pecked one of the man's eyeballs repeatedly in the socket as the man screamed and writhed with pain. Blood poured from the gory socket when the falcon fluttered away and back to the shoulder of his mistress. The other men moaned and cried out as fiercely as the victim.

"The location of McAdams!" Alecto commanded. The man in her possession floundered and writhed.

"Please!" the man begged. "I don't know anything. Let me go!"

Meg gave another command to her falcon, which flew directly to Alecto's prisoner, and as the whites grew larger in the scrawny man's eyes, the falcon pecked one of the eyes to bits, which poured out in bloody tears down his cheek. He screamed and cried and flailed his body against Alecto's strong hold.

The falcon returned to Meg's shoulder, his beak dripping.

"We're dead either way!" the blond in Meg's possession cried. "Have mercy on me and I'll tell you where McAdams is. But don't let your bird near me, or I'll never speak!"

178

Meg gave the command to her falcon, which went before the blond who had just spoken and then carved out his eye with his beak.

Meg said, "Never issue ultimatums to a Fury."

"Hell 101," Tizzie said with cruel sarcasm.

Alecto laughed a rueful laugh.

Than did not share in the pleasure of his sisters as he had expected he would. He turned and looked at the frail man he held, bound at the wrists by his leather belt. "Do not tempt my sisters with arrogant words or foolish silence. Tell them where they can find McAdams. Maybe they will have mercy on you, and maybe they won't."

"There's a warehouse," the man said with heavy breaths. "In San Antonio, Texas. He has an office there on a street called Nakoma. There's a sign called 'Dougal's' on the door. The building is close to the airport. That's all I know. I swear!"

Chapter Twenty-Four: Thwarted Attack

When Todd pulled onto the gravelly drive of Therese's home, Therese said, "Stop here. You don't have to go all the way up to the house."

"Don't be silly," Todd said.

"Seriously!" she cried with full panic. "I need to walk. I'm, I need some fresh air after all that smoke."

Todd turned off the engine. "Fine. We'll walk with you, won't we Ray."

Ray shrugged. "I don't care, but I have a feeling Therese doesn't want us to."

She met Ray's gaze. "I'm just a little worried, that's all. I've had a great time with you guys, as always. Please don't be offended."

Ray shrugged again, "Who's offended?"

Todd opened his door and jumped out. "Give me your hand," he said.

As she stepped onto the huge tire, Therese listened to the quiet night air, wondering if the gods were here, or the murderers waiting for her. She took Todd's hand and jumped. "Thanks," she said softly. "And thanks for the ride. I owe you big time."

"Big time," he teased. "I'll collect. Don't you worry." He climbed back in to his truck. "Night."

"Night." She watched him back up, the crackle of pebbles spitting out from beneath his huge tires, and pull away. When she could no longer see his taillights, her knees shook.

She stepped quietly up the drive toward her house. There were no lights on—not even the porch light. She wondered whether she should take the stairs up to the front screened porch or enter through the back as she crept slowly up the drive, her heart thudding in her chest.

A sound from the dark forest behind her house startled her. She sucked in a breath and froze, just like the chipmunks on her deck always did whenever they became aware of her. Like they, Therese stood perfectly still, waiting. The dying branch of the elm was just visible in the moonlight, and it pointed at her like an omen: *You, Therese Mills!*

The fact that Clifford was not alarmed by her presence or the presence of the thing in the woods filled her with terror. He would be barking by now. He would smell her scent. He would be aware of the other thing, too.

She decided to move toward the front door, away from the woods. She slid her key from her front jean pocket and had it ready to gouge someone's eye if needed. She took a step up. The wooden board beneath her foot creaked. Otherwise, the house was silent and still.

On tiptoes, she slipped through the screened porch to the front door. Before she could put her key in the lock, she found the door ajar. She pushed it in, gently, hesitantly. She stood there in the crack of the door, vigilant. Except for the dim light of the moon washing in through a skylight above her, the living room and kitchen behind it were bathed in a curtain of darkness. The hallway to her right, leading to the two bedrooms, was in shadows, but Therese could now hear a vague sound—like someone breathing—coming from it. Her own heart pounded so loudly, and her own breath moved through her so quickly, she found it difficult to trust her hearing.

She swallowed hard and reached for a lamp, but it failed to illuminate the room. She remembered then that the bulb had burned out and hadn't been replaced since…since before everything had happened. She took a few steps into the room to find the light switch. A low whine, barely above a whisper, came from the hallway. Therese froze like a statue.

When the whine came again, Therese recognized it, and she flew for the switch. The room was showered with light. "Clifford?" She ran to the hall. Lying on the wooden floor on his side, not moving, but still breathing, was her dog. She rushed beside him on the floor. "Clifford!" He didn't move. She used her hand to feel around his body, but she couldn't find any injuries. There was no blood, but he could barely open his eyes, and his tongue was hanging from his mouth like he was dying.

"No!" she screamed, forgetting all else. She buried her face against his fur and sobbed uncontrollably now. Clifford was her best friend. She couldn't take any more loss. This was too much for one person. She would be so alone. Did Hades have a vendetta against her? She cried for her parents. She cried for Dumbo. She cried for Clifford who looked as though he were leaving her now as well. "No, boy. Hang in there. Please don't leave me." Then with a desperate wail that would have put Orpheus to shame, she shouted, "Than! Thanatos! Thaaaannaaaatossss!"

Her eyes caught sight of something silver gleaming on the small console table to her left. Whether it had already been there or had appeared after her loud cry, she did not know. On the table lay a syringe full of blue liquid with a pink square piece of paper attached that read, "For Clifford." Therese snatched up the syringe, looked closely at it, and knew what she was supposed to do. She looked over Clifford's body for a place to stab him, and, not sure of herself, but hopeful, nonetheless, thrust the needle into Clifford's haunch and pressed the medicine through the needle. He didn't move, barely flinched, and his breaths were labored. She watched him closely, waiting, hoping to see a change.

She sat there with him for what seemed like an eternity, when she noticed his breathing slow down to normal. He brought his tongue into his mouth and swallowed. After another minute, he tried to pull himself up. Though he failed, she knew whatever the blue liquid had been in the syringe was working. Tears of joy streamed down her cheeks. She kissed Clifford on the side of his face.

In another ten minutes, he rolled up to his feet, wagged his stubby tail, and licked her face. Then he ran to his bowl of water in the kitchen and lapped up the liquid till the bowl was dry.

Now that she knew her dog would live, Therese began to wonder what had happened. Surely if the killers were still in the house, or nearby in the woods, Clifford would be barking by now. She ran to the front door and closed and locked it, just in case. She checked the backdoor, too. Maybe whatever had hurt Clifford had desensitized him. She took the broom from the kitchen closet and held it like a weapon. Then, cautiously, she went upstairs to check on her other pets. Clifford followed.

Luckily Jewels was basking in the light beneath her lamp, untouched. Therese turned off the lamp, stroked her shell, and checked her water, which was still clean. Puffy was just now grooming himself after his long daytime nap. Therese's bedroom appeared inviolate until she turned toward her bed and noticed something lying in the middle of it.

It appeared to be a long silver robe made of fine silk. A note was pinned to its sleeve—a square piece of pink paper just like the one that had been attached to the syringe, and the same writing said, "For Therese." Whoever had left the syringe for Clifford had left this fine robe for her. She touched the robe, cautiously in case it was some kind of trick, and then picked it up in her hands when nothing terrible happened. Should she put it on?

Before she could decide what to do with the robe, she was suddenly aware she was no longer alone. The hairs on the back of her neck stood on end. Clifford, too, froze in his place. She was afraid to turn around, but when she saw Clifford's stubby tail wag back and forth, she knew it must be Than.

"Therese!"

She dropped the robe on her bed, turned to him, and nearly hit him with the broom.

"Whoa!"

"Sorry!" She dropped the broom and ran into his arms. "I was so afraid!"

His arms wrapped around her waist and pulled her close to his warm body. "You were supposed to wait at the saloon."

She buried her face in his chest. "I'm sorry. I couldn't stand waiting behind." She didn't want to let go. She never wanted to move from this warm, thrilling place that brought her comfort.

He lifted her chin with a finger. "I'm just glad you're safe. When I didn't find you there, I…well, then I heard you calling. I'm just glad you're okay."

She wanted him to kiss her. She thought he might when he leaned in, but then he took her hand and led her to the bed to sit down. The wide gap between them brought her back to her senses. "What happened?" She pulled Clifford into her lap when he followed them onto the bed. "Please tell me everything. Who left the medicine for Clifford?"

"I'll tell you everything. First get comfortable. It's a long story."

They sat side by side with their backs against the fabric headboard. Therese moved a little closer to Than so that her shoulder pressed against his arm. She stroked Clifford, where he curled up in her lap.

"Tizzie learned from Grahib that tonight McAdams planned to kill you," Than said. "Grahib didn't know how many would come but said their plan was to ambush you and your aunt here in the house. Apparently, they didn't know about Richard visiting." Than swallowed hard and hesitated. Then he grit his teeth. "Grahib told Tizzie the men were promised that they could have their way with you and your aunt."

Therese gasped, her mouth wide open.

184

"Then they were to kill you and burn down the house. Make it look like an accident." He clenched his jaw.

Therese took his hand, unclenched his fist, and rubbed it between both of her hands. His words frightened her, but his obvious feelings for her exalted her. "So what happened when you left me? Did you come here?"

He nodded. "The men beat us here. There were four of them. They had already poisoned Clifford. I thought he would die. I knew it would be the last straw for you. So I went to Mount Olympus to beg Aphrodite for her help. I reminded her how I tried to help Orpheus to be reunited with his true love, Eurydice. I also told her how I helped Theseus and Hercules, favorites of hers, and also Odysseus during the Trojan War. I told her our story, from the beginning when you first embraced me in your coma, and of the deal my father made with me to make you my wife. She agreed to help. I returned to the Underworld to help my sisters punish the men who came here to use and kill you, and she came here to bring you the antidote. She wouldn't administer it herself, though. She said she doesn't have the stomach for it."

Therese jumped up off the bed full of incredulity. "Aphrodite, the goddess of love, was here, in my house?"

Than smiled. "So you've heard of her, huh?"

"Who hasn't?"

"That answer will bring a smile to her face." He laughed. "So I was very relieved to see Clifford wagging his tail when I arrived. I didn't know how it would all turn out."

"Thank you for saving my dog." She threw her arms around his neck. Then she sprang up, jittery and blushing, to pick up the robe she had dropped at the foot of the bed. "I think she left this for me, too. But I don't know what I'm supposed to do with it."

Than looked at the robe as Therese held it up to him. "It's a traveling robe." His mouth turned into a broad smile. "I can't believe it. Obviously you have found great favor with Aphrodite. This is a rare gift."

185

Therese hugged it to herself. "Oh my gosh. I can't believe I have a gift from a goddess, and from the most beautiful goddess, too."

Than laughed. "She's certainly happy to hear that, I bet, but you might want to be careful not to offend others who might be watching over you."

Therese pushed her arms through the sleeves of the robe. "It's so soft." She looked at herself in her dresser mirror. "I love it. How do I thank her?"

"I'm sure she's watching you now. But you could think of something to show your gratitude."

"Yes. I'll think of something." She sat back on the bed beside Than, still wearing the robe. Clifford moved back on her lap.

"It's magic, you know," Than said, stroking her hand. "The traveling robe enables a mortal to travel like gods."

"What do you mean? Like disappear?"

"Travel quickly from one point to another without having to travel the full line. This robe will allow you to do the same, though I don't recommend that you try it alone since you don't yet know what you're doing."

Her mouth dropped open. "I will be able to vanish and appear just like you?"

"While wearing the robe, yes."

"Can you show me?"

"Now?"

She eagerly nodded her head. "Just a quick trip, maybe to your place and back?"

He jumped up off the bed. "Your aunt and her boyfriend are pulling up the drive. Go talk with them. Don't let on what's happened. And when you've come up for bed, I'll be waiting for you. We'll take a quick trip to my cabin and back, as you wish."

186

She gave him a smile and clapped her hands with excitement. Clifford jumped off the bed and ran around the room. "Thanks!"

"Till then." He disappeared.

"Wait! Than?"

He reappeared. "Yes?"

"Am I still in any danger? Will McAdams send more men to try and kill me?"

He walked across the room and took her in his arms. "He may send men, but now you have the attention of more than one god. We are watching over you. Don't worry."

She closed her eyes and sighed. When she opened them, he was gone.

In the next moment, her aunt was knocking at the door. "Therese? You awake?"

Therese pulled off the robe and gingerly laid it on her bed. "Yeah. I was just coming downstairs."

She and Clifford followed Carol down the stairs to the living room where Richard sat watching the late news.

"Did you have a good time with your friends?" Carol asked as she sat on the sofa next to Richard.

Therese and Clifford curled up together on a chair beside the empty fireplace. "Yes. Todd's truck is so awesome. I was a little scared at first, up so high, but once I got used to it, it was really cool." Then she asked, "Did you guys have fun dancing?"

Carol and Richard exchanged smiles. "A blast," Carol said. "I can't believe we've gone dancing twice in one week!" She patted Richard's thigh.

Richard laughed. "Yeah, hopefully I'm paid up for a while."

Carol punched him in the shoulder. "You hush!"

Therese smiled. "Thanks for driving. Did Jen get my text? She never replied."

Carol nodded. "She and her boyfriend seemed not to mind. Pete, seemed disappointed. They left before we did."

Therese wondered again over what Jen had said in the restroom of the Wildhorse Saloon, but before she could think much about it, something on the television caught her attention.

"Late breaking news," the anchor person said from the television. "A La Plata County inmate known as Kaveh Grahib was strangled and killed tonight behind bars by an unknown perpetrator. Grahib was arraigned several weeks ago as a suspect for the murder of a Durango couple, Linda and Gerald Mills, which took place near Fort Lewis College five weeks ago. Investigators have no leads but are looking into this case."

"Oh my God," Therese said gaping.

"I'm calling the lieutenant." Carol stood from the couch.

Richard took her hand. "It's after midnight."

"I don't care. This concerns us." Carol crossed the room to the phone at the kitchen bar, took up the business card lying next to it, and dialed the lieutenant's number. "Lieutenant Hobson, this is Carol Stuart. Would you please call me as soon as possible? We just heard about what happened to Kaveh Grahib, and we're concerned. Thanks."

As soon as she hung up the phone, it rang.

"Hello?" Carol said. "Uh-huh. Is that good or bad?" Carol paused. "Okay, thanks." Carol hung up the phone and looked across the kitchen at Therese. "The lieutenant said he's sending out another officer to guard the house and that we should play it safe for a while. So, Therese, no more walking, even with Than. Got it?"

Therese nodded.

Carol sat back down on the couch beside Richard, who wrapped his arm around her and kissed her cheek.

"Don't worry," Richard said. "I'll stick around until the police know you're absolutely safe."

188

Therese was grateful that Richard could offer her aunt some peace of mind. She knew that gods were watching over her aunt and him, and although that didn't erase the fear looming over her, it diminished it and made it bearable.

"I'm going to bed," Therese said to them. "See you in the morning."

"Are you working again tomorrow?" Carol asked.

"Through Sunday," Therese replied. "Sunday is my last day, I think."

"Good night," Richard said. "Just call us or come down if you need anything."

"Thanks," Therese said, and then she and Clifford went upstairs to her room.

As promised, Than was waiting for them, stretched out on her bed with his eyes closed. She wanted to cross over the room and climb on top of his perfect body. She was studying him when he opened his eyes and gave her his brilliant smile.

"Sleepy?" she asked.

"A little."

"Did you hear what's happened?" She climbed on the bed next to him.

He sighed. "My sisters just returned from the Underworld. Grahib's in Tartarus now. McAdams had him killed for talking. He found out about tonight's failed attack."

"I'm scared," Therese said, and though it was true to some extent, she knew she should be a lot more frightened than she was. It was hard to be frightened when she felt so safe with Than.

He took her hand and kissed the inside of her palm. "I won't let anything happen to you. Now let's get your mind off of this. Are you ready to travel with me?"

"Yes." She got up and put on the silver silk robe. "What do I do?"

"Just hold my hand. This will feel a little weird." He stood beside her and took her hand. "Ready?"

"Ready."

Everything around her was bright—so bright she closed her eyes. Her body felt as if she were wrapped in tight plastic wrap. She couldn't move and could barely breathe, and the air seemed thick and impenetrable around her. She wasn't hot or cold, but the pressure was great, as it is when ascending in an airplane, and her ears popped. All of this happened within a few seconds. Then she felt the cool plastic wrap disintegrate, and she could breathe. She opened her eyes to find herself in the living room of the Melner cabin, and sitting on the cozy furniture were Than's two sisters and someone else—a glowing man with golden winged shoes on his feet. He looked up at Therese with astonishment.

"You shouldn't have brought her here," he said to Than.

Chapter Twenty-Five: Hermes, the Messenger

Than stepped forward. "I didn't know you were here, Cousin Hermes." Hermes stood and took Than's hand. "What has caused you to grace our presence?"

Therese noticed that Hermes was older looking and not as tall as Than, though his hair was the same dark brown, but curly rather than wavy, in tight knots around his head. His beard looked much the same as his hair. His pale red robes hung to his knees, and a wide gold belt secured the robes at his waist. The belt matched the golden shoes and the helmet lying beside him on the arm of the chair. He wouldn't blend with humans as well as the others without changing his wardrobe. "I bring grave news from Mount Olympus."

"How grave?" Than asked.

Meg frowned. "You may as well sit down, Than." She pointed to a chair, her diamond bracelets jangling. Her usual black go-go boots had been replaced by brown sandals, and her white silk pantsuit gave her a less intimidating look.

"First return the girl," Hermes suggested.

"This concerns her, too," Tizzie, in green silk and her emerald set, offered. "She should stay."

Therese could not imagine how any news from Mount Olympus, grave or otherwise, would have anything to do with her.

"Very well," Hermes replied. "Please come have a seat. Tonight will be long and grave for us all."

Before sitting down, Therese asked, "Shall I make us a pot of coffee?" She offered because she needed a cup herself, and she suspected the Melner cabin was well stocked.

Than squeezed her hand. "That sounds nice. Thank you."

So he'd heard of coffee, but not tea, Therese noted. Or maybe he just didn't want to bother with asking what coffee was. Hermes seemed anxious to talk.

Than and Hermes sat down while Therese crossed over to the kitchen, which was open to the living room, so she could still hear Hermes speaking as she rummaged through cabinets looking for coffee and filters.

"Zeus sent me to warn you that Ares is supporting this man, McAdams."

Therese froze like a statue.

Hermes continued, "He hopes to protect the potency of the biological weapon McAdams has already sold to numerous foreign coups. Ares's ultimate goal is to build a strong power in the Middle East to enable a third world war. He wants to see the U.S. fall."

Therese shuddered as she scooped the coffee grains into the filter. So they had been after her mother.

Than groaned. "No wonder."

"That's not all, brother," Meg said sardonically. "Listen."

Hermes said, "In an effort to keep you from winning over the girl, who might someday be a threat to him if made a goddess, Ares went to Cupid and convinced him to shoot his arrow into a mortal man who had a chance of wooing the girl away from you. The man has been struck, and his love is growing more and more devout every day."

Than shifted on the couch. "What's the mortal's name?"

Hermes replied, "Peter Holt."

Therese dropped the spoon on the kitchen floor, splattering coffee grains everywhere. She looked for a broom as Hermes continued.

"Aphrodite is sick over this, and so is Cupid now that he knows about Ares's intentions, but there's nothing they can do to prevent the mortal from loving the girl. However, both have sworn allegiance to you against

192

Ares, and as we speak, Aphrodite is securing the support of Apollo. You know how Ares feels about Aphrodite. Angry isn't strong enough to describe how he's feeling now."

Tizzie said, "Even so, Shining Apollo will be a useful ally."

"You speak as though there's a war," Than said.

"You haven't yet heard all, brother," Meg warned.

"In response to this move of Aphrodite's," Hermes said, "Ares went to Poseidon to seek his aid."

Therese finished cleaning up the coffee grounds, fitted the filter in the coffee maker, and added the pot of water. When she returned to the living room to take her spot beside Than on the couch, she noticed the worry in his face.

"Poseidon has agreed to stand by Ares," Hermes said. "Fortunately for you, Artemis has already pledged her allegiance to the girl."

"Her name is Therese," Than said. "So Artemis sides with Aphrodite? That's highly unusual. Those sisters of yours are typically at odds."

"Yes," Hermes agreed. "But Artemis is pleased with Therese's love for the animals and the forest. It makes no difference to her what Aphrodite chooses; Artemis wants to help the girl."

Therese's mouth dropped open. She couldn't believe she had attracted the attention of so many gods. She felt afraid and excited at once.

"Hades stands with us, of course," Tizzie added.

"At least for now," Hermes interjected. "He's miffed about his son making a choice that offends Ares. He wishes you would reconsider, but he will stand by his promise."

Than grimaced. "I will not reconsider. Only Therese's choice to remain a mortal can keep her from becoming my bride."

Therese felt faint. Than's love inflamed her, but the whole god and marriage situation was overwhelming.

Tizzie said, "But even with Hades on our side, Ares has a formidable threat against us. Along with Poseidon, Ares has his three daughters—the Amazons—and his wife, Enyo, and their children."

"Not to mention McAdams and his other men," Meg said.

"What about your father?" Than asked Hermes.

"Zeus and the others are still undecided. Hera will likely align herself against Aphrodite, but that is merely speculation." Then Hermes added, "This is the biggest rift between the gods since the Vietnam War. I can only imagine how it will end."

"What do you recommend, Hermes?" Than asked in a husky voice.

Hermes shook his head. "For now, I do not know. I wish to discuss some possibilities tonight. Ares is an evil, blood-lusting ass of a war-god, and I and my father despise him, but I fear for all who oppose him."

Therese got up to check on the coffee, and although the pot was only half full, she poured the four gods and herself a cup. Recalling Than and his sisters' love of sugar, she added generous, heaping teaspoons to each of the cups except her own. She put all five cups on a tray and served them. "It's hot," she said. "Be careful."

"Mmm," Meg purred. "Delicious. You can add coffee to your new list of bribes for me. Coffee and chocolate will get you what you want from me."

Tizzie added, "Don't forget a concert to boot."

"Thank you for the coffee," Hermes said to Therese. "And what is this I hear about a concert? Do you play a musical instrument?"

Therese blushed. "The flute." She hoped she wouldn't now be asked to perform. She had just learned an evil god helped to kill her parents and was behind tonight's attempt to kill her—not to mention the fact that Cupid unwittingly locked Pete's heart on hers, which started a chain reaction among the gods, the largest rift since the Vietnam War!

"The flute! That will please Athena. She invented it, you know, though some folks credit me with it. Perhaps some music would calm us after all this talk of strife and discord," Hermes said. "If you will play your flute, I will harmonize upon my pipe."

Therese was about to point out that her flute had been left behind when it dawned on her how easily that problem could be remedied now that she had her traveling robe. The last thing she wanted to do was disappoint a god, especially one who could easily change his allegiance. Maybe if she played with him, and played well, she would win his heart. She looked at Than, "Shall we pop back over to my place to get my flute?"

He gave her his brilliant smile and stroked her hair. "Aren't you too upset to play?"

Of course she was, but she wasn't stupid. "Not for this company."

"That's a good girl," Hermes said.

Hermes smile cheered her. She stood up, took Than's hand, and together they traveled to her room where Clifford jumped from her bed and yelped with surprise.

"It's okay, Clifford," she said in a soft voice so Carol and Richard wouldn't hear. She slid her case and music stand from beneath her bed, grabbed some sheet music from her desk, and took Than's hand. "I'm ready," she said. Then to her dog, she said, "Be a good boy, Clifford. I'll be back."

Although the pressure made it hard to breathe for a few seconds, the trip to her house and back was otherwise effortless with the robe and Than's guidance. Her feet nearly fell out from beneath her both times she landed, but, fortunately Than was there beside her, with his arm around her waist, ready to catch her.

Therese played on her flute with Hermes on his pipe for a solid hour, which seemed a worthy investment since he said more than twice how much he liked her. And after, the four gods shared many stories about their lives,

195

especially in the Underworld. Therese finally heard the complete story of Hercules and understood from Than's contributions and his reactions to the others that his opinion of Hercules was very low.

"His emotions got the best of him," Than complained. "He never stopped to use his head."

Meg laughed, "I'm not sure his head would have done him much good."

"Now there's a wonder," Hermes said. "Perhaps it's a testament to the values of humankind that such a one like Hercules, with no apparent intelligence, would be considered the greatest hero among the Greeks."

Tizzie added, "His temper got the best of him. Even I know the importance of temperance."

"He killed his wife and sons while enraged," Meg said. "Normally Tizzie would persecute such a heinous crime, but Hercules *wanted* to be tormented. He begged us to make him suffer. So Apollo told his oracle to send Hercules to a king he knew would come up with a just punishment. So the king commanded Hercules to complete twelve harsh labors."

"Hercules wasn't very smart," Hermes said, "but he was resourceful. First he had to kill a lion that no weapon could injure, and he solved that problem by using his own hands to choke the beast. Then he had to kill the Hydra, which had nine heads that would only grow back multiplied each time Hercules hacked one off. He eventually seared the necks as he chopped them to keep the heads from growing back."

"Iolaus brought him the iron," Than said. "Hercules didn't think of that on his own."

"He spent a year catching Artemis's sacred stag," Hermes continued. "Then he spent another year capturing a great boar from Mount Erymanthus. Let's see, after that he had to clean the Augean stables in a single day, which he did by shifting the flow of the river."

196

"But most of his labors required no cleverness," Than said. "Just brute force."

"True," Hermes agreed. "He had to drive away the birds plaguing the people of Stymphalus, fetch the savage bull Poseidon gave to Minos, and round up the man-eating mares of Thrace. What else? Oh, yes, bring back the girdle of Hippolyta, the queen of the Amazons. You've got to wonder why Apollo didn't intervene with that one."

"Now that right there is an example of what I mean when I say Hercules allowed his emotions to get the best of him," Than said. "He acted rashly, without reason. After all the help Hippolyta gave, he assumed she was responsible for the Amazon attack stirred up by Hera. He killed her without even offering her a chance to explain."

"We should have been granted access to him *then*," Meg snarled.

"But Hermes has told of nine. There were three more," Tizzie said. "He had to bring back the cattle of Geryon, who was a three-bodied monster, and then he ran into trouble with Atlas when he had to fetch the Golden Apples of Hesperides."

"But the hardest labor of all," Hermes said, "was the last. Hercules went to the Underworld and captured Cerberus, with Hades's permission. Poor Cerberus had to find his own way back."

"That's not when Hercules most offended me, even though he tied me up until I told him of Hades's permission," Than said. "I was there when he took Cerberus, and he wasn't cruel to the poor beast. I made sure of it. It was much later, after the Fates made their deal with his friend Admetus, that he angered me."

"What happened?" Therese asked.

Hermes shook his head. "When Hercules heard that his friend's wife had died, he rushed to the Underworld to retrieve her. If only he would have waited for more explanation."

"What do you mean?" Therese asked. "What explanation?"

Hermes said, "Long before, the Fates had hinted to Admetus that his life was about to end, and Admetus begged them to let him live. They said they would if he found another to take his place. Admetus asked everyone he knew, including his elderly parents, but no one wanted to die for him, until he asked his wife. So his wife took his place and went with Than to the Underworld."

Than grimaced. "I should have stopped Hercules when he came for her years later, but he was such an arrogant ass. I took pleasure in watching him put his foot in his mouth. When he came to me and pushed me aside, I was ready for him this time and could have easily taken him, but I knew that as soon as he delivered the woman to Admetus, Admetus would die, and Hercules would realize what he had done."

"That's not Disney," Therese mumbled.

Than had heard. "What?"

"Nothing," Therese didn't want to attempt to explain the Disney story of Hercules.

Than shook his head. "What man asks his wife to die in his place? That's plain cowardice."

Something clicked for Therese just then. Than was just, not cruel. Her admiration for him multiplied like the heads on the hydra.

"What?" he asked after she had looked at him for many seconds.

"Nothing," she smiled. In her mind, she said, "I'm falling in love with you."

He gave her a huge grin, as though he had heard her thoughts.

It was four in the morning when Therese and Than returned to Therese's bedroom. Now she was utterly exhausted, and Than had just a little over an hour to rest before getting up and heading to the Holt ranch for pen and barn duty.

Than waited with Clifford curled in his lap on top of her bed comforter while she changed clothes in her bathroom. When she returned to her bed in her nightshirt, Than pulled back the bedcovers for her. Her heart skipped a beat with anticipation. She crawled in between the sheets and lay back on her pillow. She looked up at him expectantly, suspecting he wrestled with his own desire, for she could see it in his face. Kiss me, she said in her mind. Oh, please, Than. Kiss me.

He pulled the covers over her body and up to her neck and tucked her in so that she was under and he over the comforter. He leaned down close to her face and brushed a few strands of hair from her eyes. "Your skin is so soft." He rolled onto his stomach and propped himself on his elbows and touched his fingers to her cheek. He ran a finger along her lips.

Therese closed her eyes as the longing swept through her. Please, Than. Kiss me.

He moved closer to her so that when he spoke, she could feel his breath on her skin. "You feel so good beneath my fingertips."

Her breaths came rapidly, and she felt like she was flying.

He whispered, "I've never touched someone as much as I've touched you." He smoothed her hair away from her face. "I've never longed for anything as much as I long for you."

Kiss me, she said in her mind. Please, Than. Kiss me.

"But I'm afraid," he whispered.

She opened her eyes. "Of what?"

"I'll take more of you than you're ready to give," he said breathlessly.

"I'm ready," she sighed, but she was frightened and excited and nearly out of breath.

His breaths were as rapid as hers, his brow bent in agony. "I might not have the strength to let you choose. If I kiss you now, if I take you now, I

199

want it to be forever, but it's too soon, too soon for you to decide. I don't want to be like my father was with my mother."

"I want you," she breathed. "So you see, it won't be like that."

"Forever?"

She nodded. "Please kiss me."

He swallowed hard and then ever so gently touched his lips to hers.

She closed her eyes and was soaring now, spinning, her heart going wild. She touched her hands to his face and held him to her. Something electric passed between them. Oh, Than, she thought. I want to be with you forever!

He lifted his face.

She opened her eyes, and they shared a smile.

"You feel nice," he said. "But I want to give you more time. I want you to be absolutely sure. A week isn't long enough for such a decision." He kissed her lips once more and then stood up from the bed. "I'll see you tomorrow."

And before she could beg him to stay, he disappeared.

Chapter Twenty-Six: Tortured Than

Than returned to his chambers in the Underworld wishing he could be more like his father and sisters. They seemed less moved than he by feelings of compassion. They saw right and wrong, and they acted on justice.

"I'm weak. My father would find these thoughts pathetic."

If he could be more like the rest of his family, he would not be tormented now, tortured by the wrestling emotions, human emotions, disturbing every atom of his being. If he could be more like them, he would bring Therese down straight away without another thought the moment McAdams was found and brought to justice.

But he couldn't do it. He wanted to be sure she would be happy, and it seemed more and more plain to him that she could never find joy in such a dismally dark and lifeless place as his home.

He studied his rooms, looking at them as though for the first time, contemplating what Therese would think of them. The entrance was rather imposing, but he had to have Hephaestus make the jutting iron bars, like a giant jaw with jagged teeth, to keep away the constant threats by demigods. How often had Than had to listen to their arrogant claims to immortality as he guided their souls to Charon? "My father will punish you for this!" "Hermes will have your head!" "Zeus will never let you get away with this!" They spoke as though Than had any choice in the matter.

And of course, there were the powerful human souls who made themselves rich and famous, and when their threats failed to move Than, they resorted to bribery. "I can give you all the gold you desire." As if Than needed gold! The Underworld was full of it, and Than could have as much as he desired, if he desired it. But Than found gold to be worthless, overrated, and not the most comfortable material for adorning his home.

Of course, there were also the desperate souls, not necessarily powerful, but cunning, who every few centuries would find a way back to Than's door after the judges had proclaimed their sentence but before reaching their final destination. None of them succeeded in binding Than except Sisyphus and Hercules, but they had tried. The iron jaws at his entrance were made after Hercules's stunt, and since then, Than no longer had to deal with unexpected intruders.

But once one passed the intimidating entrance, the first chamber was quite pleasing. The dome shape of the rock walls provided a beautiful symmetry to everything in the room, from the leather club chairs by the cozy fireplace to the marble cabinets where he kept his goblets and wine and dishes that had been given to him by various gods, including the best wine from Dionysus. Along the opposite wall across from the fireplace flowed the Phlegethon with its bright flames illuminating all the rooms. Several instruments made for him by Hermes, Athena, and Apollo hung above the flames, and in the middle of the room were a table and two chairs. The second chair was rarely used, so seldom did he have visitors. But the occasional visitor from Mount Olympus, such as Aphrodite and her son, Cupid, Hera, Hermes, and his grandmother, Demeter, though they came for favors or information, would always find this chamber comfortable and welcoming, even if it did lack sunlight and wind. The flames from the Phlegethon produced no heat, and underground rock kept the room consistently cool, and although the humidity could be stifling at times, the running waterfall in the next chamber, where he slept, usually kept the air fresh and circulating.

From this front chamber, he entered his bed quarters, where the trickling waterfall helped him to sleep every so often when he needed rest. Unlike humans, he did not sleep every day, and not regularly, just when he needed to, perhaps once a month or less. The water fell from a high point in the dome-shaped room and cascaded over a series of rock shelves where

Than kept a collection of shells given to him over the centuries by various people, such as Aphrodite, two different sea nymphs, the Maenads, and once, even Poseidon. A thick and living stalagmite growing in the center of the room served as a table for other possessions, such as the clock given to him by his father and made of precious stones, a tablet of Cyprus and a golden quill given to him by his mother, a moon rock from Hecate, and a pair of slippers that his brother made for him of lamb's wool. Leaning against it was a quiver with a dozen arrows made of bone.

Over his bed hung a steel sword in a golden sheath, made by Hephaestus, a bow given to him by Artemis, and a shield given to him by Zeus. His bed was round and made of a silk-lined mattress stuffed with goose feathers and draped with finely woven and magical linen, a gift from Athena.

His rooms were quite comfortable for him, but he doubted Therese would think so. There was no natural light and no living things, only the underground elements of stone and water. How could she ever come to love this place after living in her log cabin in the mountains of Colorado where the birds sang freely, the sunrises and sunsets painted the wide blue skies daily, and the green, lush trees towered in forests that rustled with all manner of life?

Chapter Twenty-Seven: Persistent Pete

Saturday morning, after taking hot coffee to the officer stationed on their back deck, Carol drove Therese the half mile down the road to Jen's house, and, as usual, Clifford went, too. As Therese stood on the gravel drive waving goodbye to her aunt, she noticed Than and Pete walking toward her across the grassy field in their jeans and boots with water glistening down their bare chests and their wet hair clinging to their heads. They were talking to one another and laughing. Therese watched them in awe, thinking to herself that life could really suck, but it could be really sweet, too.

Clifford ran across the road to greet the two boys, and that's when they looked up and spotted her.

Pete jogged across the road and gave her a wet hug. "Cold, huh? Wake you up, sleepy head!"

Therese bit her lip. Cupid's arrow seemed to be working. "Thanks a lot, Pete. You just wait."

He laughed and walked on to the pen.

Than came up with a dubious smile. "Hey."

"Hey." She could feel her entire face transform into a huge grin. He just had that effect on her.

Before she could say anything more, Jen screamed twice from behind the house, and Clifford took off toward her. With lightning speed, Than ran past Therese. By the time Therese caught up to them, Pete was there, too, and Jen was screaming, "Kill it! Kill it!"

Clifford barked ferociously.

On the ground several feet away from them lay a brownish snake with a yellow stripe down its back and white stripes down its sides. It was about three feet long, thin, stretched rather than coiled, and very still.

"I think it's already dead," Pete said. "Calm down, sis. It's just a garter snake. It's not poisonous."

"I don't care!" Jen shrieked. "Kill it! It's gross! It scared the crap out of me!"

Pete grabbed a shovel from the nearby shed.

"Wait!" Therese said. "Don't kill it if it's not poisonous." She went up to the snake and touched it. Although it barely moved, it was still alive. "It's hurt." She stroked its back. "Clifford, stop. It's okay."

Clifford stopped barking and watched her anxiously. She could feel Clifford's anxiety as he paced and whined.

"It's okay, boy," Therese said again.

"What are you doing?" Jen objected. "Quit touching it!"

Therese picked up the snake gingerly with both hands. She was afraid she might further injure it if she didn't handle it carefully. "If we leave it here, it will die. It needs food and protection from predators."

Jen looked furious. "Therese, we don't save snakes. We kill them. Remember what happened to Dumbo?"

"Yes, I remember!" Therese snapped. "How can you say that?" She held back the desire to push Jen down to the ground, and she clenched her jaw in anger. She already felt burdened with guilt over what happened to the horse. How could her friend say such a thing?

"Now girls," Pete said.

"Me? How can you want to save that, that thing?" Jen shouted.

"Jen, it can't help what it is," Therese said. "And it's not hurting anyone now."

"So what are you going to do with it?" Pete asked.

"Do you have a box I can have?"

"I'm sure I can find one somewhere around here. For now, you can put the snake in the bed of my truck."

"Maybe we could put a wet towel down." Therese walked with Pete toward the garage where his truck was parked next to Jen's and the Suburban. "And maybe we could leave the garage door open?"

"Sure." Pete walked close beside her.

"I don't believe this!" Jen complained. "It's a damn snake!"

"Language," Mrs. Holt said coming out of the house.

"But, Mom. This is crazy. Therese is saving a slimy ol' snake. I wanted Pete to kill it."

"I wanna see," Bobby chirped.

Therese couldn't hear them anymore once she was inside the garage with Pete.

"I'll run inside and get a wet towel," Pete said.

When he returned with the towel, he spread it out on the bed and then helped her to lift the snake onto it. The truck and garage were hot, which was good for the snake. It wouldn't get too cold on the wet towel. Therese stroked the snake several times while saying, "Thanks, Pete. Thanks for your help."

He moved to her and put his hand on her shoulder, and the closeness of his bare chest made her shiver. He kissed the top of her head. "I don't know anyone like you, Therese Mills."

Just then Bobby burst in. "Where's the snake?"

"I'll go get a box," Pete mumbled.

Later, when they were grooming the horses, Than seemed distant. Therese was still angry at Jen for the Dumbo comment, and so she looked to the horse to soothe and comfort her as she brushed. "You're such a sweet thing," she cooed to Sugar. "Does that feel good?" Therese looked into the horse's eye and stroked her cheek. "You're so easy. Always so clean."

"And lazy," Bobby added.

Therese was grateful for Bobby, because he was the only one who seemed oblivious to the tension between the humans in the pen. If he had known how angry the two girls were at one another, he wouldn't have kept on talking in the otherwise silent company.

"Therese, did Jen tell you she and Matthew are going on a date tonight, just the two of them?" Bobby asked.

Therese shook her head.

"They're going to see a movie," he said. "But I doubt they'll be watching it."

"Shut up, Bobby," Jen said.

"Well, *excuse me*."

Therese finished Sugar and asked, "Who now, Mrs. Holt?"

"Why don't you take Annie?"

"*I'm* doing Annie," Jen griped.

"Chestnut, then," Mrs. Holt said.

Than walked Therese home with Clifford ambling behind as the trail riders showed up. Therese was supposed to call her aunt for a ride, but she felt safe with Than and wanted to be with him as much as she could. Her aunt would be cross, but she'd get over it. Therese carried the garter snake in a medium-sized cardboard box with the wet towel Pete got for her. Than still seemed distant. Maybe he thought she was stupid for wanting to save the snake. Maybe the enchantment was wearing off.

Unable to bear the silence for another second, she asked, "Do you think I'm crazy?"

He stopped in the road and turned to face her, his dark brown hair full of golden highlights from the sun. "What? Why would I think that?"

She kept walking, so he followed alongside her. "You know. The snake thing."

Hi voice was husky. "No. I don't think you're crazy."

"Then what's wrong? You're so quiet."

He let out a deep breath. "I'm having…doubts."

207

Her throat tightened. "Oh." Her heart beat so hard that she could hear it in her ears. She *knew* his attention had been too good to be true. She should have known it couldn't last. Tears pricked her eyes.

Maybe he had been in love with *love*, and she just happened to be the first girl to come along. Maybe now that he had spent some time on Earth, he realized he should put more thought into such an important decision. Maybe he concluded that Therese wasn't right for him after all.

By the time they approached her gravelly drive, tears were streaming down her cheeks, and because she was carrying the box, there was nothing she could do to hide them. She tried wiping her cheeks on her shoulders, but she couldn't quite reach. She couldn't look at him. She was so embarrassed and full of despair that she just wanted to get to her room where she could cry in peace.

"Thanks for walking me home." She turned away from him and practically ran to the house.

Once inside, she went past Carol to the stairs. "I'm tired. I'm going to lie down for a while."

"You walked home?"

"Than was with me."

"Therese, please don't take chances like that. Does Than carry a gun? Is he a police officer? He's just another kid. You have to take this seriously. Understand? If the lieutenant thinks we're in enough danger to post a guard here, you shouldn't be walking!"

"I'm sorry." She really was sorry. If she had called her aunt, she might have avoided hearing about Than's doubts.

Then Carol added, "Pete just called. He wants you to call him back."

"Okay. Thanks."

"What's in the box?"

"It's a snake. It's not poisonous. It's hurt."

"Are you crying?"

"No. I'm fine. I just need to be alone."

She expected Carol to say something more but was relieved when she didn't. She went upstairs to her room, put the box on the desk next to Jewel's tank, and let the tears come raining down.

How could he have doubts?

Before she could kick off her shoes, the phone rang.

"Hello?"

"Oh, good. You're home." It was Pete.

Disappointment flooded through her. She had hoped it was Than calling to apologize, to explain why he had been so quiet, to tell her he wanted to be with her forever. "Hi. What's up?"

"I talked Jen into letting us tag along with her and Matthew tonight, to the movies. Sound good?"

"Um, I don't know." Was he asking her out, or was this a group thing? And should she encourage him if Cupid's arrow was really at work? On the other hand, if Than had changed his mind about her, maybe Pete could be a helpful diversion from the horrible pain in her heart.

Pete added, "Don't be mad at Jen. She was just freaked out. She's terrified of snakes and thinks that garter will eventually find its way back here when you let it go."

"If it lives. I'm not so sure it'll make it." Then she said, "Hey, aren't you supposed to be on the trail ride?"

"Bobby went. I have the next one. So, do you wanna go tonight?"

Should she? What else was she going to do now that Than was dumping her? Mope around all night? She knew if she didn't do something to distract her she'd sink down into that deep dark place she inhabited in the few weeks after...her life had changed. "That sounds good. Let me check with my aunt and I'll call you back."

After she hung up the phone, she collapsed on her bed and sobbed some more. Clifford jumped up next to her and licked her face.

"Thanks, boy," she said, her voice breaking up with weeping.

"Why are you crying?" came a woman's voice which Therese did not recognize.

Therese froze. Clifford stopped licking, but didn't bark. Slowly, she turned to see an amazingly majestic woman with glowing pale skin and long black hair standing in the room across from her. She wore a white short gown, golden boots, and a golden helmet. Beneath the helmet, her amazing blue-gray eyes stared directly at Therese.

"Who are you?" Therese gasped, wondering if she should get down on her knees.

The woman smiled. "I will answer your question if you answer mine. Why are you crying?"

Therese decided to be perfectly honest. "Um. For one thing, both my parents recently died."

"Go on."

"Then a horse I was riding was injured and had to be...put down."

"Yes?"

"And now a boy I thought really liked me has changed his mind."

"I see." The woman took off her helmet. "And now I will answer your question. My name is Pallas Athena. I am the daughter of Zeus. He is my one and only beloved parent, and, presently, he is upset, like you. But his tears become showers and his rage thunderbolts."

Therese could barely breathe. She didn't move. "Is he upset because of me?" she asked in a small voice.

Athena narrowed her eyes. "Do you think so highly of yourself that you could be the cause of his sorrow, his rage?"

Therese covered her mouth and shook her head. When she could, she said, "No, m'am. Hermes said..."

"Hermes has spoken to you?" Athena hissed.

Therese wished she could disappear. "He didn't seek me out. We, we met by accident." In a desperate voice, she added, "Look, if you want to kill me, please just go ahead." Then she put her arms around Clifford and thought better of it. Who would care for her pets?

"I didn't come to kill you, but to test you." Athena's voice was no longer harsh. "I came disguised as a serpent, and you took pity on me when others wished me dead. I see you have a kind and compassionate heart, and you are worth saving. Unlike Ares and Poseidon who stand with McAdams, and Aphrodite and Apollo who stand with Thanatos, I, like Artemis, stand with you. However, both of us wish you to reconsider your desire to become the wife of Thanatos. He is a good and kind and noble god, but his ghastly life is not the kind of life for someone like you who loves all living things. Furthermore, to marry a god carries many risks, as the males are usually unfaithful. When my brother Apollo wished to marry a maiden named Daphne, she would rather be changed into a laurel and spend eternity as a tree because she feared the warring among jealous female divinities. Think before you act."

Therese at first was stunned, her eyes wide. Daphne would rather be a tree? Forever? She swallowed and cleared her throat and picked at her sleeve. "Thank you, Pallas Athena. I don't know what to say, except that I don't think it's an issue anymore, my going with Thanatos. He's, he's changed his mind."

"Good. That is as it should be." And with that, Pallas Athena vanished.

Therese sat still and bewildered for several minutes after the goddess left. When the shock of the visit finally wore off, she checked in the cardboard box to be sure the snake wasn't still there and the entire event a bizarre hallucination. But the snake was gone, and in its place was a golden heart-shaped locket. She reached into the box and took it in her hand. The locket was secured to a delicate gold chain. She opened the locket. Inside, she found an inscription in slanting, flowing letters that read: *"The most common way people give up their power is by believing they have none."*

Therese closed the locket and clutched it to her heart. She opened the locket and read the inscription again. Why had Athena given her this message?

Therese put the locket on her dresser and went to her bathroom to take a hot shower. The water running down her tense body calmed her after the strange events of the day. Although the gift from Athena made her happy, the overall disappointment she felt from Than's behavior today was like a suffocating blanket that could not be lifted away nor washed off with the heat of this shower. Once more, tears streamed down her face. She wondered how a person could never run out of tears.

Afterward she changed into a t-shirt and cotton shorts and, with her hair still wet, climbed beneath her covers to take a nap. Clifford followed her and curled up near her hip. The lack of sleep during Hermes's visit had caught up with her, so despite the despair, the dread, and the awe, once she closed her eyes, it wasn't long before she fell asleep.

Now she was in the Melner cabin looking for the restroom. "Restroom?" she asked Hermes.

He pointed to a toilet in the middle of the living room.

From where they sat around her on the living room furniture, Meg sneered and Tizzie shrugged.

"Go ahead," Than said from behind.

Therese's bladder was about to burst, so, very quickly, she crossed the room to the toilet, but with all the eyes on her, she could not bring herself to pull down her jeans and go.

"Never mind," she said. "I'm late for school."

She grabbed her backpack, sitting by the front door, and ran out to the dirt road just as the school bus drove by toward the dam.

"No!" she shouted from the middle of the road after it had gone right past her.

Then she heard another bus coming and saw its dim headlights emerging from the Holt place, so she waved her hands to flag it down, but it sped past without noticing her.

She bit her lip, and her teeth moved, like they were loose. She touched a front tooth with her finger, and the tooth fell out. Then she smiled. "This must be a dream."

She put the tooth back in place, ditched the backpack, and sailed through the air.

"Yep. It's a dream. I can do whatever I want."

She flew back to the Melner cabin and went up to Than. She was furious with him but feeling desperate. He had been the medicine that would help her get over losing her parents. If he abandoned her now, she would be left with nothing but her grief. She couldn't take that.

"I'm going to make you change your mind," she promised him. "I'm going to make you love me again." She took his face in her hands and planted a passionate kiss on his lips right there in front of Meg, Tizzie, and Hermes.

"Figments, show yourselves!" a voice came from behind her.

Than, his sisters, and Hermes vanished, and in their place were four scaly eels, whirring through the air and giggling. They flew out of the windows and the open front door.

Therese turned to see Hip standing behind her. He was tall and well-built like his brother, but his hair was blond and his blue eyes deeper set. He wore white trousers and a white open shirt.

"You still owe me a kiss," he said. "A real kiss. That last one didn't count."

She frowned. "Aren't you supposed to be guiding the dead?"

"My brother returned to give me a brief reprieve. Zeus would have eventually commanded it." He took a few steps closer to her. "My kiss? For the tour? Remember?"

"Oh yeah." She closed her eyes and puckered her lips. When he didn't kiss her, she opened her eyes to find him sulking. "What's wrong?"

"That's not how you kissed that figment you thought was my brother. I want you to kiss me like you kissed it."

Her eyes widened. Then she narrowed them. "That wasn't part of the deal. You said a kiss. You didn't say what kind." She sighed. "Besides, I don't think I have it in me to kiss anyone right now with your brother no longer in love with me and then there's Pete forced by Cupid's arrow to love me against his will."

"What? Gods can't *force* people to do anything. Humans have free will—while they're alive, anyway. Cupid's arrow can only enhance and make compelling a feeling that was already there."

"Really?" This cheered her, to know that Pete had already felt something for her before the gods interfered, that he wasn't being forced against his will to like her.

"Now can I have my kiss?"

She was a little uplifted by this news, so she put her arms around him and planted a grateful, albeit not passionate, kiss on his mouth.

"That's better." He grinned.

"Will you answer one more question?" She gave him a flirtatious smile.

"You know the fee." He put his face close to hers.

"Why did Than change his mind about me?"

Hip's smile turned into a scowl. "How am I supposed to know? Can't you ask me a question I can answer?"

"Okay, okay. Calm down. Maybe you can answer this: When will Than return to Earth?"

"Tomorrow. Though why should you care if he's changed his mind? Forget him, Therese. You can have me." He held his arms, spread wide, palms up, with a sweet but devilish grin.

"Like I said, I have a feeling you're not a one-girl kind of guy."

He threw back his head with a loud guffaw. "You know me too well. Now give me my kiss."

As she leaned in to meet his lips, she heard a loud crash and snapped awake. She sat up in her bed and looked around. She was alone with her pets. It was thundering and raining outside. Was the storm caused by Zeus's rage and sorrow?

She looked at her clock. Six o'clock! She had slept for six hours? She still hadn't called back Pete. She ran downstairs to get permission from Carol to go to the movies, and then returned upstairs to call the Holts.

"Sorry about earlier," Jen said on the phone.

"Me, too."

It was still thundering and pouring down rain when Pete and Jen drove up the drive in Pete's truck to pick her up. She huddled beneath the umbrella feeling her curly hair get frizzier with each step she took toward the vehicle. She was glad she had decided to wear it pulled back at the nape of her neck in a wide, thick barrette. At least the frizzies would stay out of her face.

Pete opened the passenger side for her and helped her in the front seat. Jen sat in back. So maybe this was a date after all.

"Where's Bobby?" Therese asked as she fastened her seat belt.

"He spent all his money on a new gaming station," Jen said. "Plus, I didn't really want him to come. He's so immature."

"Is Matthew meeting us there?"

"We're picking him up," Pete said. "That's why Jen's sitting in back. She doesn't want you anywhere near him."

"Shut up, Pete," Jen punched his arm.

215

"Yeah, right," Therese said. "Like she's got anything to worry about."

"How's the snake?" Pete asked.

Therese thought fast. "Good. I'm going to find it a home. There's a snake farm in Pagosa Springs."

"Good idea," Jen said. Then she leaned forward. "Hey, is that a new necklace?"

Therese fingered the locket at her throat. "Um, yeah. Sort of. Well, it was my mom's." Like she could really tell them a goddess named Pallas Athena transformed from a garter snake and gave it to her.

"Oh." Jen sat back. "It's really pretty."

Pete glanced at her throat. "It looks nice on you."

"Thanks."

They were silent now as Pete drove through the winding country roads with the rain beating down on the truck. Therese was glad to be with her friends, but she missed Than and still despaired over his change of heart. She knew she should stop thinking about him altogether, but she couldn't no matter how hard she tried. She peered across the bench seat at Pete looking as handsome as ever, but even his charm and good looks could not help her forget Than. It was too late. She was in love and feeling rather desperate.

Guilt flooded over Therese when she recalled she was supposed to be going to the movies with Vicki. She needed to remember to call her tomorrow to make arrangements before her feelings were totally hurt.

During the movie, Jen and Therese sat beside one another with the boys on either end. She mostly whispered to Jen, but about halfway through the film, Pete put his arm around Therese, and she stiffened. She tried to relax, to remind herself that he was her friend and this could be comfortable, but it felt totally wrong. After several minutes, she excused herself to use the restroom. Jen came with her.

"What am I going to do about Pete?" Therese asked her when they were at the sink washing their hands. "I think he likes me."

"And you don't like him?" Jen crossed her arms and lifted an eyebrow, which disappeared behind her straight blonde bangs.

"I like him a lot. But I think I'm in love with Than."

Jen slipped a tube of lipstick from the front pocket of her jeans. "Than's leaving soon. Long distance relationships suck. You should let it go." She pressed the lipstick to her lips.

"And Pete's going to college. What's the difference?"

Jen held the lipstick out to Therese.

"Thanks." Now it was her turn to apply the makeup.

"He's not going after all. He decided to stay and help mom with the horses and work gigs with his band."

"That's stupid." Therese handed over the tube and rinsed her hands again.

"He doesn't think so. And neither does Mom. She's glad he's staying."

Therese dried her hands and said nothing.

"Give Pete a chance," Jen said in a pleading voice. "Just think. If you two got married one day, we'd be sisters."

"This isn't about us."

One of the stalls on the end burst open, and out walked Gina Rizzo wearing tight jeans, rhinestone boots and matching belt, and big silver earrings. Her blonde hair was twisted up in a clip and spilling down the back of her head. "Hey, guys. What's this I hear about Pete and Therese? Are you two dating now? I *thought* that was you I saw in front of me in line. I can't wait to tell Maddy and Katie."

"We're not dating," Therese said.

"Sure you're not." She washed her hands at the sink and ripped off a piece of paper toweling. "Later, girls."

Apparently it didn't matter if your parents died. The school bitch would show no mercy.

After the movie, a lame comedy with a disappointing ending, they stepped out of the theater to find the rain had stopped and the night sky was clear and full of twinkling stars. The air was cool, so Therese zipped the front of her jacket.

"Cold?" Pete asked. He put an arm around her as he walked her to his truck.

"Let's go dancing," Matthew said from behind. "Want to?"

"Yeah," Jen said. "Great idea, Matthew. What do you guys think?"

"Sounds good to me." Pete pointed his clicker at the truck to unlock the doors. "Therese?"

"I don't know. I'm kind of tired."

"But you napped for six hours!" Jen reminded her.

Therese climbed into the truck. "I know, but I think I might be coming down with something. I don't feel that great."

Pete patted her leg from behind the wheel. "That's okay, then. Let's go home. And hey, Mom doesn't do trail rides on Sunday, so why don't you sleep in tomorrow? I'll cover your grooming for you since you're not feeling well."

"Come on, Therese," Jen said. "Don't ruin it for the rest of us. You're just upset about Than."

Therese flashed her a fierce look. "Shut up, Jen."

Pete's smile faded as he turned the key in the ignition. "Drop it, Jen."

Chapter Twenty-Eight: Back to the Dead

Than could no longer put off giving his brother a reprieve from guiding the dead, for he could feel tension building somewhere, either among the humans or the gods or both, and so, since he wasn't sure, anyway, how he should proceed with Therese, he decided this day would be as good as any to return to his duties.

Hip appeared to Than where he hovered over the deep granite abyss that seemed to have no end to the darkness below. "Thanks, bro'," Hip said, too anxious to stop and chat. He flew on by and went straight to the poppies and into the realm of the dreamers.

Than hadn't been there for a full second when he sensed the souls of many ready to be guided. He disintegrated into five and dispatched to three different regions of the world.

One of the souls in his custody proved to be a small old woman kneeling in her garden bed. Her body lay in a heap in the grass with a spade in her gloved hand and a plant with its root ball exposed, as though she were about to plant it before she died, and her hand had clutched it and stiffened. The foliage on the plant, which Than did not know, since he knew nothing about such things, was withering, dying along with its caretaker. Much to his astonishment, as the woman's soul climbed from the heap in the grass and turned toward him, bewildered as all souls of the dead were, she held in one hand a projection of the withered plant. Never before in the history of his existence had he seen a plant-like soul accompany a human. Plenty of animals, billions of them, and at times even insects, had come with him to Charon to be taken over to the other side and, unlike the humans who must be judged, guided straight into the waters of the Lethe and its everlasting oblivion. Cats and dogs and other pets sometimes came with their humans

219

when they died together, and the animals were allowed to go with their humans to the Elysian Fields; but never had Than seen a plant-like soul, and so he stood a moment, transfixed.

"Who are you?" the woman finally asked.

"Death," he answered, as he always did. "Your time has come. Take my hand."

"But I hadn't finished yet," she said. "My garden's nearly done. Look. I have one more to plant. Can you wait?"

The answer was always no, though because of the circumstances, Than hesitated before saying so. "Don't worry," he said in a calming voice, and together they hovered over the land toward the abyss, and as they flew, she spoke to him as so many others had before her.

"How will my husband manage without me? He's disabled. He can't care for himself. Who will cook for him? What will he do?"

"Someone will take over your duties. Someone always does."

"I didn't get to say good-bye. He'll be so shocked. He might even go into cardiac arrest."

"And then he can join you. Come this way."

As they approached Charon and his raft, Charon also noticed the plant and furrowed his brow. "What's this?" he asked.

The woman looked at the plant in her hand. "This? It's Lily of the Nile. I didn't get to finish planting it. I was just about to. May I go back and finish?"

Charon shook his head.

"Have you seen this before?" Than asked. He allowed the woman's feet to touch the bank of the river, knowing it would calm her.

"Yes," Charon said as Than and the woman boarded the raft. "But not often. It happened twice in Hermes's time."

"Do plants have souls?" Than asked.

"That is a question for your father, Thanatos," Charon replied.

Than disintegrated and dispatched another of himself to Hades's palace, where he found his father engaged with Hermes.

The two gods looked agitated, and when they felt Than enter the chamber, they stopped talking and turned their faces toward him.

"Is something wrong?" Than asked.

"Always," Hades said, "But I was about to ask you the same question."

"It can wait, if you're busy," Than replied.

"Out with it, son."

"All right then. " He swallowed, feeling foolish now and embarrassed. "Do plants have souls?"

Hades narrowed his eyes. "The gods are about to break into war and you come here asking about plants?"

"I said it could wait, Father. You insisted. And the gods are always on the brink of war. Questions are meant to be asked and, when they can be, answered."

Hades sat up on his throne and looked down his thin nose at Than. A hint of a smile tugged at the corners of his mouth. Then he said, "Bravo. Yes, Thanatos. How right you are."

"So? Charon told me Hermes has seen something resembling a plant soul twice. I saw one just now. What does this mean?"

Hermes started to speak, and then stopped, looked at Hades, and waited.

Hades plucked at his beard, deep in thought. "Some do," he said. "Plants have been evolving since as long as I can remember, and some have gone beyond simple sensory reflexes, such as turning to face the sun to make food. Some seem to be infused with a primitive consciousness, like those of many insects, and when it is coupled with a deep bond with a sentient being, a kind of symbiosis seems to be awakened between the sentient being and the plant being. Plant souls have never come here of their own accord, but in the

221

company of a caring human soul, they have on the three rare occasions you have mentioned. I suspect we shall see more of this in the centuries to come."

Than felt a flicker of happiness and a lightness of spirit as he pondered the ramifications of his father's words. He said, "I want the woman's Lily of the Nile for my rooms. Is that possible? She won't remember it once she reaches the streams of the Lethe. I want to change the circumstances of my dwelling by infusing it with more life. Can I keep the plant?"

Hades shrugged. "It makes no difference to me."

Another thought occurred to Than. "If I can maintain a plant soul in my rooms, what of animal souls? We have Cerberus and your steeds, Swift and Sure, but they were immortal from their birth, so I never considered adding other animals as companions down here. If I can have the Lily of the Nile without any consequences to you and to the rest of the world, why not a dog or a hamster?"

Hermes fell to the floor overcome with laughter. Hades soon laughed along with him. Than stood with his mouth agape.

"What's so funny?"

"Never in a million centuries," Hades managed to say in between laughs, "would I have ever imagined that one of my sons would come to me asking if he could have a pet!"

"How human of you!" Hermes added, holding onto his belly.

Than felt his face flush, but he stood his ground. "And your answer then I presume is yes?"

Hades nodded but could not speak, for when he looked at Hermes rolling on the floor, he broke out in another fit of laughing.

Than had other questions for his father, very serious and private ones, but he knew he would have to wait till Hermes left to ask them.

Chapter Twenty-Nine: Than's Apology

Therese was walking between her parents as they crossed the Royal Gorge Bridge, over a thousand feet above the raging Arkansas River, when she heard someone behind them call her name.

It was Gina Rizzo, and with Gina were about twenty scraggily men wearing turbans and carrying swords.

"Get them!" Gina shouted.

Therese and her parents started to run, but Therese slipped, lost her balance, and fell over the side of the bridge. Her parents reached their hands out to her from on top of the bridge, but it was too late. Therese was free falling a thousand feet toward the bottom.

She could make out various shapes in the solid granite formations all around her as she fell closer and closer to the raging river below. One group of rocks resembled a giant hand, like that of a god. That triggered an idea in Therese's mind.

I'm dreaming.

She stopped herself midair and sailed up through the gorge. She turned several somersaults in the air to be sure. Yes! She was relieved to discover she would not crash to her death against rocks or in the raging river, but even more than that, she was glad to have a means to find Than. First she would seek out Hip.

She stuck a fist out and flew out of the gorge. She hadn't gotten very far when Hip appeared.

"Nobody establishes lucidity during a free fall," he said, flying beside her. "You are spectacular to watch. What a treat."

"Why thank you. I'm glad you find me so entertaining. But I need your help. I want you to take me to Than."

"I can't do that."

She put her hands on her hips. "Why not?"

"You'll die."

"Just for a second. Just long enough to give him a message. Then you can pull me away."

He crossed his arms in front of his chest and grumbled, "Sorry. It's impossible. Got to go."

Hip vanished from her sight.

Therese decided to try another route. "Thaaaaannaaaatos! Thaaaaaaannaaaaaatos!" She would keep screaming his name until he came to her. "Thaaaaaannaaaaatos!"

The sound of her own voice woke her. "Thanatos," she mumbled, not quite the yell she envisioned in her dream. Clifford sprang to his paws and looked at her, wagging his nub of a tail. "Sorry, boy," she said. "It was just a dream."

She looked at her clock. "Ten? I slept till ten o'clock?" She sat up in her bed and rubbed her neck. It was hot this morning, and the sun coming through the trees and in her windows was unusually bright. She crawled from her covers and went to her bathroom, trying to recall the details of her dream. She knew she had been looking for Than and hadn't been able to find him. Hip refused to help her. Maybe Than had warned Hip to keep her away from him. After brushing her teeth, she came back to her room and turned on Jewel's lamp.

"Good morning, sunshine," she said in a friendly voice to her tortoise, who hadn't yet opened her eyes.

"Good morning," a voice answered. It was Than's.

She turned to the window, thinking he was on the ground below, but he wasn't. He was in the room with her. He wore the white trousers and white shirt from her earliest dreams, before he had come to Earth.

"I heard you calling me." He fidgeted with the hem of his white open shirt. "Sorry it took so long. I was waiting for Hip to relieve me."

She resisted the urge to run into his arms. He was bathed in sunlight, and his dark wavy hair looked soft to the touch. "Why did you leave?"

He scratched his chin. "I needed to give the humans a break from their dreamless nights."

She ran her fingers through her messy hair. "I wish, I wish you would have told me you were going." She rubbed beneath her eyes, hoping there weren't mascara rings.

"I'm sorry." He crossed the room and pushed a strand of her hair that must have been poking straight up over to the side.

A wave of heat surged through her. She couldn't meet his eyes. "Than, I know you've changed your mind about me. But I just want you to know, I want you to know that I haven't changed mine."

He lifted her chin. His blue eyes were bright in the sunlight. "What makes you think I've changed my mind about you?"

"You, you said you had doubts," she stammered.

His face broke into a grin. "About taking you as my wife, but not about how I feel."

"What's the difference?"

He stepped back and fell into a chair beneath her window. Clifford jumped into his lap, and Than pet him. "I've made such a mess of your life. You had an ordinary human life, and now I've pulled you into a war between gods. Not to mention the fact that you adore life and would probably despise the Underworld."

She stepped closer to him. "Go lie down, Clifford." Clifford sulked over to his pillow in the corner beneath her other window. She looked at Than, trying to muster up courage. Finally she blurted, "I don't care about all of that. God, Than, I just want to be with you. Can't you see that? Why can't that be all that matters?"

He stood up and took her in his arms.

"Just tell me the truth," she demanded. "Do you love me or not?" Tears threatened to spill down her cheeks.

He returned the intensity of her gaze. "I do," he said in a husky voice. Then he covered her mouth with his and gave her a deep, lusty kiss. "I do love you," he said again.

A hunger like she'd never known took possession of her, and she wrapped her arms around his neck. A feverish, burning sensation flamed through her skin. Her heart either pounded franticly or stopped altogether; she could no longer tell. She grabbed fistfuls of his soft dark hair and pressed her body against him. Her knees trembled. She held on for dear life.

He took her up in his arms and carried her to her bed just as she was about to fall. He laid her down on her back and knelt on the floor beside her. She took his face in her hands and kissed him.

"I love you, too," she said in between kisses. "You're all I think about." She kissed him again. "I don't want to live without you." Then she said, "And if you leave me again, I swear I'll kill myself to be with you."

He stopped and lifted his face to look into her eyes. "Don't say that, Therese. Promise me you'll never do that to yourself."

"No."

"If you love me, promise me."

"If you love me, don't make me promise."

"Then there's only one thing to do."

"What?" Fear pricked her skin.

Than grinned. "Introduce you to my parents."

He covered her lips with his and she laughed with joy. She laughed so hard, she couldn't stop. Clifford pranced around the room.

"I'm sorry," she said, still laughing, almost hysterical now. "I'm so sorry."

He laughed at her and plopped beside her on the bed. "Don't apologize. I love to hear you laugh. I rarely hear laughter."

He blushed, and she wondered why, but instead of asking, she broke into another fit of laughter.

"I can't stop. I can't breathe."

"I seem to have that effect on people lately."

His hand at her waist sobered her, and she caught her breath. "You make me so happy. I like you so much."

He rolled to his back. "I've never been happier." Then he sat up. "Hey, I have an idea." He had a curiously sneaky expression on his face.

"What?"

"Let's travel the world together today. Let's start with Paris. I've heard it's the most romantic city."

She sat up with her mouth hanging open. "Are you serious? Paris?"

"And London, and Tokyo, and Honolulu, and Cairo, and all the places I've been to but never visited properly."

"What will I tell my aunt?"

"The truth. Tell her you're spending the day with me."

With her traveling robe from Aphrodite and her golden locket from Pallas Athena, Therese held on to Than's hand in front of the Melner cabin and closed her eyes against the bright light. The invisible plastic wrapped itself around her, and she held her breath, but soon the pressure was gone and she could open her eyes.

First they arrived in Paris, in the Louvre for just a minute and held hands while they gazed at the Mona Lisa, where a fashionably dressed woman complimented her robe and wanted the name of the designer. Therese grinned at Than and explained it was a gift; she didn't know. Although it was lunchtime in Durango, the sun was just about to set here.

"How about a cruise?" Than asked.

"How will we pay?"

Than pulled out a wallet from his trouser pocket. "My father gave me this before I left. It's magical. The paper bills become the currency of whatever country I am in at the time. See?" He pulled out the bills and showed her they were euros.

They boarded a private dinner cruise near the Eiffel Tower and sat outside on deck in the cool evening. A light breeze blew from the Seine, and the soft sound of violins lingered in the air. While the sun sank behind the Eiffel Tower, they ate omelets and soup.

While they ate, Therese asked Than a few questions about what it was like to be a god.

"Can you hear people's thoughts?" she asked, taking a sip of her Diet Coke.

"Only when a person prays directly to me."

"Does that happen often?"

"Yes, but people pray to me under the false assumption that I have anything to do with the timing of their or their loved one's death, so I tune them out. It just makes me sad." He looked into her eyes and smiled. "But your prayers to me are different." He winked. "Finally, instead of begging me to postpone my visit, or pleading for me to take them swiftly to avoid the agonizing pain, somebody actually wants me just for me, for my company. You can't know how exhilarating that is."

Color rushed to her face. "Wait a minute. Do you hear me every time I speak to you in my mind?"

A huge grin crossed his face.

"The other night…" she dropped off.

"When you begged me to kiss you?" he teased. "And when you complimented my butt?"

She licked her lips. "Okay, I'm going to have to be more careful."

"Don't."

She tried to recall other times she might have said things to him in her mind. Color rushed to her face, but what did it matter? He knew how she felt. Why should she hide her feelings from him?

When they had finished eating, Than said, "Let's go see another sunset, this time in London. We have to hurry. The sun's about to set."

They leaned on the rail of London Bridge looking out over the Thames as the setting sun cast its golden hues across the water. A crisp breeze carrying the smell of rain blew into their faces. A shower was on its way. Sure enough, within ten minutes, it began to drizzle, but they stayed to enjoy it.

Therese asked another question. "Can you make yourself invisible and eavesdrop on what others are saying?"

"Yes." He looked down as color came across his face.

"You look guilty. Have you ever done that before?"

He shrugged and the corners of his mouth turned up. "Maybe."

"Have you ever eavesdropped on *me*?"

"Once or twice perhaps."

She punched his arm. "Tell me everything, Than. I mean it! I want to know!"

The rain came down a little harder now, sending chills down Therese's back.

"Let's get out of this rain first." Than put both arms around her.

They took a taxi past Buckingham Palace, and drove around until the rain stopped. Then they strolled through St. James Park as the sky turned into night. "Please tell me?" Therese asked now that there were no other people around them.

"Let's pop over to Tokyo first. It's late morning there."

They took another cab over Rainbow Bridge and gazed at the cityscape, the sun just coming up from the east.

"That's Tokyo Tower, I believe." Than pointed to the tallest tower in the city.

"Yes, sir," the cab driver said. "The tallest one there. Also known as the Sky Tree Tower."

"It's beautiful," Therese said. "Now let's go someplace where we can talk."

"How about Cairo for dessert?"

"I better call my aunt," Therese said, getting out her cell.

The cab driver gave them an astonished glance in the rearview mirror. "That may take a day of travel, sir."

"Just drop us at the nearest museum," Than said.

Although by Durango time, the hour was late, approaching ten o'clock at night, it was sunrise in Cairo. They looked out over the Pyramids of Giza and gazed for a long while at the magnificent Sphinx, with its lion body and human head, before heading to a restaurant for dessert, or what was to the other tourists breakfast. On their way to the Lakeside Café, they strolled through Al-Azhar Park and caught a glimpse of the mosques and the Citadel. The café itself was a cluster of white pavilions floating on a lake with citrus groves visible through the screens. They ordered coffee and Baqlawa, which the waiter had explained was made of many layers of paper-thin dough with a filling of crushed nuts and sugar between the layers. Once the waiter left to fill their order, Therese asked her question again.

"So tell me. When did you eavesdrop on me?"

Than rolled his eyes. "You aren't going to forget about this, are you?"

"You promised."

The waiter returned with their coffee.

"Thanks," Therese said.

Once the waiter left again, she said, "So?"

"Okay. Remember the first day you came to work for the Holts, and you had lunch with Jen?"

"No way! You were listening?" She tried to recall what she had said. Jen had liked him then, too. She shrieked and covered her mouth. She had talked about her *boobs*!

He laughed at her, like he knew what she was thinking.

"When else?"

"I may have listened in on a few of your conversations both times we went to the Wildhorse Saloon."

"Oh my God!"

"Like I said. You can call me Than."

She slapped his arm. "Quit saying that!"

"I just wanted to be sure you weren't already in love with someone else. So many guys asked you to dance. I worried you were in love with them all."

She threw her head back and laughed.

"I might not have been wrong about Pete, though. I heard you went out with him last night." Than frowned.

Their dessert arrived.

"What's this called again?" Therese asked the waiter.

"Baqlawa."

"Mmm, it looks good," Therese said. "Thank you." When the waiter left, she said, "Were you there with us at the movie theater?" She dug her fork into the pastry and took a bite. "Oh my gosh, this is so good."

"I'm glad you like it." He took a bite. "Mmm. You're right. It's delicious."

"So were you at the theater?"

"No. I had to work. But just before I left, I heard Pete call and ask you to go, and you said you'd ask your aunt."

"You were there? In my room?"

231

Than blushed. "Are you angry with me?"

"I'm only angry that you didn't make yourself visible and kiss me, especially when you saw me crying."

"Yeah. It was hard not to take you in my arms."

"I'm angry that you didn't."

"I'm sorry."

She sipped her coffee. "The waiter probably thinks we're crazy eating this for breakfast."

"I doubt it. He's probably used to international travelers. Plus, people do sometimes eat it for breakfast here."

Therese smiled. She never would have referred to herself as an international traveler, but she supposed that's what she was today. "So then you saw my visit with Pallas Athena? And you know about my locket?"

"No. She gave you a gift?" He looked flabbergasted.

"There's an inscription." She opened the locket and tucked in her chin so she could read it. "*The most common way people give up their power is by believing they have none.*" She closed the locket and lifted her chin. "I guess she wants me to believe in myself more." Then she added, "Too bad you weren't there. It was really awesome."

"Yeah, I left as soon as she transformed from the snake." He swallowed a sip of his sweet iced tea, loaded with extra sugar. "I didn't want to anger her. She would have sensed my presence."

"Did you know she was the snake all along?" She loaded her fork.

"Not at first. I sensed her later, when we were walking home from the Holts', which is part of the reason I didn't go into depth with you about how I was feeling. I didn't want her to overhear."

"Oh. That makes sense now. But you scared me, you know. I was so hurt."

232

He looked penitent. "I'm sorry. I really was thinking of you and all that you would sacrifice." He kissed the tip of her nose and asked, "Can I make it up to you with a sunset cruise in Honolulu?"

She wiped some crumbs from her nose, which he had put there with his kiss. "The sun is setting in Honolulu?"

"Yes. If we hurry, we won't miss it."

She gave him her biggest smile. "That could work."

The wind lifted her hair from her back before she opened her eyes and found herself on a catamaran holding Than's hand with the sun setting in the distance behind the Honolulu cityscape. A tourist beside her jumped and muttered, "Excuse me. I didn't see you there," and Therese stifled a giggle. God travel was amazing.

The catamaran sailed along Waikiki Beach. The ocean glistened with an orange hue, and three dolphins leapt from the water with the volcanoes spread out on the horizon behind them. According to Than, Diamond Head, its vast silhouette resembling the profile of a tuna, was the largest of the volcanoes.

She quickly called her aunt—it would be later in Durango—and told her she was next door at the Melner cabin and Than would walk her over in a half hour, when the movie he and his sisters had rented was over. She hated to lie, but who could pass up a third sunset in one day?

Over a loud speaker came a series of clicks and long and short tones, and the captain of the vessel explained that a hydrophone enabled them to hear the dolphins speaking to one another underwater.

Therese couldn't believe she could hear them so clearly. "Wow. I wish I could understand what they're saying."

"They're excited about the boat," Than said. "They get bored easily, and racing the cruise ships gives them something to do."

She smirked. "That's one theory."

233

"It's no theory, Therese."

She looked at him with her mouth dropped open.

He laughed and turned to watch the dolphins.

In a low voice, she asked, "You can understand what the dolphins are saying?"

He answered softly, so the other mortals couldn't hear, "Gods can understand all languages, including animal languages."

She couldn't speak for a minute. She had to let that sink in.

He put his face close to hers and pushed her windblown hair from her eyes. He spoke softly, again, tenderly, "That's how I knew about the snake that night with Dumbo."

"What a wonderful gift," she murmured. She looked at him intently. "That just makes me more certain of my decision."

He covered her lips with his.

Outside of her house in the dark night at half past midnight, while clouds obscured the stars and the moon, Therese and Than walked up the gravelly drive. Therese didn't want the day to end. It had been so perfect. "When will I see you again?" she asked as they approached the steps to the front of her house.

"Tonight, if you want, after you visit a while with your aunt and her boyfriend. I suspect they waited up for you. I could wait for you in your room."

Therese heaved a deep breath, desire prickling her skin. Would he touch her again the way she longed to be touched? He must have sensed the mood washing over her, because he pulled her body close to his, nearly crushing her against him, and let out a sigh.

"Mmm," she purred. "That sounds good. I'll be right up."

He gave her a sideways grin. "Talk with your aunt first."

"Right. Good idea."

Than walked her in and Therese found that Carol and Richard had, indeed, waited up for them, and she wondered if he had other powers, like seeing the future. Luckily, her aunt said she was glad Therese was having fun. They spoke briefly before Than said goodnight to Carol and Richard and then left through the front door. Therese followed him back out through the screened front porch. "Later," she whispered with a smile.

"That's a promise," he whispered back. He pecked her cheek and vanished.

Therese sighed and crossed back into the living room, taking her favorite chair by the empty fireplace. Clifford jumped in her lap. She wondered if he had anything to say to her. She'd have to ask Than later.

"Hi boy. Did you miss me?" she asked her dog.

He panted and wagged his tail.

She laughed. "I'll take that as a yes."

"Did you have fun today?" Carol asked from beside Richard on the sofa. Carol's legs were curled up beneath her, and she and Richard shared a quilt. They had the television turned on to a movie.

"One of the best days of my life," Therese said. "I wouldn't have thought it possible a month ago."

Carol and Richard exchanged looks of amusement, but then Carol said, "Be careful, Therese. You're at that age when a person gets her first broken heart."

"I'm not worried," Therese said with a sly smile.

"We might also want to discuss a curfew. Eleven o'clock sounds more reasonable than after midnight for a fifteen-year-old."

Therese sighed.

Carol and Richard asked more about her day, and Therese made up stories about sightseeing in Durango. She turned her Parisian cruise into white-water-rafting and her London-Bridge-gazing into a lift over Purgatory Mountain Resort.

"Oh, what good ideas," Carol said. "Richard and I should have come along. He's never done those things."

"You and I can go tomorrow, then," Richard said. "You can take a day off, can't you?"

"I don't want to leave Therese here alone all day."

"I won't be alone," Therese pointed to the back deck. "The officer will be here. Plus, Than and I are going to…" an idea hit her. "Than said he'd help me sort through mom and dad's clothes and things. I've decided to donate most of them to charity so someone can get use out of them."

Carol got up and crossed the room. "That's a great idea, sweetheart." She kissed Therese's cheek. "Oh, I'm so glad to hear you're ready for that."

"Maybe you want to go through mom's stuff?"

"I took one sweater I gave her a few years back." Carol returned to the couch. "I don't really want anything else, I don't think. And you should keep her jewelry and pass it on to your daughter one day."

"I guess you're right. But I won't keep all of it. So let me know if there's something you want."

"Maybe one ring to remember her by—the opal ring my mom gave her as a graduation present."

"Sure." Therese couldn't wait another minute to meet Than upstairs in her room, so she faked a yawn, said she was sleepy, wished them good night, and used every ounce of self-control to resist running up the stairs.

Chapter Thirty: Hope

Than popped down to his rooms to wash and change into some fresh clothes and then popped back up to Therese's room to wait. He felt lighter in spirit and more joyful in heart than ever in his life. Never had he imagined that Death could find a companion willing to spend eternity by his side. Lonely and desolate he had felt, though he had found some satisfaction in knowing he was bringing an end to pain and suffering, offering peace to tormented souls, and ushering in justice to the evil ones. As much as his duties had sometimes pleased him, never had they made him feel this good. Surely nothing could compare to the feeling that one is loved by and devoted to another.

He imagined now how he would alter his rooms to bring pleasure to his new bride. He would fill them with the souls of animals and plants. He glanced over at Puffy, the hamster, and Jewels, the tortoise. He could hear Clifford downstairs with the humans. He would be waiting for them and would bring them directly to his chambers. Perhaps Clifford should come down with Therese. That would make the transition easier for her, and the dog would be happier to remain with the soul his had so rigidly imprinted upon. Puffy's time was near, Than sensed, but Jewels would live another fifty or more years; nevertheless, when the time came, he would bring her soul to Therese.

And there would be music! Than would encourage Therese to play her flute in his parents' palace. Hermes and Apollo would be invited to join her. The Underworld will become a better place with her presence.

And they would swim together. He had never before thought to glide through even one of the many waters of the Underworld. Each river played a part in helping the souls of the dead to deal with their afterlife. The Acheron was a transit river on which Charon moved his ferry. The Lethe helped the souls to forget. The Cocytus provided a place for souls to wait when the judges could not reach a proper decision; it was a kind of holding place, like the human concept of purgatory. The Phlegethon was full of fire, though it didn't burn or produce heat, and helped bring light to the darkness that would otherwise envelop them. The Styx was a sacred river on which the gods made their oaths. Than had always seen the rivers as practical functions in his duties and not features to be enjoyed. Because his godly form was less sensually perceptive than his mortal form, it just hadn't occurred to him. But now that he could feel, really feel the world around him, he would remember these feeling and use them to further enjoy his surroundings down there. And he would help Therese enjoy them, too. They would play together in the Styx, which ran right by his rooms.

He would spend the rest of eternity thinking of ways to please his wife.

Chapter Thirty-One: A Lot to Sort Out

Than was waiting for her on the chair beneath her window. He had changed into a comfortable t-shirt and loose cotton trousers. He smelled clean, and his hair was wet.

"That's not fair." Therese leaned over and took in his scent, touched his hair. "You took a shower."

He gave her a devilish grin. "We have all night. Go ahead and shower, if you want."

As anxious as she was to be in his arms again, she wanted to smell good, too, and after all their travels, she could use some refreshing. "I won't be long. Oh, and while I'm in there, I want to try something."

He stood up and gave her a look of surprise. "What?" He shifted his weight from one foot to the other and clasped his hands together like a juror about to read the verdict.

She could tell then that he was as inexperienced as she. *Of course* he had never been with anyone, she thought. He said she was the first to ever touch him, to ever kiss him. "Relax and wait here. I'm going to try to pray to you, to see if you can hear me."

"Oh." He seemed a little relieved, but disappointed, too, as he unclasped his hands and fell back into the chair.

She turned on the shower and undressed as she waited for the water to get warm. Once inside with the curtain closed, and as she shampooed her hair, she whispered, "Than, I hope you can hear me. I figured out how I can thank Aphrodite and Pallas Athena for their gifts. We'll have to go to Greece, though. I hope that's okay. I want to donate my parents' clothes to charities that support their temples or their memories or something. I'll have to do a little research to get the specifics straight." She rinsed her hair and babbled on, hoping he could hear. She soaped down her body and rinsed herself, all very quickly and eagerly, and turned off the water. "Anyway, my aunt and her boyfriend will be gone tomorrow. I told them you were going to help me go through my parents' clothes. You should have seen my aunt. She seemed really glad."

She took her nightshirt from the hook on the back of her bathroom door and slipped it on along with a pair of fresh undies. Then she opened the door to her bedroom. "Did you get that?"

He smiled at her from the chair. "Every word. No one has ever prayed to me like that before."

She crossed the room and sat on his lap, appearing more confident than she looked, for she still found it hard to believe that this handsome god was her boyfriend. "Do you like my idea?"

"As a matter of fact, yes. There's a group in Acropolis devoted to memorializing Athena and supporting her values of peace and justice. They clothe the poor. There's another group on the Cyprus Island that raises money to hold an annual festival in Aphrodite's honor. They would take your donations as well. The goddesses are going to love you for this."

She played with his wet hair and kissed his forehead. "I'm glad you like my idea. So can we go to Greece tomorrow?"

"Absolutely. And that gives me an idea as well." He gave her a playful look.

She narrowed her eyes. "What are you smiling about?"

"While we're in Greece, we can go to Mount Olympus and maybe persuade my parents to meet you. My mom should already be there, so it would just be a matter of convincing my dad to leave the Underworld."

She frowned.

"What's wrong?"

240

"I'm a little nervous. You're my first boyfriend. I've never had to meet the parents of a boyfriend before, and, well, meeting yours sounds a bit, I don't know, daunting."

"Don't worry." He kissed her neck. "You'll do fine. Maybe we'll take your flute along."

Like the notion of *performing* for the gods of the Underworld was supposed to make her less worried. "And chocolate?"

He laughed. "Yeah. And chocolate."

She kissed his cheek and sighed. "I want to know more about you," she said.

"Like what?"

"What's an average day like for you as the guide for the dead? I mean, do a lot of people die in one day?"

"On average, and only considering the past ten years, about a hundred thousand people and maybe twice that amount of animals."

Therese frowned. "Per day?"

He nodded.

She looked down at the floor, her mouth suddenly dry.

"What?"

"That's so sad. What do they mostly die of?"

"Hunger."

"That seems so…preventable."

"Yeah."

She continued to gaze at the floor.

"Is there something else bothering you?"

"This is going to sound so selfish."

"Tell me. I want to know."

"Well, how would you ever have time for me?" She blushed. "Sorry. That sounds so, selfish and immature. But, I mean, think about it. When would we ever be together? It sounds like you have to work nonstop."

241

He laughed. "Now don't freak out, okay?"

"What do you mean?"

"I can be in several places at once."

Her mouth dropped open. "I don't understand. How is that possible? I mean, are you somewhere else right now?"

"Right now you have my undivided attention, but when I'm acting as the death guide, I can be at many places at the same time."

"That's hard to grasp. So there's like a whole bunch of your clones running around?"

He shook his head. "No, no, not clones. In each instance, it's me, only me, and completely me, and not an imitation of some sort. I disintegrate into many selves. Right now I am integrated into one."

"I still can't picture it."

"You know how you can be on your computer, on the phone, and listening to music at the same time? You might also be petting Clifford, eating a snack, and glancing out the window."

Therese nodded. "So?"

"Well, I can do a million more things at the same time as a human, even though I have one brain that is aware of the million things I'm doing and the million places I am at."

"Okay, I think I'm beginning to understand. But then why can't you be with me and be the guide for the dead at the same time? Why did Hip have to take over for you?"

He moved a strand of hair from her face and pushed it behind her ear. "Because as the death guide, I would endanger your life. As long as one part of me is acting in that capacity, no human could survive my company."

"Oh." She thought about that for a moment. "Then why can't you do Hip's job and be with me?"

"Because then you'd fall asleep around me."

She laughed. "That's hard to imagine." She touched his cheek. "So is there anything you can do while you're with me?"

He cracked a smile. "Oh, I can think of something."

She laughed and lightly slapped his chest. "I mean somewhere else!"

"No. As long as I'm in my mortal form, I can't disintegrate. I have to shift into my godly form."

Her eyes opened wide. "This isn't your usual form?"

He shook his head. "No. I'm brighter. Too bright for your eyes. Any more questions?" He leaned in.

She closed her eyes and shook her head.

He kissed her neck again, enkindling her quickly and unexpectedly. Her body felt like it was inflamed, the heat rising within her and flooding all of her senses. She ran her fingers through his soft, wet hair and met his lips with hers. He dazzled her, overwhelmed her, made her want to soar across the sky. Their slow, romantic kisses turned into feverish, passionate ones, and he lifted her up and carried her to the bed. He gently laid her down on her bed without moving his mouth from hers. He moved on top of her, his body hot and hard against hers. She clung to his hair, keeping his face next her hers.

"Mmm," she moaned.

He pulled away and collapsed beside her on his back.

She turned on her side to face him. "What's wrong?"

"I'm afraid I won't be able to stop," he said breathlessly.

"Oh." Then, with her heart speeding up even more in her chest, she whispered, "That's okay."

He looked at her with a mixture of shock and desire. She was afraid but overcome. He kissed her, fervently, and she felt like she would overflow with passion. Then he stopped and collapsed on his back again.

"You're killing me," she said with frustration.

He laughed. "I'm sorry, Therese. But there's something you don't know."

"Oh no. You're already married."

He broke into a boisterous laugh. "Oops. That was too loud. I hope Carol and Richard didn't hear that." He covered his mouth with his hand and they both sat there, listening for the other humans in the house.

After a few minutes of silence, Therese said, "Tell me what's wrong."

He turned on his side to face her, propping himself up on an elbow. "I talked to my dad a little yesterday about…things. You have to know that every time a god has ever made love to a human, it has always, invariably, ended in pregnancy."

Understanding washed over her, along with disappointment. "Oh."

"Human forms of birth control are powerless against the seed of gods."

She giggled at that. It struck her as funny. Not that she had any birth control anyway.

"What?" he demanded.

"Nothing. That just sounded kind of hilarious."

"But it's true. And you're not ready to have a baby."

She bit her lip. "No. You're right. I'm not."

He sat up. "I should go."

She grabbed his arm. "No. Please don't go. Stay. Sleep here with me."

He grinned. "You want to drive me crazy, huh?"

She giggled again. "No." Then she was somber. "I just don't like being away from you."

He lay back down beside her and stroked her hair. "Okay. I'll give it a try. Maybe if you talk to me, you can distract me from what it is I really want."

She giggled once more and then called to Clifford, who had been curled up in the corner on his pillow. "Come here, boy."

He jumped on the bed between them.

"Can you translate?" she asked Than.

"He's just glad you're finally paying attention to him again. He was whining a minute ago, full of jealousy."

She petted Clifford. "I already knew that."

"I know," Than said. "You can read animals really well. That's what I meant when I said you had a gift. Your conversations with the horses in the pen made sense both ways. The horses love you, especially Sugar." Then he said, "By the way, Jewels is wondering when you're going to remember to turn off her lamp. She's tired and wants to go to sleep, but she's too warm."

Therese jumped up. "Oh my God!" She snapped off the lamp. "I'm sorry, Jewels! Is that better?"

"She's sighing with relief," Than said.

"You should have said something earlier."

"I was distracted." He gave her a lusty smile, and she nearly lost herself again.

Therese flopped back down on the bed beside Than and Clifford. "What about Puffy? Has he said anything lately?"

"He wishes we'd shut up and go to sleep so he can have peace and quiet while he works. He's miffed, but he'll tolerate it. He really likes you and is glad you're finally home. He'd just rather you go to sleep."

"He said all that?"

"Here and there, throughout the evening. I had to finally tune him out."

"Why don't I hear anything?"

"He speaks on a different frequency. Most animals do."

She turned off the lamp on her nightstand and made the room dark. "That's for Puffy, of course," she whispered.

"Of course."

She climbed beneath the covers. "Coming in?"

He cleared his throat. "Um, I think I'll sleep above the covers."

She moved around beneath the sheet until she was comfortable lying against his chest. She made Clifford lie down on the other side of her so she could be against Than.

"He's jealous again," Than said.

"I know. He'll live." She nestled against Than's chest. "Are you sleepy?"

"A little."

"Gods do sleep, don't they?"

He stroked her hair. "Yes, just not as much as humans. You go to sleep, though. Don't worry about me. We have a big day tomorrow if we're going to Greece."

She kissed his chest and closed her eyes.

Therese awoke after a dreamless night to the bright sunshine coming through her bedroom windows. It took a minute for her to remember that Than was supposed to be there, that he had been beside her when she had fallen asleep. Clifford gave her a cursory glance as she sat up and wondered where Than was. Do gods use the restroom?

"Than?" she called softly as she climbed from the bed. He wasn't in the bathroom.

The clock on the night stand said it was 9:30. She wondered if Carol and Richard had left for their day of sightseeing. Only one way to find out. She and Clifford went downstairs to see if they were alone, except for the officer she knew would be on the deck.

"Oh good, you're awake," Carol said as she emptied a half-eaten bowel of cereal into the sink. She was dressed in jeans and a button-down blouse, her red hair pulled back in a short ponytail, make up perfect. "I was hoping to see you before we left. You sure you don't want to come along?"

"I'm sure. He'll watch out for me." She pointed to the kitchen window through which they could see the police officer sitting with a pastry and coffee, his feet propped on a cooler. Then Richard walked in from the guest bedroom. "Hey, Richard."

"Hey." He sat at the granite bar and opened the newspaper in the same spot her dad had always sat. He too was dressed and ready to go.

Therese sucked in her lips and sighed. "No, I really want to do this. I've decided donating mom and dad's things to charity might give me some...I don't know...closure." She put the leash on Clifford. "I'll take him to the front to do his business. Come on, boy."

Carol kissed Therese's cheek as she passed and then took Richard's empty cereal bowl to the sink. "Call me on my cell if you need anything." Then she asked, "You won't be alone, right? I mean, except for him." She nodded her head toward the officer.

"No. Than's coming to help."

"Okay. Don't hesitate to call 911 if anything suspicious happens. Even a police officer may need help. Promise?"

"Promise."

As soon as she came back inside with Clifford, and after Carol and Richard had left, Therese poured herself a bowl of cereal and said out loud, "Than, where are you? Will you please come back?" She was startled by his instant appearance by her side. "Geez, you scared the crap out of me."

He gave her a smirk. "Sorry."

"Why did you leave? I thought you were staying the night." She ate some of the cereal while she waited for his explanation.

He took her face in his hands. "You look so cute first thing in the morning." He kissed the top of her head.

"How would you know? You weren't there." She couldn't hide the slight hostility in her voice.

"Was too. I didn't leave you till dawn. I wanted a quick shower and a moment with my sisters. They had news."

Clifford put his paws on Than's jean-clad shins.

"Hey, boy. Good morning to you, too," Than said, patting the dog.

"So, what was the news?" Therese stood to rinse the bowl in the sink. "Want some?"

"No thanks. I already ate." Then he said, "The news is complicated and I'm not sure…"

She left the bowl in the sink, turned, and pressed herself against him. "Tell me. I want to know."

He toyed with her mussed up hair, straightening it, smiling. "You're so cute, and you've been so happy. I hate to…ruin that."

She wrapped her arms around his waist. "As long as I'm with you, I'll be happy."

The doorbell made her jump. "Who could that be? I'm not dressed."

Hold on. He vanished and then instantly reappeared. "It's Pete Holt."

She sighed. "Oh God. Will you get it while I run up and get dressed?"

"He won't like that."

"Too bad."

She dashed up the stairs and quickly changed into a knit top and matching short skirt. She brushed her hair out, glossed her lips, and hustled back down.

Pete lingered at the front door, a wide space between him and Than. He wore jeans and boots and no shirt and was sweaty and grimy, as though he had just finished cleaning the barn. "Hey, Therese." Pete's voice was sobered, nearly grave.

"Hey, Pete."

248

"Sorry to barge in…"

"Don't apologize."

"My mom sent me to deliver your earnings. She would have given them to you yesterday, but…Hey, are you feeling better?" He glanced at Than and back at her.

"Yeah, thanks." She gave him a hesitant nod. "And thanks again for covering for me. I hope it wasn't too much of a drag."

"Not at all." He gave Than another glance.

They all three shared a moment of awkward silence without looking at one another.

Therese finally said, "Well, hey, thanks for coming by."

"Oh, sure. Here's the money." He held up a white envelope. "I don't want to get your house dirty."

She crossed over to him and took the money. "Thanks."

"I'll give you a call later. And hey, Mom says you're welcome to come visit any time if you get bored and want to, I don't know, hang out while we work the horses."

"Thanks. Sounds good."

She followed him through the screened porch, where Pete turned to her and muttered, "Are you two going out or something?"

Therese blushed. "Um, or something, I guess."

He glanced once more in Than's direction. "Bye, then."

"Bye. Thanks again."

She felt sorry for him as she watched him leave. When he was in his truck, she waved once more before going back inside. Than was waiting for her. He, too, appeared sobered.

"You could have a good life with Pete." He said this without looking at her. "He'd make you happy, and you wouldn't have to leave. You could live among the living. You could see sunrises and sunsets. He could give you everything I can't give you."

249

She stood in the living room across from him. "Don't. Please." She could see the diseased elm through the kitchen window and a sudden urge to chop down the dying branch overcame her, but she pushed it down, thinking she was losing her mind. *She* couldn't chop it down.

He met her eyes but said nothing.

"Is that what you want?" The hostility from earlier crept back in her voice.

"This is about you, about what's best for you."

"Then quit talking like that." She stormed off to her parents' room. In her mind, she thought, "If you can hear me, Than, please follow me. Please come in behind me and put your arms around me and tell me you will never say such a thing again."

She stood there just inside her parents' room waiting. Seconds later, he swept in behind her with his arms around her waist and clasped across her stomach.

"I'm sorry," he whispered.

She turned in his arms and kissed him, closed her eyes, and touched his neck with her hands. "Me too." Then she played with his shirt and asked meekly, "Are we still going to Greece today?"

"If you wish."

"Then we better get busy. Why don't you tell me what your sisters learned about McAdams while I start bagging some of these clothes?" She went into the closet and grabbed four or five hangers with clothes and laid them on the bed. Before Than had begun his story, she said, "Oh. I remember the last time my dad wore this shirt." She swiped the tears away as they fell unexpectedly down her face.

"Maybe you're not ready for this."

She rubbed her eyes with the backs of her hands. "I want to do this."

Than sat on a chair in the corner of the room and talked as Therese created piles of her parents' possessions and then bagged them in giant black yard bags she found beneath the kitchen sink. While she worked, Than explained that McAdams was the CEO of a corrupt pharmaceutical company in Texas that bought counterfeit drugs at cheap prices from a manufacturer in Pakistan and sold them to customers at regular market prices. McAdams then split the profits with the Pakistani manufacturer, who was also able to provide forged approval certificates, valid samples for occasional testing by regulatory agencies, and pay-offs to agents when needed. The manufacturer had connections with various foreign rebels and so was able, through McAdams, to develop and sell the mutant anthrax to them. Than explained that when McAdams got wind of her mother's research at Fort Lewis College, he ordered her execution because he feared he wouldn't get paid if his customers heard that an antidote was being developed.

Then she asked, "But why would McAdams still want me dead?"

Than stood up and put his hands on Therese's shoulders. "His men weren't after you that night. They were after your aunt."

Chapter Thirty-Two: Tagalong

"**W**hat do you mean they were after my aunt? What has she got to do with any of this?" Therese asked, her face twisted up to his with confusion.

"Maybe you better sit down." Than wished he could shield her from this news.

"Okay," she murmured and sat on the edge of her parents' bed.

He stood in front of her. "Your aunt works for a pharmaceutical company, right?"

"Uh-huh."

"A few months ago she attended a professional conference in Dallas. She went to lunch with a group of attendees, all salespeople like herself, and they got to talking about where they were all from, about their families, and things. Carol mentioned how proud she was of her sister, a professor at Fort Lewis College, who was going to be honored this summer for her outstanding work. Someone asked what work. Carol talked about the antidote for the mutated anthrax. One among the group worked for McAdams."

Therese's mouth dropped open, and she sat stunned for several minutes. She looked as though she had lost the gift of speech.

Than touched her shoulder. "Therese?"

"So that's how he found out about my mom?"

Than nodded.

"Carol can't ever know this." Therese stood up and twisted her shirt in her hands. "This would absolutely kill my aunt. We can't let her know. Oh my God." She paced around the room. "Oh my God."

"She doesn't have to know." He could hardly keep up with the combination of silent and spoken prayers.

"Please don't let her know," she either said or prayed. "Please protect her, forever. I can't stand this."

Therese continued to pace. "But is McAdams still after her? I mean, is my aunt in danger?"

"I and many gods promise to protect her." Then, gingerly, Than explained, "McAdams murdered his informer, the one who lunched with your aunt, James Barber. He's in Tartarus now. That's how Tizzie discovered the connection. She got him to talk. Tizzie thinks McAdams is afraid that if the media show pictures of his informer once someone realizes Barber's missing, your aunt will recognize him and remember having lunch with him, and that she might eventually put it all together."

"Oh no."

"But Aphrodite and Cupid are with her and Richard today. They won't let anything happen to her. And even with Ares trying to thwart their every move, Tizzie and Meg are close to finding McAdams. Barber said McAdams is meeting with his Pakistani manufacturer today. Tizzie and Meg and I will be waiting for him. It won't be long now."

Than could here Therese's prayers, for she directed them to him. She was explaining to him that it was one thing when Therese thought that McAdams and his men were after *her*; but it was another thing entirely to learn the bad guys were after her aunt. Since the death of her parents, Therese hadn't been too afraid of dying. She wasn't going to commit suicide, but if death happened on its own, that wouldn't be so bad. That had been her attitude. She hadn't tried to be careful. She hadn't stayed up nights worrying about her safety. If she couldn't fall asleep, it was because she missed her parents and longed to be with them, not because she was afraid to die. "I want to be with you, so death is no longer scary," she prayed. But now that her aunt's life was in danger, now that her aunt was the target, Therese was overcome with fear and a deep desire to seek out McAdams and put a stop to him.

253

"Help me avenge the death of my parents," she said suddenly, and now he could see she was speaking, not praying. "Help me kill McAdams and protect my aunt. I don't want to wait another minute."

He put his arms around her rigid body. "Calm down," he whispered. "I'll help you. But calm down. I don't like to see you so upset."

She relaxed a little in his arms and put her head against his chest.

"Listen," he said softly. "Let's finish sorting through your parents' things and take the donations to the goddesses' charities in Greece. We want to make sure we have them on our side before we get you involved. You'll need their protection as well as mine. Maybe there's something you can do for Artemis as well, since she has also vowed to stand by you."

"I've already thought of something." She looked up at him. "I want to donate my earnings from Mrs. Holt to a wildlife preserve."

Than was full of admiration for her. "Excellent. She'll like that."

They spent the rest of the day sorting and bagging Therese's parents' clothes, shoes, accessories, and a select assortment of books, magazines, and jewelry. Often Therese would stop, hold something up, look at it and remember. Tears would flow down her face like a waterfall, but she'd slap them away and keep going, and Than felt lost and helpless, unable to comfort her. They took only one break, for a short lunch of egg salad sandwiches Therese made for them, and by the time they were satisfied, they had ten large garbage bags and four cardboard boxes ready to donate, and it was seven o'clock in the evening.

"We'll have to go to Greece in the morning," Than said. "I promised my sisters I'd help them now. I'm already a little late."

"Can I come?"

He cringed at the thought of his sweet Therese seeing the hideousness of the Furies, the blood pouring from Tizzie's eyes, the vicious snakes, the fierce falcon, the howling hounds; but, he supposed she would have to see these things eventually if she were to follow him to the Underworld and live there with him.

Therese quickly added, "I hate being on the sidelines all the time. This is about me and my family and I want to help." She clutched the locket from Athena, which she wore around her neck, and he sensed the determination to wield her own kind of power.

He looked at her, still considering.

"Unless I'd be a liability," she said.

"You're not too tired?"

She shook her head. "Please?"

"Do not leave my side, got it?"

She nodded, smiling, and prayerfully thanking him. Out loud, she said, "Got it."

"And wear Aphrodite's robe just in case we get separated."

They went upstairs to her room, where she found and put on the robe.

"If we do get separated, concentrate on your room, on this spot, with all your might. The robe will help you get back here."

"Okay."

He could feel her trembling beside him and could see her shaking as she put her arms through the sleeves. "Try it out first on your own. Think of your kitchen. Concentrate really hard on the spot in front of the kitchen sink."

Therese closed her eyes. She prayed to him the entire time, explaining that she felt a pressure against her body, like plastic wrap enclosing her, and then, a second later, he watched her open her eyes where she was standing, or stumbling rather, in front of the kitchen sink. She grabbed onto the counter to get her balance.

"I did it!" she shouted.

The police officer sitting out on her deck turned from where he had been eating his sandwich, his feet propped up on his cooler. He looked at Therese through the window. She gave him a wave to let him know everything was okay.

Than, who had been waiting for her, said, "Okay, here we go. But hold tight to my hand and don't let go unless I tell you."

"I promise." Then she said, "I better tell Officer Gomez I'm leaving."

"Good idea, but hurry. We're late as it is."

She quickly poured some lemonade into a glass and took it out to the officer. She practically ran back into the kitchen, anxious to get started on their journey.

"Where are we going?" she asked, taking his hand.

"Peshawar. A city in Pakistan."

Chapter Thirty-Three: Artemis's Gifts

Therese closed her eyes against the bright light, and held her breath as the invisible plastic wrapped itself around her. When she opened her eyes, they were standing in the early morning sun in an abandoned alley. The foul smell of urine and rotting food accosted her. She gagged.

She followed Than, stepping over rubbish and weaving through garbage cans to a dusty window in the back of a metal building. Like Than, she peered inside, but it was difficult to see anything.

"My sisters must be around here somewhere." He closed his eyes and appeared to be in deep concentration. Then he opened them and said, "This way."

"So you can communicate with your sisters telepathically, like ESP?" Therese asked as she rushed beside him.

"ESP?"

"Extrasensory perception."

"Telepathy is not an 'extra' sense for a god. Just as I hear your prayers directed to me, they can hear mine and I theirs, though the sounds can get distorted." Then he said, "Turn here."

A pack of skinny dogs, crouched around a half-eaten carcass, looked up at them and were about to bark when Than said, "Silence." The dogs obeyed and went back to what they had been doing.

Than led Therese around the side of the building from which they could see a road and a jeep approaching. Than flattened against the building, pulling Therese beside him. "They're meeting us here."

"The people in the jeep?"

"No."

Before he said more, Meg and Tizzie appeared before them. They too pressed their backs against the building, out of site of the jeep, which had stopped now. Therese could hear men talking and the jeep doors slamming shut. Then she heard laughter. The laughing stopped at the sound of another vehicle approaching.

A man Therese could not see spoke in a harsh voice. The only word she recognized was, "McAdams."

Meg signaled the others to follow her to the back of the building, back to the heaps of rubbish and garbage cans. The dogs looked up as the group passed by and then the animals returned to their carcass.

The gods and one human huddled behind the building where Tizzie said, "I've found a place in the building where Therese can hide while we use invisibility to get McAdams."

Meg snarled, "I can't believe you brought her, Than. You know Ares is against us. You've endangered her life, our mission…"

"Enough," Than said. "This is her battle, too. I'll stay beside her but will help if you need me."

Than held tightly to Therese's hand and the bright light surrounded them. They reappeared behind a metal pallet stacked high with cardboard boxes. Through the boxes, Therese could see three men gathered in the middle of a large room full of machines and assembly lines that at the time were not running. Two of the men were dark-skinned and holding weapons, but the thin, bald, white man trembling before them must be McAdams.

"May I remind you that you work for me!" McAdams shouted. "We stand to make a lot of money together, and you can't do it without me. Damn it, you cowards, put away your weapons!"

"What happened to Grahib?" one of the darker men demanded.

"McAdams had him killed," the other said. "He had his own informer killed, too. We can't trust him."

258

"But I have your money. If you kill me, you won't get paid," McAdams said. "Those other men betrayed us. I only kill betrayers. You are good men who have served me well. I can still get you the women I promised, the red-head and her virgin niece. Trust me. Money and women. What could be better?"

"Security," one of the men replied.

Than nodded, and whispered, "I know. We need him alive."

The one man said to the other, "Let's just do it. Do it now!"

They pointed their weapons at McAdams and pulled their triggers. A loud roar echoed throughout the building as Therese watched in terror. She was shocked to see McAdams standing unharmed, but then Tizzie appeared before him. She spit the bullets into her hand and gave the men an arrogant smile. Blood spilled from her eyes and snakes coiled and hissed in her hair. The two men turned on their heels to hide, one of which came to the very spot where Therese and Than were huddled.

"Go now," Than said urgently. "Go back to your room. Concentrate. Now!"

Therese shut her eyes and focused on her bedroom, but then an image of her grandmother's green carpeting in her old house in San Antonio entered her mind, and before Therese knew what was happening, she found herself standing in her grandmother's old living room in San Antonio. Everything smelled new, and the furniture had all been removed.

"Oh, hello," a woman's voice came across the room. "I'm sorry, but the open house ended over an hour ago."

"I'm, um, so sorry," Therese said. "I'll, um, just show myself out."

"Are you okay? Did you come with your parents?"

"I'm fine. My parents are waiting for me outside."

She went through the front door and recognized her grandmother's old street just visible in the dusk. The woman from her grandmother's house stepped onto the front porch and watched as Therese hurried down the sidewalk. She walked a little way further and found a cluster of trees, but before she could god-travel, a scrawny old man approached her.

"Hey, girlie, you got any spare change for a starvin' man?"

Therese turned and ran down the darkening street. She wasn't sure where to turn. Tears welled in her eyes as she rounded a corner and saw a park up ahead which vaguely looked familiar. Two teenagers were snogging on a bench, but Therese crept behind some bushes and deeper into trees where she closed her eyes.

She tried to focus on her bedroom. A strong image of Clifford waiting for her on her bed made it easier this time. She was so afraid and wanted Clifford! She hadn't been much help on this journey. How stupid she had been to think she could help the Furies! The invisible plastic wrapped itself around her, she held her breath, still focusing on Clifford on her bed, and when she opened her eyes, she found herself standing on her bed looking down at her dog wagging his tail at her.

She went downstairs and was surprised that Carol and Richard weren't home yet. Officer Gomez still sat out on the back deck, so she felt fairly safe. After letting the officer know she was home, she put Clifford on a leash and took him outside in the front to do his business. Then she came inside and grabbed a cookie from the countertop, nearly eating it whole.

Therese looked at all the bags and boxes lined up on the floor of her parents' bedroom and wondered how they would transport them all to Greece. She was too tired to think long on it, though, and before she realized it, she had curled up on her parents' bed beneath their covers, trying to smell their scents and trying to erase from her mind the scene that had transpired before her in Peshawar. Clifford sat in the corner of the room. He had never been allowed up on her parents' bed, and even though he probably knew her parents were gone, he couldn't bring himself to break the rule.

She was nearly asleep when the phone rang. She answered the one on her parents' bedside table. It was Gina Rizzo. Gina had never called before.

"What's up, Gina?" Her voice was deep with sleep.

"I just wondered if you heard the news about your friend Vicki."

Therese sat up. "Uh-uh."

"Oh. Well her mother committed suicide yesterday. She slit her wrists with a razor blade and bled to death in the master bathroom. Vicki was home when it happened. Isn't that terrible?"

Gina's voice sounded more excited than sad, and that eerie excitement drove Therese to anger.

"I've gotta go," Therese said. She hung up the phone and left her parents' room and was sick in the kitchen sink.

Through the window, she caught sight of the diseased elm tree illuminated by the moonlight. Then, in something like a blind rage, she ran down the stairs to the unfinished basement, another project her parents had planned to one day complete. She went past the washer and dryer and stack of dirty laundry. She grabbed an axe and went through the basement to the garage, which opened to the side of the house. She squeezed by her father's Chevy truck, pulled out a ladder, and dragged it uphill to the diseased elm tree.

"What are you doing?" Officer Gomez asked.

"Fixing that tree!" Then she went back for the axe. She practically dragged it out of the garage door and up the hill.

"You're going to hurt yourself. Why don't you wait until someone can help you?"

Ignoring the officer, she climbed up the ladder and stretched herself out as tall as she could and hammered the blade of the heavy axe against the dying branch. It barely made a scratch, but she brought that axe up and she struck the branch again, despite the police officer's protests. She was going

261

to save this dying tree. She was sick of watching the disease slowly suck the life from it, and she was going to put a stop to it once and for all. She struck the branch again and again, nearly toppling over once, till it hurt her arm to keep raising the axe, and then she did it several more times. She broke through the bark, but she could see that she had been right all along. She could not chop down the dying branch. She could not save the tree. She dropped the axe, climbed down from the ladder, collapsed on the dirt, and cried.

And then it began to rain.

The officer went to the overhang to get out of the rain and didn't seem to know what to say.

Clifford barked at him from the back door. She could see Clifford looking at her through the glass pane. He was probably worried she had lost her mind. He should be, she thought.

She pulled herself up, leaving the axe to rust in the rain, the ladder to stand like an unfinished promise beside the elm she could not save. She looked over at the other elm a few yards away. Her mother had said that if they did not stop the disease from getting the one tree, it would eventually spread to its twin. It seemed wrong that two such magnificent living structures should be the victims of a life-sucking fungus to be left withering skeletons that would eventually break, crumble, and decompose and then disappear from sight altogether, as though they had never existed.

"It's okay, boy!" she hollered to her dog, who had started to whine, but before she left the tree, she caught sight of something shimmering in the adjacent cypress.

She walked in the rain toward the shimmering tree, blinking her eyes several times and rubbing them. The forest was dark on this side of the house where the moonbeams couldn't reach. And maybe the rain was blurring her vision. But, no. Even with her eyes rubbed dry, the tree shimmered. Therese backed away now, frightened.

"Come inside!" Officer Gomez called out.

"Do not be afraid," the tree said. "I am Artemis, goddess of the wood, and I will not harm you."

Therese held very still, not sure if she should speak. She swallowed hard and waited.

"I am pleased with your stewardship of the forest and the animals that abound in it. You have won my heart."

Therese couldn't make out an image of the goddess, just the shimmering tree. "Thank you. I'm grateful."

"Like Aphrodite and Athena, I have gifts for you, but mine are far better than theirs. Aphrodite may have saved your dog from death, but I have given him immortality."

Therese sucked in air. Did she just say that her best friend Clifford would never die? "Oh, thank you! Thank you so much!" She glanced at Clifford still looking at her through the back door. His tongue hung happily from his mouth as the stubby tail wagged back and forth. He seemed to understand what had happened to him. He would be able to go with her now and live in the Underworld! "I don't know what to say." Tears pricked her eyes.

"Therese!" Officer Gomez called again. "What are you doing out there? Come inside!"

"Wait," Artemis commanded. "There's another. Whereas Aphrodite gave you a traveling robe, I now give to you a beautiful crown. It is made of the finest pearls and diamonds, and when placed upon your head, will make you invisible to mortal eyes. It is waiting for you on your bedroom bureau."

Therese put her hands to her cheeks. "I can't thank you enough."

"Don't forget your promise to me, Therese. The wildlife preserve. I am counting on your offering."

"Yes, m'am. I'm pleased to give it."

"Is there anything else you would ask of me?"

"No, m'am it's just…" Therese faltered.

"What is it?"

"My friend Vicki. She's all I can think about right now. Her mother committed suicide yesterday. If I can ask something of you, I ask you to please watch over her and help her, if you would."

Before Therese had finished her sentence, the cypress no longer shimmered, and the rain no longer fell, and Therese had the feeling the goddess was no longer there.

The crunching sound of gravel made her aware of Carol and Richard pulling up the drive in Carol's little red Toyota Corolla. Carol waved to her before driving into the garage beside Therese's father's pickup. Therese wondered whether it was her request of the goddess or the appearance of her aunt and uncle that had made her disappear.

A few minutes later, Carol and Richard came through the back door, Clifford scrambling out ahead of them to growl at Officer Gomez, standing beneath the overhang of the house. Carol and Richard looked across the deck to where Therese stood beside the elm, the axe, and the ladder, still flabbergasted by Artemis's visit and the news of her gifts.

"What have you been doing?" Richard asked.

"Um, I was trying to save this tree from the Dutch elm disease. Mom and Dad were going to chop off that dying branch and treat the roots, but…well, I couldn't do it."

"You should have told me," Richard said. "I'll take care of that for you."

"Sweetheart, you're soaked and your backside is covered in mud. And you could have hurt yourself."

They went inside, including Officer Gomez, who moved to the screened front porch to avoid the rain, which had started falling again. After a shower and change of clothes, Therese came back down to hear about her aunt's day while Carol made spaghetti and Richard sat on the sofa with the news turned down low. Therese showed Carol the bags and boxes she had lined up in her parents' room, and Carol was amazed by all she and Than had accomplished. Therese told her about taking the things to charities tomorrow—though she failed to mention they were located in Greece.

Therese also mustered up the strength to tell Carol about Gina's phone call and the terrible thing that had happened to Vicki. Tears streamed from Therese's eyes when she admitted to her aunt that she had been blowing Vicki off, especially the night they were supposed to go to the movies.

"I should call her, shouldn't I?" Therese asked. "I should invite her to come over sometime soon, don't you think?"

Carol put an arm around Therese, while she stirred the pasta boiling in the pot.

"Don't be too hard on yourself. Things haven't been perfect around here, either." Then she added, "But maybe it would be nice to invite her to do something."

Therese nodded. "Maybe I'll go give her a call."

Upstairs in her room, before she made the call, Therese noticed the crown inconspicuously tucked on a blue silk scarf on one end of her dresser behind her CD player. She hadn't noticed it before when she had come up to shower and change, and with the arrival of her aunt and the appearances she had at first tried to keep up, she had forgotten the goddess's gift. Now she took the crown in her hands and studied it.

A gold base with embedded diamonds was topped by a scalloped band of gold studded with smaller diamonds. Between the scallops hung teardrop pearls from a third, thinner golden band shaped in five large scallops along the front of the crown, and at the crest of each scallop was a single large diamond. The largest of them was set in the top center scallop. Therese had never seen anything like this jeweled crown in all her life.

She watched herself in the mirror above her dresser as she placed the crown on her head. She gasped when her reflection disappeared. Frightened, she instantly removed the crown and sighed with relief when she could once again see herself gazing back from the glass.

With a mixture of trepidation and excitement, she returned the crown to her head and watched her reflection vanish. She decided to test to see if she really were invisible to mortal eyes, so she went downstairs to the kitchen and waited to see if she would be noticed.

The pasta had been drained and three plates of spaghetti sat cooling at the granite bar, but Carol and Richard sat together at the sofa speaking in muted tones. Therese crossed the kitchen so she could hear what they were saying.

"So are you going to tell her tonight then?" Richard asked.

"I think so. Do you think she's ready?"

"You know her better than I do. It's your call."

"I might know her, but I have no idea what's good for her. I wish I were better prepared. What a responsibility. And you're still sure it's the right thing to do?"

"Positive. It would be best for all of us," Richard said.

Therese couldn't figure out what they meant, but a part of her worried they were talking about Carol giving her up. She had suspected becoming Therese's guardian would be too hard for her aunt, leaving her life in Texas, her independence. Maybe they planned to give Therese to an orphanage, or foster care, or a halfway house for abandoned youth. She knew she was being ridiculous, but, what if? Her heart sped up as she waited to learn more details, but they stopped talking to listen to the news, and then Carol got up to pour glasses of iced tea. It wouldn't matter for long, anyway, she told herself. Therese intended to become a god. Carol wouldn't need to worry anymore.

266

Therese backed up to the stairwell, and as she tiptoed away, she heard Carol say, "I'll wait and tell her tomorrow. She's worried about her friend tonight."

That's right. Vicki. Therese went upstairs and took off the crown and called Vicki, reminding herself that there were others besides herself to think of. She sat on her bed next to Clifford and took up her phone.

A man with a tired sounding voice answered. "Hello?"

"May I speak to Vicki please?"

"Sure."

Vicki's voice sounded tired, too. "Hello?"

Tears came to Therese's eyes as she told her how sorry she was to hear about her mom. "I know what it's like to lose a parent," she muttered. "I'm sorry this happened to you."

"Yeah. Me too."

"We should go somewhere and do something and get our minds off…things."

"We have a lot of family in town for the funeral and everything. Maybe next week."

Therese wondered if she would still be human then. "Okay, but let's not wait too long."

As Therese hung up the phone, Carol called for her to come eat, so she went downstairs unable to stop herself from worrying about Vicki and how tired she and her father had sounded. She also wondered anxiously about what it could be that Carol and Richard had wanted to tell her.

After supper, Therese scuttled off to her room where Clifford was waiting for her. She still couldn't believe he was immortal. She hugged him and told him they would be together forever—if the Furies and Than could help her successfully catch McAdams. If only there had been a way to make her parents immortal, too. They could all be together—one big happy family.

Therese lay down on her bed and closed her eyes. She was anxious for Than to return. "Than," she whispered. "Than, come over."

When he didn't appear, she grabbed her laptop from her desk, sat back on the bed, and turned the computer on. She googled wildlife preserves in Colorado, found the Perins Peak State Wildlife Area west of Durango, located the website, and made an electronic contribution using her debit card in the amount she earned this summer. She would deposit the cash to make up the difference in her account later.

"Are you coming, Than?" she whispered again.

The phone rang, so she picked it up to find Jen on the other line.

"I'm sorry about the other night," Jen said. "I was rude."

"It's okay. I'm sorry, too. I was being selfish."

Jen's voice had the same tired sound Vicki's had had earlier. "Did you hear about Vicki?"

"Yeah. I talked to her earlier."

Then, out of the blue it seemed, Jen said, "My dad came home today."

Therese sat there on her bed in shock.

"You still there?"

"I'm here. Oh my gosh. Is everything okay I mean, are you glad?"

"Not really."

"Oh no. Do you want to come over?"

"Can't tonight. Unless I run away. If I run away, can I hide out in your basement for a while?"

"Jen, I'm coming over there."

"Don't. Just wait. I'll call again later, or tomorrow." Jen hung up before Therese could say anything more.

Therese hung up the phone and flapped her hands like she'd just washed them and there were no paper towels. "Oh my God." Then, in her mind, she screamed for Than.

His sudden appearance startled her. She leaned back in the bed with her hand on her mouth.

"I can't stay," he said, panting in his white trousers and open white shirt. "We're on a chase. The men from Peshawar. Can you hold on another hour or so?"

She saw the frantic look in his eyes and nodded. He vanished.

After saying goodnight to Carol and Richard, Therese went to her dresser and put on the crown, witnessing her own image disappear from the mirror. Then she slipped down the stairs and out the back door to Jen's.

Chapter Thirty-Four: Battle Rising

As soon as Therese was gone, Than clutched the hair on the heads of two men who had come to hide from his sister in the back of the warehouse in Peshawar. One of them stumbled and looked up in shock while the other shut his eyes as though waiting to be shot. Than pulled them to the center of the warehouse for their interrogation where Meg waited with her falcon.

McAdams was bound by Tizzie's serpent hair. The snakes twined around his neck and arms, hissing and flicking their tongues, dripping with the blood from his sister's eyes.

Alecto uttered a laugh of hysteria as she closed in on McAdams.

Before the gods could take the mortals' souls to the Underworld for further persecution in Tartarus, a flash of light washed over the building and the loud crack of a whip, as harsh as thunder, made Than flinch.

In the middle of the room stood Ares, accompanied by his twin sons, Phobos, also known as Panic, and Deimos, also known as Fear.

The Furies screamed a shrill, blood-curling shriek and disappeared, leaving Than alone to face the other gods.

"Hades wants these men!" Than said, standing his ground. "They belong to him!"

"You can have those two, but McAdams comes with me to Mount Olympus where I shall seek council with Zeus. Follow me if you wish."

Ares, his sons, and the mortal McAdams disappeared, leaving Than and his two terrified prisoners.

Chapter Thirty-Five: The Holts

The sun was setting behind the mountains across the lake, and a cool wind blew through the trees as Therese made her way down her gravelly drive to the dirt road leading to the Holts' place. She could hear her sneakers crunching against the pebbles and dirt, so she was invisible but not sound proof.

The horses were still out to pasture when she crept up the drive to the house where the one goat was tied to the rail by the front steps bleating like a child who hadn't been fed. A branch danced in the wind and scraped against the logs of the house, but, other than the bleating goat and the scraping tree, all was quiet.

Therese snuck to the back of the house and peered through the open window. She could see Mrs. Holt standing in the middle of the kitchen with her arms crossed, and then her hand moved to her mouth and stuck a fingernail between her teeth. She leaned against the kitchen sink like she was tired but too tense to sit down. Her bowl-shaped blonde-gray hair looked greasy, and the wrinkles in her face deeper than ever. Suddenly she walked across the kitchen, opened a cabinet, and took down a pack of cigarettes. She took the last from the pack and ditched the empty box in the trash. Her hands shook as she lit the end of the cigarette and sucked.

Bobby's voice cried, "But he's reformed now! He went to therapy! He said so himself!"

Therese couldn't see Bobby. She saw Pete leaning against the mantle of the fireplace. He wore a pair of ragged jeans and boots. His tight gray t-shirt was too short, like it belonged to Bobby and he had put in on by accident. He looked tired but tense, and as he ran his hand through his hair,

Therese had the feeling he'd been doing that motion all evening. "I just don't know," Pete said. "Mom, how do we know it won't happen again?"

Now she saw Bobby standing by the front door entryway with his hands open, like he was begging everyone to listen to him. He had a look of anguish and desperation, and again he said, "He went to therapy, Pete! He won't do it again!"

That's when she heard Mr. Holt say, "Y'all just think about it. Sleep on it. I'll come again tomorrow, see what y'all think. I'll go on back to the hotel now. Where's Jen?"

"She won't come out," Mrs. Holt said without looking up from the kitchen floor. "Just leave her be."

Then Therese saw Mr. Holt get up from wherever he had been sitting toward the back of their living room and walk to the entryway. He looked thin and old, and he didn't stand up straight. His gray hair made a shaggy ring around a glossy bald spot on top of his head. Bobby threw his arms around him before he had made it to the door.

"I've missed you, Daddy," Bobby cried. "I want you to stay. I know you can do it. I believe in you."

Mr. Holt hugged his son. He held the embrace for nearly a whole minute, his thin bowed figure looking slight beside his younger son. He said through tears, "I love you, Bobby. I love all my kids." Then he walked out without turning back to Pete or Mrs. Holt.

Mrs. Holt continued to lean against the kitchen sink and suck on her cigarette. Pete held himself up by the mantle. Bobby paced back and forth near the front door, seeming to fight an urge to run out and chase down his father. After several minutes of this, Mrs. Holt cried out, "Jen, come on out. He's gone now."

Therese watched Jen come down the stairs and walk straight into her mother's arms. Her eyes were red and swollen, her face pale, and her hair sticking out in all directions. She sobbed as she spoke. "I'm scared, Mom. Seeing him made it all come back. I thought I could handle it, but I can't."

Mrs. Holt held her cigarette away from her daughter with one hand and patted Jen's back with the other.

"He's reformed, Jen!" Bobby cried. "He hasn't had a drink in over a year. He only did those things when he was drunk."

"Leave her alone, Bobby," Pete muttered. "It didn't happen to you."

"It's her fault he left in the first place!" Bobby shouted. "If she'd only forgiven him!"

"That's enough!" Mrs. Holt snarled. "It's not her fault."

"And it's Pete's fault for telling!" Bobby cried.

"That's enough, Bobby!" Mrs. Holt snarled again, like a cornered animal.

"Mom," Jen said in small, shaky voice. "I think it's going to have to be him or me, and what I want to know is, who would you choose?"

"You, baby doll, every time," Mrs. Holt smoothed Jen's hair with a jittery hand. Then she lifted Jen's chin and asked, "But what I want to know is this: Doesn't everyone deserve a second chance? Can we just give it this one try?" Mrs. Holt put the trembling cigarette to her lips and sucked.

Jen looked like she was wilting, like she was a flower that would never stand straight in the vase again.

Therese sat outside of Jen's house in a wrought iron chair and watched the sun set behind the mountains across the lake. She wanted to knock on the door and talk to Jen, but she was afraid. She didn't know if Jen would feel like talking. So she sat there watching the sun sink behind the mountains, the hawks swoop back to their nests, and the deer come out of the trees. While she sat looking around, she thought how cruel and beautiful, how sweet and ugly, the world could be. She missed her parents, but was glad to have Than; she was sorry for Jen that her dad had returned, but was glad for Bobby; she

273

was sad for Vicki, but was glad her mother had found a way out of whatever pain life had brought her. Vicki's mom would go down to Erebus and forget everything and spend the rest of eternity in the Elysian Fields living whatever delusions of grandeur her soul desired. In Cairo, the sun was getting ready to rise over the Great Sphinx, and a new day would be dawning for Egypt, while here the sun was barely visible, and now, altogether gone behind the mountains.

"Let's bring those horses in before dark," Mrs. Holt said coming out of the house.

Therese froze. No one seemed to notice her. She watched the four forlorn figures make their way out to pasture.

While they were gone, she removed the crown and waited for Jen to get back. She had an idea. She knew what she should do.

"Artemis, if you can hear me, I hope you won't be offended by what I'm about to do."

Jen was the last of the Holts to make it back to the house, and none of them spoke a word till they spotted Therese sitting in that wrought iron chair on the side of the house, the bleating goat eyeing her from around the corner.

Pete was the first to spot her, and his face lit up like lighter fluid. "Therese! What a nice surprise." He fell into the chair beside her. The smile on his face couldn't erase the lines of worry or make him look less tired, but it was a small improvement.

"Hey, Pete."

The others caught up, one at a time, like they'd been walking in their own private worlds.

"Hey, Bobby," Therese said.

"Hey, Therese." Bobby kept walking into the house.

Mrs. Holt was next, and then came Jen, barely moving, like every step hurt.

"What's that you have in your hands?" Mrs. Holt stood, slight and bent, in front of her.

"Part of an old costume," Therese said. "I wanted to show it to Jen."

"It looks so real," Mrs. Holt said. "May I?"

She extended her leathery hands out for it, and Therese felt a panic coming on. What if Mrs. Holt put it on her head and everyone saw its effect? But what could Therese do, tell the poor woman no, you can't hold my crown?

Therese gave it to Mrs. Holt. Her heart thudded so loudly she thought for once the goat's bleating would be drowned out.

Mrs. Holt turned it around in her hands as Jen looked over her mother's shoulder. "It's so beautiful. It looks so...authentic. That must be some costume you have." Mrs. Holt handed it back, and Therese inwardly sighed with relief.

"Hey, Jen. Can I come up and visit with you awhile?"

Jen looked at her mother.

"Fine with me," her mother said.

Pete followed her into the house. When she glanced back at him, he smiled at her. He didn't seem to mind she was here to see Jen. He was just glad she was here.

Upstairs in Jen's bedroom, Therese kicked off her shoes and sat on the bedspread crisscross with the crown in her lap. Jen sat against a pile of pillows stacked by the headboard. Jen's eyes were still swollen and her face pale, and Therese noticed she had a sore on the corner of her mouth.

"I have something to show you," Therese said, her hands trembling a little. "Don't freak out, okay?"

"I can't promise anything."

"Listen, before I show you, let me explain. This is a special gift. I know this is going to sound crazy, but it has a special power. I'm not giving this to you, but I want to loan it to you."

"Therese, you're making it hard not to freak out. What are you talking about?"

Therese licked her lips. "First you have to promise me, I mean swear on our friendship and all you hold sacred, that you will never tell another soul about this."

"Okay, I'm officially freaked now."

"I'm serious."

"Me, too."

Therese sighed. "Don't be scared. I promise I wouldn't give you anything that could hurt you."

"Okay. I promise to keep your secret."

Therese's heart sped up as she lifted the crown toward her head. "Just watch what happens. And don't scream, okay?"

Jen nodded.

Therese put the crown on her head.

"Jesus! What the heck?"

"Sssh. Not too loud, Jen. I don't want your whole family running in here."

"Oh my God!" Jen jumped off the bed and backed into the corner of her room. "Okay, I'm really, really freaked. Where are you?" Jen accidentally bumped a stack off books off her table, then lost her balance and fell on the floor beside the strewn books. "Where are you?"

"I'm still here." Therese removed the crown from her head. "You want to try?"

Jen blinked. "This can't be happening." She carefully stood back up, her whole body trembling.

"Go on. Take it to your mirror and watch what happens."

With trembling hands, Jen took the crown from Therese and walked over to her mirror and placed the crown on her head.

"Holy crap!" Jen removed the crown. Then she returned it to her head. "Oh my holy crap!"

"Your crap ain't holy, Jen."

The two girls laughed, only one of them visible.

Jen took the crown off and turned to Therese. "Where'd you get this?"

"I can't tell. It's a secret."

Jen kept putting the crown on and off her head and watching her reflection disappear and reappear several more times. "I still can't believe it. I must be dreaming."

"I want to loan this to you because I was thinking…" she struggled to find the right words, "I was thinking that if your dad moves back home, you could wear this crown when you feel like disappearing."

Jen took the crown from her head and turned and looked at Therese, then her eyes gradually moved upward toward the ceiling, like she was figuring math. A smile curled onto her face and her eyes grew wide. Tears welled. She crossed the room and threw her arms around Therese. "I love you." Then she went back to the mirror, stood up a little straighter, and tried on the crown one more time.

The wind had picked up when Therese left the Holts' and walked down their property to the dirt road. Pete had offered to drive her—had practically begged—but Therese had said she wanted to walk, so Mrs. Holt had given her a flashlight and made her promise to call when she got there. Carol would freak if she knew, but of course Carol didn't know that the bad guys weren't after Therese. And without her invisibility crown, Therese would have to be extra careful when she reentered the house.

"Hold on, Therese!" Pete's voice called from the end of his gravelly drive. "Wait up a minute."

Therese stopped and shined her light on the ground in front of Pete, so he could see. He looked tall and muscular when he wasn't standing next to Than.

He came up close beside her, and the scent of him was strangely comforting. "Ooh, that wind is something, huh? A northern must be blowing in. Hey, you cold?"

"I'm okay." She *was* cold, and although it would feel good if he put his arm around her, it wouldn't be good for him. She should be discouraging him.

"You look pretty tonight. That a new shirt?"

She smoothed down the front of her purple knit top. "I've had it a while. Thanks." Then she looked at his shirt. "That Bobby's?"

"What? Oh, yeah. I'm behind on my laundry." Even in the darkness, Therese could see his face color.

"You do your own laundry? That's impressive," she teased.

"Yep. My mother is a slave driver." Then his voice softened. "Not really. She just wants us all to know how to take care of ourselves."

Therese nodded. "That's good."

"Hey, so how's Than? Seen him lately?"

Therese's heart contracted a little harder as she looked at Pete, and she felt sorry for him. She didn't want to add any more pain to his suffering. With his dad coming back and Bobby's anguish and Jen's trepidation, she knew Pete was hurting. She wished she could help. She felt guilty that she couldn't. "I saw Than earlier. He's, um, he's running an errand for his parents today." Never had that line seemed so literal.

Pete nodded. "I see." Then he asked, "He's leaving soon, right?"

Therese looked at the dirt road beneath their feet. "Yeah, I think so. In another week or so."

Then Pete dug the toe of his boot into the dirt and said, "I guess you heard about my dad."

Therese saw the pain in his face, his need for human affection and understanding, and she wanted to help. "Oh, Pete. I'm so sorry about all that. I wish I could..."

He put his arms around her and held her tight. "You're a sweetheart for saying that, but there's nothing anybody can do." With his face in her hair, he breathed in deeply, like he was taking in her scent, and then he released her with his breath. "It was good to see you again. Come by more often, okay?"

She felt guilty for feeling good in his arms. She had always liked Pete. If Than hadn't come into her life, he would have been a natural partner for her. "I will." Then she watched him turn and head back up the drive. She sighed and headed home.

Therese was glad she had been able to help Jen, but she knew the situation around the Holt family would be tense for a while, maybe even forever. She didn't know exactly what it was Mr. Holt had done to his daughter when he was drunk, but her imagination made her shudder. Bobby had said that Pete was the one who had told, so that meant Jen hadn't. Therese now wondered how long Jen had kept silent. She also wondered how miserable it had made Pete to rat out his own father in order to protect his sister.

A low roar, like a train, came from the lake. Therese shined the small circle of light across the grassy field toward the reservoir. By the light from the stars and the half moon in the sky, she saw deer running away from the water, across the dirt road, and up the mountains behind the houses. The roar grew louder, like the train was upon her. Now chipmunks scurried across the road, and the ground beneath her trembled. An earthquake? She looked all around her as panic set in. She wanted to run like the animals, but her feet were like bricks, and so she stood there, waiting.

Then she had this thought: Maybe Artemis was angry that Therese had loaned her gift to Jen.

"Pete?" She shined her light toward the Holts' driveway, but Pete was no longer in sight. She ran toward the driveway. "Pete?" Nothing.

She ran toward her house, the ground quaking beneath her feet. The dirt road cracked.

"Than!" Therese called. But before she could cry out his name again, a giant wall of cold water washed over her. It entered her mouth before she had gotten air. She lost her footing and dropped the flashlight. Underwater, she couldn't see. Her body tumbled and turned, and her hair whipped and clung to her face. She frantically tried to gain control by swimming, but she didn't know which way was up or down. Something like a tree branch scraped against her midriff, cutting the skin. She swam away from the force pulling her, but she couldn't even tell if she was making progress, and she needed air and couldn't find it.

Water entered her mouth and her throat burned and scratched, like sandpaper on fire, hard and hot and scraping everything it touched. She writhed in the water, as her father had the night he died.

All of a sudden she saw her parents drowning in front of her: her father turning his head side to side in a wild frenzy and her mother silently yielding to the terrible depths that took her. Therese called to Than in her mind as the darkness overpowered her, and she lost consciousness.

Chapter Thirty-Six: Ambush

At the gates of Mount Olympus, Than and his sisters had amassed an army to recapture McAdams from Ares and his sons. Than's heart thudded with fierce determination, for he knew that if Therese could not avenge her parents' death upon McAdams, she would never be his bride.

As soon as the Furies had left Peshawar, they had flown straight to their cousin Hermes, who had further solicited help from Demeter, Persephone, and Hecate.

But their greatest ally was Aphrodite, who stood in all her beauty, waiting for Ares, who loved her.

She was also the mother of Phobos and Deimos, who obeyed her.

When the god of war appeared at the gates with his sons and the prisoner, ready for battle, he was caught off guard by the beautiful sight of his one true love.

"Go, boys," Aphrodite said. "This is between Ares and me."

Phobos and Deimos vanished.

"Will you betray me?" Ares said gently.

"What you do is wrong, my love," Aphrodite said.

"No. What you do is wrong. Don't interfere. Humans can never rise to greatness without the challenges of the gods! Now stand back and let me through, you coddlers!"

Ares made to charge, but at once, Than and his sisters and his mother and grandmother, along with Hermes and Hecate, descended upon him in a cloud of determination and will, and it took every one of them to bind back the arms of the god of war and recapture McAdams.

Ares roared and pulled free and jumped up into the sky above them and laughed. "Take him. I have a better prisoner."

At that moment, Than heard Therese's cries from below. With bitter hatred, he narrowed his eyes at the god of war and shouted, "What have you done?"

"You'll soon discover." Ares disappeared.

Chapter Thirty-Seven: Poseidon

Therese awoke on a cold hard rock in the middle of a vast, unending ocean. She and her rock were the only things she could see for miles. She was cold and wet. Her shorts and shirt stuck to her like glue, her sneakers were filled with water, and she shivered uncontrollably. Was she dreaming?

She stood up on the rock to see if she could fly, but her feet barely lifted from the ground, she lost her balance, and she fell backward into the cold, salty water. She resurfaced, spitting mouthfuls of the yucky salt water, and clambered onto the rock. Now she was even colder, and her teeth chattered, and she shivered even more than she had before.

In her mind, she cried for Than, and she asked what had happened. She asked him where she was and would he please, please, please come and take her home. She clutched the golden locket around her neck thinking she was the least powerful creature in the world right now.

Five feet away, a man emerged, waist high, from the water. His sun-bleached hair clung to his head and neck, and his sun-bleached beard dripped nearly down to his bare chest. He appeared to be about fifty. His eyes were the blue-green color of the sea and his lips sun-burnt red and his skin bronze. His nostrils flared with anger as he lifted his trident from the water, about to speak.

Therese could guess now who he was.

"I could kill you this instant!" he roared like thunder.

His voice had startled her, and she clutched the locket around her neck, but then she took a breath and calmed herself down.

Although she preferred to go to the Underworld as a god, she wasn't as afraid of death as she had once been, before her parents were killed. *Before my parents were killed.* She had actually allowed herself to think the words she hadn't been able to think in over a month? *My parents were killed.* It was a small victory, but it made her feel like maybe she wasn't the *very* least powerful person in the world.

Poseidon raised his trident even higher, above his head.

Therese closed her eyes and waited. She couldn't believe that Poseidon was her enemy, because of all the gods she had ever read about, he had been her favorite. As a swimmer and lover of ocean life, she had always thought of him as an imaginary guardian, certainly not the foe facing her now. She had chosen him for her sixth grade mythology project.

In her mind, she was talking to him without realizing it. "You were my friend," she thought. "I've always looked up to you and aspired to be like you. I love the sea and marine life. I love to swim through water. It makes me feel so free. I used to think that if I had a past life, I must have been a dolphin, and my dream has been to go to Sea World in San Antonio and swim with dolphins. And I remember reading that you gave the horse to humankind. I love horses and help take care of my friend's horses. We lost Dumbo last week. It was so sad and I'll miss him, but I'm thankful to have known him, and I'm thankful that you brought humans and horses together. How can you, of all the gods, be my enemy? It seems unnatural. You're my idol.

"But I guess if I'm going to die now, it's fitting that it is in water. That's where my parents died, and maybe I should have died with them. I realize now Dumbo also died in water. That's strange. Anyway, I started this life in water, in my mother's womb, and now I'll end it in water. That's almost poetic.

"I do wish I could say goodbye to my aunt. I wish I could find Clifford and bring him with me. I wish I could say goodbye to Puffy and Jewels and my human friends. I wish I could see Vicki and help her deal with her mother's suicide. I wish I could be there to watch over Jen when her dad moves home. I wish I could spend eternity with Than as his wife."

284

Oh, Than! She thought of his perfect face and his strong body and the soft touch of his hands. She recalled the pleasure he had taken with his face turned up to the rain, his body moving effortlessly through the cool water of the lake, his expression of delight as he tasted her salad, the sugared iced tea, the brownies, and the other foods he had tried for the first time. She remembered their first waltz and his eagerness to learn. And she thought of the joy they took together in watching three sunsets and a sunrise in a single day. She longed to be in his arms, safe in his warm embrace.

She stood there shivering on the rock waiting for Poseidon to kill her. Why hadn't he done it yet? She opened her eyes.

Poseidon's expression had changed. His nostrils no longer flared, and he lowered his trident back into the sea, his arms hanging limp beside him.

"I do not wish to be your enemy," he said in a voice that wasn't gentle, but wasn't harsh.

I don't understand, she said to him in her mind.

"I am obliged to Ares," Poseidon said. "I swore an oath on the river Styx."

Oh. So she *would* die in water like her parents. "Are you going to kill me?"

"No. I'm to deliver you to Mount Olympus."

Therese should have been frightened by this, but she was elated.

"Before we go, I want to give you a gift, to prove I bear no personal animosity toward you." He waved his trident in the air, and a herd of dolphins sprang from the water and surrounded her rock with their heads above the surface and their eyes on her. She wished she had Than's power of understanding animal languages as they clicked their greetings to her. There must have been a dozen of them, with their mouths open in a perpetual grin, clicking their hellos.

285

"Hello," she said shyly. Then to Poseidon, she said, "What a wonderful gift. Thank you for giving me the chance to see the dolphins up close." She wished she could touch one, but she didn't want to ask and appear ungrateful.

Poseidon laughed. "I appreciate your gratitude and humility," he said, still laughing. "But my gift is better still. Would you care to ride on a dolphin's back across the sea to Greece?"

"Would I!" she shouted with glee. And to think she had just wanted to touch one. She would ride one, like they did at Sea World, something she had read about on the Internet a few years ago. "Yes! Thank you very much! What? Do I dive in?"

Poseidon laughed again, and now that he no longer had a stern face, he appeared quite beautiful. "I've never seen a happier prisoner. Yes. Dive into the water."

Therese was so excited that she dove in and swam the dolphin kick between the rock and the circle of dolphins. She added her butterfly arms so she could catch breaths of air in between her strokes, and then she swam up to the closest dolphin.

"You're a skilled swimmer," Poseidon noted. "It pleases me to see humans move so naturally in the water. I wish more were able. It bothers me that so many don't even know how to swim. The Earth is mostly water, you know."

She treaded water, her teeth chattering with the cold. "Y-y-yes. Th-thank you. Is th-there a p-p-articular d-d-dolphin I sh-should r-ride?"

"Arion there will take you. He's named for one of my sons."

The dolphin dipped his head to her in greeting.

Excited, thrilled, and totally overjoyed, Therese climbed onto the dolphin's back. His skin was slick and rubbery and hard to grasp. Her bare legs kept sliding off. She wished she had worn jeans instead of shorts.

"Hold onto his dorsal fin," Poseidon said, moving closer. "I will wrap a golden net around you and Arion's body. The net will keep you attached should you slip. It will allow you to stay underwater for long periods of time. It will also keep you warm." He raised his trident, and the net, like a fisherman's net but golden, encircled her and Arion.

The warmth instantly soothed her, and a low moan escaped her lips. The relief from the chilling cold was itself a gift. Her muscles relaxed, she took in larger breaths, and she could actually enjoy the feeling of sitting on the dolphin's back. She hugged him, circled her legs around him, kissed his wet rubbery skin, and said to Arion, "Thank you in advance. This is one of the most amazing moments of my life."

Several other dolphins swam up to her and rubbed their bodies against her. She extended her fingers through one of the openings between the weave in the net and stroked them. They clicked sounds of affection, and in reply, Therese said, "This is heaven."

"Are you ready?" Poseidon asked.

She was scared and excited all at once, and she was as ready as she would ever be. The golden net was surprisingly light and flexible. She lifted her head from the dolphin's back to face Poseidon. "Yes sir."

"We'll stop at my palace at the bottom of the sea first. It is a halfway point between this rock and Mount Olympus. Do you know where we are?"

Therese shook her head.

"The Aegean Sea. My palace is at the bottom, you see. I want to fetch my chariot. I prefer to travel over land on it. It makes for an exhilarating ride." He raised his trident. "To my palace!"

With that, Arion and the company of dolphins sprang into the air and dove down into the water with Poseidon in the lead. She could see him in front of her, swimming like a dolphin, his hair and beard flowing from his head and his green sarong flowing from his waist. He wore leather sandals that extended from his feet like flippers.

Below them the ocean world came into view. Her eyesight was improved, though she wasn't sure how. Was it the golden net that allowed her to see so many details of this spectacular vision? Fingers of purple, blue, and gold waved to them, and fish of many shapes, colors, and sizes darted this way and that, some in large schools, and others, like the huge groupers suspended near the bottom, alone. Occasionally, she caught sight of a barracuda or a shark, but most of the sea life was nonthreatening. Sea anemones and coral decorated the ocean floor where the sunbeams barely hit. Oh, she could just make out a cluster of starfish. And, ah! Look at those jellyfish! And there! A manatee! The most curious to Therese were the sea horses and their curly tails.

As they swam closer to the ocean floor, she was able to see other forms of marine life burrowing in the sand and rocks. Sting rays there! Hermit crabs! A lobster! And over there, eels, like the figments in her dreams!

Arion dodged a rock formation full of shadows and fluttered over another city of coral. Then he turned sideways as they passed through a rocky tunnel in a matter of seconds. Past the tunnel was a deep drop in the ocean floor—so deep Therese could see nothing beyond the darkness.

Into the darkness they plunged.

Although the golden net kept Therese warm, she could feel a drop in temperature as they plunged deeper and deeper into the darkness. She held on to Arion, wondering for the first time if Poseidon planned to keep her as an underwater prisoner so that she would never see the light of day again.

Then she realized this is how it would be when she was the queen of death in the Underworld: dark, gloomy, airless. A shudder made its way down her spine, and she pressed her face against Arion's back.

"I'm scared," she thought.

A new vision presented itself to her. Bright golden lights came from the *bottom* of the ocean, illuminating an amazing transparent structure. Its walls seemed to be formed from clear crystals, and it made her think of an aquarium. This must be Poseidon's palace. Without entering, she could see many figures inside of it—merfolk with tails and other, more human-like, people sitting among the furniture, eating at tables on golden chairs, and lounging on beds clustered in curtains of seaweed growing up from the ocean floor. At the back of the palace, the walls were no longer transparent and were made of something like shell, perhaps mother-of-pearl. Poseidon disappeared behind the shell wall as she waited on Arion's back, and before she had a chance to scan over the other figures a second time, a flash of white bolted toward her.

Three white stallions the color of sea foam and wearing harnesses of gold halted before her, hurling a current of water all about her. Then Poseidon appeared. "Let go of the dolphin," he commanded, after which he unwrapped the golden net from Arion and secured the net around her.

As Arion swam away, Therese cried to him, "Thank you!" and surprisingly, she could hear herself perfectly underwater. Then she turned to Poseidon. "That ride was spectacular. Thank you so much!"

"You're welcome. And I apologize in advance for what I'm about to do."

Despite the ominous sense of foreboding she felt after Poseidon's words, she asked cheerfully, "What are your horses' names?"

"Riptide, Seaquake, and Crest."

"May I pet them?"

He nodded, so she reached her fingers through a hole in the weave of her net and touched the flank of each horse. "Hello," she said softly. "How are you? You are all so beautiful."

Poseidon led her into his golden chariot, and before she had even sat on the bench behind his large, standing body, they took off in sudden lightning speed.

Up from the depths of the ocean they went, and then they were riding along the surface of the sea as though they were in a boat and not a golden chariot being pulled by horses. The wind whipped against Therese's face, and she squinted against it. For the first time since she had awakened, she could see land. Within minutes, they rushed onto a deserted beach and dodged past rocks and trees. When they neared a city, they rose above it, flying in the air. Therese peered down at the buildings and streets and cars and people below. She wondered if the people could see them flying over Greece. She looked ahead once again as a cluster of mountain peaks came into view. A light fog covered the highest of these, and the sunbeams against the fog created a majestic hue, a circle of light, like an enormous halo.

Mount Olympus, Therese thought as she gasped at the beautiful sight. And she hoped already there and waiting for her would be Than.

Chapter Thirty-Eight: Mount Olympus

Poseidon stopped the chariot before a giant wall of clouds at the top of Mount Olympus. Nothing but white stretched up and into the sky. Poseidon said, "Spring, Summer, Winter, and Fall, open the gates of Olympus so I, Poseidon, may enter with my prisoner."

A loud roar carried through the air, and a tunnel of cold wind lifted in front of them, startling Therese. At its center was a single rain cloud. As the wind settled and the rain cloud emptied its contents right before their eyes and then dissipated, the giant wall of clouds opened, and Poseidon drew the chariot forward. The wall of clouds closed behind them, and, in front of them, at the center of a golden-paved plaza, was a round fountain spraying water into the blue sky from the spout of a golden whale. At the top of this fountain, where the water arched and fell into a pool bordered with golden bricks, was a rainbow. Therese looked on with amazement.

Behind this fountain was a giant palace of white stone and ornate columns. To the right and left of the palace were separate buildings, as tall, but not as wide or deep. Poseidon guided the chariot to the right of the fountain to one of these separate buildings. The golden doors were latched open, revealing two golden chariots parked on either side with a space in between, into where Poseidon now backed his chariot.

"It looks like Hades beat us here," the god of the sea mumbled. "And Zeus's chariot has a new ding. Wonder where that came from, and if he knows of it."

A beautiful young man with long thick eyelashes and golden curls stepped forward to unbridle the horses.

After he had the chariot free of the animals, Poseidon said, "I'll take them to the stables myself, Cupid. I think my prisoner would enjoy the tour."

Cupid gave a subtle bow and disappeared.

So that was Cupid. She wondered if Cupid knew that *she* knew he had pierced Pete's heart.

Poseidon kept the golden net around Therese as he helped her from his chariot. She noticed the sandals on his feet had retracted so they no longer formed flippers for swimming. With the three stallions tied to leads, Poseidon led her and Riptide, Seaquake, and Crest across the golden-paved plaza, passing the center fountain, to the other building separate from the palace. It was the same size as the chariot shed and had the same type of golden doors latched open at the entry. As the god of the sea led his horses into the building, which Therese now recognized as stables, Therese caught sight of Than standing among a group of people at the back stall near two black horses.

"Therese!" Than said, rushing to her side.

She had barely time to blink from the moment she saw him, and now he was putting his arms around her with the golden fishermen's net between them. Her hair had dried during the journey, and it curled wildly from having dried in the beating wind. Than put his fingers through an opening in the weave to touch her hair and hold it between two fingers.

"I'm glad to see you safe," he said softly.

Her heart warmed at the sight of him, and she longed to wrap her arms around him, but the net prevented her. She gazed into his eyes and whispered, "I missed you."

"I missed you, too," he whispered back. "I'm sorry it's come to this, but I promise to protect you."

From the direction of the black horses came another man, tall like Than, but older-looking, with the same dark hair, but eyes as black as coal, and a short beard. Like Than and the other gods, he was beautiful. He walked over to Therese with an air of authority. "So, son, I finally meet your sweetheart," he said.

This was Hades, Than's father. "How do you do?" she said.

"Better than you, apparently," he replied.

"This wasn't what we had in mind," Than murmured. "She wanted to play her flute for you, feed you chocolate. This has gone all wrong."

"Better to meet like this than not at all," Therese said bravely.

"Oh boy, an optimist," Hades said with sarcasm.

Therese's face flushed. She could see the red color rise all the way to the tip of her nose.

"And sensitive to boot," he spoke again.

"Dad, can you lighten up?" Than kept his arm on Therese.

The god of the Underworld turned his attention to the god of the sea who lingered near the stall where the latter boarded his white horses. "Poseidon."

"Hades."

They each gave the other a civil nod.

During this exchange, Therese noticed Meg and Tizzie standing with their prisoner in the back of the stable. The third sister was there as well. She had fire-red hair that stood up in a Mohawk, deep black eyes, and a choker of black stones around her neck. All three Furies wore tall black heeled boots and short skirts. Tizzie wore her emeralds and Meg her rubies, and their hair was down and wild. A large bird sat perched on Meg's shoulder, and a wolf stood beside Tizzie.

The man in the middle of them she recognized as McAdams. Therese's eyes grew wide, and hot tears flooded them as she faced the mastermind behind her parents' death. She would kill him. She would make him pay. Though now, as she looked at him—short, thin, bald, with spectacles and wearing a suit that looked too big—he seemed terrified, pathetic, and about to pee in his pants.

"We will take the prisoner to court," the redheaded Alecto, said, and then the Furies and their prisoner disappeared.

293

"Poseidon," Than sneered his greeting.

"Thanatos." Poseidon gave him a tired nod. "I will entrust my lovely prisoner to you for now. You cannot break the spell of the golden net, so I have no fear of losing her, especially here among so many." And with that, Poseidon vanished.

"Don't be mad at him," Therese whispered. "He was kind to me."

Than scowled. "Some kindness. Don't you realize what he's done?"

She shook her head. "No. Oh my God, what?"

Hades turned toward the back of the stables. "Cupid, make sure my black stallions get the same amount of oats as Poseidon and Zeus's beasts. I won't tolerate special treatment, understand?"

Cupid appeared in front of him and gave a slight bow. "As always."

"I'll see you at court," Hades said to Than and Therese, and then he disappeared.

"So what's Poseidon done?" Therese asked.

"Come on," Than said. "They're all waiting for us."

Therese trembled with fear as they entered the golden-paved plaza and walked past the fountain to seven steps, each a different color of the rainbow, starting with red and ending with violet. Her new fears made it difficult for her to appreciate the two giant columns flanking the entryway, and, just inside, the magnificent foyer. But her eyes opened wide and she did not fail to notice as she stepped into a large rectangular assembly hall open to the clear blue sky, from which nearly solid beams of sunshine shot down to form a bright canopy above them.

Therese looked down from the sky to the white marble floor as she followed Than past Hades into the hall. Hades stood just inside with the Furies and their prisoner nearby. As Than and Therese passed them, a golden chair ascended from the floor, and Hades sat on it. It was apparently his throne. He sat opposite the long hall from two gods whom Therese presumed were Zeus and his queen, Hera.

"Should I kneel or something?" Therese asked Than, staying close beside him.

"No. I'll introduce you to each god, one by one," Than whispered. "Just give a subtle bow. Don't go deep. They despise groveling." Then Than spoke in a surprisingly loud and confident voice. "Gods and goddesses of the court, with your permission, it is my pleasure to introduce you to Therese Mills."

Zeus gave a nod. "Please bring her before each of us, beginning with Aphrodite to your left."

"Therese, I present you to Aphrodite, the goddess of love," Than said.

Still wrapped in the golden fishermen's net, Therese stood before Aphrodite and gave her a bow. The goddess of love was the most beautiful of all gathered there. Her hour-glass figure was accentuated by the white, form-fitting gown that ended just above her delicate sandaled feet. Without speaking, Therese met her crystal blue eyes and mouthed, "Thank you." Before now, Therese hadn't been able to properly thank the goddess for curing Clifford and leaving her the traveling robe. Aphrodite flipped her blond hair from her creamy bare shoulder and gave Therese a smile of pleasure, then dipped her head in polite greeting.

Than continued. "To Aphrodite's left is the goddess of the woods, Artemis."

Therese took four steps and faced the goddess on her throne. Also beautiful, her eyes and her gown were deep green, like the color of pine needles, and her brown hair was fastened into a knot on her head, a few stray hairs caressing her neck. Therese gave her subtle bow and again mouthed, "Thank you." Artemis bowed in return.

To Artemis's left was a double throne, and on it sat a mother and daughter, very similar in appearance, with golden brown eyes and hair the color of corn. Their hair was long and straight, as were their gowns of pale pastels. Than introduced them as his grandmother, Demeter, goddess of the harvest, and his mother, Persephone, queen of the Underworld.

"She's lovely," Persephone said.

To their left sat a red-haired, brown-eyed goddess whose gown reminded Therese of Alice in Wonderland in that it was blue with a white apron. Than introduced her as Hestia, goddess of the hearth, Zeus's unmarried sister.

To the left of Hestia and to the right of Zeus sat gray-eyed, black-haired Athena, whom Therese immediately recognized. Therese clutched the locket at her throat, and as she had done with Aphrodite and Artemis, mouthed, "Thank you," before she bowed to the goddess.

Zeus and Hera sat together on a double throne at the center back of the great hall, and though all the thrones were ornamental in design, theirs stood out because of the golden birds perched behind them. Behind Zeus perched a golden ruby-eyed eagle, and behind Hera three golden finches. Both gods gave their subtle bow after Therese gave hers.

Therese detected a hint of snarl in Than's voice as he introduced red-haired Ares, the god of war, who, along with McAdams, was responsible for her parents' death. Ares showed no anger or emotion as he gave his bow at his introduction. He was as beautiful as the other gods and as civil and polite.

Therese recognized Hermes, who winked at her when he was introduced, producing a broad smile across her face. Her smile lingered when she faced Poseidon next, for despite the fact that he was the god who had captured her, she would be forever grateful for the dolphin ride across the sea.

Beside Poseidon, across the hall from his twin sister Artemis, sat the most beautiful god of all the males. Than introduced him as Apollo, god of truth, of music, and of healing. He held his lyre upon his lap. His eyes were the same evergreen as his sister's, and his hair was the same golden brown. Next to Apollo, and directly across from Aphrodite, was Aphrodite's husband, Hephaestus, the god of the forge, who appeared opposite to Apollo in every way. Whereas Apollo looked young, Hephaestus seemed old; where Apollo looked strong and erect, Hephaestus appeared bowed and misshapen. His hands were gnarled and calloused, his black hair streaked with gray, and his black eyes lined with dark circles and bags beneath them. He was the only god among them not beautiful. Therese gave her bow, and he his.

The Furies moved away from their father, pulling their prisoner to the center of the hall, so that Than and Therese could stand before Hades. Although he had already introduced them in the stables, Than formally presented her here before the other gods.

Hades gave a deeper bow than the others and surprised Therese by saying, "It is a pleasure to meet you, Therese. I speak on behalf of all the gods when I welcome you to our court. I am only sorry that it could not be under better circumstances." He gave Therese a pleasant smile, and his coal black eyes sparkled in the sunlight.

Zeus cleared his throat. "Thank you, Hades. Thanatos, bring the prisoner to the center of the hall beside the Furies and the other prisoner." He then addressed the others "I believe all present are aware of the situation at hand. The Furies want to avenge the death of two souls by punishing their killer, Steven McAdams. Ares and Poseidon have captured Therese Mills in attempt to negotiate for McAdams's release. The girl for the man. We shall first hear from Ares, then Hades, and finally, Poseidon. If other Olympians have opinions, we will hear them, but remember that only the Olympian gods may speak in a court hearing unless I say otherwise. We will then come to our decision and pronounce our judgment. Ponder this: should Hades take both, one, or neither mortal soul before us?"

Therese gasped. None of the outcomes would allow her to avenge her parents' death and become a god. If Hades took McAdams's soul, Than's deal with his father would become impossible to carry out. You can't kill a soul. And if McAdams were granted his freedom by this court, how would she find and kill him on her own? Wouldn't the gods have to honor the judgment of the court? Wouldn't that mean Than and his sisters would be prohibited from helping her? She looked at Than, and he met her eyes with sympathetic understanding.

"No," she said in her mind to all of the gods around her. "I can't let this happen." She clutched her golden locket and waited.

Ares stood before his throne. "I do not deny the clear discrepancy between these two prisoners. One is vile, contemptible, though he has served me well; the other, kind and good. But sometimes good people must be sacrificed for the greater good. You all know as well as I that human power must be spread through many countries, and one among them has become too strong. It is no secret that I believe the fall of the United States will set this imbalance straight. McAdams, the prisoner who was not introduced and who cowers there in the middle like a pathetic toad, must be spared the torments of hell because in his crimes he served me. To make my demands more appealing, Poseidon and I have taken as our prisoner the object of Thanatos's desire. We will free her upon the release of McAdams and with an oath upon the river Styx to never enact that punishment upon him." Ares returned to his throne.

Therese felt herself go limp. Than's hand was fast around her waist. Ares was a persuasive speaker. She felt all hope was lost. She could never become a god and spend eternity with Than if the gods agreed with Ares. She had to be permitted to avenge her parents' death.

Hades now stood and took a few steps toward the middle of the hall. "Since when has Ares cared about the fate of his human instruments? He's not here to protect McAdams. His real purpose is less noble. He knows that my son, Thanatos, struck a bargain with me. I swore on the river Styx to make his sweetheart a god if she personally avenged the death of her parents. Ares fears the conflict that might ensue, the leverage he may lose among us, if the daughter of his victims were to become like him. In fact, he would

298

rather see me take both souls now and damn McAdams to a fate worse than that of Tantalus than see Therese Mills become a god. My daughters, the Furies, have learned that this cowering toad, as Ares has so perfectly described him, has been manufacturing and selling fake medicines to humans. Think of all those other souls in my care who have died because they did not have their proper drugs. If justice is our concern today, then choose justice. I urge you all to free the girl and watch her avenge the death of her parents and the death of those not represented here today."

Therese perked up with renewed hope. She felt a new respect for Than's father, and, in her mind, she prayed to him, "Thank you, Hades. That was an awesome speech."

As he took his seat upon his throne, Hades met her eyes and gave her a subtle nod.

Zeus cleared his throat. "Poseidon?"

All eyes turned to the god of the sea who now stood before his throne. "I have nothing to add. I defer my turn to my cohort, Ares." Poseidon sat back down.

Ares stood and said, "I see the merit in Hades's speech."

Therese's mouth dropped open in surprise. She looked up into Than's eyes, but he seemed wary.

Ares continued. "Hades agreed to make the girl a god, and his condition was that she should avenge the death of her parents. But I ask you, would that be accomplished by allowing her to simply walk up to him, imprisoned, and slit his throat? Haven't the Furies already done the hardest part of the avenging? They have worked day and night tracking his whereabouts, and they have taken him captive. What role has the girl played in any of that? And so she walks up and cuts his throat and that merits her to be here among us gods? Any pathetic wight could do the same."

"What do you propose?" Zeus asked.

299

Therese's face fell. She looked again at Than and met his worried eyes. This was not going well at all.

"I propose," Ares started, "that we place the two of them in a contained arena with invisible walls far from civilizations; that we allow them each the same weapons—a sword and shield—equitable in all ways; that the gods may watch and make suggestions, but not intervene; and that these two humans fight to the death. The victor lives and is set free; the loser goes straight to the Underworld, a soul among the dead."

"That's barbaric!" Aphrodite cried.

"Unfathomable!" Apollo shouted.

"Fair!" Hades said. "But I say let the girl choose between these three: first, set them both free to live and find their fates without interference from the gods; or, second, have me take both souls to the Underworld, neither made a god nor given his just punishment; or, last, fight the battle to the death, as Ares has suggested. If the girl chooses the latter and wins, she becomes a god."

"Agreed!" Ares snapped, eagerly it seemed to Therese.

Than gave Therese a hint of a smile, but she could not return it. Maybe he assumed she would choose the first and live a safe, and perhaps long, life. But it would be a life without him, for her chances of finding McAdams and killing him on her own were so remote as to be insignificant. Maybe he assumed she would choose the second and go peacefully with him to the Underworld a dead, unfree, soul. She doubted he thought she would choose the third.

"What?" he whispered.

She shook her head.

Zeus then said, "So, Therese, which do you choose?"

She walked to the center of the hall and looked around at each of the gods, settling her gaze on Ares. "If I choose the third—"

"What?" Than shouted. He ran to her side. "Don't even consider it! Therese! Listen to me. McAdams will kill you. He's small, but stronger than you. You might suffer abominable---"

"Let the girl speak," Ares said.

Therese bit her lip. "If I choose the third, to fight McAdams to the death, which I have a feeling is the choice you most prefer, will you swear on the river Styx to protect my aunt and all my loved ones until they die their natural deaths?"

"You have my word," Ares said with obvious satisfaction.

She met Than's pleading eyes. "No, Therese," he begged. "Don't do this. Choose the first. I'll find a way to come back for you."

If she chose the first, McAdams would be forever hunting her and her aunt. She didn't want to live a life in fear. Plus, there would be little hope of killing McAdams without the Furies' help, which meant life without Than.

If she chose the second, she would die a painless death and join her parents in the Underworld, but there would be no chance of a happily-ever-after with Than since her personality and freedom would be gone.

If she were to choose the third and die at McAdams's hand, she would join her parents in the Underworld. And if she were to succeed in killing him, she would become a god and be with Than forever. Plus Ares would guarantee the safety of her loved ones regardless of the outcome. With the third choice, she couldn't lose.

Her heart hammered in her chest. "I choose the third," she said. "I choose to fight."

Artemis and Athena lifted their fists simultaneously and shouted, with smiling faces, "Yes!"

Aphrodite covered her face with her hands and wept.

Ares smiled triumphantly.

The others looked wary, even afraid for her.

Chapter Thirty-Nine: More Gifts

"Then let us proceed," Zeus commanded, lifting his arms.

"Wait!" Than objected. "Permission to speak, Lord Zeus."

"Permission granted."

"Both of the prisoners are exhausted and hungry. Ares will see a better fight if he permits them one more meal and night of rest." He looked at the other gods and then back at Therese, unable to believe that it had come to this.

"Hear, hear!" several shouted all at once.

"Agreed!" Ares said. "The battle should begin in twelve hours. That will give Hephaestus plenty of time to wield two equal weapons and two equal shields all made from the same metal."

"But before we adjourn," Hades said, "I need clarification. Ares said the gods may watch and make suggestions but not intervene. Specifics, please."

Everyone turned to Ares. "Yes. We need specifics," Ares agreed. "We shall be an audience like that in the Roman coliseum of old. We can watch from our thrones and shout our suggestions and encouragement. But no gifts shall we give them! No magic help at all! We may encourage and offer guidance, but the humans must fight without magic. Are all agreed? Are these rules specific enough?"

"Hear, hear!" several exclaimed.

"Agreed!" Hades said above them all. "Now remove the net from your prisoner!"

As soon as the golden net vanished, Therese flung her arms around Than. "I'm so sorry!"

He held her tight and dipped his head to kiss her shoulder, feeling that this would be the last, the very last chance he would have to hold her as she truly was, as a full and complete being. He felt tears stinging his eyes and desperation gripping his heart. He had come so close to finding love and happiness for all eternity. So close. He would have been better to never have met her. Then he wouldn't now be possessed by such pain and anguish.

"Why are *you* sorry? I'm the one who got you into this disaster!" He held her more tightly. "You chose to fight to be with me. If gods could die, I would die right now of grief."

"You have a lot of confidence in me," Therese said.

Aphrodite's weeping continued to sound throughout the hall.

"I'm sorry," Than replied. "I shouldn't be so pessimistic. Of course you have a chance of winning."

"It's slim, but it's there," she murmured.

Others had gathered around them, so she lifted her face from Than's and separated her body from his. He felt he would cry.

Poseidon spoke first. "You may sleep in my chambers, Therese. I prefer my palace beneath the sea." He gave her a friendly smile and touched her shoulder in a fatherly way.

"That's so nice of you," she said meekly.

"And I will weave you fresh sheets from silk," Athena said. "They will help you sleep." Athena fingered the locket around Therese's neck. "Like this gift, they are not magical, only comfortable and soothing. I will have them ready in an hour."

It brought Than great pleasure to see the goddess's support of Therese.

"I'm so grateful," Therese said.

"And I will serve you a delicious, filling meal," Hestia said, with eyes that were pools of chocolate. "Just come to the banquet hall when you are ready to eat."

"Thank you," Therese said to Hestia, whose red hair reminded Than of Therese's.

To Than, she said, without speaking, "I'm so sorry. She's so lovely."

"And you shall use my pillow," Artemis offered to Therese. "It is made of the softest goose feathers." Artemis's evergreen eyes against her fair skin stood out like the first leaves do in the melting spring snow.

"That sounds lovely," Therese said. "Thanks so much."

To Than's mind, Artemis communicated, "She is strong. Stay hopeful."

"And I will play my lyre in my chamber beside yours," Apollo said to Therese. "You will hear the soft lullaby through the walls."

Than was overwhelmed by the support of so many. Apollo was a great ally, and Than would remember this.

"That would be comforting," Therese said in her sweet voice.

Apollo's mind was full of sympathy for Than, "Hold her while you can."

"And I shall harmonize on my pipe," Hermes said, "from the chamber on the other side."

Hermes winked at her, like a kind uncle, and Than felt himself moved by his generosity.

"Thank you so much," she said. "I'm truly grateful."

Aphrodite wiped her beautiful eyes and said, "And I will lend you my silk eye mask. It will keep light away and soothe your tired eyes."

Therese said, "Oh, I will definitely need that. Thank you."

To Than, Aphrodite silently communicated, "I am full of the greatest sorrow."

"And before you sleep," Persephone said to Therese, "my mother and I shall bathe you in warm mineral water to relax your tired bones."

Both mother and daughter, with their long hair of corn and their deep chestnut eyes, put a hand on Therese's shoulders, and Than saw the family they might have made.

"That sounds so nice. I don't know how to thank you enough."

Hades took his wife in his arms and kissed her cheek. "Lovely idea, my love."

Persephone gave her husband a smile.

Demeter asked Therese, "Would you prefer to bathe before or after you eat?"

"After, please. I have a feeling I will want to go immediately to bed after such a treat, though I'm not sure I'll be able to eat."

McAdams stood alone except for Ares, who spoke to him in quiet tones, and Than noticed Therese was looking at him with astonishingly kind eyes.

"You don't feel sorry for the murderer, do you?" he asked softly.

"Of course not. But this doesn't seem fair, the gods giving me attention. When I kill him, I don't want Ares to have any room to contest my win."

Hades put a hand on Therese's shoulder. "The prisoner reaps the harvest of the evil character he has sown. If none help him but Ares, McAdams can only blame himself. He has free will. Ares never forced him to do his evil deeds."

Therese nodded.

"I must return to my kingdom," Hades said. "I'll see you in the morning."

"Thank you."

"I must go as well," Poseidon said. "But I, too, will return tomorrow."

"Goodbye and thanks again."

Than stood with her in the great hall as the gods made their exit. He was grateful for a little more time, but the anguish was almost unbearable. He took her face in his hands and gently put his lips to hers as tears welled in his eyes and fell down his cheeks.

Chapter Forty: The Last Supper

Than led Therese into the banquet hall where an oblong table of gold with twelve matching ornate chairs stretched the expanse of the room. Unlike the assembly hall, this room did not open to the sky, and the white ceiling was trimmed in golden crown molding on which was painted a continuous grapevine. In the center of the ceiling hung an enormous gold and crystal chandelier, with five gradated layers of circular curtains made of teardrop crystals. Than pulled out a chair for Therese, and they sat together on the farthest end of the table, where Hestia now entered from another door to bring them plates of food.

"Mortals are not allowed to eat the food of gods," Hestia said, "but I hope you will find this meal of vegetables and rice the next best thing." Hestia laid out the food along with a basket of rolls and a cup of butter as Therese thanked her over and over. Hestia returned with cups of wine. "This will help you sleep."

Therese ate even though she wasn't hungry. She knew she needed to keep her strength. She was so nervous that she couldn't really taste the food. The wine, though, tasted strong and she couldn't decide if she liked it, but she forced the entire glass down. She wanted to sleep.

As she ate with one hand, she held Than's hand with the other. She couldn't touch him enough. This might be their last night together. As a soul in the Underworld without freedom and personality, she would no longer be attractive to him, and, because of the River of Forgetfulness, she would likely no longer appreciate him. Although she was frightened, she ate for strength, and she tried to savor every bite, every moment of this last meal, this final night.

"I will be there watching over you," Than said. "I will be the one shouting the loudest."

She gave him a brave smile. "Just think, tomorrow I may be a god like you, and we can begin our life of eternity together."

He smiled back. "You're right to think positive." He stroked her hair and kissed the hand he held with his.

Therese frowned.

"What?" Than touched the lines on her forehead. "What happened to your positive thoughts?"

"I'm worried about my aunt. I wish I could get a message to her. She'll be wondering where I am, freaking out, probably assuming the bad guys have captured me."

"I've already thought of that." He gave her a wry smile.

"What? What did you do?"

"I called Jen and asked her to call your aunt and tell her you were spending the night with her. I told Jen that you and I wanted to spend as much time together as possible before I leave. Jen was glad to do it."

"Jen thinks I'm staying with you at the Melner cabin?"

He nodded.

"She probably thinks we're, I mean, I bet she suspects we…"

"What?" He gave her a flirtatious smile.

Therese's appetite returned, and she popped part of a roll into her mouth.

Before they had finished their meal, Zeus entered the banquet hall and approached the end of the table where the two of them sat. Therese worried she was sitting in his seat and started to get up from her chair, but Than, holding her hand, kept her down.

Zeus wore a robe of gold silk, and a golden crown adorned his head. His brown hair was cropped short, but, despite his beauty, his beard appeared unruly, reminding her of a brown version of the beard of Santa Clause. "I

308

have a gift for you, too," he said. "You are a brave mortal, one of the bravest to cross my path. If you wish, once you have eaten your fill, it would be my pleasure if Thanatos would accompany you on a ride of my most treasured steed, Pegasus."

Therese squealed with delight. "Oh my God! That would be so awesome! Really? We can ride Pegasus? Oh, Than, let's go! I can't eat another bite!"

Zeus's laughter thundered through the room as Hestia came in to clear the plates and glasses. Therese thanked Hestia once again, and then she and Than followed Zeus to the stables.

Pegasus's coat was so white that it glowed like the headlight of a car, and Therese couldn't look directly at it. Squinting, she reached her hand to stroke his flanks.

"Unlike the other gods, he can't shift into a form that would benefit your eyes. His brightness, though, isn't as bright as ours, so you can handle it, right?"

"Yes, if I squint." She stroked his mane.

"He's saying how good that feels," Than translated. "Apparently he hasn't been petted in a while."

This made Therese that much more determined to give him a good brushing. She asked for a brush, and, to her surprise, Cupid appeared with a golden one. She took it, thanked him, and he disappeared.

"He's practically purring," Than said as she brushed Pegasus. "But don't exhaust yourself. You have a big day tomorrow."

"Such a kind and giving heart," Zeus muttered. "It's too bad. Well, I'm off. See you tomorrow. Thanatos, I trust you to bring Pegasus back in one piece."

"Yes, sir," Than replied.

As soon as they were alone, Than took Therese in his arms and pressed his warm lips to hers, then to her cheeks, and then her neck. A sigh escaped her, and then a moan, as desire swept through her. But Than stopped and looked at her. "I know how badly you want to take this ride on Pegasus, so finish brushing, and let's go. But hurry. I'm jealous of the pleasure you're giving him."

Therese giggled and arched one of her brows.

Because Pegasus wore no saddle and tack, Than helped Therese mount his white bare back just behind his wings. Than then climbed behind her and asked Pegasus to give them a tour of the skies above the mountain range. Although Therese was excited, she recalled what happened the last time she rode a horse, and she filled with anxiety. This is different, she told herself. Pegasus is immortal and he knows what to do. I don't have to control him.

At Than's request, Pegasus went into a canter across the golden-paved plaza and then, just as Therese thought they would crash into the chariot shed, he lifted up into the sky.

Than explained that the sun always shone above Olympus, but Pegasus would take them over and outside of the wall of clouds so they could see the stars and moon and natural landscape.

The rush over the wall of clouds brought a scream of exhilaration from Therese's lips. Then suddenly the day was night and the stars, so close and numerous, illuminated the mountaintops below. Than pointed out Mytikas, the highest peak, and pointed to the city of Macedonia, its bright lights illuminating the dark night, and the small village of Litohoro, where little lines of smoke rose from rooftop chimneys. Therese felt a sinking feeling in her chest at the view of all those homes in the village, because it made her think of her home and how, no matter what happened on the battlefield tomorrow, she would never see it again.

Than sensed this change in her mood. "Are you ready to go back?"

She nodded and held on as Pegasus plunged back over the wall of clouds to the palace of the gods.

Once Pegasus had been returned to the stables and thanked again and again by Therese, Than led Therese back up the rainbow steps into the palace walls. He took her past the foyer and into the assembly hall, where Hades's throne had vanished back into the marble floor, or perhaps all the way down to the Underworld, Therese didn't know which. Than explained that each of the gods possessed a private chamber behind his or her throne, and he led her now past Poseidon's throne to the chamber door. When he opened it, they saw Demeter and Persephone sitting in chairs. Persephone held glass bottles filled with colorful liquids, and Demeter held two white towels draped over one arm.

"We've drawn your bath," Persephone said, standing from the chair.

Demeter also stood. "It's this way, in Poseidon's spa."

"I'll meet you back here in a while," Than said. Then he kissed her cheek and vanished.

The walls of Poseidon's chamber were lined with pale blue silk curtains gathered in pleats as if to simulate the sea. His canopy bed lay in the center of the room, and white gauze, like foam from the sea, hung from the canopy down in piles on the floor. The bed coverings were also white and looked to be made of silk. Green tassels, like seaweed, skirted the bed.

"Athena just dressed the bed with her new sheets," Persephone said. The goddess was small, petite, and not quite what Therese expected the Queen of the Underworld to look like.

"Artemis left her pillow there for you," Demeter added. She was only a few inches taller than her daughter and also petite. For the goddess of earth, or agriculture, Therese had expected a mountain of a woman.

Persephone pulled back one curtain of gauze to expose the pillow. "And Aphrodite placed her eye mask on top of Artemis's pillow." The white silk object looked like a luxurious comfort on this solemn, dreadful night.

As Demeter opened the door to Poseidon's spa, she said, "Hera came by, too, and left a nightgown for you to wear. She said it will protect you from any god wishing to force his way on you tonight. Although it's magical, you can change out of it in the morning so as not to break any of the rules of your battle. It only works while worn."

Therese hadn't thought of that. She couldn't imagine one of these noble gods—except maybe Ares—trying such an ignoble act. Then she recalled Athena's story about Daphne, the maiden with whom her brother Apollo once desired and how she would rather be a tree than face the wrath of jealous female divinities. Apparently some male gods had problems with fidelity.

Persephone took Therese's hand and led her into the spa.

The spa was amazing. She wondered as she gazed at the huge tub if all the gods had such elaborate baths or if the one belonging to the god of the sea was special. The tub was shaped like an open clam. The bottom shell was filled with water, and the top shell was a mirror. Persephone emptied one of the colorful liquids into the water, creating a mound of foamy bubbles that glinted with the light thrown off by the many candles lit throughout the otherwise darkened room.

"We'll leave while you undress and climb beneath the bubbles," Persephone said. "We want to give you some time to yourself, but we'll return in a little while to wash your hair and to give you a facial and hand massage."

Therese's brow flew up. "Are you serious? I'm getting a facial and massage by goddesses? Oh my. Thank you sooooo much!" She couldn't believe it. Then she realized why she was getting such special treatment. They all expected her to lose, and they felt sorry for her.

She clutched the locket around her neck and wished she were home in her own bed, in he own bathroom.

Then she thought of Than and her love for him strengthened her. She would show them.

After undressing and using the other facilities—so gods do use the restroom!—Therese climbed into the clam-shaped tub and moaned with pleasure at the warm and soothing water. She was able to stretch her body straight, and a soft waterproof pillow, also shaped like an open clam, but turned on its side, held her head in place.

Now that she was alone, her thoughts went to the impending battle, and the fears took possession of her. She gnawed on the inside of her lip as she tried to relax. She could have chosen the first option and be in her own bed right now. She'd have Clifford curled beside her, Puffy running in his wheel across the room, and Jewels poking her head above the plastic walls of her little house. Therese's aunt would be downstairs, her best friend would be down the road, and Pete would be there to comfort her, to love her, and to make her happy.

But McAdams might come after her aunt.

And her parents wouldn't be there.

And she wanted Than.

She wasn't sure how she had gotten to this point where she felt like she couldn't live without Than. She wondered if Cupid had pierced her heart or if this was her own doing. But, regardless of who was to blame, she loved him, and she could not imagine life without him.

She closed her eyes and prayed, "Than, come back for just a minute. Give me a quick kiss, and then leave before your mom and grandma return. Please, oh please, come back."

When she opened her eyes, he was there beside the tub sitting on a marble bench shaped like a fish. His hair was wet, and he had changed from the open white shirt and trousers to a pale blue of similar design. The blue in the cloth brought out the crystal blue of his eyes, which sparkled with the reflection of the candlelight.

He leaned over the water, slowly, taking in the view of her, though her body was covered by bubbles—perhaps it was just the idea that she was

313

naked—and ever so slowly, too slowly, oh please don't make me wait, he touched his lips to hers and swept her mouth, her cheek, her chin, her neck with the warmth and moisture of his mouth and tongue. She fought the urge to pull him down into the bath with her as she took fistfuls of his wet hair and kept his face to hers. When she pressed her mouth more firmly to his, he vanished, her hands suspended in empty air, and Persephone and Demeter entered the room.

Talk about frustration.

But her frustration was soon replaced by pleasure as Persephone took Therese's long hair and bundled it in her hands, working through a freshly scented shampoo.

"Is that oranges I smell?" Therese muttered like one drugged.

"Mm-hmm," Persephone softly replied.

Persephone massaged her scalp, sending chills down Therese's neck and back. Then Demeter was at her right hand massaging lotion into the palm, between the fingers, along the back of the hand and wrist.

"Oh my god-desses," she moaned.

The other hand received the same treatment as Persephone rinsed the shampoo and now lathered in a conditioner, more scents of citrus wafting through the room. Again Persephone massaged her scalp, and Demeter continued to knead her palm, squeeze her fingers.

"I will let the conditioner sit in your hair a few minutes while I apply the exfoliating mask to your face," Persephone explained.

Now Persephone was massaging Therese's forehead, temples, cheekbones, jaw.

"Oh," Therese sighed.

Demeter placed Therese's left hand back in the tub and Persephone finished applying the mask.

"When the mask feels dry, wash it off and rinse your hair," Persephone instructed her.

"You'll find your towels on the bench to your right," Demeter said. "And the gown from Hera is hanging on the back of the door."

Another woman entered the room and said to Persephone, "Thanatos wishes to speak with you, my lady."

"Thank you, Hecate." Persephone turned back to Therese. "Good luck to you, sweet girl."

"Thanks so much," Therese managed to say. Tears pricked her eyes. Perhaps she had already died and gone to heaven!

The three figures vanished from the room and left Therese alone.

After a few moments, Therese dried and put on the white silk gown from Hera and extinguished the candles the goddesses had lit. Then she left the spa and went to the large canopy bed in the middle of Poseidon's chamber where a small bedside lamp in the shape of a mermaid had been left on for her. She pulled back a fluffy down comforter and silk white top sheet, moved the eye mask from the goose feather pillow, and climbed inside the bed and pulled the covers over her. Her whole body relaxed. Every muscle, every bone, every neuron firing at the synapse seemed to respond to the most comfortable bed and sheets and pillow she had ever slept on. She put the eye mask aside for now and prayed for Than to return.

He was there beside her in an instant, and a good thing, too, for she had nearly fallen asleep. He lay above the covers and she below, like the last time they spent the night together. He stroked her wet hair.

"You smell so good," he said. "And you feel so soft."

She reached her arms up and took his face in her hands. "This may be our last night together," she whispered. "So I want you to…"

"Shhh," he whispered, putting a finger to her lips. "Don't talk like that. What happened to being positive? I know what you want, and believe me, I want it to, but I won't give it to you tonight. You have to wait, to fight for it." He kissed her, and kissed her, and then he groaned, "So you better win."

She kissed him back, ran her fingers through his now dry hair, and took pleasure in his caresses. They caressed one another for several more minutes, neither really wanting to stop, but both knowing it would be better in the end. Then she put on Aphrodite's eye mask and snuggled against his chest just as the most beautiful music she had ever heard began to sound through the walls. Apollo played the lyre and Hermes the pipe, and the beautiful melodies lifted her spirits again and carried her to heights of optimism that gave her the feeling, as Than lay there stroking her hair, that nothing could stop her now.

Soon after, she fell asleep.

Chapter Forty-One: The Battlefield

In the morning, Than gave Therese a pair of jeans, a shirt, clean undies, and pair of socks he had brought her from her house.

"You went through my underwear drawer?" she asked.

He gave her a wry smile.

"How are my pets?"

"Your aunt and her boyfriend are taking good care of them."

Luckily her sneakers had dried overnight. After she changed, Than led her to the assembly hall where the gods and goddesses were just now coming in from either their chambers behind their thrones or the banquet hall or, in the case of Poseidon and Hades, the chariot shed.

Once the gods and goddesses were seated, Hephaestus presented McAdams and Therese with the golden sword and shield he had wrought and forged for them. Ares belted the sheathed sword around McAdams's waist while Than did the same for Therese. Therese pulled the blade from the sheath. It was surprisingly light.

Than stood close by and whispered, "Be careful with that thing. I can't be killed, but I can still feel pain."

She gave a nervous giggle and returned the sword to its sheath, watching McAdams with a wary eye.

Than grabbed her hand and pulled her closer, so that they were breast to breast. "Speaking of pain, if McAdams, you know... I won't let you suffer. I'll take your soul, and I'll take you straight to your parents."

She swallowed hard and gave him a frightened nod. Then he kissed her once more before taking his seat beside his father.

McAdams had dark circles beneath his eyes and bags that would put those of Hephaestus to shame. He looked pale, almost languid, and Therese actually felt a little sorry for him. She wondered where he had passed the night and what comforts Ares, and perhaps other gods, did or did not provide.

Then she remembered how she had watched her parents die, and anger rose within her. She would kill him.

"We all know the rules," Zeus announced. "So let us begin."

Therese nearly jumped from her sneakers when the assembly hall vanished and in its place was a clearing surrounded by woods. Pines, cypresses, elms, hemlocks—all trees Therese recognized. Beyond the clearing, the sun at high noon pierced through the canopy of leaves onto a deer here, a squirrel there. Cardinals, sparrows, jays, and other birds whose names she did not know flittered from tree to tree, just like they did in the bird atrium at the San Antonio Zoo. Ants burrowed in the dirt around her feet, and white limestone rocks, pink granite rocks, and other kinds, too, were partly buried in the earth, partly exposed.

The thrones had disappeared, but the gods and goddesses sat on tree stumps in the clearing in the same formation in which they had gathered at the hall on Mount Olympus. For all Therese knew, they had never left the court, and all of this nature around them was a vast illusion.

Suddenly with a roaring thunder, the ground beneath them lifted up, like the floor of an elevator, and both Therese and McAdams stumbled and fell with the trembling earth. The clearing rose at least thirty feet so that the gods could look down upon the forest surrounding them below, like the reverse of a coliseum in that what was once the battlefield in the center had become the audience seating, and what was usually the audience seating was an outer circular battlefield. But unlike the audience of a coliseum, this battlefield was ripe with life and natural structures. Behind Zeus, mountains of pink granite jutted up from the forest below, exceeding in height the level of the gods' platform. Beyond Poseidon, Therese could make out a river bordered by forest. A stream ran from the pink granite mountains, into the

318

river, and then circled around Apollo and Hephaestus and plunged into a roaring fall to a deeper canyon behind Hades. The water pooled into a smaller body of water at the bottom of the deeper canyon. Another stream ran into a fall behind Aphrodite, but the trees were so thick on that side of the forest, that Therese could not see through them. Among the trees behind Demeter, however, she thought she saw fruit. If her plan was to outrun and hide from McAdams, this would be a long battle, and fruit would be necessary to keep going. Otherwise, she and her enemy wouldn't need to kill one another. They would starve to death.

Therese and McAdams stood up on opposite sides of the platform staring at one another with fear and anger. Therese wasn't sure what to do, and McAdams appeared as indecisive. All of the gods sat around them on their tree stumps, waiting. Aphrodite's face was stained with tears.

Than, still close by, spoke in a low voice. "My best advice is to avoid hand to hand combat."

"Then how will I kill him?" Therese muttered without taking her eyes off McAdams.

"Set traps, if possible, and keep far away from him. You're in better shape and can probably outrun him, but he's stronger." Than could not keep the desperation from his voice. "Please be careful."

Therese kept her eyes on McAdams as she backed away from him towards what had now become a cliff edge behind the tree-stump thrones of the gods. A person would certainly die if he or she fell from the platform and into the canyon woods surrounding them below. But the rocky ledges could be navigated the thirty or so feet to the bottom, and it seemed to Therese there could be caves in the canyon walls. She decided she should descend behind Demeter and collect whatever fruit she could carry, and then run for a hiding place until she could think of another plan.

McAdams charged at her, however, and gave her no choice but to climb down the cliff edge behind Hades. Therese threw her shield down and it plunged, then slid, and finally came to a stop near the bottom of the deeper canyon at least a hundred feet below. She turned and clung to the rock wall, quickly finding her footing as she scaled down the side. She looked up and saw McAdams standing above her. He wasn't climbing down after her...yet.

"Oh, Than, I should have run to the trees!" she said in her mind, praying frantically, even though she knew he could not help her. "My plan was to collect food and stay on the run till he got weak. But look at me clinging to these walls! This is stupid! What am I doing? I'm going to kill myself slipping on these stupid rocks, and he'll win by default! I've already dropped my shield!"

"Your plan is sound!" Than called after her. "You can still do it!"

Then it dawned on Therese, something she hadn't thought of before! She could speak to the gods through prayer, and they could answer her! She would have to call them by name so Ares would not hear. Ares would inform McAdams. But the other gods, the ones she knew were on her side, she would speak to them!

She increased her pace down the canyon wall and lowered herself to the bottom. Her shield lay below in the deeper canyon, but she decided she would be faster without it. Since her goal was to avoid hand to hand combat, why be burdened with it when her hands could be free?

She ran along the base of the upper canyon wall toward the thick forest behind Demeter. In her mind, she said, "I'm thinking I should collect food, Than. And then hide. Do you agree?"

"Yes!" he shouted.

Then another thought hit her. She would ask the gods questions that could be answered with yes or no, so as to prevent McAdams from overhearing her plans.

"Artemis, Athena, Aphrodite," she said in her mind as she ran. "If you can hear me, shout out my name, so I know."

"Therese!" Artemis cried.

320

"Therese!" Athena echoed.

"Therese, my dear!" Aphrodite sang.

Therese looked up and saw McAdams had not descended to the forest. He stood there hovering over the cliff edge watching her. She wondered what he was doing. Perhaps he had the same plan of waiting untl she wore herself out.

"Demeter, Persephone, Hades," Therese prayed as she disentangled herself from the thick undergrowth, twigs snapping beneath her feet. "Say 'yes' if you can hear me."

"Yes!" Demeter cried.

"Oh, yes!" Persephone said.

"Smart girl!" Hades hollered. "Yes!"

Therese was filled with a renewed hope as she picked her way through the branches of trees and shrubs, some stiff like spears, others flexible like snakes, toward the fruit trees. The woods were now so thick, that she could no longer see McAdams. "Than, has McAdams climbed down from the platform?"

"No!" Than shouted.

So maybe he *did* plan for her to wear herself out. She found a narrow stream and sighed with relief. The woods had become so thick that only little spots of sunlight pierced through the canopy of leaves above her, and she couldn't tell which way she was going, but the stream would now be her guide. Layers and layers of rotting leaves covered the ground beneath her, and she had to be careful to step over the occasional fallen branch or decaying log.

Another idea struck her.

"Than and Artemis, should I attempt to make spears from these fallen branches?" she prayed. "Just say yes or no. If it would be a waste of time say no."

"Yes!" Artemis said.

"Ask me another question!" Than cried.

Ask another question? What question? She stared at the sticks.

"You want me to use the sticks for something else?" A thorn bush scratched her arm. "Ow," she muttered.

"Yes!" Than shouted. "Recall what I said earlier!"

"Is McAdams still up there?"

"Yes!"

What had Than said earlier? He had said to avoid hand to hand combat, to run, and…to set traps! "You want me to use the sticks to set traps?"

"Yes!" Than answered.

"But I have no idea how to do that!" She groaned as she bent over and picked through the sticks on the ground, looking for strong ones.

She saw several bruised apples among the sticks and leaves, most of them rotten, but when she looked up, she could see ripe ones on the branches within her reach.

"I should pick fruit, Than, Artemis, and Athena, but carrying it now will hold me back. I should store it someplace. I should find somewhere to hide, to store my food and my weapons. I could booby-trap it!"

"Yes!" all three voices rang out.

Therese pulled off her shirt and bundled fruit inside of it. She found nuts on the ground and further up the stream, grapevines. She plucked as many grapes as she could fit into the makeshift bundle, gathered up the edges, and carried it in one hand and her collection of sticks in the other.

Think, she told herself, standing in her bra and jeans with her bundle draped over her back. Originally, she had planned to climb the granite rocks jutting up above Zeus, but only because she thought a lookout was necessary. Now that she had figured out she could use prayer to keep tabs on the whereabouts of McAdams, she wouldn't need the lookout. She would need to hide, and she would want to make it as hard as possible for McAdams to get to her.

She stood there, thinking. "Is McAdams still up there?" she prayed to Than.

"Yes!" he shouted. "But hurry! Don't waste time!"

He wanted her to set traps, but she didn't know how to do that. Think, Therese! Okay, McAdams would eventually need food if she managed to stay away from him long enough, so he would come here, to this part of the woods. This would be a good place to try and trap him, or at least weaken him with an injury. But how?

She shuddered. She was not cut out for this. Strategically planning how to hurt and kill someone went against her grain. Remember your parents, she told herself. Remember the last time you saw them!

She forced herself to visualize her father writhing in frenzy as the water washed over him, suffocating him. She forced herself to see her mother, bleeding at the neck, blood pouring from her mouth as she yielded to her death. She clutched the golden locket around her neck. I can do this!

Than said not to waste time, so maybe she should start sharpening the sticks until another idea came to her mind. She followed the stream out of the thicket where the undergrowth thinned out and looked for a place to sit and work. She saw a fallen log up ahead that would serve as a bench. On her way to the log, the ground dropped below her and she fell flat on her chest, dropping her bundle, apples flying everywhere. She had landed in a hole about two feet deep and four feet wide.

"Ow! She scrambled to her feet. "Oh, damn!" Leaves stuck to her skin and fell in her bra as she gathered the apples, leaving the nuts and most of the grapes, which had fallen beneath the rotting leaves. She heaped the apples back onto her shirt, bundling it back up. Luckily they still looked good, no bruises. Her knee, on the other hand, would definitely have a bruise. It had been stabbed by a sharp rock. At least her jeans had protected her skin.

A flash of inspiration.

She could use this hole to set a trap, and she could look for similar places in the ground. She would sharpen sticks at both ends, drive them into the bottom of these holes, and cover them with dead leaves.

"Than!" she said in her mind. "I've got it!" She told him her plan.

"Yes!" he shouted. "But hurry!"

"Is McAdams still there?"

"Not for long!" Than yelled.

"What is he doing? Oh, wait, you can't answer that. Is he watching me?"

"No!"

"Is he making plans?"

"Yes! Yes, hurry!"

Now Therese was filled with worry over what McAdams might be doing up on the platform. She took her collection of sticks to the large fallen log, sat down, and unsheathed her sword. The sword was too long to whittle the wood, so she drove the blade into the ground and used it like a cheese grater, rubbing first one end and then the other of each stick against the blade. The sword was so sharp that it didn't take her long to produce a large mound of sticks sharpened at both ends. Now she needed to find a big rock so she could drive each stick into the ground.

She ran around the fallen log looking for a rock. There has to be a rock in these woods! Panic threatened to overtake her as she dug through the layers of leaves and came up with nothing, over and over. Then she remembered where she had hurt her knee in the bottom of the hole and looked there. Yes, sharp on top but smooth on the bottom where it was wedged into the ground, it was the size of a large brick. She dug it from the earth and went back for her sticks. She had made the sticks a little more than a foot long and now she hammered them into the ground, a foot apart, so that they stuck up about eight inches from the bottom of the hole. Once she had impaled the bottom of the hole with the sharp, jutting weapons, she grabbed armfuls of dead leaves and hid the trap.

Then she picked her way back to the fruit trees to gather a few oranges, this time looking more closely at the ground for small dips where she could set more traps.

"Therese!" Than cried.

"Is McAdams climbing down?"

"Yes!"

"Is he coming after me?"

"No!"

"Where's he going? Is he headed for the rocks behind Zeus?" That's where she would have gone, for the lookout.

"Yes!"

"He hopes he'll see me better from there," she muttered.

"Exactly!"

"He's waiting for me to wear myself out, and then he plans to come for me!"

"Exactly!" Than's voice sounded desperate.

Therese trembled wildly. "I'll set more traps. Shout if he heads this way."

"I will!"

A movement in the wood caught her eye, and she froze, waited. She took a slow step and looked beyond the tree where she had seen the flash of something brownish. Now she saw it was a wild horse there with her in the wood. At first, she smiled, comforted by the vision. Then she thought of the traps. The animals!

Again in her mind, she asked, "Than! Artemis! The animals! What if they hurt themselves on my traps? Can you warn them somehow?"

"No!" Artemis called out.

"Ares!" Than shouted.

Ares? "Ares will understand where the traps are."

"Yes."

"But how can we warn the animals?"

"Your scent!" Artemis cried.

"They'll avoid the traps because of my scent?" She found herself whispering rather than praying in her head.

"That will be our message! To avoid your scent!" Artemis shouted.

Therese looked at the horse. It made her feel less alone. She took an apple from her bundle and held it out. The horse's nostrils flared, but it didn't move toward her or away. Therese tossed the apple toward the tree. The horse trotted away.

Of course. The apple carried her scent. He had already been warned.

She spent at least two hours sharpening sticks, driving them into holes, and covering the holes with leaves, but she began to fear she might be wasting her time. What if McAdams never came this way? What if he killed her before he got hungry? She was wearing herself out. Was this worth it?

Then she slapped her forehead. Maybe she should have tried to mount the horse. She might have had a better chance against McAdams if she came at him from above on horseback.

Too late now.

She should set more traps, but she should seek a path he was sure to cross.

She gathered more fruit—oranges and pomegranates, and stuffed them in her shirt, but they wouldn't all fit. Then she had the idea of tying the hem of the shirt in a knot and stuffing the fruit *inside* the shirt rather than gathering the edges all around. More fruit would fit this way. She wanted to collect as much food as she could because with all her traps out here, she didn't want to have to come back this way and risk injuring herself in one of them. That would be ironic, she thought.

As she tore her way through the woods back toward the deeper canyon, she stopped whenever she found a good dip in the ground to set up another trap. She'd set down her bundle and the big rock she used for hammering, sharpen a dozen more sticks at both ends on her blade, and then stake the sticks firmly in the ground before hiding them with fallen leaves. The further she got from the thickest part of the woods, however, the fewer dead leaves were there on the ground. She realized as she followed the stream back down to the rocky canyon behind Hades that she would have to think of a different way to set traps on this side of the battlefield.

"Therese!" Than shouted.

She prayed, "Is he following me?"

"Hide!"

She looked up and realized she had now come into view of those on the side of the platform closest to her. She could see Than, Hades, and Aphrodite directly overhead. She had to remember to stay out of Ares's view. She clambered against the canyon wall and hid beneath the cliff edge above her.

"Is McAdams following me?" she asked Than.

"Just now!"

"He's just now leaving the rocks behind Zeus?"

"Yes!"

"Is he headed toward the woods or the lake?"

When he didn't answer, she said, "I mean, is he headed toward the woods?"

"Yes!"

"Good. Maybe he'll come across at least one of my traps. I think I have twelve or thirteen all around the fruit trees. But I need to think of something else down here in the canyon. There's nothing here but rocks."

327

"Yes!"

"What? I didn't ask anything." She thought back on what she had said. "Rocks? I should make traps with rocks?"

"Yes!"

But how? She thought. How could she use rocks to make a trap? The sticks went into hidden holes waiting for McAdams to happen by. They probably wouldn't kill him, but he could get cut up really bad. But falling on rocks? What could she do with the rocks? Could she sharpen them? Chip them into sharp wedges? No. The rocks could fall on him. How could she make it so the rocks could fall on him? She could throw them at him. She could gather a stockpile and keep them near her hideout so that when he came for her she could launch...

Wait! Launch?

She had to work without being seen by Ares, and she had to work fast. She crept along the base of the cliff edge scanning for possibilities. She looked down into the deeper canyon below where her shield lay useless to her and out across to the other side about a fifty yards away. Think, Therese! Think!

Then, like a bullet, it hit her.

The waterfall!

Chapter Forty-Two: The Battle

Therese filled with hope and enthusiasm when it dawned on her that she could scuttle along this canyon wall beneath the cliff edge and make her way to the roaring fall behind Hephaestus without being seen. She prayed to Than to let him know her plan.

She would find a place behind the falls to stash her food and store her rocks, which she started collecting in her arms now. She would find a lower place, visible to Ares, to set up a decoy camp. Then, when McAdams came to the decoy, she would launch her rocks at him. The rocks probably wouldn't kill him, but as with the traps in the thick part of the woods by the fruit trees, they would injure him and slow him down, hopefully enough for her to defeat him with her sword.

"Good!" Than shouted.

A blood-curdling wail rang out across the canyon and caused Therese to freeze. "Was that McAdams?"

"Yes!"

"Did he find one of my traps?"

"I think so! I can't see him!" Than called out.

Whether McAdams injured himself in one of her traps or in some other way, he was nevertheless injured, and this added to Therese's overall optimism as she scrambled beneath the cliff edge with her arms full of rocks the size of softballs. The noise of the falls thundered as she neared them and the spray hit her bare skin and chilled her, a relief after the sweat she had worked up from building her traps in Demeter's woods.

"How long till nightfall?" she asked Than in her mind. It seemed like hours had passed, and yet the sun still bore down on them high in the sky.

"Wait a minute. We never left Olympus, did we? The sun always shines, right?"

If Than answered her, she could no longer hear him this close to the crashing falls. She hadn't thought of that! How would she make it without him?

Unlike Than and the other gods, she had no powers of telepathy and could not be sure if voices in her head were inspirations or delusions. She almost turned back. In fact, she changed her mind five or six times and nearly wore herself out beneath the cliff edge with indecision. At last she decided it was her best chance of survival to go on with her plan. "I can't hear you anymore," she prayed. "But I've decided to go on anyway."

She reached the falls and found a hidden grotto behind the roaring water, but if McAdams came this way to her decoy camp, she would have no advantage for attack. Although there were many little nooks and crevices back here that she could climb onto, she would be open, visible, and vulnerable to his retaliation. She dropped her rocks in a heap, set down her fruit, and looked around.

At the furthest lip of the grotto on the outer edge of the falls, she found a nook way up high that just might work. If McAdams came through the grotto, she would see him, and she would be above him, with gravity on her side. She would also be hidden until he reached the point where she stood now. It also seemed, from down here, anyway, that she might have a view of the deeper canyon in case he came that route. The trick would be hauling the rocks and fruit up the steep wall nearly twenty feet to the nook. First she would try it empty-handed to see if it was possible.

Now that she couldn't hear Than, she felt really anxious that McAdams could be coming around the corner for her at any moment, and this anxiety caused her to tremble more profoundly than she had before. The trembling made climbing up the nearly vertical wall very difficult. She used her fingers to find places in the wall to grip, and she fished around with her

330

feet for footholds to support her weight. One false step meant falling to her death at the bottom of the canyon.

Dirt from the canyon wall got into her mouth and crunched in her teeth when she clenched them. She ran her tongue around her teeth, trying to wash it out, and she spit and gagged. She reached for another rock, keeping her mouth closed this time, breathing through her nose. A fingernail broke at the tip as she clung to another ledge, but that was the least of her worries.

Thankfully, there were plenty of strong footholds within reach of one another. When she made it to the nook, she found it was actually a cave that tunneled back into darkness. While she was glad to have all this room to store her things and move around, the unknown darkness added to her anxiety. Stop it, Therese! McAdams was the only threat worth fearing right now, she reminded herself. She walked over to the furthest edge and saw that she could indeed see most of the lower canyon from here. This just might work. There were even a few loose boulders she could move, though barely and straining with all her might. Maybe if she scooted them to the edge and found something to give her leverage, she could launch them from the nook. She needed a branch or heavy stick, but there were none around. Would her sword work, or would the rock break it? She unsheathed the sword and tested it, gently at first. The blade gave. It was too flexible. She'd have to find something else. She returned the sword to its sheath.

The sheath! It was light, but it was solid and firm. She unbelted it from her waist and tested it out. It would work! This could be her saving grace! She looked around for other such boulders and found four more loose enough and light enough for her to drag to the edge of her cave.

She re-belted her sword and sheath and climbed back down, quickly but carefully, to carry up her bundle of fruit between her teeth. Then she took the empty shirt back down and filled it with six of the softball-sized rocks. Any more than that might throw off her balance too much or be too heavy and slip between her teeth. She'd have to make a third trip down for the remaining six. She hesitated. If McAdams spotted her, she'd lose the element of surprise. Was it worth getting the remaining rocks? She decided to go for it.

Climbing up with the bundle between her teeth was not easy. She held on by the back molars, where her jaw was stronger. She couldn't swallow properly, so she let the drool drip down her chin. Most of it was absorbed by her shirt. The rocks pressed against her neck and chest as she pulled herself up the wall. Her neck was sore from both the weight of the rocks and the position in which she had to hold her head in order to clear the rocks with her body. But her shirt wasn't big enough to tie around her back or neck and still hold her bundle.

Now she had twelve softball-sized rocks she could throw at him and seven watermelon-sized boulders she could launch at him with her sheath. It was time to set up her decoy camp, and she'd have to move quickly since McAdams could be gaining on her at any time and she would not hear Than's warning. She gathered up three apples and put them in her shirt to take with her.

Oh! Another idea struck her. She couldn't hear Than, but maybe she would be able to hear several gods if they all shouted at once. She concentrated on all of them but Ares. She couldn't risk giving away her position to him. "If you can hear me, please oh please scream yes as loud as you can when I get to the count of three. One, two, three!"

Faint, but audible, she heard the whisper of a yes.

Awesome!

Again, with great concentration, she focused on all of the Olympian gods except for Ares. "If you think McAdams is still in the forest, when I count to three, please scream yes. One, two, three!"

Again, faint, but audible, like a breeze across the canyon, she heard the gods say, "Yes."

Awesome! That meant she had time to set up her decoy camp. She cautiously but quickly scrambled down the wall from her cave back to the grotto floor behind the falls. Then she scaled further down beneath the grotto to the deeper canyon floor, all the while being careful to keep herself hidden behind the falls to avoid Ares's watchful eyes. She hadn't heard him communicating with McAdams so far, but that didn't mean he wasn't doing so now that McAdams was down in the woods.

During her decent down the wall, she sought cliff edges, nooks, anything that might offer passage past the falls where she could be visible across the canyon from the platform and the lower edge of the forest. She needed to be seen in her decoy camp, but her entrance and exit to it should be hidden. She was getting nervous that this wasn't going to work. Maybe she should head back to her real camp and simply wait.

But she had come this far, and this was the perfect plan if she could make it work.

"If you can see McAdams, on my count of three, please say yes. One, two, three!"

"Yes!"

Oh, no! She was expecting a no. If they could see him, where was he? "If he has made it to the edge of the deeper canyon, please say yes on my count of three. One, two, three!"

"Yes!"

Oh my God! "Is he near the larger of the two falls? One, two, three!"

"No."

She felt some relief, but she couldn't see it in her hands, for they trembled so badly now, she could barely grab hold of the canyon wall. She climbed down a few more feet and found another nook. It tunneled beneath the cliff edge above it, into the wall of the canyon, about five feet or more and extended out past the falls. If she were to follow it to its length, she would become visible. It was now or never if she was going to set up this decoy camp. With shaking limbs and chattering teeth, she edged her way out and looked across the canyon at the gods.

A memory of touring Mesa Verde, the ancient cliff dwellings in southwest Colorado, with her parents three years ago swept through her mind.

"Than, if you can see me, wave! I want Ares to see me, and McAdams, too!"

Than waved. She waved back and blew him a kiss. Then she saw McAdams across the canyon at the smaller fall below Aphrodite. He was without his jacket and tie, and his white shirt was stained with blood and dirt. His black pants were torn and also stained, and as he moved forward, he walked with a limp. Unlike her, he held his shield, but this, too, was smeared with blood and dirt. Either he had fallen or at least one of her traps had worked!

Still, as she looked at him, trembling like her, fumbling along the rocky quay at the top of Aphrodite's smaller waterfall, perhaps closer to death than she originally thought, she found it hard to feel joy. Therese! Remember what he did to your parents! Remember what you have to do to be with Than! The anger at her parents' brutal, painful murder and the hopeful expectations of living eternally at Than's side renewed her determination. Either McAdams would die, or she would die trying!

She opened her bundle and took out an apple. Standing in sight of McAdams, she bit the apple and retreated back into the cave, leaving her shirt and the other two apples visible. Then she worried she was being too obvious in her attempts to lure him. She ran back to the edge and snatched her bundle and dragged it back out of sight. She went to the edge one more time and limped around, trying to look weaker than she was, and then she got down on her knees as though in supplication to the gods, and prayed, "Than, I'm not really injured. I am trying to appear weaker than I am to lure McAdams here. This is my decoy camp. I have another set up for attack."

She noticed how badly she trembled now that she was trying to hold still. She kept praying, "I love you, Than. I can tell the end is near. No matter what happens, after this I will be with you always, either as a god like you, or a soul among the dead like my parents. If you can hear me, please wave to me one more time."

She watched him lift his arm up to her and wipe his eyes with the other hand. She wished she could see the details of his face, but he was too far away. She looked over at McAdams. He was drinking from the top of the smaller falls. Now he washed his face. She couldn't see the details, but the overall smear of red was horrible.

He deserves this, she reminded herself.

She took several bites of the apple, and looked up again at Than. The other gods had crowded around him, probably realizing that this canyon was where their game would end. Surprisingly, she felt ravenous, and ate her apple down to the core. Then, looking once more at the bowed figure of McAdams, she tossed the core to the canyon floor to lie beside her shield, and she retreated to the back of the cave and out of sight of all.

From the back of the cave, she tunneled toward her real camp behind the roaring falls. She climbed back up to the grotto with her bundle between her teeth, and then rested there a moment, wondering which direction McAdams was going now. After ten or fifteen minutes, she climbed the rest of the way to her upper chamber where she had stored her food and rocks. She was still hungry, so she bit into another apple while she waited.

She couldn't see McAdams, but she could see the lower canyon if he tried to cross it. She doubted he would attempt it since he was apparently injured. More than likely, he would come the way she had, behind the falls, and so she mostly looked down in that direction. She had her sheath unbelted and her sword on the cave floor close by. She rested the sheath over a rock to form a lever and tucked the sheath beneath one of the watermelon-sized boulders ready to launch it at McAdams when he came.

While she waited for signs of McAdams, she ate another apple and an orange. She was thirsty, and the juice quenched that thirst. She had planned to save more of the food in case McAdams dragged this battle out over the course of days, but once she had started eating, she had found it too hard to stop. Her food supplies were diminishing, and this filled her with new anxiety.

But she couldn't stop herself from eating another apple.

On top of having only a few pieces of fruit left after her binging, she was getting sleepy. She wasn't sure how many hours had passed, since the sun hadn't moved from its position at high noon in the sky, but boy, oh boy, could she use some sleep! She knew, of course, that McAdams would find and kill her in her sleep and that closing her eyes for even a moment was out of the question.

The adrenaline that had rushed through her body earlier when she had heard the gods warning her of McAdams's pursuit had waned somewhat when she saw him, bloody and limping and trembling. And now that she was full and resting in this somewhat safe cave, the adrenaline seemed to have gone out of her body completely.

Think of your parents! But even her attempts to force the images of her dying parents into her head could not pull her from this sudden fatigue and sleepiness. She would not share this with Than. She had been about to pray, "I'm sleepy," to him, but now she realized it would only make him that more fraught with anxiety. No, she would bear this burden alone. She stood up and paced around the cave, like an animal in a zoo.

A movement in the lower canyon caught her attention. She couldn't believe her eyes. McAdams had climbed down into the lower canyon and had picked up her shield. What would he do with it? Wait. He tossed it aside. He was looking for something. What? He picked up the apple core she had tossed and was ravaging it like a starved animal. He had it eaten in an instant, seeds and stem and all, and then he looked around, trembling and pathetic.

336

He went to the small reservoir at the lowest point of the deeper canyon, the pool to which both falls spilled into, and drank. This body of water wasn't nearly as large as the one behind Poseidon—only about ten feet at the widest point—and Therese guessed it must empty into the ground and spring out again somewhere else. Then she remembered this was Mount Olympus, and all this was an illusion. The water didn't have to flow anywhere. It could just disappear.

McAdams continued to look around, over his shoulder, as though he feared *he* were the one being pursued. This thought made Therese giggle slightly. So *he* was afraid of *her*? He thought *she* was coming for *him*?

From her height she could probably hit him with one of the softball-sized rocks, but her chances of missing him were high, and she would give away her location. Plus, he looked so pathetic, like a lame animal, and until he outright attacked her, she might not have it in her to further injure him. But then how long would this battle drag on? How long would she have to hang out here in this dark cave waiting for him to come for her? Shouldn't she just end it now if she could? Launch her rocks and try to crush him to death? Wouldn't she starve to death otherwise?

"Should I attack?"

"Yes!" the barely audible answer came.

She watched McAdams scramble along the canyon floor toward her decoy camp. Perhaps he wouldn't drag this battle out after all. He seemed anxious now, almost lustful. He climbed the wall of the cliff edge furthest from the gods directly beneath her decoy camp. It was time to launch her attack. It was now or never.

Therese took a deep breath and, as she exhaled, she emitted a loud grunt, which she knew no one could hear because of the falls. But as she grunted, she took up a softball-sized rock and threw it at him. She missed, but without thinking, she threw again and again and again, until all twelve softball-sized rocks were gone, and she hit him more than once. He cowered

337

beneath her with his arms over his head, sliding down to the canyon floor. She lunged against her sheath and launched the first watermelon-sized boulder. It dropped a foot or two away from where he crouched, so quickly, before he could move, she launched the next, and bam! It hit its target. He fell over onto the canyon floor, grasping his left shoulder, where the boulder had hit, and moaned. She couldn't hear him but she could see his mouth moving. Now she moved her lever to another boulder and launched it directly on his chest. It hit him and then bounced and rolled away, breaking into smaller pieces. Although she couldn't hear his wails, she could see his face, and she could see he was in terrible pain and agony. Shuddering at what she had done, but not allowing herself to think on it, she launched another boulder and hit her mark again.

McAdams rolled over onto his hands and knees and crawled away from her. Blood poured from his shoulder, which he continued to hold with his right hand. He scrambled away, out of her reach but not her sight, and he sat against the canyon wall, breathing rapidly.

It was time for her to go to him. She belted on the golden sheath and found her sword on the cave floor. She returned the blade to its sheath and prepared to descend. You can do this, she told herself. Then to the gods, even to Ares, she said, "I'm going to end this."

Although she dreaded what had to be done, the feeling of imminent victory lifted her spirits as she climbed down from her cave to the grotto below. McAdams was no longer in view from here, but once she worked her way out past the falls, scaling down toward the deeper canyon, she could see him again sitting and slumped against the rocks.

"You killed my mom and dad!" she shouted as she got closer. "I had to watch them die! Your gunman shot my mom in the neck! My father drove off a bridge trying to dodge the gunman's bullets, and he and my mother drowned right before my eyes!"

McAdams's eyes were wide and his breathing rapid. She was within ten feet of him. She drew her sword. It was dirty from use, but it would still do the trick.

"Please don't kill me," McAdams begged in a shaky voice.

"Kill him!" Hades shouted. "Do it now and be a god among us!"

"Kill him!" the gods shouted.

She looked up at them gathered above her, and even Ares had a look of lust on his face.

She looked back at McAdams lying there quivering, bleeding, tears welling in his eyes. She looked for a place to stick him. Should she slit his throat? Stab his heart?

She shuddered as she raised the blade, still not sure where to pierce him.

"Kill him now!" Hades yelled. "Slit his throat! Think of what he did to your parents!"

Therese gritted her teeth and raised the blade higher, shaking and breathing so rapidly. This was it! This was it! Do it!

"Wait!" she screamed. "Isn't this enough? To prove I could kill him? Can't you make me a god without me having to follow through?"

"No!" Hades shouted. "A deal is a deal! He deserves death, and so much more! Kill him!"

Again she looked at him, trembling worse than she. Tears fell from his eyes. He had wet himself. What had she become? He looked at her like *she* was the monster, *she* the villain. Was she? Had she become as bad as he?

What was so very different about them now? He had killed her parents for money, and she was going to kill him now for love and immortality. Wasn't she better than this?

"No!" she dropped her arm to her side. "I won't kill him!"

She expected McAdams to take his sword and lunge at her, but he didn't move.

Suddenly Hades was at her side holding her hand with the blade to McAdams's throat. "Finish the job!" Hades commanded.

Now Ares was there with McAdams's sword at Therese's throat. "No divine interference!" Ares said through gritted teeth.

All the gods appeared around them. Hades didn't move Therese's blade from McAdams's throat, and Ares didn't move McAdams's blade from her throat. They stood there with the other gods encircling them.

"Ares, she won!" Than demanded. "Put down your blade!"

"There's no victory until death!" Ares said. "No one has won yet. Back away, Hades!"

"Foolish girl!" Hades said, letting go of her hand and retreating to the ring of gods. "Stupid, cowardly girl! You had this won! You can still win! Plunge your blade into this despicable excuse for a human!"

Ares returned McAdams's blade and stepped back to the circle of gods.

"Come on, man!" Ares said. "Don't let yourself get beat by a girl. Stand up and kill her!"

But McAdams didn't move.

"How long should we wait here while this man dies?" Aphrodite asked. "This is clearly a victory for the girl!"

"Hear, hear!" many voices shouted.

Hades moved to the center of the circle. "I swore on the river Styx that she would become a god if she avenged her parents' death. She's failed to do that. McAdams has yet to get his just dessert! This is no victory! This is pathetic and shameful! The girl does not deserve to be a god, especially among the Underworld! What kind of wife to Death would such a one as this make? She can't even end the life of the man who destroyed her parents and brought the worst of human suffering upon her!"

"Kill him!" Artemis pleaded. "You can do it, Therese!"

Than looked at her expectantly. She met his hopeful eyes.

340

"I'm sorry." Tears fell from her eyes. "I refuse to kill him. I just can't do it. I can't take a life!" She threw her sword down to the canyon floor.

"Kill her, McAdams!" Ares said. "This is your chance!"

Therese looked at the quivering, bloody man who had wet himself, and he looked at her. He didn't move from his spot.

As much as she despised him, she hated herself for her injuries to him. "Apollo," she asked silently in her mind, "Can you heal him?"

He gave her a look of astonishment and then slowly shook his head.

"Oh, this is an outrage!" Hades cried, guessing the meaning of the exchanged looks between her and Apollo. He took up her sword from the canyon floor and plunged it into McAdams's chest.

A collective gasp echoed throughout the canyon. Suddenly Ares had McAdams's sword at her throat and Than stood in front of her protectively.

"Back down, Ares!" Than cried.

"Gods and goddesses of the court," Ares said. "Would you not agree that Hades has broken the rules?"

"At no fault of the girl's!" Athena objected. "Father, she is innocent!"

"Back off, Ares and put down the weapon," Zeus commanded. "Let us think what to do."

Ares took a step back.

Suddenly Hip appeared next to the body of McAdams. He gave Therese a sheepish grin and disappeared with the hazy soul of the man, but the mangled, lifeless body still lay there on the canyon floor.

"Back to court!" Zeus commanded.

Chapter Forty-Three: The Court Decides

Than wrapped his arms around Therese. She leaned into him and closed her eyes with exhaustion. The ground beneath her shifted. When she opened her eyes, she was back on Mount Olympus inside the assembly hall standing— leaning, really, on Than—in the center of the court. Everything had returned to its original luster. The white marble floors were no longer a clearing on a platform above woods with ants burrowing near her feet. The tree stumps had returned to elaborate thrones, and all of the gods were seated on them, except for Than, who held her in his arms.

The mangled body of McAdams was no longer in sight, and through the foyer, Therese could see the golden whale fountain spraying up its heavenly water with its magnificent rainbow on top. Although she couldn't see it, she imagined the battlefield had disappeared and had been replaced with the giant wall of clouds surrounding the palace.

"Fellow gods and goddesses," Zeus said from his position on his throne. "I motion that we take some time to contemplate the decision before us, to rest after so many hours of sitting here watching with anxiety, and to eat the comforting foods we love. Does anyone second my motion?"

"I second it," Aphrodite said.

"All agreed?" Zeus asked.

"Aye."

"All opposed?"

No one, not even Ares, objected. Therese suspected he wanted time to think of some really good punishment for her.

"Good," Zeus said. "We will reconvene in two hours."

The gods and goddesses stood up from their thrones, but unlike the day before, when they had eagerly gathered around her professing their gifts, none but Aphrodite approached her and Than.

"They are all disappointed in me," Therese muttered as she watched them quietly leave the assembly hall.

Than and Aphrodite both looked down to the marble floor.

"And you are disappointed, too," Therese said.

Than tightened his hold on her. "I won't lie and say I'm not disappointed. We could be husband and wife and spending eternity together right this instant." He sighed.

"I should have had Cupid pierce your heart days ago," Aphrodite said to Therese. "You wouldn't have hesitated for the sake of love."

Than swallowed hard. "No. I wouldn't allow it, and even now, as things turned out, I don't regret my decision. I wanted her to love me without Cupid's help."

Therese bit her lip. "You think I don't love you enough? You think that's why I didn't kill him?"

Aphrodite lowered her eyes to give them privacy.

Than pulled Therese against him and kissed away her lines of worry. He kissed her forehead, her eyelids, her cheeks, and her mouth. "No," he finally said. "I know you love me. You wouldn't have chosen to fight otherwise. You could have gone free."

She leaned her head against his chest. "I'm so sorry I couldn't go through with it."

"I'm not," he said, and he kissed the top of her hair. "Your mercy and compassion are part of why I love you so much. You're so different from my father and sisters. They want justice at any price. But you, my sweet Therese, you love and respect life."

"How ironic that she would fall in love with Death," Aphrodite murmured. "Listen, I will leave you two alone, but first I have to do something about Therese's appearance. Just look at yourself."

She pulled a mirror from the air and held it before Therese.

Therese shuddered at her reflection. Twigs and leaves were tangled in her wild hair, her face was smeared with dirt, her bra, which was once white, was a dull gray and stained with sweat, and her jeans were dirty and torn. She looked like a savage.

Instantly Aphrodite made Therese clean and fresh, dressed in a beautiful gown of pale blue silk. Her red curls were swept up in an arrangement on her head, jewels hung from her ears and around her wrist. Her golden locket from Athena sparkled with polish on her throat. Silver sandals adorned her feet.

"Just like Cinderella," she laughed. Then, more seriously, she said, "Thank you, Aphrodite."

The goddess of love smiled and replied, "Although foremost I want you to look spectacular during your final moments with Thanatos, I also suspect the other gods might have more mercy on you looking so angelic."

"You're probably right," Therese said. "Thank you."

Aphrodite turned and left the hall.

"Hungry?" Than asked her when they were alone.

She shook her head. "I just ate a ton of fruit. Can we just sit down for a while?"

"You're tired, I'm sure."

"Yeah. I'm pretty tired, but I'm too nervous to sleep."

"I could take you for a ride on my father's chariot."

"I doubt your father would allow that."

"I won't ask him."

"You think that's wise?"

344

He shrugged. "I know my father. His mind is made up. Our little ride won't change anything. Besides, I could pop to your house, gather the items you want to give to charity, and pop them back into the chariot. We have two hours. This may be our last chance to get them to the goddesses' charities."

"And that could sway their decision today."

"Possibly."

She laughed.

"What?"

"It just seems odd to use your father's fancy golden chariot to deliver my parents' old clothes to charities."

He gave her a hug.

"Could I see my aunt and uncle?"

Than shook his head. "No. You'll have to remain in the chariot over Mount Olympus. I'll make a few trips back and forth with the bags and boxes while you hang out overhead."

Than and Therese went down the rainbow steps, into the golden-paved plaza, and to the stables to the back stall where Swift and Sure, Hades's black stallions, were boarded. Therese stroked their necks and spoke to them in soft tones. The feel of the animals soothed her.

"They love you already," Than laughed.

Than led Swift and Therese led Sure across the plaza to the chariot shed where Cupid helped them bridle the horses for their journey.

"This is our secret, Cupid," Than said, and Cupid winked in reply.

Hades's golden chariot had a bench seat like Poseidon's, but there was a second bench in back as well. And where Poseidon had trim of waves and ornaments of marine life, Hades's chariot was trimmed with golden flames.

Therese and Than sat beside one another. Than took the reins. Like a shot of lightning, they darted out of the shed and into the sky, high above Mount Olympus. Than put an arm around Therese's shoulders and she curled against him. She wished this moment could last forever, but it seemed to pass by too quickly. Than slowed the chariot down to an easy glide and it hovered, like a hot air balloon, far above the palace.

"I'm so glad to get away for a little while and have a few moments alone with you," Therese said softly. "I have a feeling Ares may insist I be condemned to death, which I really don't mind. I look forward to seeing my parents. But I am so sorry I won't be the same, for your sake."

"I'll love you no matter what," he murmured. "Don't think about that now." He leaned over and kissed her.

She squared herself to him, taking his face in both her hands. Oh, how she would miss these kisses! She moved her fingers over his face—his cheeks, his jaw, his sexy brow. "I won't forget this face. The Lethe River will not make me forget your beautiful face!" She kissed him again.

"I don't think you'll be condemned to death," Than said. "So quit thinking about that now. Just kiss me."

She kissed him, eagerly, but then she pulled back. "You don't think they'll make me a god, do you?"

He shook his head sadly. "No. My father swore an oath on the river Styx. You won't be made a god." He kissed her forehead. "But if they release you, I promise I'll come back for you, not to guide your soul to the dead, but to make you my queen. I don't know how I'll do it, but I swear I'll find a way."

"You think they're going to release me, back to my home in Colorado?" This thought had not occurred to her. It didn't sound like such a terrible option to her anymore. She missed her aunt, and she missed Clifford, Puffy, and Jewels. She missed Jen and her other friends. She missed her cabin across from the lake.

"I shouldn't have told you that. I don't want to build up your hopes in case it goes otherwise. But I don't think Artemis, Apollo, Athena, and

Aphrodite will stand for your murder. And Zeus will side with them over the others."

"What about Hades and Ares? They both want me dead now!"

"I don't know. That's our biggest concern. But, please, please shut up and kiss me."

After a long, luscious kiss that set Therese's soul on fire, Than said, "Hold that thought while I get the donations."

"You're going to leave me up here by myself?"

"Swift and Sure will take care of you. And I'll only be gone a few seconds at a time." He kissed her and then vanished.

Instantly he returned with a black yard bag full of her parents' clothes in each hand. He made several such trips until the chariot was overflowing. Then Than took up the reins and told the horses to head for the island of Cyprus.

The rocky shoreline came into view within a matter of seconds. Than pulled the chariot to a stop just above an enormous stone castle. Then, leaving Therese inside the chariot once again to hover in the sky, he disappeared and reappeared several times as he unloaded half of the donations with the society devoted to Aphrodite's annual festival. Then Than returned to the chariot and did the same for Athena's charity in Acropolis.

When they returned to the skies above Mount Olympus, they still had time to cuddle and kiss in the chariot before the court would reconvene.

"Now, where were we?" Than asked with a husky voice as he covered her lips with his.

"Mmm," Therese sighed. "I don't want to ever forget this moment. She was still fairly sure she would be condemned to die and taken on the Lethe River—the river of forgetfulness—to the Elysian Fields. "I won't allow myself to forget how good it feels to be in your arms, to be kissed by you."

A trumpet sounded throughout the air, and Therese immediately thought of her friend Ray, who played the trumpet in her high school band. Next she thought of Todd and his ostentatiously high truck. She thought of Vicki in the wake of her mother's suicide. And she thought of Jen, Bobby, Pete, and Mrs. Holt all doing their best to deal with their fragmented family as it tried to piece itself back together again.

Than pulled the chariot back into the shed and left the horses for Cupid to tend to and then gave Therese his hand and led her from the chariot, past the fountain, up the rainbow steps, and into the assembly hall where all the gods awaited on their thrones.

Hades gave his son a look of admonition as Than led Therese to the center of the court.

Therese felt her whole body quaking. This was it.

Zeus cleared his throat. "The first to speak on the matter at hand shall be Ares."

"Look at her standing there so lovely," Ares said sharply, standing from his throne and walking toward her. "No doubt Aphrodite's doing. Therese Mills, by appearances, could, perhaps, fit in among us gods. But Hades swore an oath on the river Styx, and no oath sworn on that river leading to his kingdom has ever, since the beginning of time, been broken. We must not allow him to make her like us no matter how badly his son desires it. She shall not be made the queen of Death!

"In addition, Hades should be punished for his interference. Who knows what different outcome might have been prevented by his hasty action? Not only shall she not become a god, but Hades must be made to swear that if any of us were ever persuaded to retrieve her from the Underworld," here Ares looked directly at Than, "that Hades would send the Maenads to rip the offending god to shreds once a year, just as they once ripped Orpheus when he stormed back to the Underworld for Eurydice the second time."

348

A gasp echoed through the court, and all the gods and goddesses looked at one another with solemn eyes as Ares returned to his throne.

Then Zeus said, "Hades, what do you have to say?"

Hades stood up. His eyes looked around the court and fell on his son, standing beside Therese. "It pains me to see my son so unhappy. Therese could have helped us all to avoid this had she done the deed herself. It's true I struck the final blow that killed McAdams, but only because I owed it to my souls, her parents, who deserved to be avenged.

"It is because of her cowardice that we stand here, indecisive. I agree with Ares that she should not become like us. I accept the punishment of sending the Maenads to rip apart any who would drag her from my kingdom. But I wish Ares and the rest of you to consider this: Does this girl, though cowardly, deserve to die? I pride myself on my just ways, and I say to you today, we should send her to her mortal home *alive*. Believe me, Ares, you who crave victory over me, she will suffer far more alive than in the Elysian Fields frolicking with her parents among the asphodel. You took away her parents, and now we take away her one true love if we condemn her to life, far away from Death. Believe me, Ares, when I say she will suffer." Hades returned to his seat.

Zeus then asked, "Poseidon? Have you any words regarding her? She was your prisoner."

Poseidon stood. "I agree with Hades. Send the girl to her mortal home alive." He returned to his seat.

"Hear, hear!" other gods and goddesses shouted.

"Send her home alive!" Artemis said.

"Send the girl home!" Athena echoed.

"Send the girl home alive!" others shouted.

"Ares?" Zeus asked. "What say you?"

Ares stood from his throne and took a few steps toward Therese. "You made me promise on the river Styx to protect your loved ones if you

349

chose the third option, which you did, and so I do, but I did *not* promise to protect *you*! Send her back a mortal girl to her mortal home, as Hades has said. Let her suffer in life without Death."

Applause rang out among the gods.

"On one condition!" Ares shouted.

The Olympians quieted down to listen to Ares's next words.

"I will agree to let her live if everyone here swears on the River Styx not to make this girl like us. She must live as a mortal and die as a mortal and none of us shall change that."

The gods and goddesses stole glances at one another, some content, others outraged.

"Shall Ares be called the king of Olympia now?" Poseidon asked. "How is it your son can make such demands, brother?"

Zeus plunged a thunder bolt down to earth and shouted, "How dare you!"

Therese wasn't sure if Zeus was mad at Ares or Poseidon, but the mystery was solved when Zeus turned his angry face toward his brother.

"Ares has every right to ensure a fair outcome, Poseidon. Do you not see how this girl's life is an affront to him, who was promised that by her hand alone his servant, McAdams, would be destroyed?"

Poseidon gritted his teeth but held his tongue.

"I say we honor my son's request. What say you, Hades?"

Hades clenched his fists at his side and gave Therese a nasty glare. "It's just. I agree with Ares."

"Then it's done," Zeus said. "Let us swear."

"I swear," the Olympian voices rang, Than's among them.

Therese looked at Than with mixed feelings. "I don't want to leave you," she said to him. "Can't you please take me with you?"

"I'll come back for you, somehow some way, I promise. I will never give up. I will spend your whole life finding a way to make you my queen."

350

"Don't take too long." She reached her lips to his, but before she made contact, he and the assembly hall and all the gods disappeared, and she found herself standing on the gravelly drive to her house.

Chapter Forty-Four: Sleep Returns

Therese stood in front of her log cabin in the dark of night wearing the pale blue gown and silver sandals from Aphrodite. She walked up the drive to the house wondering how long she'd been gone and what kind of trouble she would be in and what she would say about the way she was dressed.

When she opened the front door, she found Carol and Richard curled up on the sofa watching television. They both gave her a look of surprise, and their mouths dropped open.

Oh, boy. I must have been gone a week. Here it comes.

"Wow, you look great," Carol said. "This makeover is a *major* improvement over the one Jen gave you yesterday. Don't you think, Rich?"

"No contest. That black wig was a little weird. No offense, Therese."

Okay, what were they talking about? "Um, thanks."

"Did you have a good time?" Carol asked. "Jen told us you might sleep over again tonight. I'm so excited you've been having such a good time together, especially with school getting ready to start up again. Sleepovers during the week will have to stop then, you know. So, did you have fun?"

She thought over what she had been doing however many days it had been. "Um, yeah. Great time. I'm going upstairs to call Jen. I stupidly forgot my overnight bag at her house. I'll be back down in a little bit."

Clifford pranced down the stairs and nearly knocked her over. "Clifford!" She squatted down and hugged his neck. Tears flooded her eyes. "Hey, boy! I'm glad to see you, too!"

"You act like you haven't seen him all day!" Carol laughed.

Therese climbed the stairs to her room wondering what in the world had been happening here and how long she'd been gone. She noticed Jewel's lamp was on, so she flipped it off. Fresh lettuce and tomatoes and water had been given to her by someone. Puffy also had a full dispenser of water and fresh food. What had been going on?

She went to the phone to call Jen.

"You're back!" Jen said. "Oh my God, I was wondering when you'd come home. I was so worried. What happened? Are you and Than together now?"

"Sort of. I don't know. He had to, um, he had to go back down…south."

"Oh. I'm sorry. I guess you're pretty bummed out."

"Yeah. Thanks for covering for me, though. How did you do it?"

"I used the crown to sneak around your place to take care of your pets the first day after our *sleepover*. The second day I dressed up in a wig and a big gaudy dress and told them I was you and that I had given you a makeover. I whipped through the house fast before they noticed anything funny about you. Then today, I used the crown again to feed your pets, and I called them from here to say you might be staying over again."

"So I was only gone for two nights?"

"And three days. Wait, you don't know how long you were gone? Did you guys get drunk or something?"

"Or something." Therese sat on the edge of her bed. Clifford leapt up beside her, and she stroked his fur.

"So give me the details." Then Jen added, "unless you're too bummed."

"I am pretty bummed, and I'm really tired, but maybe we could get together tomorrow. I could come by just before the trail rides, see the horses, and we could visit then."

"That would be great! Plan to have lunch here."

"Sounds good." Then Therese asked, "Did your dad move home?"

"Yeah."

"Everything going okay?"

"I don't know. It's better with the crown. I can't thank you enough."

"Good. See you tomorrow." Then she asked, "Oh, wait. Think we could invite Vicki?"

"That's actually a great idea. I've wanted to call her. This gives me a good excuse. I'll call her now. See you tomorrow."

Therese hung up the phone and looked at herself in her dresser mirror. So she had been gone three days and two nights. Jen had taken care of her pets using the crown. She had also made an appearance yesterday pretending to be Therese. Carol and Richard had no clue she'd been fighting for her life before the gods of Olympus, that she could have won had she not taken pity on the man who had her parents killed, and that she could be a goddess right now with the love of her life for all eternity.

She called Vicki and made arrangements to meet at Jen's tomorrow morning. Then she changed from the gown and hung it up in her closet wondering if she would ever have an occasion to wear it again. Maybe prom. She smiled at the thought of wearing Aphrodite's gown to prom. She put on her nightshirt and lay down on her bed. It wasn't quite as wonderful as Poseidon's, but it sure felt good to be home. Clifford curled against her, and she stroked his fur and kissed the top of his head. At least one of them was immortal.

Although she was tired, she went downstairs to spend some time with Carol and Richard. She curled up with a blanket in her favorite chair near the fireplace, and Clifford joined her on her lap. She stroked his fur as she asked Carol and Richard what they'd been up to.

Carol said, "First of all, I've been waiting to tell you that the lieutenant called. They found the body of the man they believe was responsible for your parents' death. His name was Steven McAdams. Apparently, he was distributing counterfeit drugs all over the world and this had something to do with your mother's work at the college. They also have two men from Pakistan in custody. The men confessed to helping McAdams.

354

They turned themselves in, can you believe it? The lieutenant said something must have scared them into confessing. Anyway, he's closed the case and assures us that we're safe."

Therese smiled. "That's great." She wondered if details about the anthrax antidote were omitted by the lieutenant wanting to spare her aunt, or by her aunt wanting to spare Therese.

Carol looked at Richard, and he gave her a nod.

"Actually," Carol said, "we've wanted to talk to you about something, else, too."

Oh yeah, Therese thought. She remembered now that they had wanted to tell her something important that would affect them all, but right now she didn't think she had the strength to hear it.

Richard piped up, "We really think this would be good for all three of us. We hope you think so, too."

Therese filled with dread.

"Richard and I are getting married," Carol said.

Therese looked at Carol and then at Richard and back at Carol. This was the news? "That's awesome." Is that why Carol might need to leave her?

"You think so?" Carol asked.

Therese nodded and gave her a forced smile.

"And, well," Carol started again, "we were kind of hoping that you would let us adopt you, so that both of us could be your official guardians."

"You don't have to answer right away," Richard said. "You can take some time to think about it. But, as another guardian, I could help your aunt. I could give consent if you needed medical attention and Carol was out of town, or if you needed something simpler, like a permission slip signed. It's okay, though, if you don't like the idea. And we thought we'd all three live here in this house together."

She was so filled with relief to learn that they wanted her—that they *both* wanted her—that her eyes flooded with tears, and the tears spilled down

355

her cheeks. "I don't know what to say," she said softly. "This is, like, the best news you could give me. The past few days have been so hard. I mean, I had fun with Jen, but I also had to say goodbye to Than. He and his sisters went back...south. And," the tears were turning into sobs, "and, I don't know if you noticed, but we gave Mom and Dad's things away, and, um, and I'm just so relieved that you want me. I was scared that you would leave me, too."

Both Carol and Richard got up from the couch and kneeled on the floor beside her chair. They took her hands in theirs and kissed them. Carol stroked her hair. "Oh, sweetheart," Carol said. "I would never leave you. I'm so sorry you ever even had that thought. I will always be here for you." She kissed her cheek again.

"And I know we're not that close yet," Richard said. "But I will be here for you, too. Did you notice I chopped off that dying branch of the elm outside?"

"You did?" Therese's face lit up. She ran to the window above the kitchen sink to take a look. It was dark outside, but the dim light of the moon showed the elm's new profile. She turned and beamed at Richard across the room.

"And I treated the roots of both elms. I think they're going to make it."

Therese skipped around the kitchen bar and threw her arms around Richard. Then she threw her arms around her aunt. Then she put one around each of them and said, "Thank you. Both of you. Thank you so much."

Clifford lifted his face to hers and licked her tears, making the three humans break their embrace and fall back laughing.

After staying up with Carol and Richard a little while longer, sleep began to take possession of every limb and every muscle on Therese's body. She said goodnight, gave them each one more hug, and dragged herself up the stairs to her bed with Clifford following behind. She crawled beneath her covers, allowing Clifford there, too, and he nestled against her. He knew, unlike the humans downstairs, that she hadn't been home for three days, and now he wanted nothing more than to stay glued to Therese for as long as she would allow.

She turned off her bedside lamp and lay back on her pillow. It wasn't Artemis's goose feathered pillow, but it would do. Her sheets weren't quite as soft or clean as Athena's had been, but they felt just right. She had no eye mask or silken gown, but she had her dog and her other pets, and she was happy.

And although she couldn't have Than, he said he would come back for her. She had to believe that. She had to have hope. One day he would find a way to make her his queen.

And although it wasn't now, she still had her prayer. She would talk to him, and she knew he would hear. And he would be glad to hear her voice over so many others begging him to stay off his visit or to take them swiftly without pain and suffering. Her prayers would be like a breath of fresh air, as he had once told her himself.

"Oh, Than, I miss you already. I wish I could feel you next to me, holding me, kissing me. But I won't make you sad tonight. I want you to know that I'm happy. My aunt and uncle are getting married, and they're going to adopt me. We're all three going to live here in this house together. Can you believe it?" She continued to tell her stories—of what Jen had done in her absence, including the bit about the black wig, how Clifford was stuck to her like glue, how her uncle-to-be had saved the elm trees in the back of her house. She told him what Jewels and Puffy were doing, how she would be having lunch with Jen and Vicky tomorrow, how she couldn't wait to go for a ride with Todd and Ray in Todd's truck again. Band camp would be starting next week. She really needed to start practicing on her flute. Maybe she and her friends would get together this weekend and play their instruments together. And on and on she went, talking to Death about the life she loved and treasured.

And before she knew it, Therese was standing on a muddy bank. Fog curled around her, so she couldn't see far, but she could tell that the water was flowing in a narrow gorge between two enormous granite mountains. "Mom! Dad!" Her shouts were stifled by the thick fog. She couldn't open her mouth and yell as loudly as she wanted. "Mom! Dad!" She looked around the empty bank. Her bare feet sunk into the mud. Tall blades of grass as high as her knees grew in tufts along the shore. Mosquitoes swarmed over one area of the water. Three large boulders leaned in a cluster on the left side of the shore against the base of steep, massive wall of rock.

She recognized this place.

She leapt into the air and flew her breaststroke above the river. She told the fog to disappear. Down below, she willed Charon to look up at her from his ferry. He was alone rowing toward the bank, perhaps coming for some poor soul.

"Tell my parents I said goodbye, will you?" she cried out to Charon. "Tell them I love them and will miss them and will one day be with them again!"

The old man looked at her and waved.

She took that as a yes. Maybe they wouldn't remember her. But maybe they would.

She turned a few somersaults in the air and then headed back toward the bank. Below she saw two figures, and one of them she could tell, even from this height, was Than. She charged down toward him.

"Hello, my love!" she cried, hovering just in front of him, but without touching the icy water near her feet. Already she could feel herself growing weaker, and she found it more difficult to breathe.

Charon paddled his long stick through the water toward the bank.

"Therese!" Than said beaming. He started to reach out to her, but then thought better of it, and took several steps back. "I love your prayers. Please keep talking to me! But don't linger here another minute, and try to avoid this place. We can't have you die before I figure out how to make you a god! Go! But keep talking to me! I'll come back one day!"

Therese blew him her kiss and, reluctantly, flew away before she felt any weaker.

For all she really knew, he could have been a figment. She might have invented the whole scene. But it didn't matter. She wanted to believe in it, and that was enough for now.

She found herself flying over the San Juan Mountains when Hip came up from behind.

"It's good to be back," he said, flying beside her.

Yes, she thought without speaking. It wasn't bad.

********THE END********

Please enjoy this first chapter of the second book in the Gatekeeper's Saga:

Chapter One: Sleep and Death

Therese Mills let out a shrill, gleeful scream. "You're back!" She practically flew into Than's arms, running across the gravelly drive of her Colorado log cabin, the small pebbles working their way between her bare feet and flip-flops. She kept saying, "You're back!" over and over with profound disbelief. The ten months since she had last seen him at Mount Olympus over the dead body of Steve McAdams had seemed an eternity.

"You feel so good," Than murmured as his lips caressed her now-moist skin, hot beneath the summer sun and his even hotter body against her. He stopped, ran his fingers through her short, red curls. "Nice."

"Not too short?"

"I love it. Makes your adorable dimples stand out more." He kissed her again, his hands moving along her bare waist. "On your way for a swim?"

She was wearing the same bikini from last summer shortly after she and Than had met at Jen's ranch down the road. She smiled now at the memory of their swim in the lake. The lake was actually a reservoir tucked in a small valley between the San Juan Mountains. Only five homes, including hers and Jen's, spread apart and wedged in the mountains, shared this spectacular view.

"Care to join me?"

"What about your aunt and uncle?"

"They're inside, working. They won't bother us."

He covered her with more kisses.

360

They were kissing on her gravelly drive one minute and at the bank the next, holding hands on the jetties, about to jump. A hawk soared over the valley beneath the early morning sun.

"Did we just god travel?" Therese asked Than.

He gave her what seemed an arrogant smirk that said, "Of course."

Before she could ask another question, Than had stripped down to his white boxers and was pulling her into to the frigid water, and she was screaming gleefully again.

"It's so cold!"

"It's awesome," he said. "I've missed you, and all of this, more than you can know."

He held her close, keeping her warm, and was about to kiss her again when they heard the crunch of footsteps along the jetties.

"Pete!" Therese cried, surprised. He had been her rock since last summer, a shoulder to cry on, a friend—maybe more than a friend since Cupid shot his arrow into Pete's heart—to keep her from losing her mind. She pulled back from Than and gave Pete an awkward smile. "Feel like a swim?"

"Hey, Than," Pete said with what seemed like a forced grin. "How's it going?"

"Hey, Pete. How's your family?" Than ran his fingers through his dark wavy hair, maybe in an attempt to appear casual and unaffected by Pete's sudden appearance.

Pete's blond bowl hair cut from last summer had grown out, and he hadn't bothered to cut it. Therese had told him she liked it long. Just now he had it tied back in a ponytail at the nape of his neck. He wore his blue jeans and boots and a long-sleeved shirt open in front, exposing his tanned chest and abdomen. He looked really good, for a mortal.

"The family's okay. Summer is our busy season, you know." Then Pete added, "Need a job?"

361

"This is a quick visit," Than replied. "But thanks anyway. Tell everybody I said hello."

"You should do it yourself," Pete said. "They'd be happy to see you."

Pete's family—the Holts—ran a trail riding business down the road, and last summer, Than had taken a job as a horse handler when their usual hands had to take time off due to a death in the family. Therese later suspected Than had arranged it all so that they could meet—in the flesh, that is. They had already met when she was in a coma after her parents were killed by one of McAdams's Taliban spies. She had followed her parents to the Underworld, but had assumed it was a dream, and, as she had always been a lucid dreamer and able to manipulate the events of her dreams, she had been especially bossy and flirtatious with the god of death and with his brother, the god of sleep. She couldn't have known then that it had all been real and that the god of death, unused to receiving affection, would fall in love with her and follow her back to the world of the living.

But she was glad. More than glad. She was absolutely thrilled. And now he had finally come back for her. But what would she tell Pete?

She could see the pain in Pete's face despite his forced smile.

"Are we still on for the movies tonight?" Pete asked.

Therese could feel the blood leave her face as Than studied it. Surely he, a god, had been aware of her slightly-more-than-friends relationship with Pete. "Umm. I'm not sure, Pete. Can I give you a call?"

Jen stepped up beside Pete with her arms folded across her chest. "Hey, Than. What's up?"

"Hey, Jen. It's good to see you."

Jen, who like all the people in Therese's life had remained ignorant of Than's true identity, was pretty steamed that Than hadn't called or written for ten months. Therese also knew Jen wouldn't be too happy that Therese would drop Pete for Than.

"It's been a while," Jen said. "I thought maybe, I don't know, that you'd fallen off the face of the earth."

"Not exactly," Than said.

"You might have called," Jen said accusingly.

"It's um, complicated."

"Yeah, right. They don't have phones down south in Texas."

"Jen," Therese said sharply. "Give it a rest."

"We're still going to the movies tonight," Jen insisted. "You and me and Pete and Matthew. I already paid for the tickets online and the movie's sold out."

"Take Bobby," Therese said.

Pete clenched his jaw. "Come on, Jen. We've got work to do."

Pete walked away, and when he was out of sight, Jen, who stood there with her arms crossed, said between gritted teeth, "Don't you dare hurt my brother. Our family has been through enough lately. You should know."

Jen referred to the return of her father after three years of estrangement. Therese didn't know the details, but apparently Mr. Holt had hurt Jen in unmentionable ways while drunk, and after years of therapy and being sober, had returned for a second chance. Therese had loaned Jen her invisibility crown, a gift from Artemis, so she could disappear if her father ever fell off the wagon. But Jen had no idea how the crown worked or how it came to be in Therese's possession.

In fact, it was the existence of the crown from Artemis, the locket from Athena, and the travelling robe and gown from Aphrodite that had always assured Therese when she was feeling low that the events of last summer hadn't been imaginary.

Before Therese could reply, Than's sister Meg, one of the Furies, appeared beside Jen. She too had her arms crossed, and her blonde hair, blonder and longer than Jen's and curly where Jen's was straight, blew about her face like a gilded sunburst. "This is wrong, Than!" she roared. Her face

363

was pale and her lips bright red, like fresh blood. "You're screwing with the lives of mortals, not to mention the lives of gods."

Jen's mouth dropped open. "What is she talking about, Therese?"

Therese felt her face go white. Why would Meg expose their identity to Jen?

"Back off, Meg!" Than shouted. "This is none of your business."

"Of course it is, dear brother! We are all in danger after the oath we took on the River Styx at Ares's command. Do you wish us all to be ripped apart by the Maenads?"

Therese cringed at the memory of Mount Olympus. Therese had broken her deal with the Olympians by refusing to kill McAdams, which would avenge the death of her parents. You couldn't refuse the gods and not face consequences, she supposed.

But Meg's words confused Therese. The Maenads, women drunk with the wine of Dionysus, could only rip apart someone who dared rescue Therese from the dead. That's not what Than was doing.

What was he doing, anyway?

Now Tizzie, another of the three Furies, stood beside her sister with her hands on her hips. Her dark, serpentine curls hung loose about her shoulders and caressed the chain of emeralds around her neck. Where her sister was pale like the moon, she was dark like midnight. "Let her go, Than. She's been doing fine with the mortal. Let her live a natural life with Peter Holt."

"Therese, you can't hurt Pete!" Jen shouted. "You just can't!"

"You can't hurt Pete!" the two Furies joined in. Their voices became a chant.

Therese took Than's hand. "Get me out of here," she muttered. "Before they kill me."

Suddenly with the sound of an enormous train, the water parted like it must have when Moses commanded the Red Sea.

"What in the world?" Therese stood beside Than, shivering on the rocky bottom.

"Get in!" Poseidon's chariot came out of nowhere, pulled by his three magnificent white steeds, Riptide, Seaquake, and Crest. Poseidon's sun-bleached hair and beard were dry and blowing in the wind against his bronze face, his blue-green eyes scrutinizing them. "What are you waiting for, kids? Get in!"

Than helped Therese into the chariot, and before they had fully sat in the seat beside Poseidon, they were whipped from Lemon Reservoir into the summer sky.

The wind hit Therese's face and stung her now watery eyes. She looked back to see all three Furies following them. Meg and Tizzie were joined by their red-headed sister, Alecto. They were flying through the sky in Hades's chariot, pulled by his two black stallions, Swift and Sure.

Poseidon slapped the backs of his white steeds. "Faster!" he called.

This can't be happening, Therese thought, clinging to Than. The Furies would never reveal themselves to Jen. She gave Than a dubious look. He smiled and kissed her.

Her heart sank in her chest as they soared above the clouds. "Than," she said in his ear. "Tell me this is real!" Despite the threat of the Furies on their tail, she would rather this all be real and her be sitting beside the love of her life than the alternative.

He took her face in his hands and kissed her. She kissed him back longingly. Without letting go of the kiss, she realized the chariot was plummeting, falling back to the earth, to the sea. What sea?

"I wish you'd kiss *me* like that," Hip, Than's brother, the god of sleep, said beside her. He had taken Poseidon's reins.

Therese looked at Hip. "What happened to Poseidon?"

"You mean the ugly figment you mistook for Poseidon?"

365

"No, Hip!" Therese shouted. "This isn't a dream!" She wrapped her arms around Than and buried her face in his fine chest.

"You've gotten better and better at believing in them over these last ten months," Hip said.

"What do you care?" Therese hissed.

"You know the answer to that," Hip said.

"Leave us alone," Than said.

"Shut your figment up," Hip said to Therese.

"He's no figment!" she insisted.

Hip took out a hand-held mirror and put it up to the three of them. Only two faces gazed back. Than's was invisible.

Therese looked at Than with astonishment. He looked real when she wasn't staring at his absent reflection. He smiled at her, but now that Therese knew for certain he was a disgusting figment, she couldn't bring herself to smile back or to lean in at his attempt to kiss her.

"Figment!" she cried. "I command you to show yourself!"

Than disappeared, and in his place was the laughing eel-like creature. It flitted in the air around them and then flew away. She looked back to see the figments that had once been Furies twirl and sail away, laughing at her.

Therese moaned. "When will he come for me, Hip?"

Hip brushed a strand of his blond wavy hair behind his ear and then pulled back on the reins. He looked a lot like his fraternal twin brother: same awesome golden body and gorgeous blue eyes; but whereas Hip's hair was blond, Than's was dark brown, almost black. Therese had been tempted more than once to give in to Hip's jealous demands for affection. Hip was a womanizer who visited many girls at night in their dreams and had his way with them. Therese had managed to keep him at bay in her own dreams, but it wasn't always easy. He was good at seduction.

"I don't think he ever will," Hip said, pulling hard on the reins but unable to slow the steeds. "It's not his place. He's got a job to do."

"It's not fair," she complained.

"Life isn't fair," Hip smiled. "Only death is. Ask my father. That's his favorite line."

Therese wiped the tears from her eyes and choked down a sob. "You could take me to him," she said with an accusing tone as they continued to plummet toward the sea. "You know you could."

"I've promised him I wouldn't," Hip said. "It would kill you. You already know that. In fact, this conversation is beginning to sound like a scratched-up CD that skips back to the same spot."

"Just take me for a moment. I'll leave before I get too weak. Take me once and we'll never talk about this again."

"I swore on the River Styx."

Her eyes widened. "You never told me that before. Why didn't you tell me you swore an oath? I'd have given up by now."

"I tell you in every dream, Therese. You choose not to remember. Now wake up and leave me alone. I've grown tired of your company."

For more information about Eva Pohler Books, visit http://www.evapohler.com.

Made in the USA
San Bernardino, CA
08 January 2020